Second Impressions:

When Darcy Met Elizabeth Again

A Pride and Prejudice Variation

*By JP Christy
and A Lady*

Dedication

This is dedicated to the readers and writers of Jane Austen fan fiction. I have read more than 100 variations, and I look forward to reading more of your clever imaginings with these wonderful characters.

By the Way

Between 1796 and 1797, Jane Austen wrote a book called "First Impressions", which was rejected by a publisher. She revised the book in 1811 and 1812 and named it "Pride and Prejudice," which was published in January 1813.

My working draft of this novel was "Their Hearts Did Whisper," paraphrasing a quote from "Pride and Prejudice." (*Her heart did whisper that he had done it for her.*)

Contents

Prologue, 20 April

"Your mother sent an urgent express letter here? Why?" Darcy asked.

"Because this is where she expected me to be."

Standing in the vestibule of his cousin's London townhouse, Colonel Randal Fitzwilliam accepted the folded page from Inglesby, the impassive butler who had served the Darcy family for more than two decades.

As the Colonel broke the slim red-wax seal impressed with the Earl of Kestevyn's crest, Inglesby said, "The express rider would have waited for your reply, sir, but I told him you had not returned from Kent and that I did not know when you would return."

The Colonel nodded at Fitzwilliam Darcy. "Blame him."

Inglesby told his employer, "Your mail is on the desk in your study, sir."

Darcy thanked his butler and asked if any urgent matters awaited his attention. After being told there were not, he gave Inglesby the usual instructions to send washing water to his bedroom suite and the guest room. He added, "We will have trays of simple fare in the drawing room in, say," he turned to his cousin, "an hour, Fitz?"

"Sooner than that, if you, please, Inglesby. We rode away from Rosings Park as if the devil himself were chasing us." The Colonel gave the butler a hopeful look. "Bread, cheese, cold meat, and a bottle or two of claret?"

"Will a half-hour suit you, sir?"

"It will suit me perfectly."

After Darcy dismissed his butler with a nod, Fitzwilliam said, "Need I remind you that we stayed an extra week at Rosings at your insistence?" He unfolded his mother's letter and said with surprise, "It is very brief—perhaps the shortest message my mother has ever sent." Then he read aloud, "Is the engagement settled between Darcy and A. de Bourgh?"

Feeling bedevilled on the matter of marriage, Darcy growled, "Why do women—even those who are not happy with their married status—assume that a single man in possession of a good fortune must be in want of a wife? It is as if they consider *me* the rightful property of one or another of their female relations or friends. Tell the Countess that I am not engaged to Anne. And if by 'A' she means Aunt Catherine, assure her I am not engaged to her ladyship either." He strode briskly up the staircase and disappeared into the corridor of family bedrooms.

Knowing the townhouse well, the Colonel went to the study, where a quill and inkstand waited on the desk. After writing "not engaged" at the bottom of his mother's letter, he re-addressed it and gave it to a footman to post.

≈≈≈

In his bedchamber, Darcy gave his travel clothing to his valet and sent him away. Now, alone in the comfort of his city sanctuary, he washed away the sweat and dirt from his journey to London. As he dressed in the clothing his valet had laid out, he tried to make a mental list of tasks to be done before he left for his estate in Derbyshire. But he could not stop ruminating on his disastrous proposal to Miss Elizabeth Bennet at Hunsford Parsonage on Lady Catherine de Bourgh's estate, Rosings Park.

Within a month of meeting Elizabeth in Hertfordshire the previous September, Darcy acknowledged that although the lady had more than one failure of perfect symmetry in her form, her figure was light and pleasing. He was also captivated by her easy playfulness and her often-impertinent conversation. Upon leaving Hertfordshire in November, Darcy was relieved, for he feared that were it not for the inferiority of Elizabeth's relations, he would be in danger of offering marriage to her.

But in March, when Darcy encountered Elizabeth unexpectedly at Rosings, he admitted to himself that his feelings for her were impossible to conquer despite her small dowry and her family's want of propriety. Thus, he had proposed to her yesterday afternoon, certain of her acceptance. To his astonishment, she replied angrily, "I have never desired your good opinion, and you have certainly bestowed it most unwillingly."

Darcy muttered to his reflection in the pier glass, "I may have bestowed my good opinion somewhat reluctantly but not unwillingly. Could Elizabeth expect me to rejoice in marrying into a family whose condition in life is so decidedly beneath my own?"

He had felt embarrassed and resentful at her shocking rebuff. Now, he was ashamed he had admired Elizabeth, and he disdained her for her stupidity. *That she should believe the lies of a scoundrel such as George Wickham about my character is unforgiveable!*

This morning—after a sleepless night—Darcy pushed a lengthy letter into Elizabeth's hands in which he explained his actions. Then, he and Colonel Fitzwilliam left Kent with only a terse farewell to their de Bourgh relations. During the drive to London, Darcy dozed fitfully; he was exhausted yet could not stop ruminating on the previous day's events.

*I wish I could have spoken to Elizabeth after she read my letter—if she **did** read it. I am confident she will never repeat what I revealed about my sister's attempted elopement last summer with Wickham, but does she believe what I wrote about him? Does she believe my excuse for separating Bingley from her sister Jane? And does she suspect that I was not entirely truthful in my letter?*

Darcy gazed out the windows overlooking the terrace. The sun's heat brought to mind how his whole person had seemed to burn with humiliation at the manner of Elizabeth's rejection. *How could she have criticized me with such vehemence? My proposal honoured her! I feel fortunate to have escaped the certainty of an unhappy future with that harridan. Well, it is doubtful we shall ever meet again, but if we do, she shall learn the truth of what I once told her: I cannot forget the follies of others or their offences against myself. My good opinion once lost is lost forever.*

When he looked again at his reflected image, Elizabeth's words echoed in his mind:

> *Your arrogance, your conceit, and*
> *your selfish disdain for the feelings of*
> *others were such that within a month*
> *of meeting you, I knew you were the*
> *last man in the world whom I could*
> *ever be prevailed on to marry.*

Chapter 1, April 27

Morning at Rosing Park, Kent

One week after the abrupt departure of Mr Fitzwilliam Darcy and Colonel Randal Fitzwilliam, Miss Elizabeth Bennet sat in a coach while her cousin, Mr William Collins, stood on the dirt lane and blathered a pompous farewell in the voice he used when he preached in Hunsford Parsonage. Outwardly, she was a pattern card of graciousness. However, as she sat with her travelling companion, Miss Maria Lucas, she silently prayed, *Step away from the door, you buffoon!*

Collins was on the point of closing the coach door when suddenly, and with some consternation, he reminded the ladies that they had forgotten to give a farewell message to his patroness, Lady Catherine de Bourgh.

Alarmed, Maria looked at Elizabeth, who, at twenty, was some four years older and wiser. As Elizabeth searched her thoughts, hoping to unite civility and truth in a few short sentences, Collins added, "Of course, you will wish for me to humbly convey your respects to her ladyship and her incomparable daughter, Miss de Bourgh—and, *of course*, to express your admiration for the glory of Rosings Park, the finest estate in all of Kent."

"Oh, indeed we will," Elizabeth quickly assured him.

"And I shall give the ladies your thanks for their condescension."

"Those would be my very words," she said while Maria nodded energetically.

Collins smiled smugly as he closed the door. Elizabeth smiled with relief as they drove away. She thought, *What an infuriating, depressing visit! Had it not been for the estate's many interesting walking paths, I would have gone mad!*

Maria had a different view. With much excitement, she declared, "Good gracious! I cannot believe we have been here for six weeks, Lizzy! It seems but a day or two since we came. And yet so many things have happened."

Elizabeth nodded, thinking, *More than you know, dear girl.* In her reticule was a letter from Fitzwilliam Darcy, the insufferable master of a grand estate in Darbyshire. His letter—which he pressed into her hands on the morning after his insulting marriage proposal—was full of revelations that had shaken her world. She had read the letter three times on the day he gave it to her and at least once each day in the week since. With every rereading, she felt moments of annoyance toward Darcy but also pangs of shame. She wondered, *While it is impossible that he and I shall ever meet again, what would I say if we met?*

Maria interrupted her musings. "What did you think of Lady Catherine?"

"Elegant and reserved." In her thoughts, she added, *Her ladyship was a snob through and through—arrogant and eager to maintain the distinction between herself and we country mice.*

"As for her daughter," Maria said, "from the way that Mr Collins described Miss Anne, I expected to meet a fragile, sickly young lady. He said that whenever he called at the manor, she retreated to her room with a headache or other ailment. Yet, in our company, she seemed quite healthy."

Murmuring her agreement, Elizabeth thought, *I suspect the lady's infirmities are an excuse to avoid your ridiculous brother-in-law.* She felt a fresh wave of relief that she had been wise enough to reject Mr Collins' marriage proposal.

"Will you tell your mother that two marriageable men were here?" Maria asked with a giggle.

"Colonel Fitzwilliam made no secret of his need to marry a wealthy woman. As for Mr Darcy, well, he did not make a favourable impression on Mama. She considers him rude and excessively proud."

"Well, I need not ask what you think of Mr Darcy! He scowled at you as fiercely here as he did in Hertfordshire. No lady could enjoy such scrutiny."

"No, I suppose not." Elizabeth would never reveal that Darcy's scowl was, in fact, his intense gaze of admiration.

Maria smiled to recall Lady Catherine's other nephew. "I thought Colonel Fitzwilliam was charming. He enjoyed your company, Lizzy."

"It is a pity the Colonel cannot afford to marry for affection, but even if he offered for me, Papa would never permit me to follow the drum."

"From the way your sister Lydia dotes on the officers of the -------shire militia, she seems to desire that very fate."

"Lydia desires the admiration of officers in red coats and the opportunity to dance away the night with them. The reality of being a soldier's wife would not appeal to her." Sighing to herself, Elizabeth thought, *If I had any hope that Lydia's hoydenish behaviour had gone unnoticed by our neighbours, Maria has quashed it.*

"I am disappointed that Lydia will not be at Longbourn when we return, for I would love to tell her about Rosings Park. In the letter you received from Mr Bennet a few days ago, did he tell you when Lydia would return?"

"He did not mention it."

"Charlotte has made the parsonage very homey, don't you agree?"

"Indeed." *Had I been chained to such an obnoxious husband as Collins, I would have built a barn with my bare hands, so I could claim I was too busy to spend time with that fool!*

Maria lowered her voice as if afraid someone would hear her over the creaking carriage and the noise of the wheels rolling along the hard-packed dirt road. "I feel that my sister married beneath her and that Mr Collins does not show her the respect she deserves. I know he is your cousin, Lizzy, but what are your feelings?"

Elizabeth smiled. "I feel you are correct, and I feel **happy** that soon we will be in London with Aunt and Uncle Gardiner and Jane."

That was a truthful answer; however, a more truthful answer would have been, "I feel **too** much!"

Despite her outward appearance of calm, Elizabeth was buffeted by a storm of emotions. *While I am relieved to be away from Mr Collins, I am sorry to leave Charlotte with only his unpleasant company. I am also ashamed and angry that I let myself be fooled by Wickham's handsome face and sad tale, that I did not recognize his deceitfulness until Mr Darcy revealed it. As well, I am insulted by Mr Darcy's opinion of my family, yet I must admit the truth of his embarrassing charges. And I am confounded that he was certain I would welcome his proposal. Oh dear! I am even flattered—a bit—that he wanted to marry me. The truth I cannot tell you, Maria, is that I am nearly overwhelmed by all my feelings!*

For much of the ride, Maria cheerily described the events of their visit to Rosings Park as if Elizabeth had not seen or experienced them with her. Maria had confided that while she did not expect to have a remarkable life, she faithfully wrote a detailed account of her days so that a hundred years hence, those who read her words would know about the life of a gentleman's daughter—or, in her case, the daughter of a knight. Thus, Elizabeth suspected that Maria was practising for when she would memorialize their visit in her journal.

Although Elizabeth appeared as if she were listening, for much of the journey to London, she was meditating on a tall gentleman with handsome features, a noble mien, and a proud air that declared him to be above his company and above being pleased.

≈≈≈

Midday at Flint Rock Castle, Yorkshire

As Colonel Randal Fitzwilliam lunched in the small dining parlour at the Kestevyn family seat, he occasionally glanced at the day-old newspaper by his plate. When Beatrice Winifred Fitzwilliam, the Countess of Kestevyn, entered, he stood. "Good afternoon, Mother. I did not expect you; else, I would not have started eating without you."

Wearing a distracted expression, she fanned herself with a letter. "We have scarcely spoken since you arrived, my goodness, was it two days ago? I trust the time you spent in London was productive." Rather than take her usual seat at the end of the table, she gestured to the footman that she would take the chair opposite her son. After the footman seated her, he left to fetch her meal.

"The army is still content with my service." He sat again. "I have not been avoiding you; we have played whist twice."

"You know I cannot have a serious talk during a game."

"A serious talk, Mother?"

"I am told that successful hunters seek out their prey when the animals are distracted with eating, so here we are."

The footman returned with a plate of lightly boiled carrots, peas, and turnips, and a side dish of Coquetdale cheese and brown bread. The Countess frowned at her plate and then at the footman. "I see a bowl of cream sauce."

"Yes, my lady. Cook was concerned that the vegetables were not sufficiently flavourful."

"Cook and I have had this discussion. No cream sauces at lunch." She handed him the offending dish. "Please bring my concoction of vinegar, herbs, and olive oil."

"Yes, madam. Shall I tell Cook that you wish to speak with her later?"

"Put the dish of sauce in her hand. *In her hand*. I have every confidence she will understand."

"Yes, madam." The footman bowed and left.

"I like Cook's cream sauces."

"Cook and I reached an agreement—or so I thought. Cream sauces are only served with supper. She is not pleased that I have embraced your cousin Anne's regimen of simple meals. My midday repast consists of vegetables, cheese and brown bread, and fruit for dessert. No white bread and no meat; clear tea instead of wine. Anne has never looked healthier since her stay at that health spa in Epsom." Leaning forward, she studied the plate her son had pushed aside. She said, "You ate chicken."

"As you see; however, I shall end my meal with tea and that dish of chopped pineapple." He added in a mutter, "I do not know what wine pairs with pineapple."

The footman returned with the Countess's preferred vegetable dressing, and she told him that he could remove her son's plate. "Randal, enjoy your pineapple. Do not wait on my account."

"Thank you, madam, I shall."

After the footman left, she began an interrogation that she had been mentally refining for several days. "So then, to confirm, Darcy and Anne are *not* officially engaged."

"Darcy declares they are not."

"I shall write to Catherine today. Anne has had at least six years to bring Darcy up to scratch. Thus, I shall tell the de Bourghs I am encouraging him to find a wife elsewhere."

He regarded her warily. "Where is elsewhere, madam?"

Unfortunately, the Colonel took a bite of chopped pineapple immediately after he asked this question; thus, his mouth was full when his mother replied, "Lady Irene."

As his choking subsided, he mopped up the pineapple juice on his chin with his napkin. "You want Darcy to marry your eighteen-year-old granddaughter?"

"Darcy would improve with a little more brio. If he married her, she could teach him to be livelier."

"Irene is only a little older than his sister! Do you truly imagine Georgiana would respect—would welcome—Irene as Darcy's bride?"

"I dislike speaking ill of my children, but your sister Martha has not been a good mother to her only daughter. All her attention goes to the three boys. No wonder Irene is untutored and younger than her years. It's a pity we could not send her away to the army as we did with you following your second year at university. You were behaving like some feckless ancient Greek at a bacchanalian debauch. The army tamed *your* wildness."

The Colonel was sipping his tea as she spoke; however, upon hearing why his father purchased an army commission for him, his mouthful of tea went the way of the pineapple. His mother frowned. "Good lord, Randal! Have you forgotten how to feed yourself?"

Leaning across the table, he snatched his mother's napkin. After wiping his chin and the front of his regimental jacket, he coughed to clear his throat before saying, "So, Father bought my commission in the cavalry not because Napoleon was ravaging Europe but because he thought I needed *taming*."

"You say that as if it were a bad thing," she said, puzzled.

"I assure you, Mother, that my second year at university was *not* a bacchanalian debauch, and if you give me a month in London or Liverpool, I can show you what extreme indulgence in hedonistic pursuits looks like."

She ignored his offer. "You said that Darcy did not go directly to Pemberley after you and he left Rosing Park."

"We spent a few days in town, and then I came here, and he went to Nottingham. He had business there, and he planned to visit his late father's valet. He will probably arrive at Pemberley today."

The Countess smiled. "Oh, excellent."

Mother and son enjoyed their food in silence for several moments; then, he felt a pang of suspicion. "Are Irene and Henry still here?" His niece and eldest nephew were the children of Martha and her husband, the Earl of Harwich.

"Oh, *now* you notice their absence."

Something in her tone pricked Fitzwilliam's memory. "In January, Father and Harwich decided that Henry would remain at Flint Rock Castle so Nigel could teach him about managing an estate." He laughed. "Does my elder brother enjoy tutoring his nodcock of a nephew?"

"That is a conversation for another day," she glowered. "As we speak, Nigel and Henry are at my dower property."

"And wasn't Irene going to stay here, too, so you could prepare her for her come-out next year? Where is Irene?"

His mother looked at him innocently. "She is on a visit."

≈≈≈

Twilight at Pemberley in Derbyshire

When Fitzwilliam Darcy reached Pemberley on Monday, he was greeted by Inglesby, who had arrived from London a few days earlier. As Darcy divested himself of his hat and gloves, his butler told him that Georgiana and her guest, Lady Irene Northam, were in the music room.

Did I know Irene would be visiting? When we saw her at Flint Rock Castle last December, I don't recall inviting her. Did Georgiana invite her? Darcy wondered. He asked, "When did Lady Irene arrive?"

"Last week, sir. The Countess of Kestevyn brought her."

"Aunt Beatrice *left* Irene here? For how long?"

Inglesby gave him a bewildered look. "Were you not informed, sir?"

"No, else I would have advised you *and* the housekeeper *and* my sister's companion. Is the household ... adapting?"

Inglesby *almost* smiled at his tone. "All is well, sir."

As Darcy approached the music room, the conversation within brought him to a standstill.

"... my brother has never stayed so long at Rosings," Georgiana said. "He will be surprised to see you, Irene."

"Grandmama Beatrice says Darcy needs a lady who will inspire liveliness in him," came the reply.

Darcy scowled, thinking, *I do not know what Aunt Beatrice means by "liveliness". It is not as if I nap or fall into a drunken stupor while in company.*

"Perhaps, if Brother had a livelier nature, he would know why I dislike being abandoned in the countryside."

Darcy wondered, *Abandoned here? After she was nearly kidnapped, Pemberley should be a sanctuary for her.*

"Ah, but Pemberley is wonderful," Irene said wistfully.

Pride surged through Darcy, and he smiled.

Georgiana said, "You are welcome to have the country; I shall take the town."

"Well, I predict *I* shall be the first to marry because *I* will marry your brother. And then I shall take you to London for the season. I will be like your mama," Irene teased.

"*Elder sister*," Georgiana said. "I suggest you improve your chances with William by lighting a candle to Hera, the Greek goddess of marriage. Or perhaps you should sacrifice a chicken or a sheep to her."

Darcy scarcely heard Irene's laughter at his sister's suggestion; his mind was roiling with shock. *Irene wants to marry me? Where has this nonsensical notion come from?*

Since his only proposal had been rejected, marriage was a sensitive subject. He paused in the corridor for several minutes, struggling to master his annoyance. When, at last, he drew a calm breath, he entered the music room and greeted the young ladies. After telling them he would take supper in his suite so he could review his correspondence before retiring early, he said he looked forward to speaking with them tomorrow.

Upon leaving the music room, Darcy told Inglesby to inform Mrs Annesley, his sister's companion, that he would speak with her in the morning. However, vexing thoughts interfered with his plan to have an early night. Thus, much later and after he confirmed with a servant that Georgiana was alone (for he did not want to risk meeting Irene tonight), he knocked lightly on her sitting room door.

Georgiana was lounging on the settee with a book of Greek mythology in her lap. When her brother entered, she made a little moue. "This is the first time you have been home in more than a month to wish me a good night."

Darcy sat in the bergère. "You were welcome at Rosings."

"Aunt Catherine is so bossy, and Cousin Anne has become quite boring since spending all those months at the health spa in Epsom," she replied peevishly. "You found Anne dull, too, when we were at Flint Rock Castle in December; otherwise, you would have proposed to her. It is possible for a lady to be too educated."

"Did you invite Irene to visit Pemberley?"

Georgiana laughed. "Oh, so that is the **true** purpose of this chat. After you delayed your return from Rosings for the second time, I wrote to Aunt Beatrice and told her how lonely I was. I expected her to invite me to the castle. Instead, she delivered Irene, who seems to think that because she is two years my senior, she knows everything worth knowing. Still, I have enjoyed our duets."

Beatrice is a clever old bird. Rather than burden herself with two spirited chits, she leaves them for me, Darcy thought. "I am pleased Irene is here to be company for you."

"Why did you stay so long at Rosings? Was it because of Miss Elizabeth Bennet?"

"Where did you hear that name?" Darcy thought his voice sounded odd, and he hoped his sister did not notice.

"You mentioned her in several letters. She is not from a titled family, is she?"

"Mr Bennet, a gentleman, has an estate in Hertford-shire."

"Do you intend to court Elizabeth Bennet?"

"I doubt that I shall ever see her again. Hertfordshire is a long way from Derbyshire."

Georgiana studied him. "But you liked her."

"I like many people."

"Not in my experience."

Crossing to the settee, Darcy pressed a kiss on the top of his sister's head. "Good night. We shall talk in the morning."

"First, I must ask—if you were going to make an offering to win the favour of a Greek goddess, would you sacrifice a chicken or a sheep?"

"If I thought this was a serious question, I would remind you that we do not sacrifice animals."

"The lamb we had for supper might disagree."

"Good night, Georgiana." As Darcy left the sitting room, he reflected that perhaps it *is* possible for a female to be too educated.

Chapter 2

Derbyshire

On the following morning, Mrs Annesley was already in the breakfast room when Darcy entered. After greeting her, he prepared his plate at the sideboard. "I am surprised the young ladies are not here yet."

"Miss Darcy and Lady Irene take breakfast in their suites." She did not mention that this had been Georgiana's habit since he went to Rosing Park.

"I spoke with my sister briefly last night. She seems interested in Greek mythology."

Waiting until Darcy had seated himself, Mrs Annesley said, "I have been her companion since the end of last August, sir. I felt we were developing a friendship, but lately, she has taken me in dislike."

Stunned, he asked, "Does Georgiana's mood have anything to do with Lady Irene's presence?"

"I do not believe so. Simply stated, sir, the situation is not pleasant for either Miss Darcy or myself. I suggest that you seek another companion for her."

"I am confounded! Georgiana spoke of you with great fondness when you joined our household. What changed?"

"I wish I knew. After we returned from the Earl of Kestevyn's estate in January, she became melancholy. Then, when you went to Kent in March, she complained about being abandoned in the countryside."

But this is her home! Darcy asked, "My sister knows I visit Rosings every spring to assess the estate's condition. Surely, she did not blame you for my absence."

Mrs Annesley gave a small shrug. "I believe she blames you, sir. And because you engaged me to be her companion, she considers me 'your creature'—"

"Did Georgiana say that to you?"

"She did."

He started to rise from his chair, intending to confront his sister, but Mrs Annesley's voice stopped him. "I do not believe Miss Darcy wishes to restore our friendship. If there is some way to compel one person to like another, I do not know it."

Suddenly, Darcy's thoughts were filled with a memory of Elizabeth berating him for his graceless proposal. He sighed. "Nor do I, madam."

"I am not the companion your sister needs. As she now has Lady Irene's company, I shall tender my resignation."

"Do you have another position?"

"I have, sir, but my new employer agreed to wait until I spoke with you. I did not wish to put this matter into a letter as I thought you might have questions for me."

After a silence, Darcy said, "No questions, but I appreciate your consideration. And I apologise for any unpleasantness you have endured."

≈ ≈ ≈

As Darcy approached the music room, he was relieved to hear a composition by Federigo Fiorillo rather than a conversation; he had almost convinced himself that Irene's intention to marry him was a jest. Standing in the doorway, he thought the two young ladies were a sight worthy of a painting, with Georgiana playing the pianoforte and Irene playing the harp. However, his appreciative mood was disrupted when his sister noticed him and scolded, "You are interrupting us."

"I haven't said a word! I am content to listen to your lovely music."

"Is that your only reason for joining us?" Irene asked.

She is not flirting with me, Darcy told himself. "As I have been gone for the past month—"

"Five weeks and three days," Georgiana corrected.

Why is she so peevish? She has scarcely uttered a pleasant word since my return, Darcy wondered. "I wished to speak with each of you to learn what you have been doing in my absence. So, Georgiana, if you would kindly join—"

"Oh, please speak to Irene first. She is, after all, our guest, and she outranks me." Sighing, his sister added, "I am merely the granddaughter of an earl; Irene is the granddaughter *and* daughter of earls." When Darcy did not immediately agree, she said, "There is also a difficult section in this composition that I feel inspired to conquer now."

Although he did not believe her, he smiled at Irene. "Cousin, will you join me in the garden parlour?"

Irene gave Georgiana a grateful smile, hoping her suggestion was a sign of approval for a match with Darcy. She would have been disappointed to know that Georgiana merely wanted to delay what she suspected would be an unpleasant conversation.

As Darcy followed Irene into the garden parlour, she crossed to one of the large windows overlooking the rose garden at the front of the manor. "Was this not Lady Anne's morning room?"

"You have a good memory; Mother passed some years ago." He gestured for her to sit.

When he joined her on the sofa, Irene smiled. "I believe I have surprised you, sir."

"You have, yes."

"Grandmama Beatrice said I have grown more than an inch since we were in company several months ago."

"Have you?" He wondered, *Why did she tell me this?*

"Grandmama says I have filled out in other ways, too."

Oh, this is not the conversation I planned, he thought.

"Grandmama says you and Anne will not marry."

"We were never engaged. As a farmer, I do not encourage cousins to … marry." *Well, I can't say **breed** to Irene, can I?*

"I am your cousin removed by a generation. A second cousin is hardly the same, is it?"

"When we were at the Kestevyn estate last December, your father was quite adamant that he would not accept a Darcy marrying into the Harwich family."

"You misunderstood. When my father thought Georgiana had a tendresse for my brother Henry, he said he would not allow a match between **them**. He is determined that his heir will marry the daughter of a duke or marquess. However, Father is far less interested in whom *I* marry. Mother favours you; she mentioned that it would be nice to have even a small claim on Pemberley through me."

Martha Northam wants a claim on my family estate? The Earl of Harwich is not land-poor; what a greedy lot! But in fairness, we all have more estates than we need.

Irene sighed. "I had my eighteenth birthday in February, yet I have not had my come-out!"

"I thought you were staying at Flint Rock because Aunt Beatrice was going to prepare you to be presented at court."

"Mother bullied Grandmama into that, but after Aunt Sophie and her companion went off to a house party, Grandmama said she was not up to the task. She has no more interest in me than my parents do."

"I do not have the pleasure of understanding you."

"With the birth of each brother, my place in our family diminished. To my mother, I am a distraction from her duty to raise the next generation of Harwich men. To my father, I am a pawn to be sacrificed for his prestige," she said bitterly.

I never had much respect for Martha or her beetle-browed, braggart husband, Darcy thought. "An undeserved fate," he heard himself say as he took one of Irene's hands.

"Georgiana is not a pawn for your prestige, sir."

"Indeed, she is not!"

"You are my best hope for a happy future!" she implored.

After a silence, he smoothly pulled his hand away from hers. "You are always a welcome guest at Pemberley, but—"

Without waiting for him to finish, Irene ran out of the parlour.

For a long moment, he closed his eyes. *My world has turned upside-down. The daughter of an inconsequential country gentleman has rejected my proposal, and the daughter of an earl wants to marry me to save herself from her parents. And now, I need to apprehend the rift between Georgiana and Mrs Annesley.*

Darcy looked at a side table to see what liquid fortification was at hand. Seeing only a decanter of sherry and several dainty glasses, he groaned softly, came to his feet, and walked the short distance to his study. Cut-crystal decanters and glasses were arranged on a silver tray, but he chose the plain pewter goblet for the generous measure of brandy he poured. This was his favourite, not only because it was a gift from his grandfather but because he enjoyed its solid simplicity.

After sending a footman to summon Georgiana, Darcy settled on the sofa under the window, thinking, *I will not sit at my desk. I do not want her to fear a scolding.* Even before he finished his drink, the footman reported that the young lady had asked for her brother to join **her** in the music room.

Do I want to make this a contest of wills? Darcy sighed. "Has Georgiana been behaving differently of late?"

The footman looked discomfited. "I have not noticed, sir. Mrs Annesley would be better suited to answer that."

"I was told that Georgiana has been avoiding the lady."

The footman said hesitantly, "That may be so, sir."

"Please bring another bottle of brandy here, and put a bottle in the garden parlour as well—and some glasses larger than those silly little goblets."

≈≈≈

This time, Darcy did not linger in the doorway; he swept into the music room and stood beside the pianoforte. "So, why are we here instead of my study?" His tone was not annoyed, but it was provocative.

Georgiana was surprised to be confronted. "I ... I do not know why I told the footman that. Perhaps the devil whispered in my ear."

For a long moment, they stared at each other. Then, flicking a bit of lint off his sleeve, Darcy said casually, "Mrs Annesley is leaving."

She squealed with delight and leapt up to embrace him. "How wonderful! She is such a dreary creature. Had I known this was your news, I would have run to your study!"

As she flung her arms around her brother's waist, he thought, *There she is—the happy girl I always picture*. Then he recalled his conversation with Mrs Annesley. "You liked her well enough after Ramsgate. What changed?"

"*I* have changed. But Mrs Annesley does not see it. She treats me as if I were still a foolish child."

"You are angry with her," Darcy guessed.

"Yes. No. Sometimes. But how would *you* know that? You have seen so little of me in the past year. I am so bored here, William!"

"Bored? You have your horse, your music—it is peaceful and safe here."

"Pemberley is *your* sanctuary; to me, it is a gilded gaol."

"It will always be your home."

"No, it will always be *your* home. When I marry, I shall live with my husband."

"What about your friends? The young ladies who shared the sobriquet 'The Three Graces of Derbyshire' with you?"

"Have you forgotten? Isabella married a marquess in February of last year. And after Adeline became engaged last April, she moved to Wales. We did not attend her October wedding because it was so far away."

"You have other friends."

"Not *true* friends. The other ladies are jealous of me because I am the best horsewoman in the county. Of my few friends, two are visiting spa towns with their families, and one has gone to Lombardy to stay with a cousin—while **you**, sir, left me to rusticate here."

"Do you wish to visit a spa?" He hoped she did not.

"I want to go to London. I am a young lady; society is necessary to me. My spirits will not bear solitude."

Struggling to suppress a smile at her theatricality, Darcy said, "Georgiana, being in town during the summer months is akin to roasting in the bowels of Hades. The place swelters and stinks—and all who can afford to flee do so."

"There must be a pleasant place **somewhere** that we can go. Scotland, perhaps?"

He shrugged. "I suppose Glasgow or Edinburgh would be an agreeable change. But not for the entire summer. Is this something you have discussed with Irene?"

A frown creased her brow. "No—I am not certain I want Irene's company for an extended time. You aren't going to marry her are you?"

"At the moment, marriage is the furthest thing from my mind," Darcy lied.

≈≈≈

London

When Elizabeth and Maria arrived at the home of Mr and Mrs Gardiner at midday on Monday, they were warmly welcomed. During tea and supper, Elizabeth was content for Maria to dominate the account of their visit to Rosings Park, for she was still untangling her thoughts about Fitzwilliam Darcy. Elizabeth was also watching Jane for signs that she was melancholy over the abrupt departure of her suitor, Charles Bingley, from Hertfordshire last November.

On Tuesday evening, as the Bennet sisters helped each other dress in their shared bedroom, Elizabeth wondered, *What should I tell Jane? I do not want to mention that Mr Darcy discouraged Mr Bingley's interest in her. At least my silence on this matter spares me from having to confess my misjudgements of Mr Darcy and Mr Wickham.*

Suddenly, she realised that Jane had mentioned Bingley. "I was wool-gathering. What did you say?"

"Last autumn, I thought Mr Bingley was exactly what a young man ought to be with his pleasant countenance, good humour, and unaffected manners. However, now that I have had some months to reflect on his behaviour, I consider him shallow and insincere."

Elizabeth was relieved by her sister's sanguine attitude. Indeed, after her many readings of Darcy's letter, she had concluded that if Bingley was so easily discouraged, he was unworthy of Jane's regard. "I agree. So then, what can you tell me about the guests who will join us at supper?"

Her cheeks turned pink. "Mrs Warren is very amiable, as is her unmarried son, Mr Emery Warren."

Elizabeth grinned. "Details, please."

"Mr Warren is nine-and-twenty, and he resides with his widowed mother and two younger sisters. Although he does not joke often or strive to charm, he is pleasant and sincere. When I first met him, I did not think, 'Ah, here is a gentleman who will make me forget my disappointment.' However, he has a steadiness that made Mr Bingley seem like a rattlepate in comparison." Jane laughed softly before saying, "Also, Mr Warren took me for a drive in his phaeton."

"Oh, did he! Why did you not mention this in a letter?"

"It was only last week, Lizzy! So then, what do you have to tell me about Mr Darcy?"

"There is little to say about the gentleman," she deflected. "But should we talk about Lydia? A few days ago, I received a short letter from Papa about her near-elopement with Wickham a month ago. A *month* ago, Jane!"

"Perhaps Papa was too embarrassed to mention it sooner. You warned him that if he did not trouble himself to check her exuberant spirits, she would soon be beyond the reach of amendment. Papa's letter to me was also short, but Mama's letter gave details about Wickham being forced to quit the militia and Lydia being sent to Aunt Morton."

That Mrs Bennet had **not** written to her second-eldest daughter was unsurprising; Elizabeth knew she was not her mother's favourite child. "May I read Mama's letter?"

"Of course." Jane gave her a knowing look. "I see by your expression that you understand—Lydia is at **Kyrewood**, our aunt's academy for 'difficult young ladies'."

"Thus, our parents have tasked the redoubtable Honora Bennet Morton to amend Lydia."

"Papa still refers to his sister as 'the martinet', yet he is relieved that Lydia is in her hands."

After the sisters imagined Lydia's life at Kyrewood for several moments, Elizabeth asked, "Should I pity Lydia for her current circumstances?"

Jane shook her head. "She brought this on herself. In truth, I am relieved that her reckless actions longer threaten our family's reputation. I also think Kitty will be less inclined to skirt propriety in Lydia's absence."

Elizabeth nodded, thinking, *I wish I could tell this news to Mr Darcy, tho' I doubt it would improve his opinion of us.*

"Shall we go downstairs, Miss Elizabeth?"

She smiled. "I have carried the title of 'Miss Bennet' for six weeks in Kent. I am happy to return it to you, Miss Jane Bennet."

≈≈≈

At supper, Elizabeth and Maria were introduced to Emery Warren, a business associate of their uncle, and his charming mother, who was coming out of mourning for her husband of many years. Elizabeth thought, *Mrs Warren is a spirited lady. She is happy to be out in the world again.*

Although Mr Warren was less exuberant than his mother, he was an amiable, well-informed gentleman who did not dominate the conversation or condescend to the other guests—and he gazed at Jane rather often. Elizabeth was pleased that her favourite sister was not suffering from Bingley's defection.

After Mr Gardiner mentioned that he was leaving early in the morning for Bristol, Mrs Warren chirped, "Mrs Gardiner, you and your nieces are welcome to send word to my son should you need a gentleman's assistance in your husband's absence." As Mr Warren coughed into his napkin, an amused silence followed; however, Mrs Warren disregarded his embarrassment. "Well, Emery is a very useful man and a caring brother to his two sisters."

"Thank you, Mother." His voice was roughened by his cough. "I am, of course, at your service, ladies."

Elizabeth gave him an arch smile. "We shall not trouble you after Thursday, sir, for Jane, Maria, and I return to Hertfordshire that day." She wondered, *Is Mr Warren even aware that his gaze lingers on Jane?*

Mr Gardiner shifted the conversation to the reason for his departure. He and two other gentlemen were partners in a leased warehouse in Bristol, and now they wanted to purchase a comparable warehouse. He also talked about the sights he hoped to see in Bristol, and after he concluded his remarks, Elizabeth thought his visit sounded as much like a holiday as a business trip.

Chapter 3

On Wednesday afternoon, Mr Warren called to farewell the ladies. Ordinarily, Elizabeth would have spent his visit planning remarks to tease Jane with. However, less than an hour earlier, Mrs Gardiner had learnt that her father was seriously injured. The butler, who was new to the household, was so flustered that he revealed the ladies might not receive guests because of their distressing news.

Warren handed the butler his hat and walking stick as he asked, "Are the ladies in the drawing room or the parlour?"

"Parlour, sir," the butler stammered.

Warren strode there briskly and found Elizabeth and Jane sitting on either side of their aunt while a worried-looking Maria Lucas watched from the window seat. Crossing to Mrs Gardiner, he knelt and took one of her trembling hands. "How may I help you, madam?"

In a breathy voice, she replied, "I am going to Lambton, of course, but I—the details—"

Jane interrupted, "Tomorrow, Maria and I shall take the children to my father's estate in Hertfordshire. When my uncle left this morning, he travelled with his business associates, so Aunt insists we use the family coach."

Elizabeth said, "And I will accompany Aunt to Lambton in Derbyshire. We were about to send a footman to inquire about the timetable for travelling by mail coach."

Without hesitation, Warren said, "Allow me to suggest an alternative. Miss Bennet, you and Miss Maria and the children can travel in my coach so that Mrs Gardiner and Miss Elizabeth can take the family coach to Derbyshire."

Mrs Gardiner fell back into the sofa cushions, sighing with relief. "Oh, Mr Warren, I won't witter some foolishness so that you must coax me into accepting your offer. I welcome your generosity with gratitude."

Warren smiled and released her hand. "Then it is settled, madam. The children and the ladies will travel in my coach, and I will accompany them on horseback. My coach seats six, so there is also room for a nursemaid, whose presence will vouchsafe the ladies' reputations."

Elizabeth was giddy with relief, knowing she would not be spending nearly three long days in a mail coach, which was certain to be crowded and malodorous. "Please tell your mother that her son is not only useful, he is a kind-hearted rescuer of ladies in distress."

≈≈≈

As Elizabeth descended the staircase with Jane on Thursday morning, she said, "Before Charlotte received a proposal from Mr Collins, she told me her philosophy of responding to potential suitors. She feels it can be disadvantageous to be reserved, and she recommends that, at the beginning of an attachment, women show more affection than they feel. She said very few of us have enough heart to be in love without encouragement."

"I am happy I did not show Mr Bingley more encouragement," Jane said. "After experiencing his dizzying attention and sudden disappearance, I have more confidence in myself now. And I view Mr Warren with clearer eyes than ever I saw Mr Bingley."

"Do you wish to encourage Mr Warren?"

"I do." Jane smiled. Elizabeth smiled, too, and squeezed her sister's arm.

≈≈≈

Mr Warren arrived on horseback, followed by a large travelling coach containing his mother. Mrs Warren said, "If we ladies take turns holding the two-year-old and the four-year-old on our laps, we will be comfortable enough. I am told the journey will not last longer than a few hours."

The Gardiner daughters, aged six and eight, exchanged relieved smiles. They were pleased that no one suggested *they* sit on anyone's lap.

"I am happy for your company, madam." Jane was pleased that she would have an opportunity to introduce Mrs Warren and her son to the Bennets.

"Well, I have always wanted to see Hertfordshire," Mrs Warren said.

"Have you, Mother?" Warren struggled not to smile.

She regarded him from under raised eyebrows. "I do not share **all** of my thoughts with you, sir. And if you are not grateful for that, you **should** be."

Mrs Gardiner enjoyed their light-hearted remarks. "I confess, Mrs Warren, I have moments when I am over-whelmed by my fears. My father's accident happened four days ago, and it will be at least two more days before I reach him. However, because of your kindness, we will reach Oaklands—my father's estate—quickly and comfortably. I appreciate your help more than I can say."

"Last night after Emery told me of your terrible news, I meditated on your situation. In my heart, I believe that all will be well with your father. Some changes will come from this difficulty—I refuse to say 'tragedy'—for there will be happy changes." Tapping her temple with her forefinger, Mrs Warren said, "I have a bit of the gipsy in me. I do not see death hovering near you."

Surprised, Elizabeth looked at Warren. The staid gentleman nodded. "My mother does tend to know these things. I have learnt to trust her impressions."

≈≈≈

Lulled by the gentle rocking of the coach, Elizabeth was content to let her thoughts drift without conscious direction, but every so often, she spoke to distract her aunt from her worries. "Do you think Keziah has heard about your father?"

"As you know, my sister lives in Cornwall, but I do not think I have told you she is breeding again."

"Thus, given the distance and her condition, you do not expect her to come to Oaklands."

"While I suspect Keziah would enjoy a respite from her five children, if she did travel to Derbyshire, her husband would insist that she bring their brood."

"And chaos is not conducive to an invalid's recovery."

"Not at all!" Mrs Gardiner agreed.

She teased, "Are you cautioning me not to cause chaos?"

Mrs Gardiner laughed. "*Not at all*, my dear."

"What did you write to Uncle before we left?"

"That my father was injured, that you were accompanying me to Lambton, that Jane had taken the children to Longbourn, and that Mr Warren and his mother were delivering them. I did not write about my worries. Edward has his own." She flicked a glance at her maid, who was dozing on the backwards-facing bench and then whispered, "I know you can keep a secret, Lizzy, so I shall share the burden of a private matter with you."

"Does it involve the warehouse in Bristol?"

"Yes. The lessor of the warehouse Edward currently uses recently informed him and his partners that the terms of the lease would change upon its renewal in mid-May. The gentlemen were surprised by both the short notice and the revised demands. If another warehouse cannot be got, then Gardiner Enterprises may need to retrench. Edward's partners invested because of their confidence in him, so his reputation may also suffer."

"From what little I know of Uncle's business, he deals fairly, and he is not a fool. I am confident of his success."

"I should have asked Mrs Warren to predict that outcome," her aunt joked but with an undertone of worry.

"Mayhap her *impressions*, as her son called them, extend to the entire Gardiner family." Grinning, she added, "Do you suppose Mrs Warren is meditating on Jane as a potential daughter-in-law?"

"Jane and Mr Warren would be a good match."

Elizabeth nodded, and her thoughts soon drifted from Jane's possible suitor to her own rejected suitor. *Who would be more surprised if Mr Darcy and I met in Lambton? Him, I think, for I doubt he imagines I would travel so far from Longbourn. But he is in London now—that is where Colonel Fitzwilliam said they were going. Still, if Mr Darcy and I do meet, what then? Though his pride was hurt, I cannot believe he suffered in any other way.*

Mrs Gardiner remarked, "In the letters you sent from Hertfordshire last autumn, you mentioned not only Charles Bingley but also Fitzwilliam Darcy. And during your recent sojourn in Kent, you mentioned Mr Darcy was present there as well, tho' you had little good to say of him. At my family estate, you will be in his neighbourhood, for Pemberley is less than seven miles from Oaklands."

Elizabeth said, "When I insisted on coming to Derbyshire, I thought only of you, Aunt. I believe Mr Darcy is in London, but if he is at Pemberley, it is unlikely I will encounter him. He is very proud; I do not envision him spending time with neighbours whose wealth and status do not equal his."

"My brother is better acquainted with him than I. When Abel was at Cambridge, Mr Darcy was also there."

Elizabeth asked, "Have they kept the relationship?"

"Abel once said that Mr Darcy was not an intimate friend, but he was a reliable one."

≈≈≈

On Friday afternoon at a posting house in Warwickshire, the Gardiner coachman predicted they would reach Oaklands by sunset. At this news, Mrs Gardiner smiled with relief. "While I am eager to see my father, I am also concerned for my brother. No doubt this situation has been difficult for Abel."

"Do you call him 'Abel' or 'Abelard'?"

"I introduce him as 'Abelard', but I call him Abel."

"Is he named for your father?"

"Ah, Lizzy, I forgot you have not met Squire Joseph Selby yet. The Selby household is rather informal; everyone calls my father 'Squire' and my brother 'Mr Abel'."

"I met Abel so briefly four years ago. Will he remember me? I am not that skinny girl with braids."

"You have a womanly form now, Lizzy, but your lovely face is unforgettable."

Elizabeth had not forgot Abelard Selby; he was a handsome, strapping fellow some seven or eight years her senior. She recalled his curly dark hair (worn unfashionably long), his brown eyes, and a smile that some would call impertinent. *We are well matched in that regard*, she thought. Then a less-welcome memory pushed into her thoughts. On the afternoon they met, Elizabeth, Jane, and Mrs Bennet arrived at the Gardiner home just as Abelard was departing, having spent a week with the family.

Mrs Bennet was all politeness in Abelard's presence, but when the front door closed behind him, she said in a loud whisper, "Such a poor, unfortunate man!"

Mrs Gardiner regarded her sister-in-law coolly. "The only unfortunate thing about my brother is that some people mistake his slow speech and limp as terrible tragedies rather than a not-uncommon consequence of a difficult birth."

"Oh, well, he is a pleasant-looking man. Do you not think so, Jane? Lizzy?"

"Very much so," Elizabeth said.

"Of course, we are more than our looks," Jane said. Elizabeth knew her sister was sensitive about comments that lauded appearance over character.

"Of course," Mrs Bennet agreed. After a pause, she whispered loudly, "But is your brother all right in the head?"

Jane gasped, Elizabeth cringed, and Mrs Gardiner asked harshly, "My dear Frances, would my father entrust the management of his estate to my brother if Abelard were not 'all right in the head'?"

Then Mrs Bennet did something neither Jane nor Elizabeth had ever seen her do: she apologised without adding an excuse. "I am deeply sorry for my foolish question, Vivian. I should have known better than to show such ignorance. Please forgive me."

≈≈≈

Even before the Gardiner coach rolled to a stop on Oaklands' gravelled drive, the manor's front door opened, and Abelard stepped out onto the porch, closely followed by a woman who appeared to be of an age with him.

Eagerly watching through the coach window, Mrs Gardiner murmured, "How tired Abel looks. He is using the cane Edward and I gave him several Christmases ago. Usually, he is too proud to use it. Oh, my dear little brother!"

While waiting for the footman to lower the coach's steps, Elizabeth asked, "Who is the lady with him? If Abel is married, I did not hear of it."

"That is Mrs Susan Harcourt—we call her Mrs Susan, and I am certain she authored the letter I received about Father. She lived in Lambton until a smallpox epidemic took her parents and siblings; she was eighteen then. She left to live with a cousin outside Newark-on-Trent, but she returned several years ago after she was widowed. Susan has been the housekeeper at Oaklands ever since. She is a treasure."

Elizabeth studied the couple, who stood nearer to each other than was typical for a gentleman and a housekeeper, and her instinct told her they shared a special camaraderie.

≈≈≈

The vestibule at Oaklands was square, and opposite the front door was a broad staircase. On both the left and right sides of the room, an archway opened to a corridor. The vestibule's dark wood panelling was dado height, and the pale green wallpaper above it was decorated with small clusters of pink and yellow roses.

Elizabeth bobbed a shy curtsy when she greeted Abelard, but he would have none of it. "I feel I know you very well from Vivian's letters. Might I embrace you as if you were my cousin, Elizabeth? I feel too young to be your uncle by marriage or any other means."

Delighted by his open-heartedness, she replied, "Indeed you may, sir, if you allow my impertinent observation that you are even more handsome than I remember." She stepped unselfconsciously into his open arms. When she pulled away a moment later, she noted that his face was pink and that Mrs Gardiner and the housekeeper were chuckling softly.

Mrs Gardiner said, "You *do* grow more handsome every year, Abel. What is your opinion, Mrs Susan?"

She drew out the word "well" before adding, "Handsome is as handsome does. But I will allow that Mr Abel's appearance has matured into an attractive gravitas."

"Enough of this teasing, ladies. Cousin Elizabeth, may I present Mrs Harcourt—well, Mrs Susan to our family— without whom Oaklands would crumble into ruins." It was the housekeeper's turn to blush.

With the introductions concluded, Mrs Gardiner said, "Abel, I must go to Papa."

Mrs Harcourt gestured at a tall, sturdy footman. "Toby will assist your footman with your trunks, Mrs Gardiner, and I will see to Miss Bennet and your maid."

After those assurances, Mrs Gardiner and Abelard disappeared down a corridor, and the housekeeper led Elizabeth and the maid up the broad staircase. She explained, "When Mr Selby—we call him 'Squire'—is well, he uses an upstairs bedchamber. However, as his leg is broken, we have created a suite for him on the ground floor."

At an open doorway, Mrs Harcourt told Mrs Gardiner's maid, "This is your mistress's room. Through the dressing room is a small chamber with a window. It is furnished as a bedroom, so I trust you will be comfortable there." The maid thanked her and entered the bedroom, and the Gardiner footman trailed her with a trunk and a portmanteau.

When Elizabeth followed Mrs Harcourt into a bedroom across the hall, she was delighted to see the cheery blaze in the fireplace. "I bless your thoughtfulness, madam!" The room's yellow walls also seemed to add warmth to the room.

Mrs Harcourt smiled at the compliment. "I shall send up some washing water so you may refresh yourself. I presume you are sharing Mrs Gardiner's maid." The footman, Toby, brought in Elizabeth's luggage and left to fetch water.

"I am accustomed to seeing to my own needs for the most part, although, on occasion, I shall probably ask Aunt's maid to help me with my hair. At Longbourn, my father's estate, there is but one maid for my four sisters and myself."

"Ah, I must caution you that you will encounter a precocious eight-year girl here. She is my daughter, Cassandra, and she is happy to answer questions or show you around if no servants are available. We have a small staff in our quiet household."

"I look forward to making her acquaintance. I have three younger sisters."

"Pardon me, Mama," a soft voice said from the doorway.

Mrs Harcourt chuckled. "Cassandra, come greet Miss Elizabeth Bennet. She is Mrs Gardiner's niece."

As mother and daughter stood together, Elizabeth could see the similarities and differences: coarse auburn hair pulled away from lightly freckled oval faces, and smiles in which there was a small gap between their front teeth. Cassandra had blue eyes, a slender frame, and sun-browned skin; Mrs Harcourt had brown eyes and a sturdy frame.

Cassandra curtsied gracefully. Returning the gesture, Elizabeth said, "Elegantly done, Miss Cassandra. If your mother agrees, I should like to be called Miss Elizabeth. I know that when my eldest sister is absent, I am 'Miss Bennet', but it sounds too formal for my aunt's family."

The girl looked at her mother, who nodded and said, "I shall see you at dinner, my dear." Cassandra curtsied again and departed.

"No doubt you have noticed we are not much for formality at Oaklands. When the Selbys offered me the position of housekeeper, it was understood that my daughter would remain with me. Squire is like a kindly grandfather to her, and she adores Mr Abel." She smiled self-consciously and said, "Yes, I call him Mr Abel."

"Happy families create their own happy customs. May I call you 'Mrs Susan'?"

"Please do." She left so Elizabeth could change out of her travel clothing and rest.

There are some people for whom one feels an instantaneous dislike, such as Mr Collins. There are others whose nature is so unreadable that one feels bewildered and annoyed in turns, such as Mr Darcy. However, one sometimes feels an instantaneous affinity after being introduced to a new acquaintance. That blessed perception resonated within Elizabeth when she met Susan Harcourt.

≈≈≈

When Cassandra came to tell Elizabeth supper would be served shortly, Elizabeth said she would tell her aunt. At her knock, Mrs Gardiner opened the door, her face pale and tear-streaked. Elizabeth pulled her aunt into a gentle embrace. "Is your father very ill?"

"The accident was only six days ago, yet he does not recall it. He was asleep when we entered his room, and after we woke him, he was confused. It was all so unsettling!"

"I will stay with you as long as you wish."

"Thank you, Lizzy. Thank you for coming with me."

"Dinner will be served shortly, but if you prefer to have a tray in your room, I will advise Mrs Susan."

"No, I want—I *need*—to be with my family."

≈≈≈

Rather than sup in the dining room with its rectangular table that seated twenty, the evening meal was served on a smaller oval table in the breakfast room. Elizabeth was not surprised by the absence of Squire Selby or the presence of the housekeeper and her daughter. Abelard said, "When we dine *en famille*, Mrs Susan and Miss Cassie join us."

Well before the meal ended, Elizabeth's ears had attuned themselves to Abelard's manner of speaking. On the few occasions she could not understand him, he correctly read the wrinkle of confusion on her brow and repeated himself. Usually, her confusion was due to her unfamiliarity with the topic, for his knowledge of agricultural matters far exceeded hers. When she asked to see the estate-made seed drill, Mrs Gardiner called her the quintessential country miss.

≈≈≈

Only Abelard was present when Elizabeth came to breakfast the following morning, and he told her about the accident that nearly killed his father. She learnt that Squire Selby was both an inventor and an improver of inventions. More than twenty years ago, he built a threshing machine based on the one invented by Andrew Meikle in 1786.

Abelard said, "It worked well for its time, but the newer design would make threshing more efficient. I want to have one built for Oaklands, but Squire is reluctant. He was trying to prove the fitness of the old thresher—and himself—when he climbed on it. But it collapsed under him. The fall broke his leg, injured his ribs, and knocked him senseless. I thank Providence that my steward and workmen were there to help me get him out of the rubble."

"Providence indeed that his injuries were not worse!"

He added, "We won't need a thresher for awhile, so I hope Squire can help make a more modern version. He needs to feel that he contributes to the estate's success."

"I shall leave it to you and Aunt Gardiner to choose the best time for me to meet your father. Is he the sort of man who insists that his ills and injuries are of no consequence?"

He grinned. "Why, without meeting Squire, you have already sketched his character, madam."

That afternoon, with Abelard standing by, Mrs Gardiner introduced Elizabeth to her father. Joseph Selby, wearing a dressing gown over his nightshirt, was propped up by pillows into a sitting position in his bed. Although a thin blanket covered him from the waist down, the rigid edges of the splint that held his broken leg immobile were discernible.

Squire's fleshy nose was well-suited to his square face, and his skin was weathered by sun and time. As for his thick grey hair, it appeared to have been hastily combed. He said gruffly, "How fortunate, Miss Bennet, that you are a lady of leisure and could accompany my daughter."

Hearing amusement in his tone, Elizabeth smiled. "Oh, indeed, sir. We ladies of leisure welcome diversions in new places. I had thought to go to Italy, but I doubt the Dolomites could match the grandeur of Derbyshire."

He chuckled but then grimaced and ran his palm lightly over his side. "Lambton's cruel apothecary, Mr Leighton, forbids me from laughing until my ribs are fully healed."

Mrs Gardiner tsked. "I shall his recommendations over the rantings of Righteous Jordan James."

Seeing Elizabeth's puzzled look, Abelard explained, "Righteous is the local madman. Calling himself half-saint and half-demon, he makes concoctions from recipes he claims to receive from the Lord. Last year, after being charged with manslaughter, he was held in gaol for about two months. When the magistrate decided that other factors caused the death of a local farmer, Righteous was released."

Squire said, "It is whispered that he was freed because he threatened to put a curse on the magistrate's family."

"A man to be avoided," Elizabeth said.

Before she, Abelard, and Mrs Gardiner left the old gentleman to rest, he commanded, "Call me 'Squire', Miss Bennet. Everyone does. After so many years, it is more my name than the one I was christened with."

"Then I hope you will call me Elizabeth, Squire." She offered her hand, and he shook it weakly.

≈≈≈

On Sunday morning, Mrs Gardiner urged the house-keeper to take Elizabeth to church in Lambton. "Abel says you have scarcely set foot out of doors since Father's accident, Mrs Susan. You need some respite, and my niece could find none better than you and Cassandra to introduce her to the village."

A Dartmoor pony pulled the Selbys' estate-made cart, which had a generously proportioned bench; thus, the two women and the girl were not crowded. As Mrs Harcourt drove, she told Elizabeth that although the Selbys had moved to the neighbourhood only about twenty-five years ago, the family had been given a pew near the front of the church in appreciation for their help to the community. Elizabeth wanted to ask where the Darcy family pew was, but she felt too shy to mention the name.

Because the ladies arrived early, the little church was still half-empty, so Mrs Harcourt was not rushed in her intro-ductions to the parishioners and the parson. Mr Samuel Porter was a lean, middle-aged man whose welcoming pres-ence and compassionate sermon were everything one hoped to find within the walls of a church.

After services, Elizabeth and the Harcourts were slow to exit because they were beset by neighbours offering kind wishes for Squire's recovery. When at last, the Oaklands ladies stepped onto the broad steps in front of the church, Elizabeth took a moment to gaze around. There, among the cluster of coaches, she saw Fitzwilliam Darcy, who was shar-ing the bench of an elegant open carriage with his driver.

When Darcy glanced over his shoulder to confirm that Georgiana and Irene were settled in the open carriage, he saw Elizabeth Bennet staring at him wide-eyed and open-mouthed. As their eyes met, the cheeks of both were quickly overspread with the deepest blush. Then Elizabeth's mouth snapped shut, and she looked away.

The first and most insistent idea spinning in Darcy's mind was that she had come to see him, and he wondered, *Is*

Elizabeth here to apologise? Did she come because she regrets rejecting my proposal?

When Georgiana noted her brother's stunned expression and heard him whisper, "Elizabeth", she followed his gaze. Upon seeing the young lady, who, by now, was looking away, she frowned. *Who is this interloper? An upstart, a lady—if she is that—who clearly aspires above her station. What is she to my brother?*

Darcy watched while Mrs Harcourt took Elizabeth's elbow and led her away with Cassandra trailing them. Indicating the ladies with a nod, he asked his driver, "Ives, is that the Selbys' housekeeper?"

"Aye, that's Mrs Harcourt and her little girl. Terrible thing about Squire. At his age, he shouldna been climbing on that old thresher. Shall we go, sir?"

"Yes."

After Ives guided the team of horses clear of the other carriages, Darcy asked, "Was Selby seriously hurt?"

"Indeed he was, sir. The accident happened about a week ago, and the gossip is he can't walk. But his daughter—you pro'bly knew her as Miss Vivian before she married—come from London to look after him. She brought her niece."

"I do recall Vivian Selby. Whom did she marry?"

"A Mr Edward Gardiner. He's in trade, but he has the manners of a gentleman and the mind of a scholar. He and Miss Vivian are a good match—so says everyone."

Darcy wondered, *Did I find Elizabeth irresistible because of our differences—because I believed she was an unsuitable match?*

≈≈≈

Mrs Harcourt asked gently. "Have you seen a ghost?"

"I thought Mr Darcy would be in London."

"Oh, so you've met the brooding master of Pemberley."

Elizabeth gave her a small smile. "If he also broods in Derbyshire as he does in Hertfordshire and Kent, then at least he is consistent in his moods." After hesitating, she asked, "Was one of those young ladies Miss Darcy?"

"Aye, the scowling one with blonde hair. The plump young miss is Lady Irene Northam. Her father is the Earl of Harwich. She's been in the neighbourhood little more than a week, and already there are rumours that she intends to marry Mr Darcy."

Elizabeth thought, *Well, that explains his presence here and why he looked as surprised as I feel.* She asked, "Does Lady Irene's family live in the county?"

"No. She is the eldest granddaughter of the Earl and Countess of Kestevyn."

Eager to conceal her turmoil, Elizabeth strove to present a calm demeanour. However, after tea, she slipped away from the manor; in her perturbed state of mind, she rambled alongside the shallow stream bordering the kitchen garden. As she reflected upon what she now knew of Wickham's history with the Darcys, she blushed, feeling her shame anew. *I wish I could see Mr Darcy with perfect indifference, but I cannot. Vanity, not love, has been my folly.*

≈≈≈

Sipping a fine claret in his study after supper, Darcy mused on the unexpected appearance of Elizabeth Bennet. On the drive from Lambton to Pemberley, he had scolded himself for thinking Elizabeth had come for him. *Why would she, after I insulted her and her family?*

Darcy had thought he would feel disdain or perhaps anger if they met again. Instead, he felt confusion, apprehension, and a tiny spark of delight. When a voice in his thoughts scolded, *I am not happy to see her*, another voice disagreed, *I am happy—unexpectedly so—to see her here.*

He murmured, "I should visit the Selbys. Our families have had an amicable association for more than two decades, and Abel and I were friends of a sort at Cambridge."

Chapter 4

Elizabeth had tasked herself with two commissions at Oaklands: to ease Aunt Gardiner's worries and to be a useful member of the household rather than a burdensome guest. Thus, she eagerly volunteered to make the mile-and-a-half walk from Oaklands to Lambton when an item from the village was needed. Her first such errand occurred on the Monday after seeing Darcy at church.

At her urging and Mrs Harcourt's prodding, Mrs Gardiner agreed to leave Squire's bedside and accompany her niece to the village. When Elizabeth told Squire with charming impertinence that he must promise to be no worse for the wear when Mrs Gardiner returned, he gave her a feeble smile. In a whispery voice, he said, "Only if you promise to return my dear girl no worse for the wear, too."

On the walk to Lambton, Mrs Gardiner led her niece along a tree-lined path running near the main road. Within half an hour—which seemed shorter because of their pleasant conversation—the ladies were in Lambton. Elizabeth watched her aunt relax as she spoke with the shopkeepers and townspeople. When Mrs Gardiner and Elizabeth went to the apothecary, Mr Leighton apologised for not having ready his tincture for sluggish bowels. "Come back on Thursday."

As the ladies walked back to Oaklands with a few small purchases, Elizabeth warned that she intended to cajole her aunt into making this walk with her at least once per week.

≈≈≈

Mrs Gardiner saw that the outing had rejuvenated Elizabeth, so at breakfast the following day, she asked her niece how many days had passed since she had enjoyed a ramble in the countryside. "I took my last such walk the day before I left Rosings Park," she replied wistfully.

"As this is your first time in Derbyshire, I know you want to explore, so I insist you take time for yourself after luncheon." She agreed, grateful that her aunt understood her.

After receiving directions from an Oaklands groom—and politely declining his offer of the pony cart three times—Elizabeth set off for the area where Abelard was thought to be. In the stillness of the sunny day, the songs of birds and the hum of insects seemed loud but not unpleasantly so. "It is the sound of country life," she murmured.

Quite soon into her walk, Elizabeth found her thoughts turning to Darcy. *If I had accepted his offer of marriage, I suppose I would take my rambles across a similar landscape. I should like to see Pemberley if I could do so without Mr Darcy's knowledge. I cannot imagine he that would want me there—nor would Miss Darcy, given the way she looked at me. They are a family of only two. No wonder he wishes to marry Lady Irene.*

Families fascinated Elizabeth. Being well acquainted with the turmoil of the Bennet home, she appreciated the calmness of the Gardiner household in London. At Hunsford Parsonage in Kent, she had watched uncomfortably as Charlotte Lucas Collins strove to manage her obstreperous husband. At Oaklands, she heard hints of the sometimes contentious push-pull between an elderly father and his adult son. Mrs Gardiner said she was unsure whether Squire was being cautious or competitive.

Less than an hour into her mind-clearing, heart-quickening ramble, Elizabeth reached a pasture where cows and sheep ignored each other as they grazed within the confines of a split-rail fence. Loosely tethered on this side of the fence, a grey mare nibbled white clover and alfalfa. Walking among the ewes and lambs, Abelard paused often to examine an animal; thus, he did not notice Elizabeth until she called, "May I join you, sir?"

Seeing her, he waved. "There is a stile a short distance—"

Before he finished speaking, she had scrambled over the rail fence. "Do not tell Aunt Gardiner I did that," she called.

"Did you walk? You are welcome to drive the pony cart."

"The offer was made several times; however, I find great pleasure in long rambles."

He gestured at the horse. "I prefer short rambles. My Gipsy is a clever mare who knows my abilities well."

As Elizabeth strolled with Abelard, he told her that more than thirty of his fifty ewes—most of which were four or five years old—had birthed twins. She knew the lambs would be weaned soon, for, after eight weeks, grass was more nutritious than mother's milk.

Abelard said, "I do not know how long you and Vivian will stay, but if you are still here at month's end, you can watch the shearing. When the weather is hot, unshorn sheep begin to attract flies."

"Aunt will not want to leave until Squire is much better."

"Vivian said you were in Kent before coming to Derbyshire. Do you mind being away from Longbourn?"

"Not at all! I am excited to explore the countryside here." Then, she blushed. "And, of course, to assist your family."

He laughed. "Your time with us should not be drudgery. There will be an assembly in Lambton on Friday, and I have cajoled Mrs Susan into attending. If you go, too, she cannot cry off. She needs a bit of relaxation."

"Are the assemblies here popular?"

"Very. You will meet everyone for miles."

Such as Mr Darcy? Elizabeth wondered. *Will he be more inclined to dance in this neighbourhood than in Hertfordshire? Would he again declare me tolerable but not someone he would choose for a partner?*

≈≈≈

From her penchant for rambling, Elizabeth had developed the ability to note landmarks and directions quickly, and her skill was further enhanced after Uncle Gardiner presented her with a small compass. With this in hand, she often rambled off beaten paths because she could reliably assess how to reach her destination. Thus, after leaving Abelard, she headed back to the manor by a different route.

Upon cresting a low hill, she saw that the meadow ended at a stacked-stone wall; beyond that was a road which, according to her compass, led to Lambton. Across the road, a dense thicket filled the space between the road's edge and a stream. Although Elizabeth was at least twenty feet away, she noted that various cuttings were arranged in small piles atop the wall. Curious, she investigated. As she gently stirred a small heap of adder's-tongue ferns with her finger, she wondered who put them here and why.

"Get away, you thief!" yelled a lean, leathery man who burst out of the thicket, brandishing a knife.

Palms facing outward, Elizabeth hastily stepped back, her heart thundering. "I am not a thief, sir! I was simply curious as to why these are here." She was grateful that the wall, which was about a half a foot wide and taller than waist height, separated them.

"They are my supplies. *Mine!*" Dressed in ragged, ankle-length trousers, a stained long-sleeve cotton shirt, and a woven straw hat, the man glared with the menace seen in the fierce gaze of guard dogs. Moving very quickly, he grabbed her wrist with one dirty hand while waving his knife with his other. Elizabeth could not look away from the blade, which was the same length as the wood handle; this knife was more suited to skinning a cony than cutting a flower stem.

"Nor thieves nor the greedy nor drunkards nor slanderers nor swindlers will inherit the kingdom of God," he bellowed. "Jesus said thou shalt not steal! Matthew 19."

A gentleman's voice spoke over the agitated man's rantings. "In Matthew 19, Jesus also says, 'Thou shalt not murder'. Release the lady, Righteous."

At once, Elizabeth and her attacker stopped struggling and looked toward the voice. A handsome man who looked to be of an age with Abelard and Darcy sat astride a black gelding, which he cautiously manoeuvred closer to the man.

Shifting her gaze to her assailant, Elizabeth wondered, *Is this the madman, Righteous Jordan James?*

"Didn't hear you coming, sir," Righteous said.

"Your shouts drowned out Paladin's hooves."

Righteous squinted at him. "I made you a love potion many years ago. Did you win your lady?"

The gentleman chuckled. "That was so long ago, sir, I do not recall."

"Let me go!" Elizabeth slapped the arm that held her.

Righteous tightened his grip. "So then, sir, help me get this thief to the magistrate."

"I was not stealing!" she protested.

"So you say, but the magistrate does whatever I tell him."

"What precisely did the lady take?" the gentleman asked.

Using the knife blade as if it were a finger, Righteous combed through the cuttings on the wall. As he was no longer waving his weapon—and as the gentleman was distracting him—Elizabeth used her fingernails to pinch the loose skin on the arm that held her. Howling in pain, Righteous relaxed his grip, and she jerked free. As she dashed up and over the hill, she wished she could have thanked the gentleman James but thought him intelligent enough to assume her appreciation.

≈≈≈

Within an hour, Elizabeth reached Oaklands and asked the maid, Polly, to bring a pitcher of water to her room so she could tidy herself. Polly said, "Mrs Gardiner is in the parlour, and she has just asked for a tea tray. Shall I tell her you will join her shortly?"

"Yes, please."

As Elizabeth descended the staircase a short while later, she considered how to describe her misadventure. She told herself she had not been in danger because of the wall between Righteous Jordan James and herself. *But if I say nothing and he attacks another person, that would be on my conscience.*

Upon entering the parlour, she realised the decision was not in her hands, for the handsome gentleman who had interceded on her behalf was having tea with her aunt. After Mrs Gardiner introduced him as her cousin Trevor Selby Knowles, he inquired about her well-being. After Elizabeth thanked him for his intervention, the two of them recounted the event that brought them together.

"I know you well, Lizzy. You prefer to understate your adventures rather than have anyone worry about you." Mrs Gardiner's tone was a gentle scold.

"I shall know how to avoid the fellow in future, Aunt, for I cannot expect your cousin to always be on hand."

Sensing Elizabeth's desire to change the topic, Trevor mentioned his surprise that the letter his mother had posted last week had not yet arrived at Oaklands. "As Squire is her only brother, she is most anxious about his welfare. In her letter, she asked that I be allowed to bide here awhile so I can be of assistance. I know our respective branches of the family have not been close in recent years, and I accept the blame for my part, so I hope to make amends during my visit. I am a curate now." He gave Mrs Gardiner a wistful smile.

Aunt never mentioned an estrangement between Squire and his sister. And in what way did Mr Knowles contribute to the discord? Elizabeth wondered.

≈≈≈

Alone in his room that night, Trevor was relieved that the Selbys had not sent him away. He mused, *Yes, Oaklands is firmly in Abelard's hands, but if Squire's obvious frailty worsens or takes him from this Earthly sphere, perhaps I can insinuate myself with the family to such a degree that I can give up the church and remain here.*

He wondered about Elizabeth's presence. Was she a kindly niece who was Mrs Gardiner's travelling companion, or had she set her cap for Abelard? She could hinder Trevor's plans if she aspired to be Mrs Selby. As for the housekeeper, she was a pleasant-looking woman but also a servant, a widow, and the doting mother of a young girl.

As for Toby (the footman who might be a butler-in-training) and his twin sister Polly (the plain-spoken maid), they were too young to have much influence in the household.

"I shall be on my best behaviour while I learn the lay of the land," Trevor murmured before blowing out the candle in the brass chamberstick.

≈ ≈ ≈

When Elizabeth walked to Lambton on Thursday, Trevor accompanied her. Although she believed Mrs Gardiner needed respite more than this young gentleman, she did not mind his company. He had been at Oaklands for less than a full day, so she was determined not to make premature assumptions as she sketched his character.

They spoke in the usual manner of strangers who are explaining their places in the world; thus, Elizabeth learnt that he was the second son of a baronet, and Trevor learnt that she was the second of five daughters of a country gentleman with a small estate in Hertfordshire.

Trevor did not mention that he despised his profession, nor did Elizabeth mention her small dowry or that the family estate was entailed away from the female line. These facts could be revealed later or never. Elizabeth's intuition labelled Trevor as a pleasant fellow but not inclined to engage in deep discussions; however, she hushed that thought. *I must wait until I know him better.*

When she considered the possibility of seeing Darcy, she reminded herself firmly that he would likely send a servant if he needed something from the village. Still, she knew she would look for him.

Upton reaching Lambton, Trevor and Elizabeth parted at the apothecary shop with the understanding that after Trevor visited an acquaintance, he would meet Elizabeth at the bookshop in about an hour. As he walked to the Mute Ploughboy pub, he saw a well-maintained carriage driven by a coachman in Darcy livery. The vehicle's top was down, and the occupants were two young ladies of a similar age.

Grinning, the curate bowed deeply, expecting his theatricality to charm them. When Georgiana told the coachman to stop, Trevor said, "It is you, isn't it, Miss Darcy? We have not met in some years. May I refresh your memory? I am Trevor Knowles, a classmate of Darcy's."

Although Georgiana did not recognize him, he was a handsome fellow and made a magnificent leg. She greeted him with cool amusement and introduced Lady Irene. Trevor said he looked forward to attending tomorrow night's assembly and hoped to see the ladies there. Georgiana was noncommittal, but Irene bubbled with good cheer, and Trevor wondered if he had made a conquest. When Georgiana said they had an appointment with the modiste, he bowed again, and the carriage drove away.

While Upton Parnell waited for Trevor to join him at the Mute Ploughboy, the pub nearest to his office on High Street, he sipped a tankard of ale and considered how he might amuse himself now that his old school chum was in Lambton. Although Upton was a year older than Trevor, they had attended some classes together at Cambridge. *I led that chuckle-headed cub into some of the most colourful scrapes of his life. I wonder if he is as tractable today as he was before he became a curate and I became the cursed son of an obscure baron in this backwater.* There was a bitter edge to his thoughts.

After Upton had completed his studies in the year '04, he persuaded his father to allow him to move to London, where he learnt the law by working with two of his uncles who were solicitors. His four years in town were the happiest time of his life. He was competent enough in his work that his uncles gave him more remuneration than the quarterly allowance from his father. Upton relished being a respectable young gentleman with enough coin to pay for his entertainments. More often than not, however, he manoeuvered others into footing the bill, for his true talent was playing puppet master to impressionable people.

Then tragedy struck—Parnell Senior was granted a barony, so he called his heir back to Lambton. Upton clearly remembered his deeply felt discontent during the three-day coach ride from London to Lambton. He could have completed the journey in two long days, but he was in no hurry to return to Parnell Downs. *What is the point of being the heir to a barony if I am rusticating in this sleepy town?*

Upon returning, Upton found he was expected to take over his father's office. "We Parnells have always been solicitors. It is because of my legal expertise and my business contacts that I was granted a title," the new baron said. "I paid for your education and gave you a generous allowance when you were in London, so I expect you to burnish your reputation here while you wait for me to cock up my toes."

Saying "no" was out of the question. Thus, for the past several years, Upton had performed legal work for little minds (or so he told himself). His only pleasures were his relationship with a widow in another town with whom he rendezvoused about twice a month—and playing puppet master. By now, the people of Lambton had taken his measure, so they limited their time with him to legal matters. Upton *was* a competent solicitor—and, the locals agreed—he was a shite-stirrer.

Upon hearing of Squire Selby's accident, Upton spent two days considering how he might squeeze a bit of entertainment from this situation. *It is only logical that Squire's nephew should call here—even though Trevor Knowles resides in Macclesfield at his father's estate. I don't know what I will do with that spoony fellow if he comes to Lambton, but I shall write him and see what happens.*

That was a week ago. Today, as Upton mulled over the possibilities, Trevor entered the pub. Just inside the door, he was greeted by the barmaid. With a pang of jealousy, Upton thought, *He still has that boyish face that ladies like.* Although he could not hear their conversation, he was certain Trevor was asking for a pitcher of ale. When he gestured at Upton's table, her flirtatious smile faded.

Upton silently sneered, *Is she still offended by my friendly behaviour at New Year's? Silly chit—everyone was drunk that night.*

Trevor was in a happy mood as he took the chair across from Upton's. "Thank you for your letter, sir. Else, I would still be enduring dreary visits with parishioners."

"Well, as you are a Selby on your mother's side, I was certain you would be interested in your uncle's welfare. How did you explain your unexpected arrival at Oaklands?"

"I expressed surprise that my mother's letter to them had gone astray—a letter in which she explained that she was sending me to be useful to Squire's family."

"Let me guess—this was a letter your mother never wrote, let alone posted."

"Truth to tell, Mother was not best pleased when I took a leave from my position as curate to come here."

The barmaid arrived with a tankard and a jug of ale, taking care to stand beyond Upton's reach. As Trevor topped off his friend's drink, he said, "She already knew of Squire's accident because Cousin Vivian had written to her. Unfortunately, there are still some hard feelings about my perceived disrespect for Abel. Still, as my father said, this is a difficult time for the Selbys."

Ah, yes, your dear father—the tight-fisted curmudgeon who kept you on a short leash at university, Upton thought. After sipping his ale, he said, "*My* dear father has encouraged me to visit the Selby family, too. Although Father stepped away from his work as a solicitor when he was made a baron, he still enjoys advising me about potential clients."

"I thought you handled the Squire's legal needs."

"Not since Abel became involved in managing Oaklands. It seems he also holds a grudge about some of our pranks."

Trevor conceded, "Our pranks were not always kind, but they were amusing. Well, *I* thought they were, although neither Abel nor Darcy had much of a sense of humour."

Upton shook his head in disgust. "If only the barony had been granted a decade ago, I would have been spared the tedium of studying the law. But Father insists I maintain the Parnell firm for a few years at least."

"Do you handle legal matters for the Darcys?"

"As Parnell Downs is cheek and jowl with Pemberley, one would expect that. However, when I took over the practice, Darcy ceased to be a client. He doesn't like me any more than Abel does, and the feeling is mutual. I sometimes fantasize about how much I would enjoy humbling Darcy, but I have yet to devise a worthy scheme. Do you recall George Wickham? Now *there* was a fellow with a devilish sense of humour. He would know how to throw a rub in the way of the Proud Prince of Pemberley." Upton grinned at a memory. "Haven't seen Wickham in an age. Have you?"

"I encountered him quite by accident two weeks ago. Prepare to be amused—although *I* am an ordained parson, it is Wickham who has been infected with religiosity."

"You are joking!"

"Here's a scandal for you. Wickham was in the militia in Hertfordshire, but he was caught dallying with a gentleman's daughter. He was given the choice of resigning on the spot or being subjected to army discipline."

"So he resigned and quit the neighbourhood."

"Yes, and not long afterwards, Wickham was soundly beaten for cheating at cards. He swears he was dying when an angelic lady saved him. The lady has a church of sorts for her personal version of Christianity."

"Did he attempt to entice you into the lady's flock?"

"We had a bit of a falling-out when I attempted to entice *him* into accompanying me to a brothel the next town over."

Slouching in his chair, Upton groaned. "Wickham passed on a trip to a bawdy house so he could worship an angel? Sometimes I think the world is upside-down. You are the son of a baronet, and I am the son of a baron."

"*You* are an heir; I am merely a second son."

"We are educated, respected gentlemen who lack the resources we need to live as we deserve. You don't want to be a parson any more than I want to be a solicitor."

"Our fathers had no imaginations; for us, it was the law, the church, or the army," Trevor said glumly.

"Nonetheless, we are not servants or labourers—or mere gentlemen like Fitzwilliam Darcy and Abelard Selby. Yet, those fellows have far more wealth than you or I will ever have. And why? Merely an accident of birth."

"Too true." Trevor touched his glass to Upton's before taking a deep drink of ale. The men, scarcely thirty, never acknowledged it was also an accident of birth that afforded them privileges that many of their generation could never hope to have. Nor did it occur to them to have imaginations beyond what their fathers chose for them.

Trevor brightened. "On my way here, I encountered Miss Darcy and Lady Irene Northam. Help me with the family tree, Upton; how are the ladies related?"

"Ah, Lady Irene is the only daughter of the Earl of Harwich; he married Martha Fitzwilliam, the Colonel's eldest sister, and she has begat one heir and two spares."

"Lady Irene looks younger than Miss Darcy."

"As I recall, Lady Irene is a year or so older, but Miss Darcy's near-permanent frown ages her."

"What does little Miss Darcy have to frown about? She is rich and pretty and comes from a good family."

Upton smiled smugly. "I shall tell you the worst-kept secret in Lambton. Last summer, Georgiana visited Ramsgate and would have eloped with Wickham if Darcy had not stumbled onto the plot."

"What about the Northams? Do they have money?"

"Not as much as the Darcys, but they are plumper in the pocket than you or I."

"Rich wives—that is what we need. I doubt an earl would welcome my suit. But perhaps Miss Darcy?"

Upton laughed. "You are dicked in the nob if you think Darcy would allow you near his sister. So, tell me about Elizabeth Bennet. I saw her at church, but I wasn't introduced."

"Her father is a gentleman of modest means with a modest estate in Hertfordshire."

"Hertfordshire ... do you suppose Miss Bennet knows our Mr Wickham?"

Trevor smiled speculatively. "Possibly. I shall make a mental note to ask her."

Before the men parted company, Upton got Wickham's direction, telling Trevor he might seek out their former confederate. "Perhaps when I see him, the novelty of his being a decent fellow will have worn off, and he will have a suggestion for dealing with Darcy."

Whistling an old drinking song, Upton returned to his office and penned an anonymous letter to Wickham, care of the manor where the religious woman resided. While he doubted that his old confederate had truly changed, he was sure there would be fisticuffs and verbal fireworks if Wickham came to Lambton and encountered Trevor or Darcy.

≈≈≈

For Elizabeth, purchasing the tincture from the apothecary was the work of a few minutes; thus, she had nearly an hour to spend at the bookshop, whose windows displayed choices for a range of readers. After greeting the owner, Mr Timmons, to whom Mrs Gardiner had introduced her, she began exploring the shelves of new and used books in a large, somewhat dusty room that adjoined the shop's front room.

When her hour was nearly spent, she returned to the front room to ask Timmons if he had books about agricultural matters. He thought he might and said he would send his granddaughter, Lily, to help search. Elizabeth laid a slim volume of William Wordsworth's poetry on the rectangular oak counter, saying she would purchase it whether or not she found a book for Mr Selby.

Chapter 5

The appointment with the modiste took less time than expected, but Georgiana was not ready to return home, so she decided to visit the bookshop. Irene said, "I cannot imagine that Lambton's bookseller has works that are not in Pemberley's magnificent library. Have many of those books have you read?"

"I do not keep count." Georgiana did not like being reminded of her ignorance of her family's legendary library, which she considered too full of dull books.

One step inside the doorway of the bookshop, Georgiana stopped abruptly, and Irene bumped into her back. Peering past Georgiana's shoulder, she saw Elizabeth Bennet conversing with the bookseller at his counter. "Do you know her?" she whispered.

"Do you not recognize her? She is the impertinent miss who stared so boldly at my brother after church."

"Did she? I did not notice."

"As I recall, you were fussing with your fan at the time."

"It is broken. I need a new one," Irene said.

Georgiana scolded in a low voice, "You have scarce been at Pemberley for two weeks, yet you have broken three fans." "Do not buy another lace fan; they are too delicate for your rough handling. I insist that your next fan be wood." Then she gestured for silence so she could eavesdrop.

Timmons said, "I shall send my granddaughter, Lily, to help you search."

"I shall look on the shelves again to see if there is some other book Mr Selby might enjoy." Elizabeth patted a slim volume lying on the counter. "As for this, I shall purchase it." She returned to the room with its crowded bookcases, oblivious to the presence of the young ladies.

Timmons rang a small bell, and Lily, a tireless twelve-year-old, answered his summons. After a few words with him, she followed Elizabeth.

Still whispering, Irene asked, "Can I purchase a pretty wooden fan in Lambton?"

"Yes, but not today. I need your help in putting that encroaching mushroom in her place. Surely, you noted the inferiority of her gown. Her condition in life is decidedly beneath our own. I have no doubt she is a fortune hunter."

It took a moment for Irene to make sense of Georgiana's complaint. "You believe the lady is pursuing Darcy?"

"Do you doubt it?"

Irene thought, *Well, yes, as she is here instead of seeking him out.*

When Irene made no reply, she added, "Would you prefer to see that chit cozen William into a degrading alliance? I thought you wished to marry him."

Georgiana strode to the counter and cheerfully greeted the bookseller. "It is always a pleasure to spend time in your shop, Mr Timmons. And today, I have brought my cousin, Lady Irene Northam, who is my guest at Pemberley."

Timmons saw Miss Darcy once per month—at most—when she came to ask about the latest novels. "The pleasure is mine, Miss Darcy." He turned to Irene and added, "My lady." Addressing Georgiana again, he said apologetically, "The only recent arrivals are a political treatise about the French Revolution and a book about voltaic piles."

She ran her fingers lightly over the book Elizabeth had left. "Ah, but you have the poetry of William Wordsworth."

"It is not new; I am surprised your library does not have a copy. That is the second of Mr Wordsworth's two-volume set published in 1807."

"I shall purchase it." Ignoring the bookseller's pained look, she opened her reticule.

"I am afraid that copy is spoken for, Miss Darcy."

Georgiana looked around, wide-eyed. "By whom? I see no one here but ourselves."

At that moment, Elizabeth's voice reached the people at the counter before she came into view. "Alas, I could not find what I was seeking. I shall purchase only the poetry book."

Emerging from the room of bookshelves, Elizabeth saw Timmons and Georgiana facing each other across the counter—and the lady's hand was resting possessively on the volume chosen for Mrs Gardiner.

The bookseller said apologetically, "Miss Darcy, that book is promised to this lady. Allow me to introduce you. Lady Irene, Miss Darcy, may I present Miss Elizabeth Bennet. Miss Darcy is from one of Derbyshire's best families, and Lady Irene is her guest."

Lady Irene was the shorter of the two and had a plumper figure, and from the way she looked at Georgiana, Elizabeth sensed she was taking her cues from her hostess. Georgiana had a graceful and womanly appearance, but there was nothing inviting in her manner. Turning to Elizabeth, she exclaimed, "Oh, surely, madam, you would not deny me my fondest wish, for I have been seeking this book for months!"

Although her demand was more winsomely expressed than Lydia's, Elizabeth still heard an intent to manipulate. This was not about poetry; it was about power—and she was in no mood to capitulate to this young woman who had glared at her so fiercely last Sunday. She asked, "How long would it take to obtain another copy of this book, sir?"

"With my connections to other shops, no more than two or three days," Timmons said, grateful for her solution.

"Two or three days?" Georgiana moaned.

At the theatrical quality of her distress, Elizabeth struggled not to smile. Instead, she asked, "Are you in good health, Miss Darcy?"

"Why, yes, I am very well," she replied defensively.

"Then you are likely to live long enough for Mr Timmons to obtain another copy," Elizabeth said sweetly, thinking, *Arrogance and a sense of entitlement seem to be Darcy family traits.*

"But—"

"And my aunt, who has travelled from London to oversee the care of her injured father, will have this volume of poetry to distract her from her worries."

"But I—"

"However, if another copy does not arrive within a week, perhaps my aunt will lend you this book. She is a pattern card of kindness."

After a tense silence, Georgiana smiled slyly. "If that is your aunt's character, then she would not mind my having this as she waits for Mr Timmons to obtain another copy."

"Ah, but *I* would mind, for I have seen my aunt's worry and am determined to soothe her feelings however I can," Elizabeth said in a voice that was as firm as it was pleasant.

With a huff of displeasure, Georgiana flounced out of the shop with Irene in tow. Staring after her, Timmons asked, "Does Miss Darcy want me to obtain the book?"

Elizabeth shrugged. "I do not know, sir. So then, I shall purchase this and return in a few days to see if you have a book to recommend for Mr Selby."

After completing her transaction, she approached the partially open doorway and heard Georgiana complaining, "She insisted on buying the *only* book I wanted—such selfishness!"

Taking a deep breath, Elizabeth reminded herself that she had done nothing wrong. Stepping out of the shop, she saw Georgiana and Irene sitting in a fashionable carriage while Darcy, on horseback, listened to his sister railing about her mistreatment.

In calm tones, Elizabeth interrupted. "But I selected the book before you came to the shop."

"Miss Bennet," Darcy said haltingly.

"Mr Darcy. How pleasant to see you, sir."

A slow smile replaced Darcy's wary expression. "And you. Are you well, madam?"

"I am. Mr Timmons kindly introduced me to Lady Irene and Miss Darcy. I regret that your sister will not have the immediate pleasure of the book I purchased for my aunt, but Mr Timmons says he can obtain another copy in a few days."

"What is the title?"

"It is the second in Mr Wordsworth's set 'Poems in Two Volumes'."

Does Georgiana not know we have that book at Pemberley? Darcy glanced at his sister.

Georgiana whined, "William, it is so dreadfully warm. May we return home now?"

"In a moment." He turned to Elizabeth, "I heard Squire Selby had an accident."

"He has a broken leg, among other injuries. This book is for my aunt. She is understandably concerned about her father, and poetry helps calm her mind."

"Please tell Squire that we wish him a speedy recovery."

The approach of Trevor and Upton was unnoticed until Trevor called, "Darcy! Haven't seen you in a few years."

Darcy's reply was brief. "Yes, it has been awhile." To Elizabeth's ears, he had not missed Trevor's company.

Upton said, "Not so many years for us, Darcy. Still happy with your London solicitors?"

"Yes."

Upton greeted Georgiana, and as she was introducing Irene, Timmons came to the doorway. "Lily found the other book you wanted. I vow she knows the shop better than I."

Georgiana asked sweetly, "Will you read your two purchases simultaneously?"

"This is for Mr Selby."

Darcy began, "Nothing for yourself—"

Because Timmons did not hear Darcy, he spoke over him. "Do you wish to see the book before I wrap it for you, Miss Bennet?"

"I do, sir. Thank you."

After Elizabeth entered the shop, Trevor presented himself as an authority on the Selby household. "Squire has been greatly cheered by Mrs Gardiner and Miss Bennet."

"Will-YUM! May we go?" Georgiana growled softly.

Darcy gave his sister a stern, sidelong look before fare-welling Trevor and Upton. Then, after telling the coachman to drive to Pemberley, he rode alongside. No one spoke until they reached the edge of town.

Irene still harboured hopes of marrying Darcy, so her tone was polite rather than jealous when she said, "I assume Miss Bennet is not from Derbyshire."

"No. We met in Hertfordshire last year. I accompanied a friend, Charles Bingley, who had leased a property there. The Bennets have a small estate in the neighbourhood."

"Miss *Elizabeth* Bennet." Darcy knew Georgiana emphasised the forename to remind him that he had mentioned the lady in his letters. "Did Mr Bingley fall violently in love with her?" Turning to Irene, she said, "William's friend Mr Bingley falls violently in love with every lady he meets. But Miss Bennet is so plain, I doubt Mr Bingley would give her a second glance. Did you not think her plain, Irene?"

For the first time, Irene considered what being Darcy's wife might mean beyond separating herself from her parents and brothers. She mused, *If I marry him, I will have to navigate Georgiana's snipes and bad temper.* She shrugged. "I was meditating on the new fan I hope to buy."

"Will Miss Bennet be at the assembly?" Georgiana said.

"Possibly," he said, thinking, *Do I want to see her? Would she want to see me? I wish I had never met her. No, I don't wish that. I wish ....*

Irene interrupted his thoughts, asking, "Darcy, may we go to a shop where I can purchase a fan? Mine is broken."

And if we return to Lambton now, will I encounter Elizabeth again? He said, "Georgiana, will you lend Irene a fan?"

She huffed in annoyance. "Very well. Show me your dress, Irene, when we are at home."

He said, "And I will find the poetry book for you."

"You have it? I rather thought you would," Irene said.

"Do not trouble yourself, brother. I have lost interest."

Irene said, "Well, *I* wish to read it. I am eager to know why you and Miss Bennet wanted it."

As am I, Darcy thought.

On the ride home, he mused, *I should have said more. If Elizabeth perceives my silence as indifference—or worse, as censure—she may give me the cut direct. I do not regret what I wrote in my letter; she needed to know Wickham's character. But the tone of my writing—I cannot think of it without abhorrence!*

≈≈≈

Elizabeth and Trevor had little conversation as they walked back to Oaklands; each was lost in thought. Elizabeth could not tell whether Darcy had felt more pain or pleasure in seeing her, but he certainly had not been unaffected. She felt herself blushing over the perverseness of the meeting. *His behaviour was so altered; never had he spoken to me with such gentleness. I do not know what to make of it.*

≈≈≈

At Pemberley, Darcy asked Mrs Reynolds to send a tea tray for three to the garden parlour. Although Irene stood with him, Georgiana was already ascending the stairs. He called after her, "Sister, join us within a quarter-hour."

"I have a headache," she said over her shoulder.

"Come to the garden parlour anyway. Our conversation will let me know whether I need to find a physician to examine your head." For an instant, Georgiana paused on the staircase, her spine stiff. Then, she ran up the steps.

"Will this be a private conversation?" Irene asked.

"No, I count on you to be present." He did not admit he wanted her account because he doubted his sister would be forthcoming. Within a quarter hour, Darcy and Irene were having tea in the garden parlour. When he checked his pocket watch a short while later, he noted that his sister was almost ten minutes late. "Irene, will you carry your cup?"

She nodded, for she had a suspicion about their destination. Upon reaching the suite, Irene opened the door for Darcy and followed him in. Georgiana was reclining on her settee, and she looked up in alarm. "Has a quarter-hour passed? I lost track of the time. And why are you carrying that tray rather than a footman?"

With a "thud", Darcy set the tray on the low table in front of the settee. "Oh, did you want servants to hear our discussion?" Smiling, Irene closed the door to the corridor. Darcy picked up his cup and settled into a bergère while Irene sat in the matching chair.

With her brother and Irene sitting in the chairs at either end of the table, Georgiana felt trapped. *I shall not start with an apology. I must show strength.* It never occurred to her that apologising could be a demonstration of fortitude. She said, "Miss Bennet and I wished to purchase the same book. That is all."

"She seemed unaware that you had taken her in dislike."

"Irene!" Georgiana exclaimed in a squeak.

Darcy gave his sister a sardonic smile. "If you thought your feelings about the lady were a secret, then you have not been as subtle as you imagine." When she made no reply, he said, "I am still waiting for an explanation as to why you made such a fuss outside the bookshop—and, I suspect, inside it, as well."

Georgiana sniffed disapprovingly. "She gave her opinions most decidedly for a young woman of her station."

Remembering how Elizabeth was not cowed during conversations at Rosings Park, Darcy smiled. "Aunt Catherine thought so, too. However, like yourself, sister, she is a gentleman's daughter."

"Aunt Catherine was in Hertfordshire?" Irene asked.

"No, Miss Bennet was a guest at the parsonage at Rosings. Her friend is the wife of Aunt's parson, Mr Collins. In fact, Collins is Miss Bennet's cousin once removed."

Irene thought, *So, Darcy has been in company with this lady in Hertfordshire and Kent, and Georgiana is jealous. This bears watching; I need not take sides yet.*

Darcy said, "I would like you to be more gracious, Georgiana. We are the most prosperous family in the neighbourhood. Let us not be thought the most arrogant as well."

Georgiana rose and made ostentatious curtsies, first to her brother and then to Irene. "Excuse me, please, while I reflect on your wisdom." She retreated to her bedchamber and closed the door.

One of Georgiana's least favourite words was "why", particularly when it was followed by "did you", "do you", or "are you". Her actions tended to be guided by fiercely felt emotions rather than careful consideration. Thus, when Darcy challenged her about her behaviour, she was very annoyed. Even if she could have explained her actions, she did not want to be asked to do so. Thus, she blamed the interloper, Elizabeth Bennet, for both her own behaviour and her brother's disapproval.

≈≈≈

The Silver Birch Inn in Lambton was unique among the local inns because it had a large, rectangular hall on the upper floor used for assorted gatherings and entertainments, including assemblies. It was unfurnished save for some twenty chairs lining one wall. At one end of the room was a dais for the musicians; at the opposite end, a dozen small tables bordered the dance floor.

To the frustration of Irene and Georgiana, Darcy dawdled before departing Pemberley on Friday evening. (They were unaware of his ambivalence about attending the assembly.) Thus, by the time they arrived, the first set was ending. Many young men were cautious about approaching the Pemberley ladies, for Georgiana was known to be high in the instep, and Irene was an earl's daughter. Darcy did not notice; he was scanning the crowd, searching for Elizabeth. When he saw her, she was looking toward the small tables.

As Elizabeth watched Abelard seat himself, she whispered, "Does Abel ever dance, Mrs Susan?"

"He tried when he was younger. It did not go well."

Elizabeth frowned, distressed because Abelard could not participate in one of her favourite activities, and *that* was her expression when Darcy saw her.

Thinking she was frowning at him, a stern look settled on his countenance—and *this* was what Elizabeth saw when their eyes met. Each froze for an instant; then, she looked away and did not see that Darcy had also turned from her.

He wondered, *Why did she have such a disapproving look? Was Georgiana so unpleasant at the bookshop? Where can I go to avoid Elizabeth?* He glanced around and quickly settled on the French doors to the balcony.

Some distance away, Elizabeth muttered, "The balcony." *I will retreat there until he has chosen a partner. He seemed pleasant enough yesterday. Did Miss Darcy's tale of my villainy inspire his disapprobation?*

Not wanting to look like a mouse running for cover, she took a roundabout way through the crowd before slipping through the open French doors into the darkness. What she did not know—and what Darcy did not consider—was that the long, narrow balcony was accessible by two sets of French doors some fifteen feet apart.

Neither was aware that they had come to the balcony from opposite ends. As Elizabeth took slow, deep breaths to calm her racing heart, a voice in her thoughts scolded, *I cannot avoid him forever. Better to plan now what to say when we meet. Better to understand what I feel than to be surprised—*

"Are you following me, madam?" Darcy's voice, tight with tension, interrupted her thoughts.

She turned to face the far end of the balcony, and in the dim light, she saw the man she had sought to avoid. Primly, she said, "I could ask the same of you, sir. How did you come here? I watched these doors for several minutes."

"There are also doors at this end." Realising he might have erred in his assumptions, Darcy asked, "Then, you did not follow me to berate me?"

She huffed, "I could ask the same of *you*! In truth, I was avoiding you. I planned to wait here until you found a partner and joined a set."

"Why? Yesterday, you were quite civil. Pleasant even."

"High praise, indeed, from Mr Fitzwilliam Darcy! Yet only a few minutes ago, you glared at me."

"Because you scowled at me. I was bewildered."

"You were glaring."

"Because you were scowling!"

"I was not scowling! I was frowning at Abel."

"What did Selby do to merit that?"

She tsked. "I was frowning because I was sad that Abel does not dance—an activity I dearly love."

"So you were sad on his behalf—"

"And you glared because you thought I was frowning—"

"Scowling. I thought you were scowling at me. But I did not intend for my expression to be a glare. I was ... disappointed that you were angry with me."

"Which I wasn't," she corrected. "And so we came through different doors to avoid each other."

After a silence, he said, "I thought you didn't wish to see me because I had forced my ungracious letter upon you."

"Ungracious? Not at all, sir! The letter perhaps began in bitterness, but it did not end so. The adieu is charity itself. And I am grateful to know about Wickham's true character."

"You believed me." Relief surged through him.

"I did—I do." Unconsciously, Darcy and Elizabeth drew nearer as if pulled by a longing for a connection. "But tonight, when I saw your ... look of disappointment, I thought you did not wish to see me because of my angry words at Rosings." Hesitantly, she added, "I had hoped we might meet again under less fraught circumstances."

"As did I."

"I have considered what I to say to you, for I regret—"

Irene's voice pierced the intimate moment. "Darcy, are you out here?"

He jerked around to face the door through which he had entered and then hurried to intercept his cousin. Before Irene took more than a step onto the balcony, he grabbed her elbow and led her into the ballroom.

As Darcy partnered with Irene for the Roger de Coverley, his mind was full of questions, *What does Elizabeth regret? Refusing my proposal? I cannot ask her that in a ballroom, but if I could dance with her, I could ... we could ... perhaps she would have some words so I might understand her.*

After that dance set, however, he watched another gentleman claim Elizabeth. Not wanting to dance with any other lady, he ran his gaze over the tables at the edge of the dance floor. Noting Abelard's amused look, Darcy crossed to him. "May I join you, Selby, or are you waiting for someone?"

"Oh, I shall be quite forgotten until the ladies of Oakland have danced themselves into exhaustion."

Darcy was comfortable with Abelard's measured pace of speaking. He was happy not to feel rushed to reflect upon the speaker's words. "Do you mind being a spectator?"

"Not a bit. I can speak with my neighbours."

*How can I ask him about Elizabeth without **seeming** to ask about her?* Sitting at the table, he said, "Having your sister here must be a comfort."

"It is. And it has been a great comfort to Vivian to have her niece here. Elizabeth and her sister Jane were at the Gardiner home when news of Father's accident was delivered.

Vivian's husband, Edward Gardiner, had gone to Bristol on a business matter. So, Jane took the Gardiners' four children to Hertfordshire, and Elizabeth accompanied Vivian."

"I didn't know your sister's married name is 'Gardiner'."

"Edward is a good businessman and a very good husband and father, which is a great relief for any brother. Elizabeth's mother, Mrs Frances Bennet, is his sister. I believe you met the Bennets in Hertfordshire last year."

Oh dear Lord! What has Selby heard about me? In a strained voice, Darcy said, "Yes, I met the family."

"And recently, you saw Elizabeth in Kent."

"During my annual visit to my aunt, Lady Catherine de Bourgh." He waited anxiously for Abelard to say more.

At that moment, Mr Timmons arrived with three cups of punch. As he set a cup before Darcy, he said, "When I was at the punchbowl, I saw you take my seat." Pulling over a chair from another table, he sat. "Well met, Mr Darcy, for I have a question. Does Miss Darcy want me to order that volume of Wordsworth's poetry? When she left the shop yesterday, I was uncertain about what she wanted."

*I am well acquainted with **that** feeling,* Darcy thought. He said, "My apologies for any confusion. Pemberley's library has all of Wordsworth's works, including the volume Miss Bennet purchased."

"I thought as much. I have heard about Lady Irene, so I was pleased to see the face that went with the name."

Abelard said, "Servant gossip says you will marry Lady Irene, Darcy."

With a noise that was half groan, half chuckle, he said, "Servant gossip is usually more accurate than that. Lady Irene is a guest, but she is not my betrothed."

The men made casual conversation and glanced at the dancers occasionally. Darcy was answering a question about winter crops when Abelard abruptly interrupted him, saying, "I know this song. The set is about to end. If you wish to dance with Elizabeth, I suggest you go now."

"Observant as ever, Selby." Smiling, Darcy strode away. Whilst a ballroom was not an appropriate place for a private conversation, he wanted to be near Elizabeth. She accepted his invitation to dance, and as they moved through the steps of the Boulanger, their talk was careful and banal. However, before the dance ended, both felt that rapprochement was within reach.

In her bedroom that night, Elizabeth marvelled that Darcy, whom she had been certain would avoid her as his greatest enemy, wished to preserve the acquaintance. *That we have spoken of the bitterness between us—at least a little—I now have confidence in my own strength and shall never be embarrassed again.*

≈≈≈

The following day, a wagon from Pemberley arrived at Oaklands bearing the estate-made bath chair that Darcy's father had used in the last months of his life. It came with a note in which Darcy said he would call when he returned from the Earl of Kestevyn's estate, Flint Rock Castle, in some two weeks.

Riding in Pemberley's well-sprung Dormeuse carriage (a favourite of the late Mrs Darcy), Irene, Georgiana, and Darcy made the four-hour journey to the Kestevyn family seat, Flint Rock Castle. Darcy felt that his scheduled departure from Pemberley on the day after the assembly was a blessing. It afforded him time to meditate on the unexpected appearance of Elizabeth Bennet and removed the temptation to dash off to Oaklands on impulse.

He reminded himself, *I must not be impulsive. Unlike Bingley, I have responsibilities. A sister and a young cousin who need my care in ways that Bingley's two sisters do not.*

He glanced at Georgiana, who had tucked herself into a corner on the forward-facing seat and was dozing. When he glanced at Irene, he discovered she was studying him with a speculative gaze. Giving her a perfunctory smile, he returned to his pocket-sized, leather-bound diary.

Among his notes, lists, and musings was an important reminder: Speak with Beatrice about Irene's situation. However, there was no reminder to reflect upon how Elizabeth would have finished her sentence that began, "I regret." He knew this puzzle would dominate his thoughts until he spoke with the lady again.

Relaxing into the carriage squabs, Darcy mused, *Are my feelings more than an infatuation? Elizabeth Bennet is one of the handsomest women of my acquaintance, but her character is even more appealing than her appearance. That she travelled so far to be a comfort to her aunt ....*

"How long until we reach the Castle?" Georgiana asked in a sleep-slurred voice.

He consulted his silver pocket watch, a gift from his father. "If no disaster befalls us, we should arrive in less than forty minutes."

"What sort of disaster?" Irene asked.

Georgiana rolled her eyes. "William **always** says that." She settled back into the corner and was soon dozing again.

Darcy studied his sister's face. *Is Georgiana a disaster yet to come? It is illogical that the minor contretemps over a book caused her dislike of Elizabeth.*

Confident that Georgiana's attitude was of no consequence, Darcy returned his thoughts to Elizabeth. *When she sees Pemberley, she will understand my pride in my heritage. I thank Providence for bringing her here. As Lambton has little competition to concern me, I can take my time to deepen my acquaintance with her.*

Chapter 6

While Georgiana and Irene were settling into their rooms at Flint Rock Castle on Monday afternoon, Darcy joined Colonel Fitzwilliam on the terrace for a brandy. He remarked, "I did not know that Anne and Aunt Catherine would be here."

"I refuse to take the blame; however, after I returned from Rosings, Mother asked me to confirm that you and Anne were not engaged. Then, she wrote to Aunt Catherine that she intended to push a match between you and Irene."

"Why didn't you tell me about her plan?"

"By the time I learnt this, Irene was at Pemberley. It was too late to raise the drawbridge and lower the portcullis. And I was certain Irene would mention it to you."

"She did."

"Will there be a battle royale between Irene and Anne for your affections?"

Darcy chuckled. "I doubt there will even be raised voices. Neither lady has a genuine matrimonial interest in me. Indeed, based on a brief conversation, what Irene wants most is to escape her parents."

"One would expect my sister to be kinder to a child of her own sex, but Martha sides with power—specifically, that arrogant arse she married. They are not overtly cruel, merely disinterested. The last time I mentioned Irene to Harwich, he seemed not to know her, and when he remembered her, he said a widowed marquess had expressed an interest. Irene hasn't even had a season, yet her parents are contemplating a match with some old widower! I would not blame her if she ran away with a tinker."

"Where are Harwich and Martha now?"

"Using their connections to find the Right Schools for the younger sons. Meanwhile, the Harwich heir is shadowing my brother to expand his knowledge of estates. Nigel deserves our pity for being burdened with Henry."

"Is Henry still behaving like a lordling?"

"According to a recent letter from Nigel, Henry is worse every day. The pup is utterly obsessed with the trappings and distractions of his class."

"Happily, Irene is not like that," Darcy said.

"Does she get on well with Georgiana?"

"I have enjoyed hearing their duets on pianoforte and harp." At once, he recalled Georgiana saying, *I am not certain I want Irene's company for an extended time. You aren't going to marry her, are you?*

≈≈≈

During supper, the conversation began with family news, and Georgiana was proud of her restraint; a full ten minutes passed before she asked why Irene's eldest brother was not joining them. The Countess said, "Henry is with Nigel on estate business. The boys return here every week or so, but I know nothing of their schedule."

Fitzwilliam teased, "I shall tell my thirty-seven-year-old brother that you referred to him as a boy."

"Then, Nigel and Henry could return at any time?" Georgiana pressed.

"Yes, and be off again just as unexpectedly. It is of no matter; I manage perfectly well without them. Truth to tell, Henry is inclined to create little dramas with his demands, so I prefer his absence." She chuckled. "I was present when Nigel said something that made Henry fly up into the boughs. Then Henry declared that as both he and Nigel were viscounts, they were equals; thus, Nigel had no authority over him. Nigel said they would never be equals while Henry acted like a brat."

Lady Catherine tsked, "I hope Henry outgrows that."

By the time the strawberry and almond tartlets were served, the conversation had meandered through royal gossip, London scandals, and planned journeys for July and August. Anne asked, "How is life in Lambton? Although I have not been there in some years, it lives in my memory as the quintessential English village."

Georgiana sighed. "It is the quintessential **boring** village, home to two hundred and eight families, but scarcely thirty worth knowing."

Darcy asked Irene, "Are you bored?"

"No. I enjoy riding in the beautiful countryside. I have my music—and you and Georgiana—and there are such wonderful books in Pemberley's library."

He wondered, *Is this flattery to show me she would be an amiable wife?* Apparently, the same thought occurred to Georgiana, who said smugly, "One can scarcely expect Irene to criticize the estate of her possible future husband."

Even if Irene had not blushed, Darcy would have seen her discomfort. "Thank you, Irene. I wish my sister appreciated Pemberley as much as you do."

Georgiana laughed hollowly. "It was a joke!"

"You were rude," the Countess said.

"Not as rude as a lady I met the other day. She made such a fuss about a silly book," Georgiana said defensively.

Darcy stared at her. *Surely, you are not going to speak of Elizabeth Bennet.*

"I was attempting to purchase a poetry book I had wanted for some time, but a lady—if one can call her that— insisted on buying it." When no one commented, she added, "This lady, who I am certain is a fortune hunter, came to Lambton to pursue William."

Now all eyes shifted to Darcy.

"I met Miss Elizabeth Bennet in Hertfordshire last year, and when I was at Rosings recently, she was a guest of Aunt Catherine's parson."

"I recall Miss Bennet—a charming lady!" Fitzwilliam said. "We talked most agreeably of Kent and Hertfordshire, of travelling and staying at home, of new books and music. She kept me well entertained."

Darcy recalled those conversations, not because he participated—which he didn't—but because they were so spirited that they drew his attention. The Colonel added, "I cannot envision her snatching a book from you, Georgiana, so that she could purchase it herself."

Lady Catherine regarded her niece through narrowed eyes. "I grant that the lady is an impertinent creature, but she was never rude."

"Nor would I call her a fortune hunter," Anne said.

Looking at his sister as he spoke, Darcy said, "Miss Bennet came with her aunt to Lambton because her aunt's father was seriously injured in an accident. She bought the book because poetry helps to calm her aunt's mind."

"Very considerate of her," the Countess said approvingly.

Georgiana said resentfully, "Well, none of you were there at the bookshop to see her."

"I was. Miss Bennet had selected that book before we arrived, and you tried to cajole—or bully—her into relinquishing it." Irene met Georgiana's scowl with a serene stare that said, *I am not afraid of you.*

"Also, that book is already in our library." Darcy wished he could ask her, *What is your purpose with this nonsense?*

At once, Georgiana's eyes were teary. "You all misunderstand me!" She pushed aside her unfinished tart. "Excuse me, please. I have a headache." She hurried out of the dining room before Darcy and Fitzwilliam had time to stand.

≈≈≈

When the others retired to the drawing room to drink tea, coffee, and port, no one mentioned Georgiana. Afterwards, Lady Catherine and Irene retired to their suites.

"Whist," the Countess announced, "it is the price of my hospitality." Her love of cards for ha'penny stakes was well known to her relatives and neighbours, so Anne, Darcy, and Fitzwilliam followed her to the small parlour she had designated as her card room.

Early into the first hand, Darcy laid down a card. "Aunt Beatrice, why did you send Irene to Pemberley?"

She laid a card on top of his. "Georgiana wrote to me that she was lonely."

"You could have invited Georgiana here. I thought *you* were going to prepare Irene for her come-out."

"I feel sorry for Irene, so I agreed for her to come to Flint Rock, but I intended for Sophie to guide the girl."

The Colonel exclaimed, "You intended for my unmarried, youngest sister to prepare Irene for her presentation? The Surprise stammers!"

The Countess glared indignantly at him. "As I have told you, do *not* refer to Sophie as 'The Surprise'. The ten-year gap between your birth and hers is not that uncommon! Sophie has already been presented at court and has had a season; she understands what Irene needs to know. Also, her companion, Mrs Jenkinson, is quite competent."

When Darcy glanced at Anne, she said drily, "No doubt you are thinking that if my former companion is so competent, why didn't *I* catch a husband during my three seasons?" She played a card and added, "I have never thought highly either of men or matrimony."

"Where are Sophie and Mrs Jenkinson?" Darcy asked.

"Sophie received a last-minute invitation to a house party, and off they went," his hostess said, clearly annoyed.

"And so Irene is at Pemberley because—" Darcy began.

The Countess snapped, "After rearing five children, I am tired! Let us discuss something else. Anne, is Lady Phillipa still at Rosings? I know she was your mother's companion for all those months you were health at the spa in Epsom, but has the arrangement continued?"

"Lady Phillipa is Mama's unofficial companion. As a widowed viscountess with few resources, she is more comfortable with us than in that shabby townhouse outside London. And her collaboration with Mama has benefitted the neighbourhood. You know Mama loves to be useful."

"How many towns in Kent have received libraries courtesy of Aunt Catherine's generosity?" Darcy asked.

"Seven."

Fitzwilliam said, "We saw less of Lady Phillipa this year than in past years."

Anne said, "She is not in good health, and her wits are starting to wander. She will live out her days at Rosing. However, until I find another companion and another cause for Mama, I shall not be able to visit my friend in Denmark." Regarding the Countess with a speculative gaze, she said, "You are, as ever, the consummate hostess, Aunt Beatrice, but I sense you are separating yourself from demands that do not interest you."

The Countess folder her arms and sat back in her chair. "Yes, in September, some friends and I have planned a card-playing holiday. We are calling it our 'Whist-full adventure'." At the blank looks around the table, she repeated, "***Whist-full*** adventure. We eight ladies shall stay a few weeks each at a property that is the exclusive domain of one of us—say, a pied-à-terre or a dower house."

"*I* think it is clever, Aunt. How long do you plan for this adventure to last?" Anne asked.

She shrugged. "Several months at least. We are simply freeing ourselves from the judgemental gaze of society and the demands of, well, our demanding families. Just the companionship of good friends and whist."

"What of Father?" the Colonel asked.

"The devil take your ridiculous father! He won't notice my absence until he wants something a countess can provide that his ladybird can't." She ran her gaze over the table and smiled. "Ah, I shall take another trick! Lovely."

Much later, after Darcy dismissed his valet for the night, he sat in a leather-covered armchair before the fireplace, gazing at the glowing embers. Despite being attired in his nightshirt and dressing gown, he was not abed. Instead, he was meditating on Elizabeth's presence in Derbyshire. He accepted that her arrival had nothing to do with him; still, she did not behave as if she wanted to end their association. He continued to be haunted by the question, *At the assembly, what was she going to admit that she regretted?*

≈≈≈

After breakfast, Anne, Darcy, and Fitzwilliam relished a bracing race across the pastures surrounding Flint Rock Castle. When they reached the stream that watered a copse of beech trees, they rested their horses. Fitzwilliam breathed deeply and exhaled slowly. "When I ride across these fields, I pretend I am one of the landed gentry. Alas, as a second son and a mere colonel, I suffer from want of money." He gave Darcy a wry grin and added, "Despite my need for a wealthy wife, I am safe from my niece's matrimonial predations."

He dismounted smoothly, and as he helped Anne off her grey gelding, she said, "King Felipe the Fourth of Spain was forty-four when he married his fourteen-year-old niece. To keep the power in the family, you know. You are thirty, and Irene celebrated her eighteenth birthday in February—"

"Stop! Not only do I have no interest in marrying someone I consider a child, I would never want my sister Martha to be my mother-in-law," he exclaimed. "However, Irene does need to be rescued from the Harwiches."

Anne said, "I may have a solution, but first, I am going to resolve *your* situation, Fitz."

"I have a situation?" he asked.

Darcy was still astride his horse, so Anne poked him in the leg with her riding crop. "Get off your high horse, and let Fitz use that diary you carry everywhere."

"I write my private thoughts in it!" he protested.

"Then tear out a page and lend Fitz your pencil."

"Why?" both men demanded.

"I will prove Fitz need not marry a wealthy woman."

Darcy dismounted and reluctantly tore a page from his pocket diary. Handing Fitzwilliam the items, Anne cautioned, "Do not write large; it seems Darcy does not like to share his paper. Now, how much will you receive if you sell your commission?"

Fitzwilliam sat on a tree stump. "Not more than five thousand pounds; likely less. I could not buy an estate with that." At her gesture, he noted the sum on the paper.

Darcy said, "About a decade ago, an acquaintance of mine bought a one-hundred-acre estate in Sussex for about thirty-five hundred pounds."

"Darcy, how many estates do you own?" Anne asked.

"Three; however, I may add one to Georgiana's dowry."

"And Pemberley is the largest," Anne said.

Darcy grinned. "But, of course, fit for the master!"

"I suggest that you give Fitz one of your lesser estates."

For several silent moments, the men considered her suggestion. At last, Fitzwilliam asked, "Where are the lesser estates, and how 'lesser' are they?"

"The year after I inherited, you visited the properties with me in the north of Derbyshire and in Staffordshire."

As the Colonel contemplated this, Anne said, "And I will give you fifteen thousand pounds. Not a loan, a gift."

Fitzwilliam looked from Anne to Darcy. "Assure me this is not a game you are playing."

Anne said, "I am quite serious. Darcy?"

Darcy nodded. "Yes, why not? If these gifts will keep Fitz off the battlefield—"

"And if you promise never to whinge again about needing a wealthy wife, you may take us at our word," Anne said.

"What will Aunt Catherine say about your giving me such a sum?" The Colonel struggled to contain his excitement.

"Recall that Rosings and all its resources are mine except for my mother's widow's portion and her right to occupy the dower house. Not that I intend to dislodge her from the manor anytime soon."

Fitzwilliam threw back his head and laughed. "I can quit the army! I can marry a lady without considering her dowry."

"You *will* have to worry about all the problems that come with having an estate," Darcy reminded him, "but you already have experience with that."

"This is so unexpected. And I can marry *anyone*!"

"Well, you *will* need the lady's consent," Anne said.

"And you must not assume she will accept your proposal," Darcy said. *Will they surmise that I am speaking from experience?*

The Colonel's expression was contemplative. "I could marry Elizabeth Bennet. She is clever and witty and lovely."

Anne glanced at Darcy and saw what she expected to see: shock that was turning into worry. "Fitz, I believe the lady already has a suitor. You have had this notion for, what, three minutes—and you have not yet chosen an estate. Settle that matter before you pay your addresses to anyone."

"Yes. Right. I need to be sensible, practical, and ...." Laughing again, he tossed the pencil and paper into the air.

Darcy said, "You also need to return my pencil, so we shall remain here until you find it."

When Fitzwilliam squatted to comb his fingers through the grass, Anne smiled; Darcy gave her an answering smile and a nod. Abruptly, he rose and offered the pencil. "Here. Thank you. Thank you both! If this is a joke or a dream—"

"It is not," Darcy said.

"I could raise horses or hunting hounds. And I could marry anyone." As he walked back to his horse, he began to whistle an old folksong, "My thing is my own".

"Thank you for agreeing with me," Anne murmured.

Darcy said, "Thank you for your sensible suggestion, and let me know how I may help Irene."

"For now, letting her stay at Pemberley is sufficient."

≈≈≈

At the manor, Darcy sought out Irene and invited her to stroll in the castle's formal garden. With a heavy sense of dread, she took the arm he offered and walked with him. Upon reaching a wrought-iron bench painted in the Countess's favourite shade of red, he gestured for her to sit.

"If this will be a short rejection, I prefer to remain standing," she said.

"You break my heart." Darcy sat and asked, "Sit with me, please." With a shuddering sigh, she sat, and he took her hand. "This conversation is neither a rejection nor an offer of marriage. You are a victim of rather stupid parents—and you may quote me to both of them."

She laughed with relief. "I shall save your words for just the right moment, sir."

"Anne and I are considering how to mend *your* heart, for life in the Harwich household sounds unkind. Until we find an alternative, you are welcome to stay at Pemberley. No, you are *always* welcome, but I think you can do better ... well, except for our library. Marriage, of course, is the usual path for acquiring a new residence, yet—"

"I am not even ready to be presented at court," Irene interrupted bitterly.

"Have you no aunts on your father's side to help you?"

"My grandmama, the Countess of Harwich, gave birth to six sons and then died."

Darcy winced. "I certainly hope there was more to her life than that. At any rate, Anne and I will find the right lady to guide you. I will also bear the expense of ensuring that you have what you need to be the equal of your peers."

"Will the lady reside with me at my father's estate?"

"I think it best if you live in or near London so you can enjoy the entertainments that everyone will discuss. You have a vivacious nature, so when you are officially out in society, you will shine like the jewel you are."

Smiling, Irene leaned against his shoulder. "I believe this is the kindest rejection in the history of the world."

Darcy laughed. *She truly is a dear girl*, he thought. Impulsively, he kissed the top of Irene's head.

Abruptly, Georgiana's voice shattered the moment. "Ah, you are together. Should I wish you happy?"

Irene sat up straight, but she felt confident rather than embarrassed. "I wish everyone happy." She kissed Darcy's cheek, rose and curtsied, and returned to the manor.

≈≈≈

Later that night, when Georgiana said she was ready to retire, Darcy said he would walk her to her room. When they were out of hearing of the others, he said, "You confound me. I cannot tell if you like Irene or not. You have been rude to her in the presence of others. Yet, she tolerates you."

"I have not been rude; I have been boldly clever, saying things that others only think."

"You give yourself too much credit."

"Irene tolerates me because she wants to marry you, even though you are merely a gentleman."

Amused, Darcy said, "I have always thought that being gentleman was a point of pride."

Georgiana groaned. "Ours is the only branch of the family without titles. Uncle Kestevyn is an earl; Aunt Beatrice is a countess; Aunt Catherine and Irene are 'ladies', and even Randal and Anne are honourables. But what are we Darcys? Nothing! We have the same honorifics as our housekeeper and butler."

"How tragic," he said drily. "We shall have to console ourselves with the knowledge that our estate carries no debts and generates an income of ten thousand per year."

"I want to be Lady Georgiana!" she pouted. "Surely, there is an earl, marquess, or duke who needs some of Pemberley's resources and has a daughter or sister in want of a husband. Such a wife could throw me in the path of titled gentlemen."

"You would sell me to the bidder with the loftiest title?"

"I know you would enjoy the prestige."

"So that the Prince Regent can impose upon me for funds for his next architectural whim? No, thank you."

"You would not pursue a title—not even for me?"

"Not for anyone, dear girl."

≈≈≈

On the following afternoon, Anne was happy to accept Darcy's invitation to play chess, for the cousins were well-matched in the game. They had moved only one piece each when the Countess bustled into the room and kissed their cheeks. "Thank you for your generosity to Randal. Of course, the Earl will not approve, but only because he wants all boons and blessings to flow from him. Thus, I am also pleased that your generosity will annoy my husband."

"A servant said Fitz left for London today," Darcy said.

"He is very eager to sell his commission, and *I* am very happy he will settle down."

Anne said, "I am also considering how to provide Irene with a better situation. I must talk with her before forming a plan, but I am determined she will have a pleasanter future to contemplate within a month or two."

"Excellent, my dear! I am grateful for your efforts. She is a sweet child but too energetic for me. The lady you spoke of at supper last night—Miss Bennet—would she be a suitable companion for Irene?"

Darcy answered, "No, she is a gentleman's daughter and does not need paid work."

"Well then, I shall leave the matter in Anne's hands." She squeezed her niece's shoulder affectionately and left.

Darcy told Anne, "I, too, need your assistance. As Mrs Annesley now has a new situation, I must find a companion for Georgiana. Do you have any sug-gestions? Perhaps Mrs Jenkinson?"

"After she gets Sophia fired off, she will retire, and I will give her a generous pension. Jenkinson was my friend, my confidant, and my champion."

"Is there someone you can recommend for Georgiana?"

"I would not burden anyone with such a capricious charge. You have done your best, but she is never content."

Darcy was surprised, but as he reflected on Anne's words, he agreed that Georgiana was rarely pleased. "I do not know what would bring her happiness. Anything she asks for, I happily provide, so I am bewildered by her habitual petulance *and* her animosity toward Miss Bennet."

"You like the lady. I noticed that at Rosings Park."

"I do, yes, although I can't predict what will come of that. I thank you for warning Fitz away without mentioning me."

"Georgiana might disapprove of any lady you choose."

Hesitantly, he asked, "Do you like Georgiana?"

After a silence, Anne admitted, "I used to, but she has become selfish and spiteful. If you are wondering why I have not said so before now, it is because you did not ask. No one wants to hear their relations disparaged—certainly not if the speaker's opinion was unsolicited."

≈≈≈

Several days later, Darcy was in the library when the butler interrupted him by softly clearing his throat. "Pardon me, sir, but the Countess requires a fourth for whist."

He sighed. "It is too much to hope, Ashton, that *you* are her chosen fourth?"

"It is, sir. The game is afoot in the blue parlour."

Darcy put aside his book. "Please bring me a brandy there—and I want a glass from my Uncle's private store."

"If you do not tell the earl I gave it to you, I will not tell the earl you demanded it."

When Darcy entered the blue parlour, the Countess said, "Ah, good, you are here. Nigel and Henry returned a short while ago. Ordinarily, Nigel partners with me, but he is in a foul mood, writing a long letter to Harwich about what a wretched boy Henry is. I am told Henry is sulking somewhere with Georgiana." She waved a finger at her nephew.

"Do not let Harwich trick you with a taradiddle about educating Henry. That is what he told Nigel."

As Darcy sat opposite the Countess, Lady Catherine asked, "What taradiddle did Martha tell you, Beatrice, so you would agree to prepare Irene for her come-out?"

"Martha, devious creature that she is, appealed to my vanity, praising my knowledge of the qualities a woman must possess to be considered an accomplished lady."

Lady Catherine sat back in her chair. "Martha is not wrong; you understand what matters—that a lady respects tradition and understands her duty to her family."

The Countess said, "She must have a thorough knowledge of music, singing, drawing, dancing, and modern languages. But no Latin or Greek; *not* a blue-stocking."

Lady Catherine mused, "To be truly accomplished, a woman must also have a certain *something* in her air, her walk, her voice, and her expressions."

Her sister-in-law nodded. "And to all this, she must have character and be in the habit of improving her mind."

Anne looked from her mother to her aunt. "With that formidable yet vague list of qualifications, I am surprised that the two of you know *any* 'accomplished' ladies."

Before the Countess or Lady Catherine could reply, Darcy said, "I hope you can broaden my education. I am at a loss to understand Georgiana, her petulance, her moodiness. She is inexplicably emotional, although I suppose that is common for young females—" He interrupted himself. "Aunt Catherine, you smirked at Aunt Beatrice!"

"The 'inexplicably emotional' element has nothing to do with Georgiana's sex and everything to do with her age."

Lady Catherine agreed. "It is true. During those years of change between childhood and adulthood, all young people's brains become disordered, resulting in excessive sensibility. Irrational emotions can suddenly flare during the most mundane situations. As a lad, my brother could be as emotional as a frustrated puppy!"

The Countess tapped a playing card on the back of Lady Catherine's hand, which lay between them on the table. "Darcy has his I-do-not-believe-you look."

"Convince me," he said.

She asked, "Do you not recall when Nigel got into a fistfight with Randal over who would be the first to drive the new phaeton? In those—what did you call them? Years of change? Nigel was such a hothead. I felt fortunate that Randal was usually quite calm. Ah! And I have yet to meet a lady who injured her hand because she punched a door or a wall when she was upset. Yet, I have known four men who did so—including Harwich when he was newly married."

Darcy asked, "Anne, have you no example to add?"

She grinned. "I do, actually. When you were fifteen and I was thirteen, I ate the apple tart you asked Cook to put aside for you. What a fuss you made! When you saw the empty plate, you flung it to the floor and broke it. One would have thought I had stolen your favourite horse and saddle."

An embarrassed smile overspread Darcy's face. "I had considered that tart to be my reward for my hours of studying Marcus Aurelius' meditations of Stoic philosophy."

"Yet your response was not Stoic," Anne teased.

"I *was* rather emotional, but I was just a lad."

The Countess took a trick. "That is the point, sir. Georgiana's brain is not yet matured."

"But it will mature, won't it?"

"To one degree or another," Lady Catherine said.

"That is not reassuring," Darcy grumbled.

"My remark was meant to be truthful, sir."

≈≈≈

Lying in bed that night, Darcy was certain he had never felt less like sleeping. When he contemplated his sister's behaviour, he felt at a loss to curb her incivilities, which tested his authority. When he considered Fitz, he hoped that one of the lesser estates would suit him. When he considered

Irene, he hoped Anne could devise a plan to help the girl. However, when he reflected upon Elizabeth, he felt overwhelmed by uncertainty. *I still feel as attracted to her as I did when I proposed—no, my feelings are stronger. But is she interested only in resolving the misunderstandings between us?*

It occurred to Darcy that Elizabeth's desire to protect Jane matched his own habit of protecting Bingley from his foolishness regarding young ladies. He had also realised how insulting his assumptions about the Bennets were. However, it was Anne's point about unsolicited fault-finding resonated most strongly with him. With a new and unsettling perspective, he recalled the details of his proposal, which had included a litany of harsh criticisms about the Bennets. "I owe Elizabeth an apology," he murmured to the darkness.

Chapter 7

During Trevor Knowles' first few days at Oaklands, he was charming, respectful, and he took pains not to be a bother as he learnt the habits of the household. Then, after spending some afternoons riding around the estate, he began phrasing suggestions as if they were questions. Gradually, his manner became more condescending than amiable.

When he could, Trevor met with Upton in his office, where, over glasses of claret, he asserted that the Selby estate should be his. Upton encouraged his ambitions. The "what if" questions he casually asked were often absurd, although Trevor seemed oblivious. Nor did Upton dwell upon the likelihood that people would be injured if his schemes were implemented.

While Elizabeth was unaware of Trevor's meetings with Upton, she did notice that he was becoming more assertive in his opinions. In his conversations with her and Mrs Gardiner, he spoke wistfully about the misfortune of being a second son. Yet, despite his longing for an estate, Elizabeth realised he was less knowledgeable than he presented himself to be. In a letter to Jane, she described Trevor as a handsome fellow but said he reminded her of Wickham and his lament of being denied a parsonage by Mr Darcy.

≈≈≈

On a sunny afternoon, Mrs Gardiner sat in the parlour, gazing absently out the window. Had she paid attention to the view, she would have noted Owain, the estate's newest field hand, trimming the low hedges bordering the gravel drive. At the point where the drive curved back to the main road, she might have looked with an appreciative eye at the little wilderness area where a towering Spanish chestnut tree shaded a granite bench for two. But Mrs Gardiner was not paying attention; she could not see beyond her worries.

When Elizabeth came to the parlour, she hesitated at the threshold. *How weary Aunt looks.* She entered and knelt by her aunt's chair. "Have you heard from Uncle?'

"Yes, and for another week at least, as there are complications. Edward sounds very tired."

"Does he sound as tired as you seem, Aunt?"

Mrs Gardiner gave her a startled look and then smiled. "Thank you for that, Lizzy. You have interrupted my melancholy thoughts."

"I have a favour to ask. I suspect you will tell me 'no', but you **must** say 'yes'."

As Elizabeth took a breath in anticipation of making her argument, her aunt said, "Yes, I will walk with you."

Very soon, bonnet strings were tied beneath chins, parasols were resting on muslin-covered shoulders, and the ladies were strolling toward the little wilderness. While it was not Mrs Gardiner's habit to burden anyone with her concerns, she was relieved to admit that she **had** concerns. "My father is not healing as well as I had hoped; his memories are confused. Also, my dear husband writes that his business may be at risk. At least I have no fears about the welfare of my four little darlings; I know Jane oversees their care as if they were her own. Still, I cannot stop the shadows of a gloomy future from colouring my thoughts."

Elizabeth was silent for several moments so she could consider her aunt's concerns and give her aunt time to reflect. Then, she said, "My philosophy is that when one ruminates too long upon either **what might be** or **what was**, one loses what is pleasurable about **this** moment."

Her aunt teased, "I thought your philosophy is to think only of the past as its remembrance gives you pleasure."

Elizabeth laughed. "My philosophies are not mutually exclusive. If I mused upon the matter, I might find that I have even more philosophies. However, such musings would interfere with my enjoyment of this moment with you."

"I fear you have seen more of my father's sick room than of the countryside."

"My rambles have been delightful, and I have learnt much from Abel." She nudged her aunt with her shoulder. "I envy you having a brother who is so knowledgeable and kind. The inconvenience of having only sisters is that I had no opportunity to watch a boy grow into a young man who would introduce his friends, thus, enabling me to understand which behaviours are typically masculine and which are personal qualities."

"Are you thinking of anyone in particular, Lizzy?"

"Mr Darcy is described as the brooding master of Pemberley. But I have never seen Uncle Gardiner brood—nor Charles Bingley. If anything, Mr Bingley lacked the gravitas I observed in Mr Warren. As Jane mentioned in the letter we received yesterday, she seems quite taken with Mr Warren, and I approve."

"Have you formed an opinion about Trevor?"

"I cannot tell if he wants to be seen as a tragic fellow who has been denied his life's dream or a bold fellow who can forge his own destiny."

"He, Wickham, and Upton Parnell—you danced with him at the assembly—were confederates at Cambridge. While they said they were just having a lark, I disagree; larks are not cruel. Although Abel has said little about what he endured from them, I know it was unpleasant. On more than one occasion, he and Mr Darcy joined forces against that trio of terror. Because of those 'larks', my parents banished Trevor from Oaklands."

Elizabeth had been quite popular at the assembly, so she struggled to recall which of her partners was Upton Parnell. "Thinning blond hair combed back? Dressed more foppishly than is typical in Lambton?"

"Yes. Abel says that given how few people like Upton— much less trust him—he is eerily well-informed about other people's business. To quote our plain-speaking cook, Upton likes to stir the shite just to raise a stink."

≈ ≈ ≈

After returning from church on Sunday, Elizabeth slipped away to spend time in nature, hoping to settle her mind.

When will Mr Darcy visit Oaklands? By my calculations, he might return to Derbyshire on Saturday next. Thus, the earliest he is likely to call would be after church on the twenty-fourth. Of course, he will be calling on the Selbys, not only **me***. Will he bring Miss Darcy and Lady Irene? Will his conversation be polite but nothing of substance? How can I be so confused about my feelings for such a vexing man! Do I want his good opinion or not?*

≈≈≈

In the afternoon, Elizabeth and Mrs Harcourt sat on the granite bench in the wilderness area and watched Trevor play quoits with Cassandra. Mrs Harcourt murmured, "That is the most effort I have seen Mr Knowles put forth."

Elizabeth replied, "I cannot fathom why he remains here. Abel does not need him, so other than keeping Squire company in the evenings, Mr Knowles has no purpose."

A frown creased Mrs Harcourt's brow. "Squire's recovery has seemed slower of late. I asked the apothecary, but he assured me this is not uncommon."

Pressing his hand to his chest, Trevor exclaimed, "Ah, Miss Cassandra, you are too skilled for me. I cede the field." He bowed first to the girl and then to the ladies on the bench before sauntering to the manor. At the front door, he stepped aside so Polly could emerge with a tray of lemonade. He spoke to her and, after she shook her head, he went indoors.

Cassandra had collected the quoits, and she called, "I shall come back for my lemonade after I put these away."

As she hurried off, Polly stood before Elizabeth and Mrs Harcourt, holding out the tray so they could each take a glass. "I have written a new song."

Elizabeth looked surprised; Mrs Harcourt did not and urged, "I long to hear it."

To the tune of "Yankee Doodle", Polly sang, "Some men when they drink too much, they get a little randy. Mr Knowles is not that sort tho' he's drunk all the brandy."

"**All** the brandy?" Mrs Harcourt exclaimed.

"Well, that is what I said when he asked for more. Only this week, he finished a full bottle but asked me not to speak of it. Of course, I said I would not."

Elizabeth laughed. "And so you sang, Polly. Clever girl!"

Sneering, the maid said, "As if I would put the interests of some sneaksby over my loyalty to this household!"

Mrs Harcourt asked, "Does Mr Knowles drink alone?"

"I have seen him enter Squire's room in the evening, and in the morning, two brandy glasses need a wash."

Elizabeth said, "Too much alcohol is bad for an invalid. Perhaps ending those tête-à-têtes will reverse his decline."

"Draughts, cribbage, neighbourhood gossip." Mrs Harcourt ticked off each activity on her fingers. "When Squire improves, he may be up to a game of chess. With you, Mrs Gardiner, Cassie, and myself, Mr Knowles will have no opportunity to impose himself on Squire." She smiled at the maid. "Thank you; your songs are always informative."

Cassandra raced out of the manor. "I have come for my lemonade." After the girl collected the last glass on the tray, she sat on the grass at her mother's feet, and Polly left the ladies to their conversation.

"I assume this was not Polly's first song," Elizabeth said.

"She sang a particularly memorable one about a baker who added chalk to his bread to whiten it. When the song spread through Lambton, the rogue closed his shop and moved away." Mrs Harcourt sighed, "Now I must consider how to tell this to Mr Abel and Mrs Gardiner."

"I will tell Aunt," Elizabeth assured her.

≈≈≈

At tea, Trevor mentioned that he wanted to purchase some brandy. Abelard, having been alerted to the ladies' suspicions, said that next week, he would speak with the fellow from whom he acquired spirits. When Trevor offered to make the purchase, Abelard declined, saying his supplier preferred that his identity be known only to a trusted few.

Following supper, Mrs Harcourt and Elizabeth kept Trevor in the parlour with inquiries about the changes he had noted in Lambton, having been away from the village for several years. When at last he brought his flask of port to Squire's suite, he found Mrs Gardiner reminiscing with her father. After a few minutes, she rose, kissed her father's forehead, and wished him good night. Then, she asked, "Will you wish Squire a good night, Trevor?"

"I hoped to sit with him for awhile—to ease his pain."

Squire said, "I am too tired for company, nephew."

Trevor started to speak, intending to coax his uncle, but Mrs Gardiner pulled him into the corridor.

Squire's valet was sitting in a hall chair, and he stood. She said, "My father is ready to sleep, Nash. I am certain you have noted that his recovery has slowed, so he is not to have strong spirits until he is more himself. Small beer and wine diluted with water are acceptable, in addition to coffee and tea. We rely on you to help us guard his health."

Nash bowed his head. "And so I shall, Mrs Gardiner."

After the valet entered Squire's suite and closed the door behind him, Mrs Gardiner began leading Trevor to his bedchamber. Although his expression was one of bewildered innocence, there was annoyance in his tone. "I fear I have been misunderstood. Has Polly said anything about me?"

"I speak with Polly throughout the day. She is a valued member of this household."

"The Selbys are fortunate to have loyal servants."

"We **earned** their loyalty by treating them fairly and showing appreciation for their good work. I have not spoken to Polly about Squire's care. Do you suggest that I do so, sir?"

He smiled tensely. "I leave such matters to you."

"As you should." With a stern look, she said, "And I have a question only you can answer."

"I am at your service."

"Why are you here?"

"To assist with Squire's care."

"And where will you go when you are not needed?"

"I ... I have not considered that."

"I urge you to meditate on that question, **Cousin**."

≈≈≈

The following day, after an early morning race—early for Trevor and Upton—they rested their horses at the River Wye. Pacing agitatedly, Trevor said, "They want me to leave Oaklands. What shall I do?"

Upton shrugged. "Leave, I suppose." Having Trevor in the neighbourhood had not been as amusing as he had hoped. There had been no public confrontations with Abelard, nor had Wickham come in response to Upton's anonymous letter. The Lambton solicitor whose favourite pastime was stirring shite was bored.

"If I am not here, how can I demonstrate that I would be a superior squire for Oaklands?" Trevor whined.

"Did the Selbys hint or state that you should go?"

"Cousin Vivian hinted that I am not useful."

When Upton laughed, he complained, "I am not a farmer nor a common labourer, so I have nothing to do! And I fear the Selbys hold our school pranks against me. They should forgive me and forget my trespasses. The Bible says so."

"Does it?"

"Doesn't it?"

"You are a curate. You should know."

"I have not **memorized** the entire Bible."

"I thought that was part of the job."

Trevor made a dismissive gesture. "What can I do so they won't send me away?"

After a contemplative silence, Upton suggested, "Be the prodigal son. Encourage their pity."

"Explain, sir."

"My father, who has a prodigious memory for familial histories, once told me that Oaklands was given to Selby by his late wife's grandmother. Squire had a falling-out with his father, which is why Fallow Deer Grove was given to your mother. Do you know nothing of this?"

"I never asked."

Upton stared at him. "You never asked?" *No wonder he does not know what is in the Bible or how to run an estate.*

"But I ask **you** now how to make myself a prodigal son."

"Tell the Selbys that in addition to visiting for the sake of your uncle's well-being, you have sought shelter at Oaklands because of an estrangement with your father. Let Squire see his circumstances being repeated in your life."

"What is the reason for my alienation from Father?"

Upton rolled his eyes. "Do you expect me to spoon-feed you every detail, man? If you cannot contrive a convincing tale, you don't deserve Oaklands. Does not the Bible say that the Lord helps those who help themselves?"

Trevor smirked. "For all the many things I do not know, sir, I am aware that sentiment is from a fable by Aesop."

Upton made a dismissive sound, for he liked to imagine that he was superior to the complaining curate in every way. "There is another lesson to be learnt from Aesop. Whatever story you contrive for the Selbys, keep it simple. Having too many details is dangerous. If they press you, say only that the matter is too painful to discuss."

≈≈≈

Consequently, over tea, Trevor showed a heretofore unseen humility as he told the Selbys, Mrs Harcourt, and Elizabeth that although he was **most** interested in Squire's welfare, he had also come to Oaklands because of a falling-out with his father. Trevor said he understood the importance of being a parson, but he believed in his heart he was meant to have an estate. However, when he approached his father with a plan to acquire a property, Baron Knowles insisted that Trevor make the church his career.

Trevor told his story well and without excessive details, but Elizabeth had seen enough of him to suspect that, at best, his story was a partial truth and, at worst, it was a bag of moonshine. When she glanced at Abelard, Mrs Gardiner, and Mrs Harcourt over the rim of her teacup, she was certain she saw doubt in their faces as well.

Still, Upton had been correct. Squire's estrangement from his father made him willing to help Trevor. After telling him he could remain at Oaklands, Squire looked to his son for confirmation.

While a full minute passed in silence, Trevor feared his perfidy was obvious to his cousin. Finally, Abelard said, "Very well. To prepare you for the future you dream of, I can arrange for you to experience the most important aspects of caring for an estate. Since arriving here, you have made no effort to learn about Oaklands other than riding through it."

"Because Oaklands can never be mine," Trevor blurted.

"No, it never can. Still, our people can teach you lessons that apply to all estates, and I expect you to participate fully."

"I will. I promise."

"Your first lesson is that every man and woman working here is your superior."

"But—"

"No buts."

"Even if—"

Abelard declared, "You must assume that everyone at Oaklands knows more than you—because they do."

When Trevor gave Squire a beseeching look, Squire nodded. "Abel is correct. That is the cost of staying with us."

"I appreciate your generosity. Thank you." The curate-who-would-be-a-squire smiled feebly.

Chapter 8

Following supper at Flint Rock Castle on Saturday, Darcy announced his intention to return to Pemberley on Monday, which was a week sooner than originally planned. He did not reveal his recent ruminations had clarified his intentions toward Elizabeth, and he was impatient to see her.

The Honourable Randal Fitzwilliam had arrived from London earlier that day after selling his commission, and he now sat with his mother on a settee for two in the drawing room. "I will go with Darcy, as I have an estate to choose."

Lady Catherine made a disappointed moue. "Darcy, I expected you, Irene, and Georgiana to stay two weeks complete. Beatrice, what have you to say about this?"

Waving her black lace fan in a leisurely motion, the Countess sighed. "I am merely the chatelaine at this humble castle, a way station used by various Harwiches, Darcys, and de Bourghs for their pleasure and convenience."

Fitzwilliam grinned. "In other words, Mother, you don't mind if we leave?" She snapped her fan shut and swatted him with it.

Darcy had not told his plans to Georgiana or Irene, so he wondered whether they would choose to remain at Flint Rock. The ladies chose Pemberley; however, Georgiana asked whether Henry could join them. Darcy was in no mood to manage the Earl of Harwich's lazy heir, so he said 'no'."

≈≈≈

After an uneventful journey to Pemberley on Monday, the Darcy siblings, Irene, and Fitzwilliam arrived in mid-afternoon. During supper, Darcy asked who would join him in a call to Oaklands on the following day. He was eager to apologise to Elizabeth—and more than eager to hear the rest of her thought from their interrupted conversation at the assembly.

Fitzwilliam said he was happy to come along, but Georgiana declined, saying, "I am weary from our journey."

Irene wondered, *Do I want to watch Darcy try to endear himself to another lady? I prefer not. My time at Flint Rock gave me much to consider.* She gave Darcy an apologetic smile. "I will join you on another day."

≈≈≈

Darcy and Fitzwilliam called at Oaklands on Tuesday afternoon. From Fitzwilliam's introduction to Mrs Gardiner, Elizabeth learnt he was no longer in the army. As for the ladies of Pemberley, Darcy said, "My sister and Lady Irene are not with us because we returned late yesterday from Flint Rock Castle. The ladies felt they would not be at their best."

"Such delicate flowers, my cousin and my niece," Fitzwilliam said innocently, but Darcy heard his mockery.

"How far from Lambton is Flint Rock Castle, sir," Elizabeth asked, envisioning a journey of many hours.

"Never more than four hours by coach. Usually less."

Although he did not want to criticize his sister or Irene for their feeble excuse, Darcy felt his face redden. Still, given Georgiana's animosity and the risk that Irene might follow her lead, he was relieved they had stayed away. With more cheerfulness than he felt, he asked after the Bennet family.

Elizabeth marvelled that Darcy spoke with good-humoured ease, and she saw approval in Mrs Gardiner's face. She wished Abel were here, for she longed to hear Darcy converse with him. As for Trevor, his whereabouts were unknown, but his company was not missed.

Mrs Gardiner rang for a tea tray, and as she poured out, Mrs Harcourt pushed Squire's bath chair into the parlour. At his direction, she situated him beside a library chair, which she then claimed for her seat.

Squire beamed at Darcy and Fitzwilliam. "I thank you for coming, gentleman, although since the assembly, Oaklands has had many visitors. While I like to pretend all this attention is for me, I have noted two types of callers in particular: unmarried gentlemen and determined mamas dragging their marriageable sons with them. As Vivian is already well settled, I can only assume that Miss Elizabeth's presence has brought new popularity to my humble estate."

Elizabeth blushed while Mrs Gardiner chided Squire for being a tease. With mock regret, Squire said, "My apologies if I was inappropriate, Miss Elizabeth. You see, I recently injured my head." That earned him more laughter.

When Mrs Gardiner thanked Darcy for the loan of the bath chair, he replied, "One could say that it has come home, for although Pemberley's carpenter built it, he followed plans drawn by Squire. Sensibly, those plans were drawn for a four-wheel chair, which is more stable than the common three-wheel model."

Bewildered, Squire asked, "I made the plans for this?" He ran his palm along the tapestry-covered padded armrest.

"Some ten years ago, I believe," Darcy said, hoping to spark a memory.

"Am I late?" Trevor asked cheerily as he entered.

Trevor greeted Darcy and was reminded he had met Fitz-william some years ago. After nodding to the ladies, he asked his uncle, "How are you feeling, sir?"

Squire was still admiring the bath chair. "I **designed** this. Mr Darcy, kindly give my praise to your carpenter for his fine work. By chance, do you still have my drawings?"

Mrs Harcourt said, "You have these plans in your study."

"Do I? Are you certain?"

With a theatrically censorious expression, Trevor exclaimed, "Never say you have been rifling my Uncle's papers, Mrs H!"

"I am **Mrs Harcourt**, sir, and Squire showed me the plans for this chair when I helped him organize his study at his request," she said coldly.

Squire looked abashed and patted her arm. "I **do** recall those hours we spent on several cold afternoons the winter before last, Mrs Susan. You patiently listened to my reminiscences as you brought order to chaos so that Abel could locate the estate records easily. You are a treasure, madam. I apologise for having such a poor memory."

Trevor, who should have looked abashed but didn't, said cheerily, "Mrs Harcourt is indeed a treasure and a very busy lady. Should you need assistance with your documents, sir, I would be happy to help."

Because Elizabeth and Mrs Gardiner were exchanging wary glances, they did not see Darcy and Fitzwilliam do the same. Squire, however, ended the discussion. "Mrs Susan and I have everything in good order. There is no need for you to trouble yourself."

Trevor prattled about nothing of note, and the others made polite conversation until Squire finished his tea and said he wished to rest. Before Mrs Harcourt came to her feet, Trevor leapt up and hurried to stand behind the bath chair. "Allow me to help you, Uncle."

Frowning, Squire twisted in his chair. "No need, sir! Mrs Susan and I shall manage."

As Mrs Harcourt wheeled Squire out of the parlour, Trevor realised all eyes were on him, and he smiled thinly. "Well, I have spent my day learning how Oaklands' stables are run, but now I am due to meet an old school chum at the Mute Ploughboy for a tankard of ale." When no one spoke, he added, "You know him, Darcy. Upton Parnell."

"Yes, Young Parnell," Darcy drawled.

I have never heard him drawl, Elizabeth thought.

Grinning, Fitzwilliam rose and told Mrs Gardiner. "The tea was most refreshing, madam, but now I crave a taste of ale." To Trevor, he said, "I shall go with you, sir."

Trevor stared open-mouthed, uncertain how to uninvite a man who had invited himself. *I shall have to watch what I say if Fitzwilliam is present—and Parnell will not be happy.*

Fitzwilliam bowed to the ladies. "I hope to see you soon, for I shall be coming and going in the neighbourhood for the next few weeks."

"But—" Trevor croaked.

Fitzwilliam said, "So it behoves me to acquaint myself with the denizens." Trevor felt trapped when the former colonel flung an arm around his shoulders. "Lead on, sir." Resignedly, he let himself be led from the drawing room.

Fitzwilliam paused in the doorway to ask Darcy, "Shall we meet in half an hour at the pub, Cousin?"

Darcy consulted his pocket watch. "Yes, I do not wish to wear out my welcome at Oaklands." After the men departed, he turned to Mrs Gardiner, "Or perhaps I have already tarried too long."

She smiled warmly. "Not at all, sir. However, I do wish to look in on Father before he falls asleep."

"If Squire feels fit enough, will you bring him to Pemberley on Saturday for luncheon?"

"I doubt he can manage yet." Noting the wishful gleam in her niece's eyes, Mrs Gardiner understood, *She wants to see Pemberley.* "However, Elizabeth, Abelard, Mr Knowles, and myself welcome your invitation."

"Splendid! Does two in the afternoon suit you?"

"It does. Now, if you will excuse me." Smiling, Mrs Gardiner left. *Taking Elizabeth to Pemberley is the least I can do to satisfy her curiosity—and mine.*

Now alone, Darcy said, "There is a prettyish kind of little wilderness beyond the drive. I should like to take a turn in it if you will favour me with your company."

Feeling suddenly shy, Elizabeth nodded. She rose and hesitantly accepted the arm he offered. As they exited the drawing room, Darcy thought, *So, all I must do is find a subtle way to ask her about the regret she started to voice when we were at the assembly.*

≈≈≈

Their walk began in silence as they followed the stepping stones to the wilderness. After making a few remarks about the Spanish chestnut tree with its trunk that was nearly seven feet in diameter, Darcy said, "For some days now, I have wanted to speak with you. Regarding my sister's behaviour at the bookshop, she is still ... well, she has not been herself since Ramsgate."

"Her insistence on having that book confused me."

"It seems Georgiana is unaware that our library contains all of Wordsworth's poetry."

"Oh." Having nothing more to say on the matter, Elizabeth said, "I had not met Squire before this visit. Abel and Aunt Gardiner say his memory is rather fragmented since the accident. Squire has said that he fell off a horse; yet another time, he said he tumbled down some stairs. But neither is true."

"What did happen?"

"One of his inventions from some years ago—a device for removing the husk from the barley grains—needed to be replaced. When he stepped onto the platform atop the machine, it collapsed under him."

"He is fortunate to have his family with him—and I include you, Miss Bennet."

"Thank you, sir. I must say that Mrs Susan is, as Squire said, a treasure."

"I was not well acquainted with her family, the Brownings. They had a cobblery and made boots and shoes of good quality. When smallpox took them, I was at university. Before Miss Browning went to live with a relation, Mr Parnell Senior oversaw the auction of the cobblery. My father said the low offers did not reflect the property's true value. However, Squire stepped up and bid twice as much as anyone else; thus, Miss Browning had at least some money when she left. Mind you, the Selbys had no use for the shop; however, more than once, I recall Squire expounding on the importance of being a good neighbour."

"The Selbys are generous people and, as sometimes happens, generous people are rewarded. The cobblery's tools are now Squire's workshop, and Abel said his father was surprised at how useful they are."

"For many years, Squire was the man to consult for solutions to a wide range of mechanical matters."

"Such as building a bath chair."

"Yes. It was distressing that he did not recall his design."

"I was more shocked by Mr Knowles' behaviour."

"The best I can say about him is that he is not as conniving as Upton Parnell. At university, those two and George Wickham amused themselves with vicious pranks and disregarded proprieties."

"I am duly warned. Little by little, I am learning about the locals. Mr Timmons has a high opinion of you; however, the apothecary—while offering no specific criticism—is concerned that you and your servants are not making sufficient use of his tonics that bolster good health."

Darcy chuckled. "He prefers to keep people healthy rather than deal with the sick. I can't quibble with his logic."

"If I have counted correctly, sir, your family has two earls, two countesses, and two viscounts roaming the halls of Flint Rock Castle. Does anyone ever get confused about whom is being addressed or discussed?"

"Well, Fitz's parents are the Earl and Countess of Kestevyn, so en famille, the earl is called Kestevyn or Edmund, and the Countess is called Lady Kestevyn or, familiarly, Beatrice. Kestevyn's heir uses the courtesy title of Viscount Ambrose; however, I call him by his Christian name, which is Nigel. Lady Irene's parents are the Earl and Countess of Harwich—Harwich despises his first name—Cuthbert—so we do not use it." His voice dropped to a theatrical whisper. "Fitz calls his brother-in-law 'the arse Martha married', but I find that too wordy. Harwich's eldest son is Henry, whose courtesy title is Viscount Bowmont. He is a sullen, easily offended lad."

"Would you like to have a title?"

"Thank you, **no**. While Georgiana's fondest wish is to be Lady Somebody-or-other, I have no interest in joining the peerage. No interest and no regrets." After a pause, he added,

"Regarding the topic of regrets, Miss Bennet, I have wondered what you *nearly* said at the assembly."

She stopped walking as she strove to remember their brief conversation on the dark balcony. Suddenly, she smiled. "Ah, yes. My last words to you were 'I regret', and then a lady called your name."

He sighed. "My cousin, Lady Irene."

"And you have been wondering what I regretted?" She gave him an arch look.

"Wondering? Not at all. I have been confused, unsettled, and tortured by your unfinished thought."

Elizabeth smiled. "Well, I was going to say that I regretted believing George Wickham's lies—and speaking so harshly to you."

"As my letter noted, my father and sister were also fooled by Wickham. And after reflecting on my ungracious proposal, I realised I had provoked you, so I apologise for my rudeness. However, in my letter, I wrote a half-truth. While I did not see Miss Bennet's partiality to Bingley, I also discouraged him because he is not worthy of her." At her surprised look, Darcy added, "I am uncomfortable discussing Bingley now; I hope you will forgive me."

"I will—I do."

As he took his pocket watch from his waistcoat, he began, "I only regret that—oh, no!" He showed her his watch. "I am late to meet my cousin."

After a moment of confusion, Elizabeth laughed. "So now it is *my* turn to be unsettled and tortured by your unfinished thought. Well, I shall see you at luncheon on Saturday, so I expect you to have a very entertaining regret to tell me, sir."

Darcy bowed over her hand and departed. Watching him leave, she mused that never had she seen the gentleman so free from self-consequence and reserve. His cordiality wiped away the last vestiges of her anger toward him, and she marvelled, *His behaviour was so different from when he put his letter into my hand at Rosing Park!*

≈≈≈

"You are late," Fitzwilliam said as Darcy sat at the table his cousin shared with Trevor and Upton. Trevor's expression was pleasant but vapid, while Upton eyed Darcy warily, acknowledging him with only a nod.

"Am I? My apologies." He gestured to the barmaid to bring a glass for him and a fresh pitcher for the table. An awkward silence followed—not unexpected among men whose recollections of each other were less than friendly. After the barmaid brought a glass and more ale, Darcy filled his glass with ale and topped off his cousin's drink. At last, Darcy said, "If I had not been late, what scintillating news would I have heard?"

Suddenly, a male voice behind Darcy asked sternly, "Don't you have an office to go to, sir?"

"I do, Father." Upton quickly came to his feet. "Good day, gentlemen." He strode out of the pub, relieved to have a reason to leave their company.

After Baron Parnell greeted the men with more civility than he afforded his son, he asked, "So, Knowles, what brings you to Lambton?"

"I came to Oaklands to help my Uncle Selby."

Fitzwilliam said, "Darcy and I also called at Oaklands."

The Baron grinned. "More competition for the hand of Miss Elizabeth Bennet, I presume. Yes, you have a grand estate, Darcy, but the Parnell name comes with a title."

Is he considering Elizabeth a match for Upton? Darcy wondered.

"Has your son taken an interest in Miss Bennet?" Fitzwilliam asked.

"Upton? He's not the man for a lady of her vivacity," the Baron scoffed. "No, sir. I have been widowed for three years, and Miss Bennet is the first lady to catch my eye. She is so charming and such a graceful dancer. New blood for the Parnell line—imagine the sons she could give me!"

I most certainly will not! Darcy thought.

At that moment, the barmaid returned. "Are you joining the gentleman, Baron?"

"Not today. I came to remind Upton he was needed elsewhere." He gave Trevor a cool look. "I remember, Knowles, when you and my son were as thick as thieves. Please assure me that the foolishness you got up to at Cambridge is well and truly behind you."

"Indeed it is, sir. I am a curate now," he replied stiffly.

Baron Parnell sighed. "May the good Lord have mercy on your flock." Turning on his heel, he left.

Trevor glared at Darcy. "Why didn't the Baron scold you? You were no angel."

Darcy shrugged. "When it came to wasting time, getting drunk, and acting the fool, I humbly acknowledge I was not in the same league as you, Parnell, and Wickham."

For a moment, Trevor toyed with his half-full glass of ale. Then he finished the ale in two swallows and rose. "I am certain my uncle needs me. Good day, sirs."

Watching him leave, Fitzwilliam said, "I thought he would empty his glass on your head."

"Wisely, he did not."

"I assume you were late because of Miss Bennet."

"I was."

"May I also assume that when Anne said Miss Bennet had a suitor, she meant you?"

"Yes, although I am not certain how Anne knew."

"Our Anne has become quite observant and charmingly bold since she recovered her health. I do not wish a life-threatening illness on anyone—well, no one I can think of at the moment—but her experience changed her. She is certainly happier."

"It also changed Aunt Catherine. At last, she treats Anne like an adult," Darcy agreed. "How was your chat with my former classmates?"

Fitzwilliam "You saw Trevor's unhappiness when I insisted on tagging along. After Parnell was reminded of who I was, he implied that you bullied him."

"I merely gave him percussive reminders that words have consequences."

Fitzwilliam chuckled. "So that is why he referred to you as 'Fisticuffs Darcy'."

"Upton is a mendacious scape-gallows. I suspect what truly bothers him is that after Baron Parnell left the firm, I ceased doing business there."

"At Flint Rock, you said there was little competition for Elizabeth in Lambton. If the squire was telling the truth about the parade of suitors—and given the baron's interest— do not act the fool by delaying your pursuit of the lady."

≈≈≈

When the Oaklands party—consisting of Elizabeth, Mrs Gardiner, Abelard, and Trevor—drove to Pemberley on Saturday, Elizabeth felt both eager and anxious as she watched for the first appearance of Pemberley woods. Their carriage entered the large park at one of its lowest points and drove for some time, and she admired every remarkable spot and point of view. She could not silence the thought, *Of this, I could have been mistress.*

Darcy was waiting on the portico, and he greeted them warmly. In the entry hall, Irene and Fitzwilliam were friendly; however, Georgiana was reserved in her welcome. Luncheon was served in a small dining room. With only eight at the table, there was a pleasant informality in the conversations over a meal that included curried chicken soup and salmon trout.

During the dessert course, which included tasty delights made with last year's plum preserves and this year's early strawberries, the conversation turned to happy recollections of summers with family. As Irene listened, her sadness made her quiet. Mrs Gardiner and Abelard took turns describing a summer spent at the seashore in Bootle. She said, "Our first visit was when Abel was four, Keziah was twelve, and I was ten. We collected so many seashells!"

"Keziah was the eldest, but she was the most timid of us when it came to splashing about in the surf," Abelard said.

Mrs Gardiner said, "And now Keziah lives in Cornwall—an easy walk to a beach—with her five children and a sixth due soon. She reminds me that we can outgrow our fears."

Irene surprised herself by asking boldly, "Do you wish to be a father, Mr Selby?"

"I do, and a dear eight-year-old girl at Oaklands has been training me for the role."

Elizabeth recounted a berry-picking adventure with her sisters. Trevor told of sleeping out of doors with his siblings on hot August nights. When Darcy shared a happy memory of teaching his sister to swim, Georgiana nodded but offered no memories of her own.

After Fitzwilliam spoke fondly of stealing a neighbour's apples with his sister Helen, who was three years his senior, Irene exclaimed, "Aunt Helen is such a proper viscountess!"

"When I was quite young, that proper viscountess was the best older sister a boy could have."

When she asked if he had stories about her mother, he searched his memory but then shook his head, no. "Martha is ten years older. She was—and still is—closer to Nigel than to Helen, Sophie, and myself."

Upon realising that the others at the table had amusing recollections of and amiable relationships with at least some of their siblings, Irene felt cheated. She wondered why her parents did not encourage friendships between their only daughter and her three brothers. Although her heart ached, she silently scolded herself, *I cannot be melancholy. Darcy will see it and be even less disposed to marrying me. And if I do not marry, I must return to a home where I may as well be a ghost for all that I matter.*

When the conversation turned to estates, Abelard spoke of a recent experience at the cattle market in Bakewell where a drunken buyer confused a cow with a bull. As Darcy and Abelard exchanged stories of such experiences, Georgiana rose and said she would escort the ladies to the drawing room for coffee and tea. The gentleman also came to their feet, but when Fitzwilliam said he preferred the company of ladies to the business of cattle, Trevor concurred.

Darcy said, "Will you come to my study, Selby, while I find the direction of the horse breeder I mentioned?"

"I will, sir. And then we shall join them for tea."

≈≈≈

In the drawing room, Georgiana studied the tea tray for several moments before addressing her guests. "Would you care for weak tea or strong tea, Miss Bennet?"

"Strong tea, please."

Trevor, who imagined he was being helpful, said, "We are all strong tea drinkers at Oaklands."

"How interesting. Irene and I are weak tea drinkers," Georgiana murmured. As she handed Elizabeth's cup to the footman tasked with delivering them, she said, "I understand, madam, that you met my brother twice before following him to Derbyshire."

"I did not follow him here," Elizabeth said coolly. "I met Mr Darcy in Hertfordshire last autumn and encountered him again at Rosings Park this spring—quite unexpectedly."

Mrs Gardiner said, "My dear niece accompanied me to Lambton after I received word of my father's accident."

"My mistake." Georgiana handed the footman a cup for Mrs Gardiner. "William stayed at Rosings longer than was his custom, although he never said why. I felt abandoned."

Fitzwilliam flicked her a leery glance before addressing Mrs Gardiner. "Does your father continue to improve?"

"He does, thank you for asking."

Trevor said, "But it would be a mistake to underestimate my uncle's injuries. One never knows when an elderly fellow such as him might have a relapse ... or worse."

Elizabeth's shocked look hardened into a glare. "I was unaware that you had medical training, Mr Knowles."

"Oh, I haven't. It's just that I am a ... a cautious fellow."

Georgiana gave two cups to the footman. "The pink one is for the cautious fellow, and the green is for Lady Irene."

Irene asked, "Did you know Mr Darcy lived in this neighbourhood, Miss Bennet?"

Aware that Irene and Georgiana were watching her closely, Elizabeth said, "I was told that Pemberley is in Derbyshire; however, when Mr Darcy and Colonel Fitzwilliam—excuse me, *Mr* Fitzwilliam—departed Rosings Park, I had heard they would spend time in London."

"Which we did," Fitzwilliam said.

Georgiana turned to Mrs Gardiner. "I understand that you live in London, madam."

"Yes, with my husband and four children."

"Daughters? Sons?" There was longing in Irene's voice.

"The two eldest are girls, who alternate between coddling and castigating their little brothers." When Mrs Gardiner's expression softened at the thought of her children, Irene stared at her teacup, hoping no one noticed her teary eyes.

"What did my brother tell you about me, Miss Bennet?" Georgiana asked.

*What little I know comes from Darcy's tale of her near-elopement with Wickham. I cannot mention **that**!* Elizabeth replied, "As I recall, he said you were a talented musician." As she smiled, she wondered, *Or did I hear that from Charles Bingley's sisters?*

"Only that?" She was disappointed. "Then what did you two speak of?"

"Do you aspire to be a Bow Street Runner, Cousin?" Fitzwilliam's tone was amused, but his gaze was wary.

Mrs Gardiner said, "This is Elizabeth's first visit to Derbyshire. I am pleased she has seen it at its springtime best."

Trevor said, "Are you enjoying spring at Pemberley, Lady Irene? At school, Darcy was very serious—a bit humdrum. But how would you describe him, my lady?"

"Darcy has been very kind to me—I am a second cousin he scarcely knew who arrived uninvited. He is a thoughtful, well-informed gentleman and diligent in caring for the estate. Happily, he is *not* a gudgeon like my brother Henry."

"I like Henry," Georgiana blurted and then seemed embarrassed by her outburst.

Fitzwilliam said, "To Darcy's virtues, we must add generosity. I left the army because he offered me an estate."

Elizabeth and Mrs Gardiner congratulated Fitzwilliam, but Trevor sighed. "I am happy for your good fortune, sir, for having an estate is exactly what I wish for myself."

For several moments, everyone drank their tea. Suddenly, Georgiana asked, "Did my brother mention that I am one of the ladies declared 'The Three Graces of Derbyshire?' The other ladies are married now, so I am all that remains."

"Now that Lady Irene is here, you have the company of another Grace," Elizabeth said just as Darcy and Abelard entered the drawing room.

"I doubt that Irene will be at Pemberley long enough to be granted that distinction," Georgiana said airily.

Irene leapt to her feet. "Thank you very much, Georgiana! First, my parents cast me out; then Grandmama sent me here because she could not be bothered with me. Now, I find I am not wanted at Pemberley either!"

"You *are* wanted here, Irene," Darcy exclaimed as she pushed past him and ran out of the room. As her footsteps faded with distance, he looked at Fitzwilliam as if to ask, *What has happened here?*

Georgiana ran her gaze around the room. "Oh dear, I fear your conversation at luncheon about your happy family memories has overset Irene."

Elizabeth was astonished, thinking, *You blame us?*

Georgiana rose. "I suppose I should go and calm Irene."

Fitzwilliam said curtly, "I am certain she would prefer my consolation to yours." His smile was tense as he said, "Mrs Gardiner, Miss Bennet, Mr Knowles, Mr Selby, while I hope never to repeat **this** experience, I **do** look forward to being in company with you again." He bowed and exited.

Having lost her opportunity for a graceful exit, Georgiana glanced around uncertainly. Finding herself the centre of attention, she said, "Kindly excuse me, but I have a terrible headache." At the doorway, she paused and told the guests. "I thank you for visiting us today." Then she closed the drawing room's double doors behind her.

After Darcy opened the doors, he told his company, "I do not know what happened here, but I suspect my sister has behaved rudely. Please accept my apology on her behalf."

With calm authority, Mrs Gardiner said, "I appreciate your sentiments, Mr Darcy, but one cannot apologise for someone else. One can be embarrassed or angry at another's behaviour, but one cannot feel regret on behalf of someone who feels no regret." Rising from the settee, she smiled. "The meal was delicious, and you were kind to invite us."

Elizabeth rose, too, and gave Darcy a sympathetic look. "Yes, we appreciated the invitation." Seeing that Trevor was still sitting, she said briskly, "Do come along, sir."

Abelard asked, "Or would you prefer to walk to Oaklands? It is a fine day for ramble." Trevor quickly stood.

When Abelard offered his hand to his host, Darcy shook it, saying, "Speaking only for myself, I am very sorry for the unpleasantness." He had not felt such confusion and helplessness since Elizabeth's rejection of his proposal.

≈≈≈

On the drive to Oaklands, Elizabeth and Mrs Gardiner told Abelard about the peculiar conversation during tea. As was their habit when Trevor was present, they spoke more circumspectly than they otherwise would have.

Abelard remarked, "And there I was in Darcy's study, speaking as if we were still students at university."

Elizabeth said, "I do not know if Miss Darcy's purpose was to show that she sees us as her inferiors or—"

Mrs Gardiner interjected, "Not only ourselves. She asserted her superiority over Lady Irene, too. When Miss Darcy spoke, I heard jealousy in her spite."

Abelard said, "Darcy would not condone her behaviour."

A wince flickered across Elizabeth's face. *If you had seen his arrogance in Hertfordshire, you might think otherwise.*

≈≈≈

At that very moment, Darcy was questioning Irene and Fitzwilliam in the garden parlour. His feelings shifted from bewilderment to anger. When his housekeeper reported that Georgiana had asked for her supper on a tray in her room, he had no objection. "I shall let my sister wonder how I shall deal with her tomorrow," he told his cousins.

Fitzwilliam thought, *But you have never tried to curb her attitudes and behaviours. Nor have I. Did we create a monster?*

Chapter 9

On Sunday morning while Irene and Fitzwilliam were at church in Lambton, Darcy and Georgiana met in his study, where he told her what he had learnt regarding her rudeness at the luncheon. Initially, she was dismissive, then defensive, and, finally, tearful.

Darcy wanted to believe his sister was still the laughing girl he had taught to swim in the ornamental lake shimmering in front of the manor. He *wanted* to believe her.

And Georgiana wanted .... Aching with frustration, she admitted to herself, *I do not know what I want.*

≈≈≈

Elizabeth was disappointed but not surprised that Darcy and Georgiana did not attend church. (Nor did Squire.) After services, however, Fitzwilliam and Irene greeted the Oaklands party with such friendliness that Elizabeth suspected they were attempting to compensate for the unpleasantness of the previous day. Before Fitzwilliam took Irene back to Pemberley, he gave a note to Abelard, saying it was intended for Mrs Gardiner and Elizabeth, too. In it, Darcy repeated his regret for the unpleasant end to their luncheon.

That evening, Elizabeth was beset by doubts and wondered whether Darcy would avoid her because of Georgiana. *I never want to cause a rift between siblings. Even if Darcy were to choose me, it would be misery to reside in a household where my husband's only sister despised me.*

Abruptly, she laughed at herself. *What transformed Mr Fitzwilliam Darcy from the last man in the world whom I could ever be prevailed on to marry to a gentleman whom I respect and admire? My hatred of him vanished ere I came to Derbyshire. Having meditated many hours on his letter, I am almost ashamed of ever having disliked him. But what are we to each other now?*

On Monday, Squire joined the family for breakfast. He was as hale as Elizabeth had ever seen him, and he declared that he longed to be out in the world. She thought, *Trading chamomile tea for brandy with Trevor did him much good.*

When Abelard told Squire his accident had occurred less than a month ago, Squire asked, "What was the exact date?"

"The twenty-seventh of April," Mrs Harcourt said.

Squire grinned. "So then, Wednesday is my anniversary. Well, I wish to celebrate by going to Lambton and showing my neighbours that I am not yet ready to cock up my toes."

"But you cannot go in the bath chair. The wheels are not made for that," Mrs Gardiner said.

"And you cannot manage on foot," Mrs Harcourt said.

"I could put a board in the pony cart to support your leg. And *I* will drive the cart, sir," Abelard said.

≈≈≈

At Pemberley that same morning, Georgiana surprised Darcy in his study, where he always started his morning with a cup of coffee and a thick slice of pound cake. Chin in hand, she leaned on the back of the Hepplewhite chair, facing her brother across his wide desk. "Have you noticed that Irene has lost weight? She says she does not crave sweets here as when she is at Harwich Hall."

When Darcy admitted he had not noticed, she said she wanted to take Irene to the modiste in Lambton. "Her gowns need to be taken in, which is quite a bit of work, so I suggested we have the modiste's ladies make the alterations on the ballgowns and eveningwear. Also, I want her to have a new gown—as an apology—which I will pay for with my pin money. And a new fan; I swear she is death to fans."

"That is a kind gesture." However, to her dismay, he did not offer to pay for Irene's gown.

"Will you escort us to Lambton?" She thought, *Surely William will open his purse when we are at the modiste's shop. Perhaps, he will buy a new gown for each of us.*

Darcy gestured at this appointment book. "I cannot accompany you, dear girl. I have meetings with two tenants and my stable master. But I insist that you have Rogers drive you. Irene is not as skilled a rider as you are, and two grooms have mentioned that she is sometimes reckless when she attempts to keep up with you."

Georgiana pouted prettily and asked, "Could not the stable master and the tenants adjust to *your* schedule?"

"I set these meetings, and for me to change them on a whim would be disrespectful."

"Ah, of course," she murmured.

After she left the study, Darcy's thoughts were filled with Elizabeth. *I should call at Oaklands today. Did that wretched ending to our luncheon give her the impression that we Darcys share a disregard for the feelings of others? Am I so faint of heart that embarrassment keeps me away? When I recall how Fitz described my sister's remarks, a mere apology seems insipid. Well, if I conduct my meetings efficiently, perhaps I can call on her this afternoon.*

≈≈≈

The young ladies left for Lambton later than Irene had expected; she did not realise Georgiana was dawdling in hopes that Darcy would escort them. Thus it was early afternoon when they entered the dress shop. While the modiste was measuring Irene, she stood at the window, staring dispiritedly at the comings and goings on Lambton's main street. *I am bored, bored, hopelessly bored!* However, her interest was piqued when the bookseller's granddaughter escorted Elizabeth to the shop. *Has a special volume arrived for the Bennet creature? I should investigate.*

Irene's voice interrupted her musings. "Please tell me your thoughts about colours. Salmon? Orange? Or lemon?"

I daresay she is brooding about food again, Georgiana thought as she faced Irene.

≈≈≈

When Lily Timmons had called at Oaklands a short while ago, Elizabeth was surprised to hear that Mr Timmons had a story he was certain would interest her. Although his use of the word "story" rather than "book" puzzled her, she was curious to see what he had to offer. Upon entering the book-shop, Elizabeth was even more surprised to find that the story was not a book but rather a person.

Timmons assured her, "I would not have allowed Mr Wickham to meet with you here had he not convinced me that he has an urgent message for an important person in the neighbourhood. We have agreed that I shall witness the conversation to ensure he does not importune you."

Wickham said, "Mr Timmons is the most discreet man in Derbyshire—or possibly the kingdom."

The previous September, when Elizabeth had been intro-duced to the former lieutenant in the -------shire militia, she thought he had a most gentlemanlike appearance: all the best part of beauty, a fine countenance, a good figure, and very pleasing address, but after reading Darcy's letter, she had dreaded seeing Wickham again. However, the man who stood before her now was a ragged shadow of the lieutenant he once was. "Who is the message for?" she asked warily.

"Mr Darcy—none other."

"How did you come to Lambton?"

"On a borrowed horse and, yes, I have the owner's permission. I live now some twenty miles distant."

"Are you in need of funds, sir?"

Wickham chuckled. "For possibly the first time in my life, I am not."

"Your fortunes have improved then?"

"In material terms, madam, I am as poor as I have ever been; however, in spirit, I have never been richer. But I did not come to speak of myself."

*If that is true, then Wickham **has** changed*, she thought. "What is the message?"

"A warning, or rather a caution. An anonymous letter told me that Trevor Knowles was pursuing Miss Darcy.

Knowles is not to be trusted. He is a schemer who is as eager for Miss Darcy's fortune as she is eager for a title. As he is a baronet's son, she may become interested in him."

"If Miss Darcy is so keen on having a title, why did she consent to ...." Elizabeth glanced at Mr Timmons.

Timmons said, "Elope with the son of Pemberley's steward? That is no secret here."

"Nor is it the truth," Wickham said. "Oh, I was in Ramsgate last August, quite coincidentally. After encountering Georgiana, I became her convenient dupe, arranging an elopement with some titled fellow. But when Darcy arrived unexpectedly, she claimed I had enticed her to run away. No doubt she feared that if she revealed her true intentions, Darcy would find the fellow and thrash him."

"Why were you helping her?" Elizabeth asked.

"As a child, she was extremely fond of me, and I thought of her as a younger sister. In Ramsgate, she told me she had a tendresse for a fellow who was a guest at a nearby estate but that Darcy was ruining her life with his interference. Thus, out of my fondness for the girl she had been **and** because she offered an irresistible financial incentive, I agreed to obtain a coach and driver to convey her and her beloved for their elopement."

"Miss Darcy was fifteen, sir," she scolded.

Wickham winced. "My involvement in her plan is nothing I am proud of. While the story she told me about Darcy's interference was not particularly credible, I was also motivated by a desire to tweak his nose. But when I went to her accommodations to tell her I had arranged for the coach and driver—and to receive my payment—I overheard her tearfully telling Darcy that I had conspired with her companion, Mrs Younge, who was a rather foolish woman but not a guilty one, to steal her away."

Surprised, Elizabeth looked at Timmons, who shrugged.

Wickham sighed. "Yes, I deserve your doubt. Still, if Knowles convinces Miss Darcy that she has a fair chance to be Lady Knowles, she might attempt another elopement. I am making amends, Miss Bennet, by telling this to you."

"And you want me to tell Mr Darcy? Do you not want a reward?"

Wickham shook his head, sad that he was suspected of scheming even when he told the truth. Timmons shrugged again. "Well, I cannot know if all that he says is true, but if Lily were of an age to marry, I would not agree to a match with Knowles. He is rather foolish and has a reputation for wanting wealth without working for it."

Wickham produced a folded page from his jacket and offered it to her. "You have heard my caution, and this is the anonymous letter. I shall leave now, and I have no intention of returning." He bowed to the bookseller. "Thank you, Mr Timmons, for making this meeting possible."

Elizabeth tucked the letter in her reticule to read later. "Is your horse at the stable?"

"For the past two hours. It took me awhile to convince Mr Timmons to summon you. He is quite protective of you."

"I shall walk with you." She farewelled Timmons and Lily and led the way out of the bookshop. As they walked to the stable, she realised Wickham was limping.

"Why are you being my escort?" he asked.

"I have some questions. Why did you not ask Mr Timmons to deliver your message?"

"Darcy admires you; he is more likely to believe you."

How did Wickham see Mr Darcy's admiration of me when I did not? she wondered. "Well, I will tell him your message. So then, did you intend to run off with Lydia?"

Reluctantly, he admitted, "I did. Lydia is pretty and lively, and she does not consider the consequences of her actions. When I am in my cups, I am rather stupid and do not think of consequences either. But I have drunk nothing stronger than small beer for the past month."

"What changed you, sir?"

"An angel, or perhaps a witch." He explained that after his discharge by the --------shire militia, he had no prospects and little money. He travelled to Manchester, where he was robbed and severely beaten after playing cards with the wrong people. "I was dying when the witch found me. She saved my life and urged me to follow a righteous path."

A voice behind them thundered, "Stay where you are, Wickham!"

Wickham and Elizabeth glanced back and saw Darcy outside the modiste's shop; his expression was fierce as he strode toward them. Elizabeth said, "Go on, I will slow him." She turned to face Darcy as Wickham jogged clumsily to the stable, which was only a short distance away. Seeing that Georgiana was following her brother and scowling, she thought, *If Wickham's tale is true, Miss Darcy would not want him telling it to me.*

When Darcy was but a few steps away, she raised her hands, palms up. "Let him depart, sir. Please."

"Why? What was he doing here?" Darcy demanded.

Georgiana screeched, "Have you added Wickham to your list of conquests, madam? Did he tell you he was my fiancé?"

"Please lower your voice, Georgiana; else, you will make a spectacle of us all," Darcy said.

Ignoring him, she sneered, "Did Wickham come to Lambton to woo you, Miss Bennet?"

At that moment, Wickham rode out of the stable, and they watched him urge his horse to speed him along the road out of Lambton. Elizabeth reclaimed their attention by saying, "Wickham came with a message for *you*, sir. Might we speak privately?"

Georgiana grabbed Darcy's arm. "If you shall speak about me, I have a right to listen."

Lady Irene called from the doorway of the modiste's shop. "Georgiana, I need your advice!"

Darcy told his sister, "Go back to Lady Irene."

"But I want—"

"Return to the modiste's shop. I shall join you shortly," he commanded.

Georgiana's glared at her brother; then, shifting her gaze to Elizabeth, she scoffed, "If you believe a single word Wickham said, you are a ninnyhammer, a fool!"

Elizabeth watched her storm back to the modiste's shop. *Oh, Wickham, I think you spoke the truth about her attempt to elope with someone else.*

Darcy interrupted her thoughts. "Well, Miss Bennet?"

"Mr Timmons sent his granddaughter to Oaklands to—"

"Tell me about Wickham!"

She gave an exasperated huff. "I did not know he was coming to the bookshop to speak with me. Mr Timmons sent for me, and he listened to our brief conversation, which you can confirm with him. Then I walked with Wickham to the stable because I had a question about a private matter. Now, shall I tell you his message?"

"Yes, if you please."

"He heard a rumour that Trevor Knowles was pursuing Miss Darcy and wanted to warn you."

"How did Wickham know you were in Lambton?"

She took the folded page from her reticule. "I do not know. Perhaps, I am mentioned in this letter he received. I have not yet read it."

He snatched it from her and examined it. "It is not addressed to you."

"It is not addressed to you either," she snapped.

Just then, Irene joined them, breathless from running. "Georgiana has fainted. We must take her home."

"Yes, we must. Good day, madam." Darcy put the letter in his pocket and strode away, oblivious to Irene's struggle to keep up with him.

Elizabeth muttered, "I am vexed with all of them!" Turning her steps toward Oaklands, she thought, *This is not my concern. Wickham should not have involved me.*

≈≈≈

My anger is showing, Darcy thought, waiting for the hostler at a small coaching inn to answer his question. The village noted on Wickham's letter was not, in fact, the location of Attics Garden Manor. Also, the hostler was a middle-aged man whose welcoming demeanour had turned cautious at Darcy's inquiry. "I hope you come in peace, sir. Miss Arabella gives sanctuary to those with nowhere to go."

"Is a man named George Wickham finding sanctuary there?" Darcy feared his nemesis was taking advantage of a vulnerable lady committed to assisting the needy.

"We don't know names—safer that way when vexed relations come looking for their kinfolk."

"I assure you I am not a vexed relation." When the hostler continued to regard him with an unblinking stare, he added, "My name is Fitzwilliam Darcy, my estate is called Pemberley, and I give you my word as a gentleman that my intentions are peaceful." *There, I have nothing to hide.*

Finally, the hostler nodded and told him how to reach Attics Garden Manor.

≈≈≈

"If you did not want me to find you, then you should have kept your letter," Darcy taunted Wickham, who sat in a library chair with one leg resting on an ottoman.

"That is true." Upon realising that Wickham was not surprised to see him, Darcy was at a loss for words. Wickham continued, "You must have seen my direction on the letter. Did Miss Bennet give it to you, or did you take it?"

Darcy's wince was almost imperceptible. Almost. Wickham tsked, "You **took** the letter from her. Did the lady have an opportunity to read it first?"

"Why did you want me to find you?"

"I would have preferred for you to take the word of Miss Bennet or Mr Timmons, but if you didn't, I was **willing** to let you find me."

"My sister was quite overset by your appearance."

"I hoped I would not encounter either of you, so I arranged to talk with Miss Bennet in the bookshop. And, no, she was not expecting me."

For a full minute, the men studied each other; Wickham knew Darcy was looking for a scheme. At last, he said, "Miss Darcy is mindful that I know a secret which puts the lie to what she told you at Ramsgate. Not then and not now do I wish to run away with her. Nor does she want such a future with me. She shares your opinion, sir, that I am beneath her touch. She has her heart set on a title."

"If there was no attempt to elope, why did Georgiana say there was?"

"Oh, your sister planned an elopement. My part was to procure a carriage and driver so that she could marry the gentleman of her dreams. She paid me well for my services— well enough for me to escape to Hertfordshire when I overheard her telling you that I tried to steal her away."

Anger jolted through Darcy. "Liar! You are defaming Georgiana!" He stepped nearer to the seated man.

Behind him, a female voice said sternly, "There will be no violence here, Mr Darcy. Step away from Mr Wickham."

He turned toward the voice, expecting to see a woman with a weapon. Although the lady was not armed, the butler standing beside her had a pistol, which was pointed at the floor. When Darcy realised he knew the woman, the shock was such that he forgot to bow before saying, "Lady -------, it has been years since we met."

In her early thirties, the tall, angular woman met his gaze unflinchingly. "At least twelve years, by my calculation. We were guests at a ball at the Earl of Kestevyn's Mayfair home. You were a lad, and I was a young bride." She indicated the drawing room with a graceful wave. "Within these walls, I am simply Miss Arabella. I use my title as a marchioness only when I move through society—a tedium I endure as infrequently as possible."

Wickham said admiringly, "Miss Arabella saved my life. She was there when the hand of Providence was not. She is a witch in the tradition of wise healers who protect life."

"I would never describe myself as a witch. That would attract the self-righteously foolish to do me harm, even in this enlightened age," she said with a wry smile, and Darcy heard her sarcasm when she said "enlightened."

"Did you never wonder, Wickham, whether Providence was punishing you for your many sins?" After making that accusation, Darcy was embarrassed.

Wickham, however, was amused. "As I lay dying after being set upon and beaten, I wondered whether I should pray, but I could not form the words. My entire life, I had expected, asked for, and prayed for a power outside myself— Providence, fate, luck, and even the Darcys—to provide for me and save me from my mistakes. But at that moment, I thought that if I could live my life again, I would rely on myself. No *deus ex machina* for George Wickham. And then Miss Arabella found me."

"Did you not think that Providence had sent the lady?"

Wickham laughed. "So, you would argue that after I renounced god, he—or *it*—sent help? Darcy, we have both known men whose sins are far worse than mine, yet god allows those scoundrels to prosper and be admired."

"My late husband being one such scoundrel."

Darcy dredged his memory for details about the marchioness and her much older husband. *When did the marquess die—ah, the year after my father.* "Condolences on the passing of your husband, my lady."

"Did you not hear the details of that vicious old bastard's unlikely demise? He was struck by lightning."

"You should congratulate Miss Arabella on her widow-hood; else, she could not have established this place."

"Attics Garden Manor is **yours**, madam?"

"Yes, a gift from my stepson, the current marquess, for my efforts to protect him and his siblings from their father. When I named the estate, I called it Ataraxia Garden. That was too foreign for the locals, so they call it 'Attics Garden'. A few local wits call this 'Attics to Let Garden'."

The word 'ataraxia' stirred a memory from Darcy's school days, but he recalled no details. "And this is a religious sanctuary?"

"If you are seeking my counterpart in religious lore, I suggest Lilith, the first woman. She was formed at the same time as Adam and from the same clay. She ran away from the Garden of Eden because she refused to obey someone she considered her equal."

"This garden is a retreat from religion and a sanctuary from the sanctimonious," Wickham said. "People who are different, but not dangerously so, find shelter here."

"As do wives, children, and servants escaping brutal masters. That is why there is no violence here—although we can and have defended ourselves," Miss Arabella said.

Darcy tried to picture her late husband. "After meeting the marquess at the ball, I never saw him again. But I recall other gentlemen praising him as a deeply pious man."

Her laugh was short and sharp. "He was a pious fraud. His sister, who had been inculcated with the same strict piety, was also in the gazebo that day. It had been raining off and on, so she, like my husband's heir and myself, was attempting to shield my husband's three youngest children from being murdered by their father. Terrified, we clung to each other as the marquess stood in the garden, waving his Baker rifle and ranting about what unworthy creatures we were. Of course, the rifle was only a single-shot weapon, but at my husband's feet were two wooden cases, each containing a brace of duelling pistols primed and ready to fire." Her recitation was matter-of-fact, but then she grinned. "Suddenly, the marquess was struck by lightning. He died instantly."

"You saw it?" Darcy asked.

"We all did. My sister-in-law, who had no love for her cruel brother, fell to her knees on the gazebo's rather dirty floor and proclaimed that the Hand of God had rescued us. Yet, when I heard this, I wondered where was the Hand of God when the marquess mistreated his children, myself, and anyone else he had at his mercy. Well, the vicious old bastard had no mercy, but neither did the deity who permitted such abuse of us."

Wickham said, "My life was never so terrible as Miss Arabella's. You told me often enough, Darcy, that I had more opportunities than I deserved. But I, too, was confused that the god behind this unjust world was so widely praised for being kind and loving." Quietly, he added, "My parents' deaths troubled me more than I would admit. I felt unmoored by the loss of them."

"Are you familiar with the works of Epicurus, Mr Darcy?" Miss Arabella asked.

"The Greek sage who lived three centuries before Jesus?"

She gave Wickham an arch look. "Do you see how we use religion as a marker for specifying historical dates? Epicurus left written works and was mentioned by his contemporaries. Yet all accounts of Jesus were written by others years after his death."

Darcy felt a twinge of discomfort at her casual heresy.

Miss Arabella continued, "In the year of solitude following my husband's death, I immersed myself in reading philosophy. What society called my time of mourning was, in fact, one of the happiest years of my life. I often meditated on these words of Epicurus: 'Is God willing to prevent evil but not able? Then he is not omnipotent. Is he able but not willing? Then he is malevolent. Is he both able and willing? Then whence cometh evil? Is he neither able nor willing? Then why call him God?' "

Darcy suddenly recalled, "Ataraxia—tranquillity and the absence of fear. Do you follow the philosophy of Epicurus?"

"I embrace his wisdom that a good life is based on peace of mind, simplicity, honour, and freedom from fear and bodily discomfort. For me, serenity and simplicity are achieved by not relying upon the creator of the universe to involve itself in my life. Like Deists, I also value rational thought, which I rely upon to avoid those mental disturbances that disrupt my peace."

"Drinking, gambling, lying, resentment—habits that shaped my life." There was no self-pity in Wickham's voice.

Darcy silently scolded himself. *These digressions do not serve my purpose. The marchioness knows enough of Wickham's history that she does not need me to rescue her.* He bowed to Miss Arabella and then turned to Wickham. "You have not said who my sister intended to elope with."

"He's a young man; I saw him once from a distance. Miss Darcy said he was titled but did not tell me his name."

"You could have told me about my sister in a letter."

"As if you would **ever** read a letter from me." Wickham chuckled. "I have learnt from Miss Arabella and Epicurus the importance of helping others. My conscience required me to alert you to the letter I had received. I sought out Miss Bennet because I saw your partiality to her in Hertfordshire; I thought you might believe her over Timmons or me. As I told her, I have no intention of returning to your neighbourhood. To my mind, sir, our business is done."

Is there anything else I want to know? After a pause, Darcy asked, "Who do you think wrote your letter?"

Without hesitation, Wickham replied, "Upton Parnell. No doubt, he presents himself to Knowles as a friend, but we both know he is no one's friend. I would not be surprised if he were also pushing Knowles in Miss Darcy's direction."

Darcy nodded, his thoughts too agitated for him to reply.

Wickham said, "When I encountered Miss Darcy in Ramsgate, I had not seen her in about seven years. Had she not recognized me, I would not have known her. However, I soon realised that more than her appearance had changed.

Consider the possibility that your sister is not the angel you believe her to be and that I am not the worst devil to walk the earth since Miss Arabella's monstrous marquess."

Miss Arabella asked, "Will you leave now, Mr Darcy?"

"Yes, my lady." Darcy bowed to her and then nodded at Wickham. "Farewell, sir."

≈≈≈

On the ride to Pemberley, Darcy rode with less urgency. He was not convinced that Wickham was telling the truth, but neither was he certain of Georgiana's veracity. It also occurred to him that his anger toward Wickham was about more than their history. When he saw his nemesis with Elizabeth, jealousy had burned through him.

"A poor excuse for my rudeness to her," he muttered, "but my sensibilities were nearly overcome." Upon hearing himself speak, he smiled wryly and thought, *I will never admit to Aunt Beatrice or Lady Catherine that even at nine-and-twenty years of age, I have not outgrown my impulse toward excessive emotions.*

First, my rudeness in Hertfordshire. Then my arrogant offer of marriage in Kent. Then Georgiana's uncivil remarks at Pemberley. What shall I say when I apologise to Miss Bennet **this** *time?*

Chapter 10

It was not yet ten in the morning when Darcy stood facing Elizabeth just inside the vestibule at Oaklands. Mrs Harcourt remained near, for Elizabeth had told her of Wickham's appearance and his warning about Trevor. The sharp annoyance Elizabeth had felt the night before had softened to a wary coolness. She wondered, *The fact that Mr Darcy is here so early and the contrition in his expression count in his favour. So, will he justify his behaviour or—*

"I apologise for my rudeness." He offered Wickham's letter. "I should not have taken this from you. "

Accepting it, she asked, "Did you seek out Wickham?"

"I did. I have known him too long and too well to be a fair judge; so, it is impossible for me to be impartial. But I did him no harm. In fact, our conversation," he paused before admitting, "was surprisingly philosophical."

As Elizabeth studied him, Darcy felt his countenance redden. Abruptly, he offered her the linen haversack hanging from his shoulder. "Oranges from our orangery."

The haversack had escaped Elizabeth's notice, so his gift surprised her. Laughing, she accepted it, saying, "Oh, Mr Darcy. I cannot sketch your character at all!"

"Will you walk with me? Perhaps in the wilderness area there or to Lambton—whatever you prefer, madam," he urged. Elizabeth gave the haversack to Mrs Harcourt with a look that said, *All is well between the gentleman and me.*

Darcy offered his arm to Elizabeth, and they strolled toward the wilderness. She assured him that her encounter with Wickham was unexpected. "As I said at the assembly, I believed what you said in the letter you gave me at Rosing." She stammered slightly, reluctant to remind him of her rejection and their argument.

"On the subject of letters, Wickham thinks Upton Parnell authored the one he received. At university, Parnell skirted the edge of propriety lest his father refuse to pay his school fees. Still, Parnell encouraged the reckless stupidity of Wickham, Knowles, and others."

"But not Young Mr Darcy?" she teased.

"Oh, in one or two minor scrapes, and that is all I shall say." Sighing, he confided, "As for what Wickham said about Georgiana, I fear I have not been a good surrogate father."

When she stopped abruptly and tugged his arm, he faced her. "At what age was that role forced upon you?"

"Twenty-two. I was scarcely a year out of Cambridge."

"How old was your sister?"

"About eleven."

"And how were you prepared for fatherhood?"

"I ... well, I had been reared to manage Pemberley but not a young girl."

"So what did you do?"

"I relied on Georgiana's governess. When my sister was fourteen, she said she was too old for a governess, so Miss Truscott was pensioned off and relieved to be, I suspect. After I engaged Mrs Younge, Georgiana was delighted, saying she was full of *joie de vivre*. And you know the end of that story."

Elizabeth thought, *I am not certain I do, but I shall not risk a disagreement now.*

They sat on the bench and, after a brief silence, Darcy asked, "Did Wickham come to you because he hoped your kind heart would compel you to listen?"

"He had no guarantee of my kind heart. He was forced out of the militia because of his scandalous behaviour toward my youngest sister. She has been exiled to Kyrewood Academy, where Papa's famously flinty sister has a seminary for 'difficult' young ladies."

"Do I want details?"

"Where ignorance is bliss, tis folly to be wise." Fixing him with a stern glare, she said, "The point is, sir, that despite knowing of your animus—and possibly mine—

Wickham came to warn about a danger to Miss Darcy and with no interest in seeing her."

"Did he tell you Georgiana wanted to elope with a titled fellow?"

"He did."

Darcy asked, "Only time will tell if Wickham has truly changed, but his caution has merit. I would not welcome Trevor Knowles into the family."

"Have you told your sister you spoke to Wickham?"

"No, I am reluctant to accuse her of something that may not be true. As you have sisters, do you have any advice?"

"She is at a rebellious age. And, no, not every girl experiences this in the same manner."

"Were you rebellious?"

Elizabeth laughed. "Oh, sir, do not assume my rebelliousness is in the past! My advice for any age is this: Do not cut yourself off from her or give her a reason to cut herself off from you."

On the ride to Pemberley, Darcy meditated upon her advice; he was grateful she understood his challenges as his sister's guardian. At the manor, he waited for Georgiana to find him, which she did within an hour. While she was surprised to hear he had called at Oaklands this morning, she was angry that he had visited Wickham yesterday. She challenged, "Do you expect me to believe Wickham came to Lambton to warn of Trevor Knowles' dubious character? That he has no interest in me? What a farce!"

"But Wickham did not seek you out. Nor could he have known you would be in the village. I must allow for the possibility that his character has changed."

"People do not change!"

Darcy protested in his thoughts, *I believe I am changing for the better, and I fear you are changing for the worse.* He said, "Anne changed, as did Aunt Catherine."

Georgiana rolled her eyes. "Oh, yes, Anne's miraculous Deliverance From Death. I am not convinced she was as ill as she and her mother claim."

Where is your compassion for your cousin? he wondered. "We weren't there, so you are free to doubt the details, but you cannot deny that Anne and Lady Catherine are more tolerant and serene."

She gave a dismissive sniff but made no reply, so Darcy asked, "Are you still determined to marry a peer?"

"Yes, but I must like the gentleman very much. I do not have such feelings for Mr Knowles. And anyway, his eldest brother could live for decades *and* produce a son who would inherit the title. As you know, English baronets are not even peers." When Darcy gazed at her without comment, she wondered, *What reassurance does he want from me?*

"Do you promise me that you will not enter into an engagement or endeavour to elope with Trevor Knowles?'

"I do. At Ramsgate, you said I am too young to marry."

≈≈≈

On the anniversary of Squire's accident, the Dartmoor pony pulled the cart along Lambton's main street at a walking pace under Abelard's sure hand. Squire sat beside him, his broken leg held straight on a board extending to the front of the cart.

Walking together on the pathway of paving stones between the roadway and the shops, Elizabeth and Mrs Gardiner kept pace with the cart. Mrs Harcourt and Cassandra followed them, but Trevor walked ahead, for no one cared to walk with him.

A high-pitched female voice called from behind them. "Squire, I am delighted to see you!" Abelard stopped the cart as a stout, middle-aged woman in a flowery muslin gown hurried to join them. "When I saw you pass our shop, I was disappointed you did not come in to greet me, but I see now you could not." The widow, Mrs O'Casey, owned the chandler's shop, so she had known the Selbys for as long as they had lived in the neighbourhood. Stepping up to the cart, she held out her hands to Squire.

He clasped her hands fondly, pleased to know he had been missed. "And I am delighted to see *you*, madam."

While the Oaklands party conversed with Mrs O'Casey outside the pub, Trevor glanced through the windows. Seeing Upton, Trevor smiled wistfully, thinking, *I wish I were drinking with you rather than ambling with this lot.*

Upton's returning smile was more of a sneer. Leaving his hat and walking stick at his table, he stepped outside. Trevor was the first to greet him. "Parnell. Lovely day to be out of doors, eh?"

"Knowles," Upton said, giving his friend a shallow nod. Then, he greeted Abelard, spoking slowly and loudly. If he saw the Selby scion roll his eyes, he gave no sign of it.

Abelard said, "My speech is slow, Parnell, but my hearing is not."

Mrs Gardiner said, "However, Mr Parnell, our father would appreciate it if you spoke slowly and loudly to him."

"Because of the accident?" Upton asked.

"Because you tend to speak so rapidly that your speech is garbled," Mrs Harcourt said.

"Mrs Harcourt is correct," Mrs Gardiner said.

"Are you improving, Squire Selby?" Upton asked.

"Well, I am out of bed, am I not?"

"No doubt Knowles has made himself useful."

Mrs Harcourt answered, "Oh, yes. Squire has kept Mr Knowles well entertained."

"I think you said that backwards," Trevor remarked.

"Did I?" Mrs Harcourt smiled innocently. She was well aware of the men's disdain for her. To Trevor, she was merely a servant; to Upton, she was the harridan who once gave him a fierce set down.

Upton still harboured resentment toward Susan Browning Harcourt. Before leaving Lambton, she had spurned his offer of carte blanche; yet, how could a cobbler's daughter expect a gentleman such as himself to offer marriage? After her angry rejection, he convinced himself that if Squire Selby had not paid such a handsome price for the Browning cobblery, Susan would have accepted him. As for her obvious fondness for Abelard (*a cripple!* Upton fumed), he told himself it was merely gratitude.

"Such charming impertinence, Mrs Harcourt," Upton murmured. He smiled at Squire. "I have always admired your liberality, treating your retainers like family."

"And why should they not, Mr Parnell? Decent people treat other people decently," Mrs O'Casey bristled.

Upton ignored her, but when he heard the barkeep calling his name from the pub's doorway, he could not ignore him. Turning to the barkeep, Upton saw that he held a hat and walking stick while the barmaid hovered at his side. "I am certain you did not mean for us to take these as payment for your nuncheon and ale, Mr Parnell."

*I did not want an audience—well, not **this** audience,* Upton thought. Taking a small leather purse from his pocket, he put a few coins into the barmaid's hand. "You will note that I have overpaid you. Put the balance aside and apply it to the charges for my next visit."

After Parnell reclaimed his items, he expected the publicans to return to their work, but Elizabeth asked a question that held them in place. "From your words, Mr Parnell, it seems you do not have loyal retainers. But do you have family, sir?"

He gave her a questioning look. "Of a certainty, madam."

"Ah. Your manners being what they are, I assumed you were raised by wolves." While Upton stared at her dumbstruck, Elizabeth asked her companions, "Are there wolves in Derbyshire?"

Mrs Harcourt said, "A few lone and lonely wolves. So few that they are hard-pressed to find company."

Upton scowled at her before turning to Abelard. "I say, Selby, your housekeeper—"

"Don't **say**," Abelard said. "Keep your breath to cool your porridge, sir, and we shall keep ours to swell our songs." To everyone's surprise, he began to sing some lines from a bawdy tune, "This young man then, being so blamed, did blush as one being ashamed."

Mrs O'Casey and the barmaid laughed with Elizabeth, Mrs Harcourt, and Squire while the barkeep remarked, "I have not heard 'Watkin's Ale' sung in many a year."

Aware of his friend's embarrassment, Trevor smiled weakly; Upton glared at him as if to say, *Speak up! Do not condone their humiliation of me.*

Squire said, "Give my regards to Baron Parnell, sir." He waved farewell to those on the street as Abelard urged the Dartmoor pony forward

Outnumbered and scorned, Upton stalked away. As the Oaklands ladies moved past Trevor, he stared after his friend. He knew Upton would chastise him for his cowardice the next time they met. *Well, I will pay for the ale and endure his foul mood. He is my only ally for my ambitions.*

After supper at Oaklands, Elizabeth sat in the parlour, ignoring the book in her lap. Through the gap in the linen draperies, she glanced surreptitiously at the little wilderness where Mrs Harcourt, Abelard, and Cassandra were crowded on the small bench, laughing and talking.

When Mrs Gardiner entered, she saw her niece's interest. "Do you wish to join them?" she teased.

Elizabeth shook her head. "They are like a happy family."

Mrs Gardiner sat with her on the sofa. "You see it. I see it. They **feel** it. Yet, no one talks about what a good match Abel and Susan would be," she said with a touch of exasperation.

"Would Squire object to the marriage?"

"Oh, such an earful Father would get from me if he were so foolish! No, I fear that Abel lacks confidence in himself in this matter—you have seen how confident he is in his work. Or perhaps Mrs Susan is the reluctant one. I do not know."

"After Squire is more recovered, you and I can join forces and hint at the happy couple," Elizabeth said.

"Oh, of course. That sort of plan *never* goes awry."

≈≈≈

When Darcy called the following afternoon to invite Elizabeth to ride in his curricle, she told him of the previous day's outing. She asked about Trevor and Upton, and although Darcy thought it unlikely that she had an affinity for either man, he felt a flash of jealousy—until she said, "Such arrogance! They see themselves as superior creatures, yet nothing in their manner or appearance supports that delusion of consequence."

"Delusion of consequence. I shall remember that," he said, amused.

Hesitantly, Elizabeth said, "When we spoke at Hunsford Parsonage, I assumed that you offered for me because you were not betrothed to Miss de Bourgh."

Darcy thought, *I offered for you because I ardently admired you, and I thought you admired me, but I prefer not to dwell on **my** delusion.* He told her, "Anne and I were never engaged and never will be."

"Is this because you are engaged to Lady Irene?"

He groaned. "No engagement there either. These nonsensical rumours make me seem like the most desirable gentleman in the kingdom—which we both know I am not."

Elizabeth's cheeks glowed pink, but there was no hesitation when she said, "I do not consider you undesirable ... not now. But I do not repine at declining your proposal. At Rosings Park, neither of us truly understood the other—or ourselves. Such confusion, such ignorance is not a sufficient foundation for a happy union."

"I know myself better now." When she met his gaze, he continued, "But I do not claim to know your heart."

"My heart." Self-consciously, she looked away. "My heart is ashamed for misjudging you."

"But what did you say of me that I did not deserve? For although your accusations were formed on mistaken premises, my behaviour to you merited the severest reproof." When she made no reply, Darcy added, "I am not betrothed, engaged, affianced, or promised to any lady in any locale in the kingdom."

Giving him an arch look, Elizabeth asked, "But what of ladies in France or the Americas or the Kingdom of Naples?"

Darcy grinned. *I have finally achieved a bit of banter with this enchanting lady.*

≈≈≈

While Elizabeth and Darcy flirted in a curricle, Trevor grovelled to Upton and paid for decent claret rather than their usual ale. After Upton's amour propre was mollified, Trevor felt free to complain again about Life's Injustices. "I have spent the past ten days working my arse off. Abel was right about one thing; I was unaware of how much I did not know. But there is no doubt in my mind that I would be a better squire than Abel. *Regardez-moi!* People understand me when I speak. I look as a squire ought to—certainly more so than my crippled cousin. It was cruel for my uncle to give him a name that would be shortened to 'able'."

Upton cautioned, "But is ten days of experience sufficient for what you dream of achieving?"

"If I have a good steward, I don't need to know much. But how can I show my uncle what I truly am?"

Suppressing a smile, Upton asked in a neutral voice. "And what are you truly?"

"A natural leader! I am well-spoken, educated, and have a gentlemanly manner."

For several moments, the men sipped their ale and reflected in silence. Then Upton said, "If the Selbys experienced more challenges—or threats—than Abel could handle, they might see you as someone to share the burden of the estate. I am reluctant to encourage you in some radical action, but if the family were temporarily inconvenienced or incapacitated, you could right the ship, as it were, and everyone would see your leadership."

"Threatened, inconvenienced, or incapacitated?"

"Oh, nothing serious—just think about it for a bit. You have always been a clever fellow. Perhaps you and Selby could be co-guardians of Oaklands while Squire recuperates. Selby would manage the farm, and you could be the face and voice—"

"And the brain," Trevor interrupted.

"Oh, indeed," Upton murmured.

Chapter 11

On the last Saturday in May, Elizabeth was at the breakfast table with Mrs Gardiner when Abelard entered and put a rough map beside her plate. "Can you make sense of this?"

She studied his sketch. "Yes, here is the dirt lane running perpendicular to the stream bordering the kitchen garden." With one finger, she traced the route of arrows on the map but stopped at a stick figure of a tree. "What is this?"

"A very old, very large oak tree. A red kerchief is nailed to the trunk, for that is where the lane splits. Follow the rightward lane until you find me. I shall be here at the place marked 'SD'."

"SD ... something delightful?"

He chuckled. "Yes, that and 'seed drill'. If you come in the pony cart, you should arrive at the field within half an hour. We will be there all day, so come when you like."

Upon finishing her meal, Elizabeth conferred with Cook and Mrs Harcourt. The former prepared a batch of cheese biscuits, and the latter provided a large basket in which she placed two earthenware jugs of small beer and half a dozen tin cups, saying, "I have no idea how many labourers are in that field today."

The Dartmoor pony, which could easily have pulled twice the weight of Elizabeth, her basket, and the cart, stepped lively under the lady's experienced hands. Shortly after noon, she arrived at the field where Abelard was conferring with two field hands. She left the basket in the cart, having decided to share the refreshments *after* her curiosity was satisfied, for she could see two seed drills parked side by side in the cleared field.

Abelard explained that they were only now planting spring barley because of April's late frosts. "We made these seed drills at the estate last winter but have not yet used them." He gestured to one of his workers, saying, "While Rafe explains how they work, I will learn whether I can trust him with my precious machines."

Rafe did indeed understand the principles and the mechanics, and Elizabeth was fascinated, certain that Longbourn would benefit from such a useful tool. At the end of Rafe's recitation, she said he had earned the ale and cheese biscuits she had brought.

As she turned toward the pony cart, the youngest field hand, Owain, yelled, "Smoke!" and pointed. A stand of trees prevented them from seeing what was burning, but Abelard did not hesitate. He easily mounted Gipsy and raced toward the smoke. Rafe, who had also ridden to the field, followed on a black gelding.

"I can take you with me," Elizabeth called over her shoulder to Owain as she ran to the cart. He sat beside her and held the basket of biscuits and beer in his lap.

When they were past the trees, they saw the wooden roof of a herder's hut in flames. "Nobody lives there," Owain said with relief.

A girl of about ten darted out from behind the hut and dumped a bucket of water on a horse blanket, which Abelard and Rafe then threw over the burning roof. However, before the men could adjust the wet blanket to cover more of the blaze, a breeze threw a handful of sparks at the nearby shed.

Small tongues of flame began to appear on the shed roof, and the girl shouted, "Peter!"

As a small boy holding a chicken under each arm scrambled through the shed door, Owain leapt out of the cart and ran to him.

The Dartmoor pony instinctively turned away from the fire. "You are a sensible creature," Elizabeth muttered, securing him in a nearby stand of trees. Mere minutes later, the hut's roof began to collapse, so Abelard and Rafe pulled off the blanket and put it on the shed roof. Elizabeth filled the girl's bucket in a stream behind the hut while the girl, the boy, and nine black chickens sat at a safe distance.

After the men covered the shed roof with the damp blanket, Owain took the bucket. "I'm tall enough to throw more water on the shed, Miss Bennet."

"What about the hut?" Elizabeth asked.

Rafe said, "Nothing to burn inside those stone walls. We'll clean it up, put a new roof on it, and it will be fine. How are Tamsyn and Peter faring?"

Elizabeth surmised that the purpose of his question was to move her to a safer distance, and she did not mind a bit. She joined the children and the chickens on the grass. "It appears that Mr Selby and Rafe saved the shed with your timely help," she said.

Tamsyn was pleased. "And *we* saved the chickens." However, Peter, who was hugging the cockerel on his lap, looked distressed.

"Are they yours then?" Elizabeth asked.

Tamsyn explained, "My uncle brought them from the Highlands at the end of March. They are Scots Dumpies. On our farm, we have a large flock of White Dorkings. You know how chickens are when you put new birds with the flock."

Elizabeth nodded. "Pecking order—they can be vicious."

"Mr Selby said we could use the shed for them."

"They almost died, Tamsyn!" the boy exclaimed tearfully.

"But you rescued all of them?" Elizabeth asked softly. When Peter nodded, she said, "Be happy for the blessing that resulted from your bravery, young sir. Do not fret about what *might* have happened."

Tamsyn said, "Scots Dumpies are creepers. That fellow left the shed door open, but the chickens are too short-legged to climb over the board blocking the bottom of the doorway."

"What fellow, Tamsyn?" Abelard sat beside the girl.

"We just saw the back of him, sir."

Peter said, "We were late to care for the chickens today because Mama was feeling poorly."

Abelard asked, "Does your mother need Mr Leighton?"

Tamsyn shook her head. "She didn't say she wanted one. She's breeding, so she feels sick in the morning."

"Tell her if she wants the apothecary to send me word."

"Yes, Mr Selby," Peter said solemnly.

Rafe came to sit with them, and Owain arrived a minute later with a bucket of water. "Thought we might wash off the smoke and ashes before we have beer."

"And cheese biscuits," Elizabeth said.

Abelard joked, "You are brash, sirrah, and if I weren't so hungry, I would take you to task."

Elizabeth rubbed her hands in the water. "Well, then, allow me to serve you."

While the children and men sat eating and drinking, Elizabeth held a Scots Dumpy hen under one arm and carried an earthenware jug to refill their cups. She had already consumed her share and wanted to return to the manor with empty containers.

When Rafe pointed to the hill beyond the hut and asked whether the man on horseback racing toward them was Darcy, Elizabeth turned to look. Abelard, who was sitting with two chickens on his lap, said, "Likely is. Pemberley is in that direction."

Someday, I shall walk to the hilltop; perhaps I can see the manor house, Elizabeth thought.

Mere minutes later, Darcy reined his horse to a stop near them. "We saw smoke."

We? Elizabeth looked to the hill again and saw Irene on horseback, approaching at a trot. Georgiana was travelling more slowly, trailed by a groom.

Abelard said, "I thank you for investigating, sir. The hut was unoccupied, so no real damage was done."

"I am relieved to hear it." With the most urgent matter settled, Darcy turned to Elizabeth. "It appears you have a new friend, madam."

"Yes, this is my fine feathered friend. I'm afraid we have finished the cheese biscuits, but if you would like a drink of small beer, we have another cup."

"Thank you, no."

At that moment, Irene arrived. Holding her horse at a safe distance, she called, "Good day, Mr Selby. Judging from your cheerful group, may I assume this was not a tragedy?"

"Merely a dash of drama, Lady Irene."

She thought wistfully, *These people have just dealt with a dangerous situation, yet they are relaxed—happy even. I wish I could sit on the grass with a pretty little hen in my lap and chat with Elizabeth and the children.*

The scene also enchanted Darcy. Elizabeth felt his gaze so intensely that she redirected his attention. "Would you say this is a typical Derbyshire herder's hut, sir?"

"Well, our typical huts have a roof on top of the walls rather than smouldering between them. Why do you ask?"

Her sweeping gesture encompassed the hut, the shed, and the hills beyond. "I have never seen a place for which nature has done more or where natural beauty has been so little counteracted by an awkward taste."

Trying not to laugh, Darcy asked, "Are you not thinking of Pemberley, madam?"

"Pemberley is **nice**, but does it offer a bedchamber under the stars as this hut does?"

"Not as yet, but it could." He wondered, *Is she imagining what I am imagining?*

Feeling herself blush, Elizabeth turned to the children and held up the jug. "Who wants more?"

Darcy thought, *Yes! More teasing conversation, more laughter, more blushes, more of you, Elizabeth Bennet.*

Georgiana had arrived, but she kept apart from the group and listened with an astonishment bordering on alarm at Elizabeth's sportive manner of talking to her brother. She cleared her throat and called, "Is all well?"

"It is, Miss Darcy," Abelard said.

"Ah, good. Irene, race with me back to Pemberley."

Irene looked at Darcy, who said, "I shall follow shortly." As the ladies rode off, trailed by the groom, he asked, "Do you know what started the blaze?"

"No. The children saw a man leaving the area but did not recognize him," Abelard said.

"He was too far away, and he went into that grove." Tamsyn pointed.

Darcy urged his horse nearer to the hut, and because he was mounted, he could see over the stone wall to the interior. "Does it seem that the fire started atop the roof?"

Abelard rose and crossed to him. "Yes, there is no sign of scorching inside the hut."

Dismounting, Darcy asked, "Have you offended anyone lately? Any recent disputes?"

What an odd question, Elizabeth thought.

"Just the usual people; no one new."

"Are you in need of a protector, Selby?" When Abelard laughed heartily, Darcy laughed with him.

Confident that his horse would not wander, Darcy left the animal unsecured and walked with Abelard to where Elizabeth sat with the children and the two field hands.

Peter wore a worried frown. "Will the man come back and take our chickens?"

In a reassuring tone, Abelard said, "The kitchen garden at the manor is fenced. We can keep your birds there for awhile, and you can visit whenever you like."

Elizabeth said, "I shall leave the beer here so that I can put some hens in the basket. If Peter and Tamsyn come with me in the cart, they can each hold a bird or two."

Rafe said, "After me and Owain make sure the fire is out, we will clear away the burned wood."

"No hurry, Rafe. There is time enough to do it safely," Abelard said.

As Rafe approached the hut, he called over his shoulder, "Got your gloves, Owain?"

"I thought I did," Owain muttered, patting his pockets. When Abelard offered his gloves, the lad accepted them with a grateful smile and trotted after Rafe.

Abel did not mock or scold—not like my father would have. He simply lent the lad his gloves, Elizabeth thought.

Mounting his horse, Darcy tipped his hat. "Selby, Miss Bennet, until we meet again."

≈≈≈

As Darcy handed the butler his hat and gloves, Inglesby said that the young ladies were having tea on the terrace. "I shall join them, and I would like a glass of brandy—no, ale. Oh, and ask Cook to prepare some plain cheese biscuits for supper—something simple."

"Cook is certain to have a recipe, sir."

When Darcy stepped onto the terrace, he saw Irene and Georgiana sitting in wicker chairs at the white wrought-iron table. "Ladies, who won the race?"

Georgiana exclaimed, "You have returned at last! I thank Providence that you could see who Elizabeth Bennet is."

"I won by a nose Darcy," Irene said. *But your sister would be in a taking **even** if she had won. She has a bee in her bonnet about Miss Bennet.*

"Congratulations. Georgiana is a skilled rider." Darcy sat beside Irene.

Georgiana wailed, "Will-YUM! You saw her with your own eyes. Miss Bennet is a hoyden. She was carrying a chicken and serving beer like a common tavern wench!"

"If you believe that tavern wenches carry chickens when they serve customers, you are woefully misinformed. Ah, here is my ale. Kindly wait until I have had a drink." Closing his eyes, he sipped the brew and imagined sharing it with Elizabeth. When he opened his eyes, he saw Georgiana take a breath in anticipation of continuing her scold, so he spoke quickly. "I saw Miss Bennet help people in need, which is more than I have seen **you** do."

Irene straightened in her chair, listening with new attentiveness. *Point to Darcy! Carry on, sir.*

Georgiana stammered, "Oaklands is not Pemberley—not ours! And, well ... but ... I would not know what to do."

"You and I were given good principles, but we were left to follow them in pride and conceit. Our parents, aunts, and uncles encouraged us to care for none beyond our family circle, to think meanly of the rest of the world."

Irene mused, *I fear the Darcys, the Fitzwilliams, and the Harwiches share that undesirable trait.*

"I do not have the pleasure of understanding you." Georgiana stalked into the manor.

Irene waited for Darcy to meet her gaze before telling him, "I cede the field to Miss Bennet, but I rely on you and Anne to rescue me from the Horrible Harwiches."

He assured her, "We will not fail you. I was sincere when I said you may stay at Pemberley for as long as you like."

Irene finished her tea in one gulp and jumped to her feet. "Even after you marry Elizabeth Bennet?" Making a shallow curtsy, she gave him an arch smile before going indoors.

Darcy grinned, murmuring. "Even after I marry Elizabeth Bennet."

≈≈≈

During supper at Oaklands, Squire said, "So, then, Abel, tell us about the fire."

"There was a fire on the estate?" Trevor asked.

Abelard replied, "Nothing of consequence, but we must put a new roof on the herder's hut in the northwest pasture sometime this summer."

Squire shrugged. "Not even a day's work for that."

"Was anyone hurt?" Trevor was annoyed at the casual manner in which they regarded the damage. *Oaklands could be under threat, yet they do not see it!*

"The only lives at risk were the Scots Dumpies in the nearby shed," Abelard said.

"But they are safe in the garden now," Cassandra said.

"Ah, good, the chickens escaped a fiery end," Trevor said.

"Are you familiar with that breed?" Mrs Gardiner asked.

Should I not know that a Scots Dumpy is a chicken? Have I given myself away? He wondered. "Well, I have heard of them, of course. They are from Scotland."

"Of course," Mrs Harcourt said sardonically.

Elizabeth said sternly, "The birds had to be rescued because they could not climb over the board across the threshold of the shed's door. They are creepers."

"Yes. Creepers," Trevor mumbled. "I suppose vagrants started the fire. Does this sort of thing happen often?"

Squire shrugged. "No. Will you pass the carrots, please?"

Trevor had hoped the fire would instil at least some worry into his hosts, a sense that Oaklands needed more oversight than could be provided by an elderly invalid and his shuffling son. When the conversation turned to seed drills and Abelard's plans for sowing the field with barley, Trevor knew he needed a different plan, a stronger threat.

≈≈≈

After supper, Abelard sat on a wooden bench next to the garden fence, watching the Scots Dumpies find tasty insects as they explored their temporary home. Elizabeth sat beside him, a glass of claret in one hand and a tankard of ale in the other. Taking the ale she offered, he said, "You spoil a man, madam—and I say that with gratitude."

"Do the chickens appear to be missing Scotland?"

Abelard chuckled. "Cook is in alt. She swears there is nothing better than poultry manure in a garden. Legend says that when the Romans invaded, the locals had Dumpies in their camps to warn when strangers approached."

"They are endearing little creatures." She nudged him lightly with her shoulder. "You and Mr Darcy have a history."

"That we do."

"Why did he ask if you needed a protector?"

Abelard smiled. "Ah, you noticed. During my two years at Cambridge, he was there, as were Trevor, George Wickham, and Upton Parnell. I knew Trevor, of course, but I knew the others only slightly. One day, a rather drunk Parnell asked if women who were breeding ran when they saw me for fear that my deformities were contagious. I did not know Darcy was standing behind me until he said, 'If you do not wish to sully your hands, Selby, I shall be happy to plant him a facer'. Well, because of my limp, I was slow to face Darcy; thus, I saw the alarm in Upton's eyes."

"I never envisioned him as a pugilist," she said.

"Upton called him 'Fisticuffs Darcy'. When I asked, 'Are you not concerned about sullying your own hands?', Darcy replied that although he was a gentleman, he was also a farmer, so he had touched shite before. Parnell nearly tripped over his own feet as he ran away."

Picturing that, she laughed.

Abelard continued, "I was proud and did not want to be pitied, so I said I did not need a protector. Darcy agreed but said he liked having an excuse to punch Upton. I asked if he had punched him often. I will never forget his contemplative expression as he counted; I believe the number was six—no, seven times over two terms."

Elizabeth said, "I have not known Mr Darcy for as long as you have, but throughout our acquaintance, he has generally been quite serious. This side of him is a revelation."

"There is more. A few weeks later, I was reading in a coffee house across the street from a tavern—some dull tome required by one of my classes. So when a man exited the tavern, swearing like a sailor, I watched him storm away. A short time later, I saw Darcy exit the tavern, so I went to greet him. I had taken only a few steps into the street when the swearing man rushed back with an ally and attacked Darcy. I learnt later that Darcy had revealed to the other players that the swearing man was cheating."

Abelard raised his left hand with its stiff fingers. "I have not got much of a left fist, but my left elbow is sharp, and my right fist is very strong. I joined the fray, and Darcy and I routed the rogues. There we were in the street—bruised and a bit bloody—and I asked, 'Do you need a protector?' So you see, although he and I are not intimate friends, we are reliable friends." He raised his tankard. "To Fitzwilliam Darcy."

Elizabeth touched her glass of claret to the tankard, and they drank. Then she asked, "Why did you leave university?"

"I was more interested in applying my scientific studies to Oaklands. Squire is an amateur inventor, but I am more interested in crops and animal husbandry. So I returned here, and Darcy stayed at Cambridge and took a degree."

"I suppose you did not see each other often after that."

"Darcy Senior's health was already failing. Thus, immediately after university, *our* Mr Darcy," Abelard grinned at her, "took responsibility for all of the family properties. In those days, Pemberley had an exemplary steward—George Wickham's father—but he was getting on in years; he passed not long after Darcy Senior."

"Such painful losses and heavy responsibilities for a young man," she murmured.

"Indeed. At the age of two-and-twenty, Darcy was managing a large estate *and* several small estates. He also had to find a new steward *and* be a parent to his young sister. As for Wickham, curse his greedy soul, he became quite demanding without their fathers to keep him in check. Well, that's the rumour, and I believe it." He smiled slyly. "And now, what is your story about Mr Darcy?"

"Ah, that story is still unfolding," Elizabeth said. *But recollections such as yours show me there is more goodness in Darcy than I once thought.*

≈≈≈

While driving to Oaklands on Tuesday, Darcy mused, *It has been some six weeks since I left Rosings in a fury, having been fiercely rejected by a lady who accused me of being ungentlemanly. Elizabeth and I are friends now, but could she see us as more? I want us to be more.*

When Darcy invited Elizabeth to ride in his curricle, the discussion about propriety—which involved Mrs Gardiner, Mrs Harcourt, and Squire—ended with the agreement that during broad daylight in this rural neighbourhood, a lady and a gentleman could drive without imperilling their reputations. Elizabeth offered examples of how some improper acts could be deemed proper under some circumstances, which amused everyone. It was clear that while she understood the importance of a good reputation, she also saw the nonsense in certain societal dictates.

Upon reaching the road to Lambton, Darcy steered the curricle in the opposite direction. Inspired by Elizabeth's practical perspective, he spoke of personal matters. He told her that Georgiana's current antipathy extended to family and friends. He also admitted his errors as a father figure. "More than once, I have taken the coward's path. Rather than deal with my sister's discontentment, I simply acquiesced when her demands were small."

Elizabeth said, "Someday, sir, you will be a husband and father. I urge you *not* to separate yourself from your children when their moods seem difficult. You and your wife should be partners in your parenting."

I wonder if she is thinking of Mr and Mrs Bennet, Darcy mused. "Have you been imagining me as a husband and father, madam?"

In the space of a few moments, Elizabeth blushed, scowled, and then laughed. "I have no answer for that."

Ask her, a voice in Darcy's thoughts urged. *Change the topic and **ask** her!* He cleared his throat. "I withdraw the question. Now, if I may, I want to speak of something else." He took a steadying breath and said, "Madam, you are too generous to trifle with me. If your feelings are still what they were last April, kindly tell me at once. My affections are unchanged, but one word from you will silence me on this subject forever."

Feeling the uncommon awkwardness and anxiety of his situation, she forced herself to speak. "While I am grateful that *your* sentiments have remained steadfast, sir, I confess that my sentiments have changed. I welcome your attentions now, and I ... wish to know you better." She did not yet trust her instincts and needed to feel that the Fitzwilliam Darcy of Derbyshire was not the gentleman she had encountered in Hertfordshire and Kent.

She did not throw herself into my arms, which would have been inconvenient as I am piloting a curricle, but she did not reject me. Darcy asked, "A courtship then?"

Elizabeth's smile dazzled him. "Yes, a courtship." They were happily in accord when they returned from their drive a short while later. To their surprise, Mr Gardiner had arrived at Oaklands with his four children and their nanny in a rented coach. Darcy remained for an introduction to Elizabeth's uncle and was invited to luncheon the next day. As he drove home, he wondered whether Mr Gardiner could sanction their courtship on Mr Bennet's behalf. *If so, that could ease our progress toward marriage.*

≈≈≈

At supper, Elizabeth did not speak of Darcy or what they had agreed upon during their drive. In his absence, she was excited yet confused; she knew she was happy rather than *felt* herself to be so.

On the following morning, the fact that the Gardiners and Abelard were present when Elizabeth entered the breakfast room seemed like the hand of Providence. After greeting them, she took a steadying breath and announced, "I have news and a request. Mr Darcy has asked for a courtship—that is my news. My request," she looked at Abelard, "is to remain here to determine whether he and I would suit. May I?"

"You are most welcome to stay," he assured her.

Mrs Gardiner said, "As we discussed at supper last night, Lizzy, your uncle and I will leave this week for London. So, I daresay Squire will be happy to have your company."

Worriedly, Elizabeth asked, "Will Mama and Papa object to my staying here awhile longer?"

Mr Gardiner chuckled. "My sister is far too busy to object to your absence. She is striving mightily to ensure that Mr Warren comes up to scratch for Jane—she can now name all of his favourite foods. She is also well occupied with writing lengthy letters to Kyrewood Academy regarding the care and feeding of one Lydia Bennet. One might feel sorry for Mrs Morton in her role as headmistress were it not for the fact that your mother is sending her enough foolscap to meet the academy's need for kindling for a year." He looked at his wife. "Vivian, do you want to tell me your thoughts about Mr Darcy in front of Lizzy, or shall we speak privately?"

Mrs Gardiner rolled her eyes. "Have I mentioned, my dear, that your subtle approach to delicate topics such as this is one of your most endearing qualities?"

"Privately, I hope you will tell me my other endearing qualities," he teased.

Abelard sat back, arms crossed over his chest. "Well, I believe Darcy is *just* good enough for you, Elizabeth. And have *I* mentioned that there is a small piece of Pemberley property we Selbys have always wanted to annex?"

Mrs Gardiner said, "Some believe it is best to know as little as possible about one's future spouse, but I disagree. Take time to be certain, my dear. You are a sensible young woman, so I am confident you will make a sensible decision. Do not allow yourself to be influenced by the knowledge that my fondest dream is to be driven around Pemberley in a colourful curricle."

Casting a mock glare, Elizabeth said, "I appreciate that all of you are taking the matter of my future so seriously."

≈≈≈

When Darcy and Irene came to luncheon at Oaklands that afternoon, Georgiana's absence was explained in a short sentence. "She has a headache," Irene said. Darcy grimaced and sighed but said nothing. Then, while Mrs Gardiner, Mrs

Harcourt, and Cassandra entertained Irene in the parlour, Mr Gardiner spoke with Darcy and Elizabeth in the drawing room. He told the young couple that he was tentatively consenting to their courtship on Mr Bennet's behalf.

"Send Brother Bennet your letter, Mr Darcy, and I will send him one as well. Do not be concerned if some weeks pass before you receive his response. Lizzy's father enjoys reflecting on the letters he receives. When he replies quickly, it is usually because he disagrees or disapproves."

Elizabeth groaned and nodded.

Later, as they descended the staircase together, Darcy asked Elizabeth, "When do you come of age?"

"September."

"Well, as it is the beginning of June, I shall get a special license if we have not heard from your father by September."

"Or I could write to Mama. In which case, we could receive a reply from Hertfordshire in the time it takes for an express letter to travel from there to here."

"I have a new appreciation for your mother, madam."

Chapter 12

Early on Friday morning, Darcy came to farewell the Gardiner family, and Elizabeth appreciated his gesture of respect. On the porch with the Selbys, he stood so near to her that the backs of their hands touched. After the Gardiner coach turned from the gravel drive onto the road, Trevor said to no one in particular, "God bless Mr and Mrs Gardiner. I can't imagine being shut up in a coach with four brats for a two- or three-day journey, even if a nanny was on hand." As he sauntered toward the stables, Mrs Harcourt flicked a disapproving glance at his back.

Cassandra, however, was bubbling with good cheer. She held up the book she had been hugging. "Look, Mr Darcy. Mrs Gardiner gave me her poetry book! I am learning words that people never speak." She skipped into the manor, followed by her mother.

Squire grunted, "How quickly and easily the girl moves. I dearly love her, but she does make me feel old sometimes."

"She makes *me* feel old sometimes, too," Abelard said as he pushed the bath chair into the manor.

Elizabeth gave Darcy an arch smile. "Alone at last."

"Yes, in broad daylight, with an open door behind us and in full view of whoever wishes to look our way. I have yet to kiss you to celebrate our courtship. May I kiss you?"

"In broad daylight and full view? I think not, sir! However, if we were to stand behind the wide trunk of the chestnut tree ...."

Darcy grabbed her hand and pulled her toward the little wilderness. "Before I do my errand in Lambton, I want to confirm that you will save at least two dances for me tonight. As we are courting, perhaps we might dance three times and risk the gossip."

"I am merely a visitor here. It is *your* reputation that would be at risk," she teased.

"You can only claim to be a visitor until we marry."

When they were behind the Spanish chestnut, Elizabeth closed her eyes, nervously awaiting her first kiss. When Darcy brushed his lips against hers, his gentleness calmed her. His second kiss thrilled her, and his third kiss sparked her desire and his own.

She thought, *I am far too sensible to marry a man based on his kisses, but were I not so sensible, I would certainly consider marrying* **this** *man for more of* **these***.*

≈≈≈

Darcy arrived early at the Silver Birch Inn; this would be his first assembly with Elizabeth as a courting couple. While Georgiana was introducing Irene to a friend who had recently returned from Lombardy, Darcy kept his gaze on the doorway of the ballroom. With uncharacteristic disquietude, he found himself imagining disasters that might keep the Selbys from attending.

At last, Abelard stepped into the ballroom with Mrs Harcourt on his arm, and Trevor followed, escorting Elizabeth. She moved with the easy gracefulness he had noted all those months ago in Hertfordshire, her fine eyes scanning the room. Darcy waited for her to find him, and when their eyes met, her joyful smile took his breath away.

Elizabeth pulled her hand from Trevor's arm and walked toward Darcy as if he were the only person in this crowded ballroom; he approached her with the same single-mindedness. As she passed one young man, he attempted to claim her attention, but she did not notice this would-be partner. When the space of only two small steps separated them, Darcy held out his hand, and as Elizabeth's palm glided over his, he savoured the warmth of her skin through her lacy gloves.

At that moment, the musicians played the opening notes of "Kiss Me Sweetly", so they joined the line of dancers for a reel. During the first half of the dance, Elizabeth and Darcy gazed at each other ardently. Having received tentative approval for their match, they allowed themselves to feel the yearning that societal customs had demanded they conceal.

But tonight, their awareness of each other blossomed with each touch.

Pricked by a spark of self-consciousness, she said, "We must have some conversation, Mr Darcy."

"I feel as if we are already communing in perfect accord," he murmured in her ear.

Stepping away in accordance with the pattern of the dance, she asked, "What are your thoughts about Lord Byron's address to the House of Lords in defence of Luddite attacks on the manufacturers who are depriving workers in Nottinghamshire of their livelihood?"

He replied, "Oh, I thought you would want to discuss the Earl of Wellington's successful siege of Badajoz that forced the surrender of the French garrison."

A gentleman who overheard this exchange scolded, "Dances are for dancing. To be fond of dancing is a certain step towards falling in love. No politics, no religion, nor serious talk about books."

By the assembly's end, Elizabeth and Darcy had danced three sets and kissed on the balcony—a perfect evening.

≈≈≈

While the Oaklands servants attended to their usual Saturday routines, Elizabeth helped Mrs Harcourt reorganise the linen closet, for she enjoyed the housekeeper's company as much as she enjoyed being useful. This is where Trevor found the ladies.

"Mrs Harcourt, as Oaklands has no butler, I am bringing my concerns to you."

"Your concerns, Mr Knowles?"

"Well, I do not wish to complain," he stammered, thinking, *You are supposed to ask what you can do for me.*

Elizabeth said, "If you do not wish to complain, *don't*."

He flicked an annoyed glance at her and then spoke to the housekeeper. "A button came off my jacket—during the wash, I suppose—so I asked the valet to sew it on, but he said he was too busy. Too busy to assist a guest! How is that possible? I cannot entrust this task to Toby or Polly."

While Elizabeth made no effort to conceal her amusement at his pique, Mrs Harcourt said, "Nash *is* too busy because he attends to both Squire and Mr Selby. You have been at Oaklands for two months, sir, long enough to know we are not hiding any servants from you. Our small staff is sufficient for our needs."

"Oh. Then perhaps you—" He opened his hand to show the ostentatious brass button. At Mrs Harcourt's scowl, he turned to Elizabeth, "Or you?"

She replied curtly, "I am neither your servant nor your mother. Sew on the button yourself."

"Me ... sew this? I have important matters to attend to."

"What important matters? What purpose do you serve here?" Mrs Harcourt asked.

"I am a guest. Guests do not serve a purpose," he huffed.

Elizabeth quickly corrected him. "They certainly do; they entertain their hosts. But it is bad form to be an **uninvited** guest for an extended period in a household where a disruptive event has occurred, such as Squire's accident."

"You think to lecture me about etiquette, madam?" Trevor scoffed, "Why, anyone who comes to call would not know if you were a family member, a guest, or a servant!"

She laughed. "That is a heavy misfortune indeed."

Frowning, he clenched his hands into fists, causing the shank of the brass button to poke into his palm. At that moment, Upton's advice echoed in his mind: *Encourage their pity.* Trevor's frown became an apologetic smile. "I have made a mull of this, ladies. Please forgive me, but I have never sewn on a button. I did try once, but I cannot do it." Sighing, he shrugged.

"That is something Mr Selby never says."

"What does he never say, Mrs Harcourt?" Trevor asked.

"That he cannot do something."

He looked puzzled. "But each of us has some *thing* we cannot do."

Elizabeth said, "Some activities require great strength or a particular ability, but most can be done if one tries a different approach." She told Mrs Harcourt, "I have heard Abel say that when an activity is difficult, he finds a new way to do it, and *voila!* he succeeds."

"Squire represents the best traditions of his generation, but Abel is the future of Oaklands. Do you not agree, Mr Knowles?" Mrs Harcourt asked.

When he made no reply, Elizabeth said, "I am told that Oaklands has only been in Squire's possession for some two decades, whereas," pausing, she turned to Trevor, "the Selbys have possessed what is now your father's estate for how many generations?"

"Six," he said tersely.

Mrs Harcourt said, "Yet, Fallow Deer Grove has changed very little according to a map Squire showed me last year."

Elizabeth said, "Abel showed me a map of Oaklands from when Squire first acquired it and a current map. The estate has grown significantly in one generation. I can only imagine how it might look in *six* generations."

"Under the right management," Mrs Harcourt said.

"Yes, under the wise guidance of someone who will do what is needed for this estate to thrive." Smiling innocently, Elizabeth asked, "Mr Knowles, as a parson, how do you plan to grow your flock of parishioners?"

He replied stiffly, "I am a curate; I do not yet have a parish." He made an abrupt bow and walked away. *Bothersome bitches! They are too stupid to know that Oaklands needs me!* He barked a sneering laugh and muttered, "As if my mother would ever sew a button on my jacket!"

After telling Polly he would not join the family for dinner, Trevor rode away.

≈≈≈

At Pemberley that same night, there was an unexpected guest for supper. Fitzwilliam had returned with the news that he was ready to claim an estate. His ebullience as he praised his future home and fantasized about his life there lightened even Georgiana's mood, for Irene had come to think of her as Our Lady of Perpetual Discontent.

When Georgiana asked what Fitzwilliam intended to do with his estate, he replied, "Besides live there in landed-gentry glory? I should like to raise hunting hounds."

Irene clapped her hands excitedly. "Oh, may I have one of the puppies, Uncle?"

"You may," he said magnanimously. "As soon as one of the litters produces a pup that is not up to my exacting standards, I shall give the useless animal to you."

Much later, over glasses of port in the library, Darcy toasted Fitzwilliam. A bottle of port and a plate of cheese and bread were on the drum table between their twin armchairs. Darcy said approvingly, "The Staffordshire estate is a good choice for you. It does not have the rich soil of the West Midlands, but the landscape is pretty, and the manor is sound. Did you frighten the servants when you appeared unexpectedly and said you would be their new master?"

"*I* charmed one and all, whereas their inquiries about you were quite perfunctory," Fitzwilliam protested. "So, what do I do next?"

"There are papers to sign, and then Daisy Meadow Lodge will be yours. Does Anne know you have chosen a place?"

"We shall speak when I go to Flint Rock on Monday."

"I will enjoy watching you flourish at Daisy Meadow."

Fitzwilliam grimaced. "Meaning no disrespect, but I **must** change the name."

Darcy laughed. "Well, if you must, you must. What name have you chosen?"

"None yet. I have been considering how estates are named. There is no mystery behind 'Harwich Hall' or 'Flint Rock Castle', but what is a 'Pemberley'?"

"A word that has more e's than it needs. So, within a year, will you bring a bride to your as-yet-unnamed estate?"

He gave Darcy an arch smile. "Within a year, will *you* visit my as-yet-unnamed estate with *your* bride?"

Cautiously, he replied, "I hope so. But Georgiana feels such animosity towards Elizabeth that she is barely civil. I do not understand it, and it weighs on me—my sister's adamant rejection of the woman I love."

"Are you asking for my advice?"

"I will not allow Georgiana to dictate my choice of wife, but if you have any suggestions for handling my sister, I am eager to hear them."

"Does Elizabeth know she is your choice of wife?"

"We are courting." As her image filled Darcy's thoughts, he chuckled and said, "*I* am courting the lovely, impertinent, brilliant, fierce Elizabeth Bennet of Hertfordshire."

≈≈≈

Because Elizabeth found herself dealing with minor matters, she came to Squire's suite a half-hour later than usual on Sunday night. She was pleased that the door to his sitting room was slightly open, for she carried a tray with two cups of tea and several ginger biscuits. Upon entering, she found Trevor sitting at the escritoire while his uncle dozed in his bath chair adjacent to it. Paper, ink, and a quill were within easy reach of Trevor, who was gently waving a piece of paper in one hand.

Elizabeth's eyes narrowed. *Is he drying fresh ink?*

When Trevor met her gaze, he smiled self-consciously and stopped waving the paper, although he continued to hold it with the blank side toward her. "Did you bring tea for Squire and me?" he asked cheerily.

She set the tray on the desk. "No. This is for Squire and *me*; we are going to play draughts. Have you been helping him write a letter?"

"Write? Oh, no. Yesterday, I received a letter from my mother, and I was reading it to him. Mother has asked me to return to Fallow Deer Grove, so I shall depart on Tuesday."

Yesterday, I received a letter from Jane, but I saw no letter for you, Elizabeth thought.

Hearing their voices, Squire spoke in slurred tones. "My sister sent a letter here? She has not written since the passing of my dear wife. You know, Trevor, it is because of me that your mother and her baronet have Fallow Deer Grove." He squinted at Elizabeth. "I prefer Oaklands; I am proud of it."

"Oaklands is a fine estate," Trevor said. "No doubt Abel gives it his best effort."

Faint praise from an envious man, Elizabeth thought. She noted a half-full glass of amber liquid near Squire's hand where it rested on the escritoire.

Squire shifted his gaze to his nephew and repeated, "My sister sent a letter here?"

"Yes, I read it to you a short while ago."

"I don't recall that," Squire mumbled.

"I shall read it to you again, sir," Elizabeth said as she grabbed the paper, but Trevor snatched it back.

Flustered, he stood. "I shall read it to Uncle again tomorrow. I do not want to delay your game of draughts." He hurried out of the room, closing the door behind him.

Elizabeth set a cup in front of Squire. "Will you drink some tea? And I have brought ginger biscuits." She sat in the chair Trevor vacated and placed the brandy glass on her tray.

Holding the cup with both hands, Squire cautiously raised it to his lips and drank deeply. As he set the cup on the saucer, he said, "I did not know I needed this. Thank you."

Elizabeth poured half the tea from her cup into his. "It is easy to be thirsty yet not know it. You do not recall Trevor reading your sister's letter?"

Squire shook his head, no. "He is a strange lad—and jealous of Abel." After dunking a ginger biscuit in the tea, he made an appreciative noise as he ate it.

"How often does he visit?"

He searched his memory. "A few years ago, Trevor hoped I could recommend him for a living at a parsonage." With a sly smile, he added, "I never would recommend him. He was cruel to Abel at Cambridge. Cruel men are not men of God."

"Indeed, they are not, sir."

He finished his tea, took a deep breath, and sighed. "I am tired tonight, Lizzy Bennet. May I call you that? Vivian does."

"Of course."

"So, if you do not mind, we shall postpone our draughts game until another day."

"I will send Nash to you." To Squire's happy surprise, she kissed his forehead before collecting the tray and leaving.

The valet was mending the hem of a shirt as he sat on a hall chair across from Squire's suite. He stood and bowed. "Miss Bennet, I did not realise you were in the suite. When Mr Knowles said he wanted to speak privately with Squire, I went to the kitchen for a cup of tea. Is all well, madam?"

"Mr Nash, I know it is not my place to instruct you, but if Mr Knowles attempts a private talk with Squire, would you tell Mr Abel or Mrs Susan immediately?"

The valet met her gaze evenly. "I appreciate your giving me a reason to intercede. Mr Knowles is ... well, I am not certain what he is."

"I believe we understand each other, sir."

"Shall I take your tray?"

"Thank you, no. However, Squire is ready for bed."

≈≈≈

Abelard, Mrs Harcourt, and Cassandra were playing Vingt-un when Elizabeth entered the parlour. The girl told her primly, "I am not gambling. I am practising arithmetic."

"That is precisely what I thought you were doing," Elizabeth assured her. "But may I interrupt at the end of this hand?" When all agreed, she set the tray on a side table and fetched a glass and the brandy decanter from the credenza. A minute later, Mrs Harcourt won the hand and collected the pile of small seashells in the centre of the table.

"Seashells for markers—how clever!" Elizabeth said.

Abelard said, "My sisters and I collected them from the shore at Bootle when we were children. So then, madam, please interrupt."

"When I went to Squire's room to play draughts, Trevor was sitting at the escritoire, and your father was nearby in his bath chair. He seemed a bit befuddled, and this glass was by his hand. I wonder if it contained more than brandy."

Abelard sampled it and then cleaned his palate by sipping from Mrs Harcourt's teacup. Elizabeth poured some brandy into a clean glass and gave it to him. After a sip, he said, "Compared to this, I taste bitterness in Father's glass."

"Perhaps laudanum? That would account for his confused state." Elizabeth saw the housekeeper's worried look.

Mrs Harcourt asked, "Where was Nash?"

"I spoke to him after leaving Squire's room. He said that when Trevor came to the suite and wanted to speak privately with his uncle, Squire dismissed him. So, Nash went to the kitchen. I trust I did not overstep when I asked Nash to inform you if Trevor attempts another private conversation. By the bye, he is departing on Tuesday."

"Did Trevor tell you that tonight?" Abelard asked.

"Yes, he said he had received a letter from his mother asking him to return to Fallow Deer Grove. From your expressions, it seems he has not mentioned this."

Mrs Harcourt asked, "When did his letter arrive?"

"Saturday he said."

Mrs Harcourt said, "I recall your letter from Longbourn but nothing for Mr Knowles."

Abelard teased, "Well, Miss Cassie, will you miss your playmate for quoits?"

The girl shook her head, no. "Mr Knowles pretends he likes me, but he always asks about the people at Oaklands. Sometimes my answers are not wholly truthful, and other times, I say I don't know." She smiled mischievously.

Abelard laughed. "Let no one scold Miss Cassie! She is protecting Oaklands and us."

Elizabeth debated whether to mention Trevor's behaviour regarding the letter. *Well, he is leaving on Tuesday, so if he does nought else to arouse my suspicions between now and then, I shall say nothing.*

≈≈≈

The dream woke Squire early on Monday morning. In it, he sat near a large round table encircled by chairs filled with men that his dream self knew, although his awake self would not recognize. These men were drinking and talking, but in their jokes, they noisily mocked Squire as if he could not hear them. Their words stirred old fears: those times as a young man when he felt like a fraud and now with the frequent moments when he felt like a useless old man. *Is that what Trevor has been hinting at? Insolent boy!*

Still, the bleak mood shaped by Squire's dream clung to him. When Nash helped him dress and mentioned the need for a new belt because Squire had lost weight, his employer snapped, "I do not pay you to comment about my person!"

At the breakfast table, Squire grumbled when Polly set his bowl of porridge before him, calling it food for children and toothless old people. Baring his teeth to the maid, he tapped them and declared that he was no toothless babe.

≈≈≈

"Mind your feet, Mr Knowles! I could have salvaged some of that sugar if you had not pranced around in the mess. Out of my kitchen, sir—out! Out! Out!"

Elizabeth was on the opposite side of the closed door to the kitchen. Hearing Cook's command, she quickly moved back. Trevor burst through the door and stumbled to stop when he saw her. "Don't go in there." Then he hurried off.

Cautiously, she opened the door and leaned into the kitchen. "How can I help?"

Cook was kneeling on the floor, brushing spilt sugar onto a flat piece of metal. Sitting back on her heels, she asked disgustedly, "Is that jolter head well away from my domain?"

"Yes." Elizabeth stepped into the room, taking care to avoid the scattered sugar.

"I am preparing a ragout for supper, and since the kitchen maid is out in the garden, I have to mind the carrots and turnips so they don't burn. Then Knowles bumbles in with a recipe and asks me to make his favourite teacake tomorrow so he can eat it on the ride home. When I said I would make his cake in the morning, he said he would make certain I had all the ingredients. This is my domain! I know what is here down to the last drop, dash, and crumb. And then Mr Jolter Head spills the canister of sugar!" She wiped her forehead with the back of her hand and sighed. "There is enough in the sugar bowl for tea and coffee today but not enough for baking."

Just then, Trevor stuck his head through the doorway. "I am the answer to your prayers, madam."

Cook waved the brush with menacing vigour. "Do not put so much as your toe in here!"

Trevor held up a carved wooden box. "I have sugar."

Meeting him at the door to keep him out, Elizabeth accepted the box, which was large enough to cover both her palms. "Why do you have this?"

"As a curate, I call on parishioners for the rector. Many of them scarcely have a feather to fly with, so when they offer me tea, it is usually a weak brew of much-washed leaves. Thus, I carry sugar to flavour it, which, of course, I share with the parishioners."

"Thank you. Go away," Cook said sternly. Trevor opened his mouth to speak but thought the better of it. Pressing his lips together, he left, closing the kitchen door again.

Setting the box on the work table, Elizabeth opened it and stared at the contents; then, she stirred it with a finger. Having swept up the spillage, Cook looked over her shoulder. "What are those little specks, do you suppose?"

"They could be insects, but I am not certain. Might I have a bowl and a sieve?"

"Miss Bennet, you are not a kitchen maid."

"I can be for a little while. It will be our secret. You have a ragout to prepare."

"Our secret." Cook gave the pot of vegetables a quick stir and then provided a bowl and a horsehair sieve.

After several minutes, Elizabeth said, "This process is working, but I think it preferable to have a sugar loaf from a shop you trust rather than *this* from a careless curate." She set aside the bowl. "I shall be back within the hour."

"Squire refuses to buy sugar made by slaves, so we get our loaves from Mr Varney, who sells sugar from India. Just tell him to put the charge on Oaklands' account."

≈≈≈

In the parlour shortly before supper, Cassandra was reading to her mother from the book of Wordsworth's poetry while, across the room, Elizabeth was re-reading the letter Darcy gave her at Rosings Park. Although she knew it so well that she could quote entire passages, she kept it in a dull-looking geography book; it would not do for anyone to discover she had received a letter from a gentleman who was not a relation.

Cassandra's voice often pierced Elizabeth's concentration when the girl asked her mother how to pronounce a word or what the poet meant. With patience and encouragement, Mrs Harcourt answered her questions.

Squire was also in the parlour, sitting in his bath chair and fidgeting with his pocket watch. The peevishness he had shown at breakfast had grown throughout the day, and he had replied curtly to the ladies' greetings when he came into the room a quarter-hour ago.

When Toby entered and requested Mrs Harcourt's assistance, Elizabeth kept her eyes on her letter. She expected the housekeeper to give the care of Cassandra to either herself or Squire; however, Elizabeth was not ready to end her musings about Darcy. Mrs Harcourt asked, "Squire, may Cassie read to you while I deal with this matter?"

Speaking in a kinder tone than the adults had heard from him today, he said, "Come read to me, child."

After Mrs Harcourt left, Cassandra sat on a footstool by the bath chair. Resting the open poetry book in her lap, she traced her forefinger under the row of words. Elizabeth closed her eyes and listened as the girl read, "There's a Cuckoo and one or two thrushes; And a noise of wind that rushes with a noise of water that gushes; and the Cuckoo's—" Abruptly, she stopped reading to ask, "How do I say this word, Squire?"

Cassandra held the book so he could see it. He replied dismissively, "Sound it out like your mother taught you."

The girl frowned. "That is a strange place to put 'g', but I shall try. Sov-er-ee-gen?"

Is the word 'sovereign'? Elizabeth wondered.

"Yes, that's correct," Squire said.

But it isn't correct, Elizabeth thought as Cassandra read the final line of the poem.

"Sov-er-ee-gen cry fills all the hollows of the sky." Cassandra's frown deepened. "What does 'sov-er-ee-gen' mean?" She held the book closer to Squire's face.

In a burst of temper, he knocked it out of her hands, and it slid across the rug. Elizabeth quickly tucked away Darcy's letter, poised to intervene. After a silence, Cassandra asked quietly, "Is reading difficult for you as well, sir?"

"How dare you ask me that!" Squire roared.

Elizabeth hurried over to sweep the frightened girl into her embrace. Just then, Abelard shuffled quickly into the parlour. "What is the fuss?"

"That silly girl claimed I cannot read." Squire was determined to be the wronged party.

"No, sir, she did not," Elizabeth protested in a firm, level tone. Her hands rested lightly on Cassandra's shoulders.

Abelard skewered his father with a fierce glare, causing the old man to shrink back in the bath chair. Crossing to Cassandra, he touched her head gently. "All his life, Squire has had difficulty reading, but he pretends he does not."

"You say that to make the girl feel better." But there was doubt in Squire's voice.

Mrs Harcourt strode into the parlour. "What has happened?" At the sound of her mother's voice, Cassandra pulled away from Elizabeth and ran to her.

Elizabeth explained, "When Squire was unable to help Cassandra with the pronunciation of 'sovereign', she asked him if reading was sometimes difficult."

Abelard told Mrs Harcourt, "Cassie asked a reasonable question and received a rude response." To his father, he said, "Years ago, Mother told us that you have an uncommon condition that interferes with your ability to read."

"I am not stupid!"

"This is not about intelligence, Father. The doctor told Mother that the human brain is an uncharted world; it gives us powers but does not give everyone the same powers."

"What doctor?" Squire demanded.

"One of the *many* doctors you sent me to."

Upon hearing this, the fire of self-righteousness that had held Squire erect in his chair was extinguished. A fear he believed he had hidden and a lie he had told for years were revealed. Elizabeth saw shame in his expression, and his eyes shone with unshed tears.

Holding Cassandra in a fierce hug, Mrs Harcourt said, "Please excuse us. I need to see to my child." There was dignity in her anger as she walked the girl out of the parlour.

Abelard called after them, "Squire will apologise. He will also have a tray in his suite. So, I beg you to come to supper."

Cassandra stopped just beyond the threshold and looked over her shoulder at Abelard. He smiled and she smiled in return; then, Mrs Harcourt led her away.

In a feeble attempt at humour, Squire said, "So you are sending me to my room?"

"I am, sir. But you will get your supper."

≈ ≈ ≈

Trevor was the first to arrive in the dining room, so he lingered in the doorway. Elizabeth came next, and they exchanged greetings. She wondered how he had spent his last full day at Oaklands but did not care enough to ask. When Abelard entered, he escorted Mrs Harcourt on one arm and Cassandra on the other. Only after everyone was seated did Trevor realise that Squire was not joining them, and he asked after his uncle.

"My father prefers to rest," Abelard said.

Trevor also noted that there was less conversation than usual. He wondered, *Is this blue mood because they will miss me when I am gone?*

≈ ≈ ≈

On Tuesday morning, Elizabeth and Abelard were in the breakfast room when Toby steered Squire to his usual place at the table. Squire gave the footman an egg from the hat in his lap. "Kindly give this to Cook."

Toby started to exit but stepped aside so Mrs Harcourt could enter. Squire met her eyes nervously. "I have apologised to Cassie for my rudeness and assured her she did nothing wrong—that the fault was mine. We spoke this morning when she was tending to the Scots Dumpies. After she graciously accepted my sincere regrets, she presented me with an egg. I also apologise to you, Mrs Susan, for frightening the girl."

"I know Cassie appreciates your apology, sir, as do I. Shall I fix you a plate?"

"I would be grateful for it, madam." As she filled a plate with selections from the sideboard, Squire greeted Elizabeth and then told his son, "I am not an unintelligent man, Abel, but sometimes I am a fool. I am sincerely sorry for any pain you suffered because of my pride about my limitations."

Abelard gave him a loving smile. "I, of all people, understand the battle between pride and shame at an inability to do some things that others manage easily."

When Mrs Harcourt set Squire's breakfast before him, he thanked her and asked, "Where is Trevor? If he is already gone, I am not offended that he did not farewell me."

"I have it on good authority that he is packing as we speak," Mrs Harcourt said.

"I suppose he will go Lambton for a last drink with Parnell," Abelard said.

As the others attended to the food on their plates, Elizabeth fretted over Trevor and his behaviour two nights ago. At last, she said, "Pardon me for asking, Squire, but do you recall drinking brandy with Trevor on Sunday evening?"

"No. Perhaps. I am not sure. Did I drink tea with you?"

"Yes, and we chatted briefly. Then you went to bed. But when you were alone with Mr Knowles, did he ask you to sign anything?"

Squire shook his head. "I am not sure."

Chapter 13

On Tuesday afternoon when Darcy arrived at Oaklands, he found the manor door open. Stepping into the vestibule, he also stepped into a prolonged farewell between Trevor, Elizabeth, and Mrs Harcourt. Cook was hovering near, clearly waiting for Trevor to stop speaking. When at last, he took a breath, she shoved a palm-sized, paper-wrapped square into his hands.

"As you requested, Mr Knowles. Have a safe journey."

Trevor raised the square Cook had given him. "With this, I am certain to be safe." After greeting Darcy, he moved into the doorway. Toby began to close the door very slowly but with a nonchalance that made it seem as if he were unaware of his actions. Trevor frowned at him, but the footman was gazing off into the distance.

With one foot on the porch and the other on the threshold, Trevor told Elizabeth. "Please write to me if I can be of service to Squire."

"Of course. Farewell, sir."

Darcy decided to move Trevor along. "That's a fine horse you have, Knowles, but he seems a bit restive. I would not leave him standing if I were you."

"What? Yes, Paladin is a prime goer," he said distractedly as the door pressed against his shoulder.

Cook exclaimed, "Oh, goodness, two wasps just flew in. Don't want any more of those!"

Darcy nudged Trevor. "Off you go. We do not want the house to fill with insects."

"Certainly not." Waving jauntily, Trevor stepped backwards onto the porch. Even before he turned to face his horse, the door closed with a solid "thud".

In the vestibule, Toby leaned against the door. "If he returns, I shall tell him the family are not receiving visitors."

"Bless you, Toby!" Mrs Harcourt said. The footman touched his hand to his forehead in a half-salute before sauntering off to attend to other duties.

Cassandra stuck her head out of the parlour. "Is he gone?" she whispered loudly.

Cook asked, "Can you peek through the window without disturbing the curtains?"

As the girl ducked back into the parlour, Darcy greeted Elizabeth, Mrs Harcourt, and Cook. Cassandra leaned out of the parlour to report, "He rode down the drive and turned onto the main road." Then she disappeared again.

Cook shook her head. "It will be a sad day for us if we need to rely on that wiseacre for help."

Mrs Harcourt assured Darcy, "This is not how we usually behave when a guest departs."

"He was more a barnacle than a guest," Cook muttered.

Darcy asked, "What was the item you gave him?"

Cook rolled her eyes. "He said that whenever he travels, the cook at Fallow Deer Grove makes him a special teacake. He called it his safe-journey talisman."

Elizabeth mused, "I would not expect a curate to be so superstitious."

Darcy asked, "Did his recipe seem special or unusual?"

"Well, it called for rather a lot of sugar. I have not yet sampled the results, but we can taste for ourselves after luncheon. Mr Knowles insisted that I make enough for everyone. I also made ginger biscuits—Squire favours them."

"Will you dine with us, Mr Darcy?" Elizabeth asked. "Mrs Harcourt and Cassie will be attending a picnic with a neighbour whose young niece and nephew are visiting."

"It would be my pleasure." Darcy envisioned himself walking with Elizabeth after the meal and perhaps sharing kisses behind the chestnut tree. The thought made him smile.

≈≈≈

Following a cold collation of bread, cheese, and roast chicken (*not* a Scots Dumpie), Cook brought out the tray containing a bowl of early strawberries and a plate of ginger biscuits and slices of teacake. When Abelard saw a bottle of Squire's favourite port on the tray, he asked, "To what do we owe the honour of your presence and Father's port?"

Cook grinned. "The port is to celebrate the departure of Mr Knowles. And I want to hear your thoughts on what Knowles called his 'safe-journey teacake'."

Squire patted the arm of the empty chair beside his. "Come sit in Mrs Harcourt's seat. We will sample his recipe together. I am certain it won't be half as good as your ginger biscuits. I see you brought six glasses. Will you have a dram of port, Cook?"

"Your private stock is not only for my birthday, sir? You are a generous master."

Seeing the cook and the squire laugh together made Elizabeth smile. When she saw Darcy's amusement, her smile broadened. *Not stuffy, not above his company—I prefer Derbyshire Darcy to all the other Darcys.*

After filling glasses for Squire and Cook, Darcy asked about the preferences of the others. Elizabeth was in a celebratory mood, so she asked for a splash of port; however, Abelard declined, saying it was too sweet for his taste. He also declined the baked goods, preferring the strawberries. Squire took four ginger biscuits and one slice of teacake before passing the tray of desserts to Elizabeth and Darcy, who each took some cake.

Cook put a slice on her plate and regarded it with doubt. "So let us see if Knowles' recipe was worth the effort." As she nibbled the confection, she recounted the sugar incident. "After spilling it on the floor, he staggered all over it before I could save even a little bit. Then he gave me a box of sugar he carries for his visits with parishioners. But I did not look in the box right away."

From her tone, Abelard sensed something was amiss. "What did you see?"

"Little dark specks. I thought they might be insect eggs or the like. They weren't proper insects—no legs."

Elizabeth nodded. "Whatever the specks were, they were quite small. We could not make out the details."

Cook gave her a fond look. "After Miss Bennet sifted some of his sugar, she thought it best to get a new loaf. Angel that she is, she walked to Lambton to buy one from Mr Varney. I added some of the sifted sugar to the batter so that if Knowles asked me, I could truthfully say I used his."

"Nothing special about the taste," Squire said after two bites. He pushed it aside in favour of ginger biscuits.

Cook took three bites before agreeing with Squire. When she said that using less sugar and adding orange juice and orange zest would improve it, Darcy grinned. "I will send more oranges before the week is out, madam." He ate less than half of the teacake slice before abandoning it in favour of Squire's fine port. Even Elizabeth did not finish her slice.

Fortunately.

Darcy was content to linger at Oaklands. After having tea and coffee in the parlour with the others, he and Elizabeth walked to the little wilderness so they could be within view but out of the hearing of those in the manor. Their conversation was so spirited that he was in no hurry to change the mood by speaking seriously about their courtship.

It was not surprising that Elizabeth was the first to be stricken by the noxious effects of the teacake. Of the four who had partaken of it, she was the smallest and had consumed the most. While sitting on the bench with Darcy, she felt an unexpected sense of nausea; then, a violent spasm wracked her slender frame. She began to stand but dropped to her knees when a second spasm gripped her. With outstretched, trembling arms, she managed to stop her forward fall as she retched violently.

In a heartbeat, Darcy was kneeling beside her, holding her shoulders and supporting her so that she did not collapse into her regurgitation. His voice was gruff with fear as he called, "Selby! Polly! Someone help!"

≈≈≈

Within an hour, Cook, Squire, and Darcy were suffering from nausea, vomiting, and painful sensations of tingling skin. As Abelard waited anxiously for Rafe to return with the apothecary, he told Polly to advise all the servants that the teacake was poisoned. "Collect whatever is left of it and lock it in my workroom so no one accidentally samples it."

Darcy was the last to be stricken; he was a young, robust man who weighed more than Cook and Elizabeth. After casting up his accounts into a basin provided by Polly, he sat on the vestibule floor with his knees drawn up to his chest. With great effort, he breathed slowly, trying to calm his racing heart. *Just a few minutes of rest, and I will be well enough to assist with the others. And Elizabeth needs me.*

The truth, of course, was that he needed to be with her.

A short while later, Abelard dragged a hall chair across the vestibule so that he could sit beside Darcy. "Can you drink a bit of small beer? The apothecary says it might help."

Lifting his head, Darcy accepted the proffered tankard with unsteady hands and took little sips.

Abelard said, "Unless you make a fuss, I shall send word to Pemberley that you will spend the night here. Should I mention that you have taken ill?"

"Say only that I am staying the night. What else did the apothecary tell you?"

"Leighton agrees that the cause is likely food poisoning and, because all of you have already emptied your stomachs, there is no reason to administer purgatives. He also said if his wife and children had these symptoms, he would have them drink as much small beer and weak tea as they could, on the hypothesis that the liquid would dilute the poison."

"Or the liquid could spread it more quickly," Darcy said.

"Yes, that is the risk. So then, how are you?"

"Nauseous. Struggling not to scratch my burning skin. And I have a terrible headache. How are the others?"

"Squire and Cook are about the same as you. All remnants of the toxic teacake are locked away, and Owain is collecting Mrs Susan and Cassandra."

"Elizabeth?"

"She is ill, quite ill."

For several hours, Darcy drank as much weak tea and small beer as he could stomach. Finally, when he ached to remove his skin to end the burning sensation, he asked for a linen bath towel. It was a short distance from the kitchen door to the stream bordering the garden. He followed the meandering flow to where it entered a copse of bushes and saplings. Although the stream was shallow, it was deep enough to cover him as he lay in it, letting the cool water flow over his bare skin. The surrounding greenery filtered the sunlight, lessening his headache and giving him some relief.

≈≈≈

Wearing only her chemise but with the hem pulled up to her knees, Elizabeth sat fidgeting on her bed. Her arms and legs felt scorched, but it was as if the fire was *in* her veins. Thus, she wiped her arms and legs with a rag dampened in a jug of water on her bedside table. She had hoped that vomiting would settle her stomach, but she still felt nauseated, and her head ached. Closing her eyes, she fell backwards onto the bed.

Late that night, her hallucinations began.

The library chair Toby had put in the corridor was opposite Elizabeth's bedroom door, and Darcy claimed it as his vantage point. Thus, when he heard her whimper, he was in her room in an instant. A single chamberstick burned on the bedside table, so he needed several moments to comprehend what he saw: Elizabeth, still in her chemise and still clutching the rag, was huddled on the floor in terror.

Darcy knelt beside her. "Miss Bennet. Elizabeth, why are you not in bed?" He spoke quietly, worried that his presence might add to her fear.

"So much blood on the ceiling and the walls," she murmured, gesturing weakly.

"There is no blood." Reflexively, he reached out, hoping a light touch would reassure her. When his fingers brushed her bare arm, she sucked in her breath sharply and pulled away.

"No, my skin will burn you!"

"Do you know me?"

"I am not certain."

"I am Fitzwilliam Darcy. We are friends, good friends. Shall I help you into bed?"

"No! Too much blood on the bed."

"Elizabeth, there is no—"

"You are trying to trick me! I am safer here."

Now what do I do? he wondered. He took the water jug from the bedside table; it felt too light to be full. "Elizabeth, if there is water here, I will pour it on the cloth you are holding. Do you understand?"

Although she did not reply, she held out the wadded rag in her cupped hands. There was just enough water to dampen it, and she immediately pressed it to her face.

"You are safe, my dear girl. I will return in a moment." Darcy let his hand rest lightly on her unbound, tangled hair, now stiff with dried sweat. Then he rose slowly, pressing his palm on the wall to steady himself.

"Mr Darcy?" At the sound of Mrs Harcourt's soft voice, his head jerked up, and he saw her standing in the doorway. "How is Miss Elizabeth?"

"She thinks there is blood in her bed, so she stays on the floor. She needs water to cool her and something to drink."

Mrs Harcourt said worriedly. "She already used all the water I brought earlier? Did she finish the small beer, too?"

Darcy looked around. "I did not see a container for it."

"I will bring more of both. Will you stay with her?"

"For as long as she will allow me."

≈≈≈

At dawn, Mrs Harcourt pushed open the door to Elizabeth's bedroom. Darcy was sitting with his back against the wall, dozing. Elizabeth lay beside him, her head on the pillow across his lap. When the housekeeper rested her hand on his shoulder, he woke slowly. Suddenly remembering where he was, he looked around for Elizabeth. Seeing her, he smiled. "She is better, I think."

"After you help me put her to bed, you must go to your bed and sleep."

"But if there is any change—"

Mrs Harcourt promised, "I will fetch you, sir."

≈≈≈

Before Darcy allowed himself to rest, he asked Toby to send word to Pemberley that he would stay another night at Oaklands. He also asked for a haversack of oranges to be brought with his change of clothing. Then he went to the bedroom Polly had readied for him and slept fitfully. It was noon when Abelard knocked lightly on the bedroom door. Before pushing the door open, he called, "I hope you are decent, Darcy."

After a silence, Darcy grumbled wearily, "Are you asking about my character or my state of dress?"

From the doorway, Abelard said, "I know what poisoned everyone. We were lucky. When you feel well enough, come see the culprit through my botanical microscope."

This news jolted Darcy awake. "I will join you shortly."

"Oranges have arrived from Pemberley with your fresh clothing. Should I send Nash to help you dress? Toby brought some water awhile ago, but it is cool now."

"Cool water is my preference. I shall pass on the offer of a valet, but I would be most grateful for coffee."

When Darcy stepped into the corridor some ten minutes later, Toby was approaching with a tray bearing cups, a coffee pot, a silver jug of cream, and a pot of honey.

"If you follow me, sir, I will take you to Mr Abel."

"How are the other patients?" he resisted the urge to single out Elizabeth.

"Squire and Cook are much recovered, and Mrs Susan says Miss Elizabeth is sleeping peacefully."

Toby paused at the open doorway of Abelard's workroom so Darcy could precede him; then, he set the tray on a large mahogany desk scarred by many years of use. Abelard was at his work table, where his botanical microscope sat beside several open books and Trevor's wooden sugar box. After he dismissed Toby, he joined Darcy at the desk, and they prepared their cups of coffee.

"Honey instead of sugar today," Darcy observed.

"The sugar Trevor gave Cook was contaminated with fungus—ergot."

Stunned, he set down his coffee cup with a "thunk" that rattled the china. "Ergot poisoning ... St Anthony's Fire? Dear Lord, we **were** lucky!"

"I know ergot has some medicinal purposes, but *sola dosis facit venenum.*"

"It is the dose that makes the poison," Darcy translated.

"The sample you see through my microscope is from Trevor's box of sugar."

Forgetting his coffee for the moment, Darcy peered through the microscope. "Those dark specks are such little things," he murmured.

"Even after Elizabeth sifted the sugar, there was still some contamination. Did you know ancient Egyptians wrote about grains that caused hallucinations and spasms?"

"You did not learn that at Cambridge."

"No. I got my real education after leaving university."

"Do you think Trevor intended to poison us?"

"I do," Abelard said in a flat tone.

"To what purpose? Is he an heir to Oaklands?"

"Not to my knowledge but, of course, I shall ask Squire. If Trevor thinks to show that we Selbys need him, I am certain he will return to rescue us."

"If he does, please send word to Pemberley." With a wry smile, he added, "I know you do not need a protector, sir, but I should like to be present when you confront him."

≈≈≈

Late in the morning on Thursday when Toby opened the manor door in response to insistent knocking, Georgiana pushed past him. "Where is Mr Fitzwilliam Darcy?"

"I believe the gentleman is sleeping in a guest room."

"Do you know who I am?"

Toby pretended he did not. "You are too young to be Mr Darcy's mother; however, ..." He trailed off with a shrug.

"Take me to my brother at once!"

"Do you not wish to remain here while I confirm he is accepting visitors?"

"There is no time for delay!"

At that moment, Polly emerged from the downstairs parlour. "I shall take you to his room, Miss Darcy." She led the way up the staircase and paused outside the guest room door, raising a loose fist to knock lightly.

Georgiana did not wait. Opening the door wide, she swept into the bedroom, exclaiming, "Aha!"

Aha indeed, Polly thought, amused. She crossed to the windows to open the heavy velvet drapes blocking the morning sun while Georgiana flung open the bed hangings and repeated, "Aha!"—but with less certainty.

Groggy with sleep, Darcy opened his eyes one at a time. "Is that you, Georgiana? Why are you yelling 'aha'?"

Polly asked, "Shall I bring coffee, sir?"

"Please do," Darcy said.

"Would you care for coffee, madam?" Polly asked.

"I am here to rescue my brother." Georgiana did not admit that she had expected to find Elizabeth in Darcy's bed.

"Very good, madam. Carry on." Grinning, the maid left.

Darcy struggled to a sitting position. "Rescue me from what ... or whom?"

"From seduction by Elizabeth Bennet!"

He laughed. "Seduction indeed! What could be more romantic than a starry-eyed couple casting up their accounts in glorious harmony? Georgiana, several of us were poisoned by tainted food."

"William, you cannot spend another night here with ... with an unmarried lady! Think of Miss Bennet's reputation."

"How considerate of you to feel some concern for Elizabeth," he said sardonically.

"You must stop referring to her by her Christian name; else, people will think you have some attachment to her."

"Well, I *am* courting the lady." Darcy was in no mood to defend his relationship with Elizabeth at the moment. "I will return to Pemberley with you and sleep in my own bed."

Feeling she had won a victory, Georgiana said, "While you dress, I shall wait downstairs."

≈≈≈

Having been alerted to Georgiana's presence, Mrs Harcourt was waiting in the vestibule when the young lady descended the staircase. "Good morning, Miss Darcy."

"I have come to take my brother home."

"Do you wish to wait in the parlour for him?"

Georgiana gestured. "That chair by the door will suffice."

"How is Mr Darcy this morning?"

"Well enough, I suppose. Where is Elizabeth Bennet?"

"Still sleeping. She has been ill recently."

"What sort of a household is this where guests are poisoned?"

"In my three years here, this is the first such occurrence."

"The idea that my brother might have died at Oaklands terrifies me!"

Is the chit always this dramatic? The housekeeper said, "Then take comfort in knowing he was only mildly affected.

"I would have been all alone in the world," Georgiana said mournfully.

In no mood to humour her, Mrs Harcourt said, "That would be a tragedy, but at least you have relations to help you. And with your wealth, you will never be without a home. When smallpox took my family, I left Lambton with a small trunk and a portmanteau. I lived with an invalid cousin who had only a meagre pension. Yet for all my sadness, I also knew I was more fortunate than many."

Being put in her place by a housekeeper did not sit well with Georgiana. "Mrs Harcourt, did you see George Wickham when he came to Lambton a few weeks ago?"

"Wickham? I have not seen the fellow in a decade."

"Rumour has it that you were never truly married—that Wickham is your daughter's father." Behind Georgiana's smug expression was her thought, *Surely Upton Parnell would not lie to me about a woman's reputation.*

"Does 'rumour' have a name, Miss Darcy? My late husband's name is written in my marriage lines. If you will excuse me, I have a household to run." She did not bother to curtsy; she simply walked away, her head held high.

≈≈≈

Owain helped Georgiana onto her side-saddle while Darcy mounted his horse. When he looked at his sister, she seemed poised to scold, even though Owain was standing by. "Do not speak," Darcy told her. "I have been ill. I need sleep, not conversation."

Upon reaching Pemberley, Darcy entered the vestibule first, ignoring Georgiana, who followed him closely as she insisted, "All I am saying is—"

"Darcy, how do you feel?" Irene bellowed to be heard.

"Better, thank you. Ah, Inglesby, I require a bath, a pot of peppermint tea—not too hot—and then I shall nap."

"Yes, sir." The butler moved with brisk efficiency while two footmen took the siblings' hat, gloves, and assorted outerwear.

"Will-YUM! We must discuss this!" Georgiana insisted.

"Not now. I am dead on my feet—and for all that, I am a lucky man."

"If you were not so obsessed with Elizabeth Bennet, this never would have happened."

Struggling to control his anger, Darcy turned slowly to face his sister. "In the words of Shakespeare, *shut up!*"

Georgiana stared wide-eyed as her brother climbed the staircase, keeping a firm grip on the bannister. Seeing his unsteadiness, Irene hurried after him and put a supportive arm around his waist.

Some hours later, Darcy woke from his much-needed nap to find a small, folded paper on his bedside table. He read the note and smiled. It read, "Miss Bennet is much better this afternoon. She hopes you will call tomorrow if you feel able."

Chapter 14

On Friday morning, Elizabeth took the housekeeper aside. "I am curious, Mrs Susan, about when I was insensibly ill, but I am a bit uncomfortable discussing it."

"Of course, Miss Elizabeth. I promise you my discretion." As she smiled reassuringly, she thought, *I would wager my best bonnet that she will ask about Darcy.*

"First, I thank you for giving me sponge baths; I know my skin had an unpleasant smell. Cassandra said the stench reminded her of dead mice."

"Well, it was not as bad as all that."

"Also, my memories of Tuesday night are unclear. I recall terrible stomach pain before I cast up my accounts. But after that ... and during my night of horrible imaginings, was I ... was Mr Darcy with me?"

"He cared for you as if you were a newborn babe." Seeing that Elizabeth was eager for details but reluctant to ask, she continued, "Because of your hallucinations, you thought your room and bedding were bloody. Instead, you curled up on the rug, and Mr Darcy sat with you."

"There was blood on the ceiling and running down the walls—or so I believed." She winced at the recollection.

Lest Elizabeth be shocked about a gentleman in her bedroom, Mrs Harcourt said, "I was in and out of all the sick room to bring small beer and clean chamber pots."

"You poor dear! How exhausting that must have been. I am grateful and humbled."

Mrs Harcourt patted her arm. "I am certain you would have done the same had our situations been reversed. But I tell you this to assure you that I witnessed nothing untoward in Mr Darcy's care of you."

She smiled shyly. "Mr Darcy is a gentleman."

With a mischievous look, she said, "The brooding master of Pemberley did not brood in our time of crisis."

Hesitantly, Elizabeth asked, "As for Wednesday night, did he stay with me until I fell asleep?"

"He stayed throughout the night. I told the footmen to set a pallet beside your bed for me. However, Mr Darcy insisted on watching over you. I left him alone, for I was desperate for a rest, but I woke him at dawn so he could return to his room without being noticed."

Elizabeth's rush of joy at hearing of his behaviour made her giddy. "I can think of no better comfort than being cared for by you and Mr Darcy. Thank you!"

"You are quite welcome."

As the housekeeper walked away, Elizabeth's heart did whisper, *He did this for me.*

≈≈≈

When Darcy came to Oaklands in the afternoon, he joined Elizabeth, Mrs Harcourt, Abelard, and Squire in the parlour. Their quiet conversation centred around a shared relief that they were recovered. Although everyone in the parlour heard the knocking on the front door, no one gave it any thought until Polly said, "What a surprise, Mr Knowles."

After Mrs Harcourt hurried out of the parlour, everyone strained to hear what was being said a short distance away. Polly stepped back to await instructions when the housekeeper entered the vestibule and said, "You have returned, sir. We did not expect you."

If her louder-than-usual voice seemed odd to Trevor, he did not remark on it. "I had not intended to impose upon you again after such a short absence, but it seems I left my Book of Common Prayer here. Did a servant mention finding it?"

"Unfortunately, a mysterious illness struck us after you departed." Mrs Harcourt shook her head sadly.

Trevor assumed this to mean that not everyone was fully recovered. "Good lord, how may I be of service, madam?"

She enthused, "How kind of you to ask, sir! But you have only just arrived, so please refresh yourself in the guest room where you stayed. Polly, take water to Mr Knowles' room. Afterwards, sir, join the family in the parlour. I shall tell Squire you are here, and you can make your offer to him."

Not to Abel—good. "I shall join the family shortly."

After he went upstairs, Mrs Harcourt ran to the parlour. In the doorway, Abelard scoffed, "How may **that** rogue be of service? By confessing his sins to the magistrate!"

She laughed. "The criminal curate's victims were due for a bit of luck, and now they may confront him *en masse.*"

"I daresay Polly has already alerted Cook to Trevor's presence. Please tell Cook she has my permission to get some revenge for herself," Abelard said.

Mrs Harcourt patted his chest with the palm of her hand before going to the kitchen.

≈≈≈

Trevor stood before the mirror affixed to the space between the windows overlooking the stables. His skin was still damp from the wet cloth he had used to wipe away the dust from his ride, so the fresh shirt he pulled over his head did not fall smoothly into place. Draping a length of linen over his shoulders, he mused, *What style of cravat should I tie? What would convey that I am a gentleman of property?* he wondered. Then a depressing thought interrupted. *What knot can I tie with sufficient competence so that it does not appear to have been crafted by a drunken monkey? Oh, bother, the Sentimentale will do.*

A short while later, Trevor stepped into the corridor and strode confidently to the staircase. As he walked, he muttered, "I must not smile. I must not seem too cheerful. This is a household of invalids."

Had he looked over his shoulder, he might have seen Cassandra let herself into his bedroom. After closing the door behind her, she took a moment to look around. The clothing Trevor had worn for his ride was in a heap on the floor, and his hairbrush was atop the chest of drawers. At the foot of the bed was a leather satchel large enough to hold more than a gentleman's change of clothing. Opening it, the girl removed a suede folio and began perusing the papers.

≈≈≈

Just before Trevor reached the parlour, he paused to arrange his expression to one of concern; then, he entered the room. Mrs Harcourt was sitting with Abelard on the sofa, Elizabeth and Darcy occupied matching armchairs, and Squire sat in his bath chair. Upon hearing Trevor's solemn greeting, Squire looked up. "Do come in, nephew. Sit there." He gestured at the bergère near him.

Before sitting, Trevor greeted each person by name; he was confused because everyone looked healthier than expected. When no one spoke, he asked, "Have I interrupted your conversation? I do apologise."

Mrs Harcourt replied sweetly, "We were discussing the strange illness that afflicted us after you left, sir."

He joked, "Perhaps, I should have stayed."

Cook entered with a cup of tea and stood just beyond Trevor's reach. "I am very pleased to see you, sir."

"Thank you, madam." He raised his hands to accept the cup, for he was quite thirsty after his ride; however, Cook did not seem to notice.

"I wanted to return your sugar box. Did you have any distressing symptoms of illness after you left Oaklands?"

"Nary a one." He wondered, *Does my expression appear innocent? How does my voice sound?*

Darcy said, "The experience was so terrible I would not wish it on anyone. Soon, all of us were sick, although none so gravely as Miss Bennet." He looked at her sympathetically.

Elizabeth fanned herself with a fan that matched her pink day dress. "My case was the most serious; I suffered terribly. I retched convulsively, yet I felt such an intense thirst. And my skin tingled painfully," she said softly. Darcy and Abelard exchanged glances, content to let the ladies lead the conversation.

Mrs Harcourt tsked, "The poor dear did not sleep at all on Tuesday night. Oh, and her confusion! There were moments when she did not know us."

"The hallucinations were the worst of my symptoms," Elizabeth said. "I was certain that blood was running down the walls, and when it touched my skin, it burned me."

Trevor stared at her, horrified. *Blood on the walls? Righteous Jordan James did not mention **that** when he sold me his powder for causing stomach pain. Something else must have sickened them,* he told himself.

Elizabeth glanced at Trevor but then looked away as if embarrassed. "There were other symptoms—sweat with a most unpleasant odour, rather like a dead animal. And a disorder of my ...." Trailing off, she gestured below her waist.

While he was distracted by Elizabeth's account, Polly came to the doorway carrying the wooden box. Cook gave her a discreet nod before handing Trevor the teacup. She asked again, "But you suffered no distress, sir?"

"I thank Providence that I did not." Grateful for the tea, Trevor took a large sip.

"Did you enjoy the cinnamon I added to your recipe?"

"Cinnamon? Oh, yes, it was an improvement. I shall tell my mother's cook about it."

Cook smiled as if pleased by his words; however, what truly pleased her was his indirect confession that he had not eaten the teacake, for there was no cinnamon in it. "Ah, here is Polly. Come along, girl, and give the gentleman his box."

After hearing Elizabeth's tale, he was reluctant to touch it. He nodded at the table between himself and Squire. "Set the box there." Polly did as asked and then moved to the doorway to watch the storm Trevor did not know was coming. Toby entered and stood with his twin, and they exchanged amused glances.

Cook said, "You will be happy to hear that we did not use all of your favourite sugar. The was more than enough left to sweeten your cup." As she spoke, she moved a few steps to the side, for she had timed her remark to coincide with Trevor taking another mouthful.

Her words registered in his consciousness just before he swallowed; thus, he reflexively spewed his tea. Wiping his chin with his sleeve, he exclaimed, "Have I been drinking—did you poison me, madam?"

"I poisoned everyone," she said cheerfully. Then her voice turned cold. "But I could not have done it without you."

They know—they know! "But I was trying to help you!"

"By poisoning us?" Abelard challenged him.

"I was just demonstrating how vulnerable you are without a sturdy, robust man to help in times of crisis."

"Is that how you see yourself? Sturdy and robust?" Mrs Harcourt laughed. "As if *you* would be a match for Mr Abel."

Darcy exclaimed, "Your crisis could have killed us!"

"Killed? Certainly not! Righteous said the substance would only cause an upset stomach." Under their scowls, he added, "Perhaps a *serious* upset stomach but only that."

"You got your poison from Righteous Jordan James? He is mad!" Abelard declared.

"It was *not* poison!" Trevor insisted.

"Do you know what he gave you?" Mrs Harcourt asked.

"Not precisely," he admitted in a weak voice.

"Ergot," Abelard said. Clearly, the word meant nothing to Trevor, so he added, "St Anthony's Fire. A fungus that infects grains. Those fortunate enough to survive ergotism often must have their hands or feet amputated."

No one spoke as Trevor contemplated the awfulness of his actions. Desperate to convince the others—and himself—that his crime was not so grave, he said, "But no one died, and no one had to suffer amputation, so, in truth—"

"We survived because Cook used only a small portion of the sugar you gave her," Elizabeth said. "I purchased a sugar loaf in Lambton to replace what you had ruined. Had we used only your sugar, we *would* have died."

Crossing his arms, Abelard sat back. "Why did you set fire to the herder's hut?"

Trevor looked around the room; seeing the anger in the faces around him, he tried to recast the fire as a positive event. "I did it for the good of Oaklands. It was a caution, an example of what could happen. Again, no one was hurt! Given the size of this estate, it is unreasonable to expect a man such as yourself—" Seeing Mrs Harcourt's scowl, he amended, "Or any man to be able to manage this estate well."

As Trevor uttered inanities, trying to deflect their questions and accusations, Squire watched intently. Thus, he was reluctant to look away when Cassandra tugged urgently on his arm. "Squire, you must see this—you **must**!"

He told himself, *I owe the girl a moment of my attention.* Although he did not look away from the confrontation, he asked, "What is the matter, Cassie?"

"You signed a paper that gives Mr Knowles authority over Oaklands," she whispered.

Squire jerked around to face her. "Read it to me."

"It is stupidly wordy—and written as if the words are yours—so I shall just read the important part. 'My recent experiences have shown me my mortality. So that Oaklands will prosper for years to come, I hereby name my nephew Trevor Selby Knowles to serve as co-owner of Oaklands in partnership with my son Abelard Selby. Abelard will continue to manage the estate's agricultural production, and Trevor will represent the estate's interests to banks and businesses. Working in harmony, Trevor will serve as the head of Oaklands, and Abelard will serve as the corpus'."

As he gasped, she added, "See, this is your signature."

Glaring at his nephew, Squire roared, "How dare you try to steal my son's legacy?" He took the paper from Cassandra and waved it. "Oaklands is not yours, and it never will be!"

"I wasn't trying to steal anything. But that *is* your signature. Miss Bennet was present when you signed it."

"I was not!" Elizabeth snapped. "I came to Squire's room after you coaxed a laudanum-befuddled man to sign a paper he did not read."

"Did you never wonder why my father's estate went to my sister and her husband—yes, *your* parents?"

In a small voice, Trevor said, "I heard you had a falling-out with grandfather, and he banished you."

Squire's laugh was harsh. "Is that your family's lore? Well, I *did* have a falling-out with the old hell-hound, and afterwards, I took my family away, and we never looked back. Now *you* have had a falling-out with me."

"A falling-out with *us*," Abelard corrected. "You are not welcome here."

To say that Polly packed for Trevor is to overstate the care with which she stuffed his few possessions into his satchel. Darcy and Abelard dragged Trevor out of the manor and dropped him onto the gravel drive. After Polly tossed his satchel just beyond his reach, Elizabeth opened it and dumped the contents of the wooden box over his clothing and hairbrush. As Rafe brought out Trevor's horse, Abelard called from the porch, "We have kept a sample of your poisoned sugar if the magistrate wants to see it."

≈≈≈

Darcy was pleased to be included in the early supper at Oaklands, which was a celebration. As he listened to Elizabeth's conversation with Squire, his respect for the Selbys grew. She said, "I am curious, sir, how you came to possess Oaklands."

"My dear wife, Laura, was from a cadet branch of the Winstone family. Her grandmother owned this property and gave it to us after *I* banished my father from our lives. Rest assured, I shall send my sister a letter about Trevor's perfidy." Squire gave the housekeeper a beseeching look, "With your help, Mrs Susan?"

"Always, Squire."

"You have never spoken of the falling-out with grandfather, only that it occurred," Abelard said.

After a hesitation, Squire said, "I was ashamed of my father; still, you deserve to know the truth about him. Because I was the heir—and our family possessed only Fallow Deer Grove, near Macclesfield—I continued to live with my widowed father after my marriage. Laura was a wonder, the way she ran the household," he recalled with a smile. Then his smile faded. "What do you remember, Abel?"

"Grandfather used to bump into me. I did not understand; I thought it was a game. But he didn't smile when he did it; he looked angry."

Squire said, "He *was* angry—at you and your mother but mostly at me. Even before my father was knighted—I was just a lad then—he had delusions of a dynasty. He was angry that Laura's first-born babies were girls. Then when you were born, Abel, all he could see was how you were different. When you were about four, some drunken fool at a supper party made a sneering comment about the Selby estate being inherited by a cripple."

Elizabeth could not suppress her gasp.

Squire quickly assured Abel, "I never thought of you as anything 'less than'. You were my beautiful, cheerful boy." Smiling, he added, "I feel blessed with you and your sisters. I hope you know that." Abelard's eyes were bright with unshed tears as he nodded to his father.

Squire spoke to Elizabeth and Darcy as if fearing that Abelard would find his words too hurtful. "My father told me I would not inherit Fallow Deer Grove unless I put Abel out of our lives. He said to find a charity that would take him or a family willing to raise him, so long as that charity or family was not in the county."

Looking at Abelard, he continued. "That very day, Laura and I packed. Bless your practical mother; she sent a servant to ask a neighbour for the loan of a wagon to take us to Warrington, where we could hire a coach. Instead, the neighbour's head groom took us to our destination, Bootle."

"Salt Breeze Cottage! Such a different world from the gloominess of Grandfather's house," Abelard recalled fondly. "I have many happy memories of that place and our relations on Mother's side of the family. Especially Granny Winstone."

"Especially Granny Winstone." Squire told Elizabeth, "She was Laura's great-grandmother. She celebrated her ninety-third birthday a week after we arrived there."

Abelard said, "She taught me to read."

"So that is why you were a better student than most at Cambridge." Darcy grinned.

"I should have asked her to teach me to read," Squire said wistfully.

"When we weren't learning lessons from Granny, my sisters and I played on the beach and collected seashells. It was a holiday for us." Abelard gazed sympathetically at his father. "Only now do I realise what a difficult time that was for you and Mother, not knowing where we would live."

Squire said, "Granny Winstone—yes, even I called her that—had advised Laura against marrying me, but she embraced me all the same. When we told her why we suddenly turned up at Salt Breeze Cottage, she said she had not wanted Laura to marry me because my father was a terrible man. As for Oaklands, it had been Granny's home with her husband. She said she was happy to give us this blessed estate because she preferred to spend winters in her townhouse in Manchester and summers in Bootle. Still, she visited us often. She lived to be one hundred and one."

Abelard raised his wine glass. "To Granny Winstone, may her spirit know how much we love our home." Mrs Harcourt poured some wine into Cassandra's water glass so the girl could join the toast.

Hesitantly, Squire said, "In my life, I have not always been right or wise, but I never meant to be unjust, Abel. Do not think for an instant that I lack confidence in your ability to manage Oaklands. My criticisms are merely echoes of an old man's fear of being a burden."

≈≈≈

Elizabeth led Darcy through the kitchen to the garden where the Scots Dumpies were scratching the soil and picking at the greenery. While he appreciated the fresh air, he knew the sun would soon set, and he would not be able to see her expressions in the darkness.

Tugging his hand, she indicated they should sit on the wooden bench where Abelard had told her some of his history with Darcy. Leaning against his shoulder, she said, "We have had such a dull week that I need the excitement of these chickens to liven my mind."

He laughed. "Oh, yes, such an ordinary week that a month from now, I shall have difficulty recalling it." His right hand was resting on his thigh, and when she clasped it with both hands, her casual touch heightened all of his senses.

"Thank you, Fitzwilliam Darcy."

"What have I done to earn your gratitude, madam?"

"There is so much I do not recall about my terrible time of illness, but Mrs Susan said you cared for me as if I were a newborn babe.

"It was my pleasure to care for you. Then and always, in sickness and in health."

Smiling, Elizabeth squeezed his hand. "I suppose I ought to write to my family about the nefarious Mr Knowles. But as Papa has not responded to your letter about our courtship, I shall assume he is too busy to be bothered with my news."

Darcy grinned at her annoyance with her father, a feeling he shared. "I want to write another letter to Mr Bennet; however, in this one, I will ask his permission to marry you if you are amenable. I love you."

At her surprised look, he winced. "I suppose I should have *first* said that I love you. Is this another awkward proposal?"

She cupped his cheek with a light hand. "Oh, no, Mr Darcy, this proposal was perfect." She already comprehended that he was exactly the man who, in disposition and talents, would most suit her.

He turned his head slightly to press his lips to her palm, thinking, *If only the sun would set so that the darkness would conceal our kisses.*

Chapter 15

People liked Charles Bingley, and he liked people. He also liked dancing, picnicking, playing cards, performing in amateur theatricals, and engaging in entertainments of all sorts. As well, he enjoyed shooting and riding, but only in the company of others. At six-and-twenty, he considered himself more mature than many of his peers; he did not drink to excess, nor wager on pointless distractions (such as cockroach races), nor take offence over insignificant matters in hopes of finding himself in a duel.

Alas, Bingley's two sisters did not share his high opinion of himself. After a fierce row with his youngest sister, Caroline, in the family's London townhouse, he sent a footman to obtain passage to Derbyshire on the mail coach. Bingley could have used his own coach; in addition to his annual income of five thousand pounds, he had inherited property to the amount of nearly a hundred thousand pounds. However, he preferred to travel for some three days in the company of strangers who were certain to be more entertaining than the company of his valet, who always fell asleep. Bingley joked that this was his preferred type of gambling; the risk was small, and he always met some interesting people.

On his first day of travel in the mail coach, Bingley had a lively conversation with two young men from Italy; they had completed their studies and wanted to see England. On the second day, Bingley had a discussion with a brother and sister of middle years whose business was publishing moral treatises, many on the topic of duty.

As the coach entered Derbyshire on the final leg of his journey, Bingley reflected on their wisdom, deciding, *It is my moral duty to get Caroline married—not just for her future happiness but for mine. If Caro were not such a harridan, she would be married now, and I would not be burdened with such an ungracious sister.*

He also blamed their eldest sister, Louisa, for not taking her in hand. Louisa had been married to Osgood Hurst for several years, so she understood what was involved in coaxing a gentleman into the parson's mousetrap. "Perhaps Darcy will have some advice for me, and *I* will bring some liveliness to Pemberley," Bingley murmured, eager to tell his troubles to his friend.

While he was by no means deficient in intelligence, he considered Darcy clever and generally superior in understanding. Bingley also knew that in social situations, his friend tended to be haughty and reserved; the master of Pemberley was well-bred, but his manners were not inviting.

≈ ≈ ≈

When Darcy called at Oaklands on Saturday morning, he brought his letter requesting that Mr Bennet approve his marriage to Elizabeth. Toby directed him to the kitchen garden, where Elizabeth and Cassandra had been replanting the beans into raised beds so the chickens couldn't reach them.

Darcy watched as his fiancée stood outside the fenced garden with her hands on Cassandra's shoulders, slowly turning her in a circle.

"Shall I return later? You seem quite busy," he called.

Elizabeth waved at him. After telling Cassandra something he could not hear, she came to stand with him. Together, they watched the girl make quarter turns, never looking up from her palms. Darcy said, "I am mystified."

"I have been showing her how to use a compass."

"A useful skill indeed."

She put her arm around his waist. "To what do I owe the pleasure of your company?"

"I would like you to read this before I send it." Intrigued, she unfolded the page. After praising his letter as thoughtful and well-written, Elizabeth insisted on including a brief note. In it, she assured her father that she could imagine no better partner for life than Fitzwilliam Darcy. He was delighted to send it along.

Darcy delivered their sealed correspondence to Timmons, whose bookshop also served as the receiving house for outgoing and incoming letters. As Darcy rode to Pemberley, he was certain that he had never been so happy in all his days. In the vestibule, a footman accepted his hat and gloves as Inglesby reported, "The young ladies are in the upstairs drawing room having tea with a guest."

"Someone has come to visit?"

"No, sir. Someone has come to *stay*."

"Has Fitz returned from Flint Rock?"

"No, sir."

For a moment, master and servant stared at each other. Then Darcy rolled his eyes. "Fine! Do not reveal this mysterious caller's identity. I shall find out for myself."

Still, he smiled as he ascended the staircase; this was an old game with Inglesby. Had the butler been concerned, he would have said the caller's name. Also, Darcy was simply very happy.

The door to the drawing room was open; thus, as he approached, he heard a man saying, "Whatever I do is done in a hurry. Thus if I should resolve to quit a place, I will be off in five minutes. When I am in the country, I never want to leave it; and when I am in town, it is pretty much the same. At present, I hope I can be fixed here for awhile."

Bingley? Why has he come? Darcy was surprised.

"But of course, you must say," Georgiana said as Darcy entered the drawing room.

Seeing his old friend, Bingley leapt to his feet. "Darcy! I would have visited sooner if I knew what charming company you were keeping."

Irene blushed and giggled behind her fan.

Oh, for pity's sake, Bingley has charmed another young miss! Darcy thought.

≈≈≈

After Sunday services, the Pemberley party met with the Oaklands party in the churchyard. Darcy greeted Elizabeth, but when he was pulled into a conversation with Abelard, Bingley stepped forward to express his great pleasure in seeing Elizabeth again, and he inquired after her family and their Hertfordshire friends.

She construed this as Bingley's wish to hear news of Jane, and she longed to know his intentions. Once or twice, she even imagined that when he looked at her, he was trying to trace her resemblance to her eldest sister.

Georgiana watched with interest as Pemberley's latest houseguest greeted Elizabeth enthusiastically. She wondered, *Is there a match to be made here? That would be an elegant solution for removing this lady from our lives.*

≈≈≈

When Darcy and Bingley called at Oaklands on Monday, Abelard was reviewing financial papers in the study he shared with Squire; thus, he joined Elizabeth and Mrs Harcourt and their callers. He was only slightly acquainted with Bingley but knew him to be a pleasant fellow. At the end of the visit, he suggested a simple picnic on Tuesday, and the ladies of Oaklands were happy to plan such a diversion.

After this news was shared with the ladies of Pemberley, Irene was surprised that Georgiana did not anticipate having a headache that would prevent her from attending. She wondered if Bingley's extensive praise of Elizabeth was the remedy for her cousin's maladies. This hypothesis seemed valid when, on Tuesday, Georgiana treated Elizabeth with rare courtesy. She did not even mind that the picnic included the Selby housekeeper and her daughter.

"Do you not find Mr Bingley handsome and gentleman-like, Miss Bennet?" Georgiana pressed. "Such an amiable man—fashionable but not a fop. His conversation is lively, and his manners are easy and unaffected."

"He is everything a young gentleman should be," she quoted Jane from last September. But she wondered, *Does Miss Darcy have a tendresse for Mr Bingley?*

Bingley, meanwhile, wondered if Darcy had a tendresse for Elizabeth. *With his habitually stern expression, who can tell? But I doubt he would appeal to a lady with her wit and brio. I am liked wherever I go, while Darcy's haughty reserve continually gives offence. I sometimes feel sorry for the fellow; alas, he cannot see himself as others see him.*

When Darcy teased his friend about his compulsive need to charm every lady he met, Bingley was eager to differentiate himself from his friend. "It does not follow that a charming man who enjoys society is less estimable than a deep, intricate character such as yourself."

Although the picnic lasted longer than was usual for such outings, Bingley was peevish when it ended; he was enjoying bantering with all the ladies. Consequently, on the carriage ride to Pemberley, he urged Miss Darcy to have a picnic very soon. "Perhaps Lady Irene could play her harp for us."

≈≈≈

When Bingley called at Oaklands on Thursday, he was alone; Abelard was busy with his steward, so Elizabeth and Mrs Harcourt entertained him. He said, "No doubt you are wondering why this is my third visit in four days. Being in your company refreshes my fond memories of my time with your welcoming family."

Without realising it, Elizabeth viewed Bingley through the prism of Jane's impression from last autumn. Thus, she was certain Bingley wanted her advice about renewing his acquaintance with her sister. Having recently received news of Jane's engagement to Mr Warren, Elizabeth felt she must discourage Bingley but had not found the right words.

Mrs Harcourt served as a chaperone, and by the middle of the half-hour call, she was certain that Elizabeth and Bingley were unknowingly engaged in a cross-purposes conversation. *It is as if when she speaks, he imagines she is saying something entirely different.*

She listened with amusement as Elizabeth tried to dissuade Bingley from pursuing Jane. However, the young gentleman was certain he had never been so bewitched by any woman as he was by her. Thus, he interpreted her remarks as an effort to convince him that she, of all the Bennet daughters, was his perfect match.

Later, when Elizabeth reflected on Bingley's visit, she was nagged by a notion that his enthusiasm for romance was greater than his sincerity. *I am glad Jane has Mr Warren as a model of genuineness*, she thought.

≈≈≈

When Bingley retired to his room at Pemberley that night, he penned a letter to his sisters in his usual hasty manner and addressed it to the townhouse of his brother-in-law, Mr Hurst. (He had correctly assumed that Caroline would relocate to the Hurst residence in his absence.) He wrote that Providence, fate, or some supernatural force had arranged for Miss Bennet to be waiting for him in Derbyshire. Insisting that she was his true angel, he also told his sisters that he recognized his past fickleness and immaturity. He ended his letter with a declaration that he intended to propose to the lady.

After Bingley's letter arrived at the Hurst townhouse in London, Caroline and Louisa discussed it at length. Caroline grumbled, "Charles still writes in the most careless way imaginable. I can scarce make out his meaning."

Louisa reminded her, "What matters, Caro, is that at long last, our brother is ready to settle down. Jane Bennet is a sweet girl—you said so yourself."

"I like Jane well enough, but does she have sufficient bottom to curb our brother's impulses? If not, he doesn't deserve her affection. And why is Jane in Derbyshire?"

"We both noticed Darcy's interest in Elizabeth when we were in Hertfordshire. Perhaps he invited her and Jane to visit. I am delighted that Charles's affection for Jane has endured. This may be the sign we have been waiting for."

"I will not believe it until I see it," Caroline declared.

"We can use Charles' coach. I shall send an express to Darcy but caution him not to tell our brother we are coming."

≈ ≈ ≈

On Friday, Darcy and Bingley met with a horse breeder in Salford. For some months, Georgiana had complained that her stallion, Apollo, was annoyingly skittish. As it was Darcy's habit to give his sister whatever would please her, he decided to surprise her with a new mount. Settling on a five-year-old bay mare named Fortuna, he told himself this gift was **not** a bribe to improve Georgiana's mood. (In the meantime, Bingley pondered what sort of horse would please Elizabeth. *I will help her overcome her fear of horses so we can ride together on the estate I purchase.*)

When Darcy presented Fortuna to his sister, her reaction was everything he had hoped. Georgiana was excited and appreciative, and he told himself, *She has out-grown her moodiness. Soon, she will embrace Elizabeth as a sister.*

≈ ≈ ≈

A trunk from the Gardiners was delivered to Oaklands on Tuesday, and when Elizabeth looked inside, she exclaimed, "It is Christmas!"

Puzzled, Cassandra reminded her that the month was June, but when the girl looked over Elizabeth's shoulder into the trunk, she gasped, "Is all of this for us to share?"

Elizabeth and Cassandra unpacked the trunk while Mrs Harcourt read Mrs Gardiner's accompanying letter aloud. It began with her hope that health and peace at Oaklands were restored; then, for several sentences, she vented her anger and disgust at Trevor's greedy actions.

As Elizabeth lifted out several rectangular bundles wrapped in paper and tied with string, the housekeeper read, "Mr Abel and Squire can no longer claim they are too busy to make decisions about the fabric for their new clothing, for my dear husband has chosen the best from his warehouses."

Cassandra untied the string of one package. Upon opening the paper, she exclaimed, "But this is not for gentlemen's clothing." Now Elizabeth and Mrs Harcourt gasped at the bright silks and printed muslins.

"Ah, but we have many more packages to open," Elizabeth said. By the time she and Cassandra had emptied the trunk, they found not only the cloth for men's clothing but also boxes of men's hats, ladies' bonnets, and gloves for all. Mrs Gardiner's letter ended with another hope—that some of the fabric would be used for a wedding gown or two.

≈≈≈

Two months had passed since Squire's accident, and for the past week, he had practised navigating the familiar hallways and doorways of the manor using Abelard's cane. Thus, when he and Abelard strolled the short distance from the livery stable to the tailor's shop in Lambton, Squire moved confidently, albeit slowly, along the paved pathway of High Street. After the Selbys' coachman carried their parcels of fabric to the tailor, he left to have lunch at the Mute Ploughboy with the coin Squire gave him.

Meanwhile, Elizabeth, Cassandra, and Mrs Harcourt took their share of textile treasures to the modiste to discuss their desired gowns. The ladies and gentlemen had agreed to meet for luncheon at the Silver Birch Inn, where the Oaklands party dined on dishes that were specialities of the inn's French cook. Even Squire, who felt the need to defend the plainer fare served by Cook, admitted that, yes, this meal was *somewhat* delicious. With wisdom beyond her years, Cassandra told him that one could like different dishes without judging one as being better.

Afterwards, as the Oaklands party strolled along High Street, Squire and Elizabeth walked arm in arm, and Abelard walked between Mrs Harcourt and Cassandra. Happily conversing, they did not notice they were near the Parnell firm until an inebriated Upton stumbled out.

He had drunk his first brandy at breakfast when Baron Parnell refused to allow him to spend a month in Bath. The Baron complained that his son had not earned a holiday. "Your best month of earnings is less than half of my worst month as a solicitor. Get yourself to the office and be useful to your clients, sir!"

That argument had occurred a bottle-and-a-half of brandy ago. Now Upton was unsteady on his feet and unconcerned about his reputation or his words. In a loud voice, he taunted, "So, you've crawled out of your sick bed, Squire? Congratulations! Could have sworn you'd stick your spoon in the wall after that stupid accident."

While the Oaklands party stared at him in consternation, Upton continued, "But *was* it an accident? You, there, Abelard, if you had managed to send your old man to his heavenly reward, I would be asking you for advice about doing the same for my old man!"

Abelard pushed Cassandra behind him, and Squire bellowed, "Clear the way, sirrah, for respectable people!"

Upton sneered, "If you had not paid such a pretty penny for the Browning's cobblery, old man, Miss Susan would have been happy to be my whore." Then he began laughing uncontrollably, paying no attention to the gathering crowd.

The solicitor staggered when Abelard landed a fierce punch in the fleshy space between his cheekbone and jawbone. As Upton's knees started to bend, Mrs Harcourt swung her clasped hands into his groin. Collapsing onto the pavement, he was nauseated by waves of pain.

Squire held up the cane. "Shall I finish off this villain?"

Mrs O'Casey's high-pitched voice cut through the air. "Oh, save yourself something to do on another day, Squire. You know Parnell will give you or someone else here an excuse to give him more of the same."

Amid chuckles from the crowd, Squire said, "I bow to your superior wisdom, madam."

"As you should. Now, will you come to my shop for a cup of tea? Just last week, I received a new order of spermaceti wax candles. Brighter than beeswax, you know."

Bless Mrs O'Casey for making something bad into something insignificant, Elizabeth thought, as the Oaklands party followed the chandler. Cassandra held Abelard's hand as she stepped around Upton. Pausing for only the briefest moment, she primly told the injured man, "You should not tell lies about my mother or anyone's mother."

≈≈≈

When Caroline and Louisa arrived at Pemberley on Friday, Darcy was conferring with his steward. Thus, he missed tea with Georgiana, Irene, and the three Bingley siblings. Once Bingley was certain that his sisters had not come to interfere with his plans, he spoke effusively about his affection for Elizabeth Bennet.

Louisa asked faintly, "Not Jane Bennet?"

Although Irene recognised the name of Elizabeth's eldest sister, she was unaware that Bingley had once shown an interest in her. Listening to him wax rhapsodic over Elizabeth's many virtues, she saw the disappointment in his sisters' faces. She also noted Georgiana's encouragement of the gentleman's interest. Irene thought, *If Bingley and Elizabeth made a match, that would put paid to Darcy's pursuit of the lady but not his deep regard. Oh, Darcy, if only you knew what was happening here this afternoon.*

≈≈≈

Upon returning to the manor, Darcy was informed by Inglesby that Miss Caroline Bingley and Mrs Louisa Hurst had arrived several hours earlier and were eager to speak with him at his earliest convenience. He grimaced; in his experience, urgent conversations were often unpleasant ones. "Tell the ladies I shall join them in an hour. Also, please send washing water and a light repast to my room."

"Would you like ale with your meal, sir?" Inglesby asked.

"Yes." Striding up the stairs, he thought, *But I shall likely want brandy after meeting with the ladies.*

Within an hour, Darcy was knocking on the partially open door of the sitting room that linked the Bingley sisters' bedrooms. Louisa regarded him with relief. "Oh, do come in, sir. We are …. Well, I don't know the word for what we feel."

Darcy sat in an armchair near the small sofa occupied by the ladies. "Did you have a pleasant journey?"

Louisa replied, "We did. We discussed at length Charles' recent letter informing us he was violently in love—that fate had given him a second chance with Miss Bennet. Of course, we thought he meant Miss Jane Bennet. It has been some ten months since he spoke of his interest in Jane. That is a record for Charles, as you know. So imagine our dismay—"

"Our chagrin and disbelief," Caroline interjected.

"Yes, all of that, when Charles said Miss Elizabeth Bennet is his angel. He plans to propose," Louisa said.

"What!"

Caroline exclaimed, "Charles has substituted one Bennet daughter for another! You know how he leaves words out of his correspondence, and there are ink blots throughout."

Darcy demanded, "You are quite certain that **Elizabeth** is the object of his affections?"

"Oh, yes. A short while ago, he asked us which of the two poems he had just penned was better," Louisa said. "When he mentioned how difficult it was to find a rhyme for 'Elizabeth', I said 'Jane' had many more rhymes."

Caroline added, "Charles was not amused."

How did I fail to see his infatuation? Does Elizabeth know? Darcy wondered. "This is madness. Your brother has been here less than two weeks."

"This is merely a ***dash*** of madness in a barrel of immaturity," Louisa said.

Caroline said, "Mr Darcy, we have to explain the situation to Elizabeth Bennet. She will understand."

"Should we not speak to your brother first? Miss Bennet believes he still has a tendresse for Jane." Fearing some capricious fate would meddle with his dream, Darcy was reluctant to reveal that he was waiting for Mr Bennet's response to his offer for Elizabeth.

Louisa said, "Let us see how Charles conducts himself at supper. Then we will know how to proceed."

For the rest of the afternoon, Darcy's thoughts were consumed by the situation. He had posted his letter to Mr Bennet nearly two weeks ago but had yet to receive a reply, and he wondered whether the Bennets objected to him. *The problem is inconvenient timing—all because my indolent future father-in-law delays responding to letters!*

Darcy also felt that he should tell Bingley of his proposal, yet he was reluctant to speak of it until the matter was settled. If his suit was rejected *after* he and Elizabeth made known their intention to marry, then her reputation could suffer, as well as his own.

During supper, Georgiana was the most vocal supporter of a match between Bingley and Elizabeth, and she took pains not to meet her brother's eyes as she praised the lady. However, the Bingley sisters stared intently at Darcy, waiting for him to Set Charles Straight. Irene also studied him, wondering why he was silent.

Finally, Darcy asked, "Bingley, did Miss Bennet tell you that she and I are courting?"

Bingley barked a laugh and slapped the table with his palm. "I *knew* you liked the lady despite disliking her family. Yes, she did! But you must agree, sir, that Miss Bennet and I are a superior match. My liveliness, *her* liveliness ... I am certain she prefers me."

Darcy scowled. "Then we will put that question to the lady the next time we are in her company." He did not believe Elizabeth preferred Bingley; she was certain Bingley still had a tendresse for Jane and said she intended to discourage him in the manner of a fond friend.

For the rest of the meal, Bingley was his usual cheery self while his host sat in sullen silence. Before the Bingley sisters retired, Darcy told them he had an appointment with a friend on the following day, but he would take them to call upon Elizabeth on Sunday. "Inconvenient timing, but I suppose a day's delay will make no difference," Louisa said, sighing.

≈≈≈

Having agreed a few days ago to accompany Abelard to Bakewell to look at cattle, Darcy was reluctant to break the commitment. Thus, he told himself that waiting until Sunday to speak with Elizabeth would not worsen the situation. By the day's end, Darcy pondered, *Why did I allow my friendship with Selby to lapse? I have more in common with this honest farmer than with the lordlings and fops who clutter my life in London. I thank Providence and Elizabeth for the chance to renew this acquaintance.*

While Darcy was in Bakewell, Bingley insisted that his sisters join him in calling at Oaklands. "You are acquainted with Miss Bennet and her family, so it would be the height of rudeness for you to come to Derbyshire but not acknowledge her presence." And so, the Bingley siblings called at Oaklands; it was a visit as awkward and unpleasant as Elizabeth would have predicted. Miss Caroline Bingley and Mrs Louisa Hurst were distant and condescending, which angered their brother and insulted their hostess. When the Bingleys departed after eighteen miserable minutes, Elizabeth took a long walk to shake off her annoyance.

≈≈≈

While Caroline and Louisa had supper on trays in their shared sitting room, Bingley dined with Darcy, Georgiana, and Irene. Darcy was in fine spirits, having enjoyed his time with Abelard. Bingley, however, was so glum that Irene, who had come to count on his cheerfulness, asked innocently, "Did you and your sisters enjoy your call at Oaklands?"

"You went to Oaklands!" Darcy silently scolded himself, *Of course—and the ladies were rude, as is their strategy.*

"Yes, I cannot decide which of my sisters was more discourteous!" Once Bingley began his garbled tirade, he could not stop. His remarks ricocheted between Caroline's boorishness, Louisa's disdain, and Elizabeth's valiant efforts to be a gracious hostess. Bingley concluded, "But Elizabeth Bennet will be the making of me! She is my angel, and I will **not** invite my sisters to our wedding!"

Georgiana clapped her hands. "Bravo, sir! I would be honoured to sit in the church in place of your sisters."

Without realising he did so, Darcy shook his head. *This is absurd! Caroline and Louisa were right; we must explain the situation to Elizabeth as soon as may be.*

≈≈≈

Shortly after noon on Sunday in the parlour at Oaklands, Elizabeth glared at the Bingley sisters, who sat on either side of Darcy on the sofa. She was very little disposed to approve of the ladies, so she focused on her fiancé.

"I find your tale of Mr Bingley's tendresse for me difficult to believe. He and I have had several conversations, but the topic has always been his affection for Jane. However, as she is now betrothed, I have been reflecting on how to tell him. Mr Bingley **did** abandon Jane last year, but he has been so sincere lately in his regard for her."

Louisa gave Darcy a stern look. "You must explain the situation, sir. She will never believe Caro or me as we have already been cast as the villains of this drama. And **you** are the one who habitually makes excuses for Charles."

Sighing, Darcy turned to Elizabeth. "Do you recall my saying that I discouraged Bingley from Jane because he was not good enough for her?"

"I do, although you did not explain yourself."

"I have been friends with Bingley for a decade. As you have seen, he is an amiable, social fellow."

Caroline said bitterly, "He is also a flirt and a fickle, spoony jingle brains! Because of Charles, I was jilted, yet he takes no responsibility for the consequences of his actions."

Louisa said, "Hush, dear, let Darcy explain our strategy."

"Strategy," Elizabeth repeated sceptically. She wondered, *Is this another attempt to keep the Bennets and Bingleys in separate spheres? More snobbery?*

Darcy continued. "Bingley falls in and out of love rapidly, heedlessly, and often. When he was younger, most young ladies gave little weight to his attentions. However, after the passing of his parents a few years ago in a coaching accident, Bingley became the head of a family with a not-insignificant fortune. Suddenly, ladies began taking him seriously."

Caroline said, "In the year '09, I became engaged to a gentleman who had a pretty sister of seventeen. When our families spent time together, Charles—true to form—flirted with the girl." Sighing, she shook her head. "She began talking about how we would be sisters twice over when I married her brother, and she married mine. Until then, I did not know she expected to be Charles' wife."

Louisa said, "Charles did not realise it either, and when he lost interest in the young lady, she claimed that he jilted her. To avoid public disgrace, we Bingleys paid for an extended vacation in Italy for the girl and her parents."

Caroline said, "My fiancé allowed me to end our engagement with the understanding that he would end it if I did not. He is married now and a father." Elizabeth saw the pain in her expression.

Lousia said, "But did Charles learn from the experience and change his behaviour? No! Thus, the three of us devised a strategy to protect ladies and avoid scandals."

"When Bingley declares he has found an angel, we discourage him," Darcy said. "We tell him that the lady has no particular regard for him. Sometimes we even say that the lady is mercenary or her family is unsuitable."

"Afterwards, we wait to see what Charles does," Caroline said. "We are still waiting for the day when he sincerely takes a lady to his heart. We will know it because he will ignore our discouragement and pursue her. To date, he never has. He simply shifts his attention to the next pretty girl."

Louisa said, "When Charles wrote that Miss Bennet was his fate because he found her again here, we thought he meant Jane. We *thought* this was evidence of his maturity."

"It was not until we reached Pemberley on Friday that we learnt *you* were the object of his affections," Caroline said.

Darcy added, "I was unaware of Bingley's feelings for you until Caroline and Louisa told me. And at supper last night, he announced his intention to marry you. I told him we had a courtship, but he was certain you preferred him to me."

The three callers waited in anxious silence for Elizabeth's reaction. At last, she said with some asperity, "Your tale is so nonsensical, I can scarcely credit it. I cannot be clear in my thoughts until I speak with—"

Suddenly, Mrs Harcourt entered. "Mr Bingley has called, and he insists upon seeing you. Shall I show him in?"

Elizabeth studied her guests' faces: Louisa looked weary; Caroline appeared girded for battle; and Darcy wore a flinty expression. "Yes, Mrs Harcourt, I—"

Bingley burst into the parlour, grinning broadly and carrying a posy. "I was certain you would see me, Miss Bennet. I know your heart as well as my own."

Feeling jolted out of her complacency, Elizabeth greeted him hesitantly. "Good day."

Noticing the occupants of the sofa, Bingley said, "So then, Darcy, did you escort my sisters here so they could pay off every arrear of civility to Miss Bennet?"

"Miss Bingley and Mrs Hurst have been most gracious," Elizabeth said. After a pause, she said, "I am happy you called today, for I have news of Jane. Will you be seated?"

Bingley dragged a library chair next to Elizabeth's bergère. "I hope Miss Bennet is well. Indeed, I hope all your family are well."

She gave him a closed-mouth smile and nodded. Bingley sat and looked around the room before realising he still held the bouquet of wildflowers—yellow daffodils, valerian, and bright blue speedwells—which he had obviously collected himself. Mrs Harcourt, who had been waiting in the doorway, asked, "Shall I put the flowers in water, sir?"

"Yes, thank you." As she exited, she gave Elizabeth a sympathetic look.

Elizabeth faced Bingley. "I do not wish to pain you, sir, but Jane has accepted a proposal from another gentleman."

"Ah, capital! Do send Miss Bennet my best wishes. She is a lovely lady."

"She is a lovely lady," Elizabeth repeated in a murmur. *Perhaps the account of his being a faithless flirt is not a Banbury tale.*

"My time with your sister was enjoyable, but she and I did not share the intimate conversations in which you and I discussed our dreams for the future. I remember such an afternoon in Hertfordshire last October as if the words were written on my heart."

This was not his first reference to a misremembrance. At once, Elizabeth grasped the significance of those bewildering occurrences. "Mr Bingley, your fond memory was of a conversation you had with Jane."

"I am reluctant to disagree, but you are mistaken. **You** were always the object of my affection. I remember our time together with pellucid clarity," he insisted.

As Elizabeth did not have a mirror, she could not see the change in her expression, but those sitting on the sofa did. "**My** mistake, sir, was in not realising that you cannot discern one Bennet daughter from another."

Defensively, Bingley grumbled, "I am certain I would never confuse Miss Mary or Miss Lydia with you."

"What of my sister Kitty?" As Bingley squinted, trying to picture the fourth of the five Bennet daughters, Elizabeth said coolly, "So, you had no special regard for Jane."

"Indeed I did not. Oh, perhaps the notion crossed my mind when I first saw her; she is quite pretty." He flashed a smile at Darcy. "However, I am grateful to my friend and my sisters who said she had no particular regard for me."

"Were you aware Jane was in London from January through April?" Elizabeth asked.

"I learnt of her presence in February when I saw her walking in Hyde Park with a handsome family. Were those your relations from Cheapside? Your sister mentioned she had family in town."

"Yes."

"Ah, I nearly forgot! Miss Bennet, I have written you a poem. Well, I wrote two, but I believe this is the best."

As Bingley reached into his jacket pocket, she said, "I do not wish to hear it."

He glanced at his sisters and Darcy and then chuckled. "No, not with an audience. Your modesty adds to your other perfections." In a quieter voice, he continued, "You can hardly doubt my purpose; however, your—"

"We have both misunderstood each other, sir. I thought our conversations were about your affection for Jane."

"Jane? No, madam. If your sister thought my natural friendliness meant more, I cannot be blamed for that. "

Elizabeth stared at him, recognizing her conundrum. *If I agree that any reasonable lady would know him for a niffy-naffy fellow, then that means Jane was a fool. But if I reveal that he **did** touch Jane's heart, I will feed his vanity. No—I refuse to bolster his amour propre!*

Caroline told her brother, "If Jane Bennet took your words to heart, then **you** are the villain for misleading her. Yes, women fancy that a man's admiration means more than it does, but **men** take care that it should."

Bingley dismissed her remark with a wave. "You do not understand, Caroline." To Elizabeth, he said, "**You** are my angel, madam. You hold my loving heart in your dainty hands." When Bingley came to his feet, Darcy rose, too, ready to protect his fiancée.

Elizabeth rose and faced Bingley. "I am most assuredly **not** your angel, sir."

Darcy pressed his lips into a line to suppress a smile. *She is a Valkyrie, and **he** is in for some of what I experienced after my proposal at Rosings. Perhaps this is what he needs.*

Bingley protested, "But you were so attentive to me."

"Was my attention equal to what you showed Jane during your **three** months in Hertfordshire? You are a mooncalf, a rattlepate, and as foolish as any lad I know."

Bingley glared at his sisters and Darcy. "What did you say to turn her against me?"

Elizabeth answered for them. "Blame yourself, sir, for it is your own words that turned me against you. Your casual dismissal of my sister to whom you paid prodigious attention before abandoning her without so much a note of goodbye."

Bingley asked Caroline accusingly, "Did you not send the Bennets a farewell letter on my behalf?"

Hearing Caroline growl, Louisa muttered, "You cannot do violence to Charles here. We are guests—it would be rude to bloody their carpet."

Elizabeth said, "Miss Bingley did. I presume you did not read the letter, sir."

"Not every word ... Caro's handwriting is better than mine, so whenever I can, I leave my correspondence to her."

Not every word? I daresay you read none of it! Elizabeth thought. "If I took your honeyed words as truth, I am certain you would soon abandon me for another lady."

Bingley looked puzzled. "Who?"

At that moment, Mrs Harcourt entered with the posy arranged in a short, porcelain jug. Elizabeth snatched out the flowers and hit Bingley on the head with them. "Take your poem and your pitiful self and leave!"

"But I ... but you—"

Before Bingley could find the words to finish his thought, Darcy grabbed his arm. "It's time to depart with whatever tattered remnants of dignity you still possess." As he pulled his bewildered friend out of the parlour, he said, "As always, Miss Bennet, it is a pleasure to spend time with you, and I shall see you soon. Caroline and Louisa, I have my horse, and you have the curricle, so I encourage you to visit Lambton before you return to Pemberley. Come along, Bingley."

As the men departed, Caroline and Louisa hurried to help Elizabeth collect the flowers from the carpet. Mrs Harcourt protested, "I can take care of this, ladies."

Elizabeth said, "It was my action, Mrs Susan, so it is my obligation."

"This is true for us as well," Louisa said, handing Mrs Harcourt a daffodil. Amused, the housekeeper accepted each blossom and returned them to the porcelain jug.

Caroline said, "Miss Bennet, we are so very sorry for our brother's behaviour—and our rudeness as we attempted to minimize his harm."

Sitting back on her heels, Elizabeth remarked, "My Aunt Gardiner says one cannot apologise for someone else. One can be embarrassed or angry by another's behaviour, but one cannot feel regret on behalf of someone who feels no regret."

After the flowers were collected, Mrs Harcourt said, "Perhaps you and your guests would enjoy a glass of port or brandy, Miss Bennet."

Louisa pressed a hand to her breast, "Oh, yes, please. A brandy would restore me."

Caroline put an arm around her sister's shoulders. "Port for me, thank you."

Elizabeth nodded. "Port."

As the housekeeper exited, the ladies seated themselves. Louisa said, "We need a different strategy for managing Charles. What we are doing isn't working."

Elizabeth said, "Not only that, you are damaging your own reputations by presenting yourselves as proud, disagreeable ladies." This time, even she heard Caroline's growl.

≈≈≈

Shortly before supper, a footman arrived from Pemberley. In the vestibule with Mrs Harcourt and Toby looking on, he handed Elizabeth a haversack of oranges and a note. "Mr Darcy hoped you would have a reply for him."

Mrs Harcourt took the oranges and told Toby, "Please fetch the other two Pemberley haversacks for this man. I do not think that even a grand estate has an infinite supply. And after I put these oranges on a tray, I shall return this one."

Now alone with the footman, Elizabeth opened the note. It read, "I love you, and I am sorry for the nonsense. The sooner we marry, the better."

In the note Elizabeth sent with the haversacks, she had written, "I love you, too, and if we do not have a letter from my father by the end of the week, I shall write to my mother."

Chapter 16

Early on Monday, Bingley generously tipped a groom to take his valet and himself to Lambton to catch the mail coach. He had farewelled no one nor thanked his host. When Caroline and Louisa heard of his abrupt departure, they asked Darcy for another night of hospitality. Louisa explained, "If we wait until Tuesday to leave, we are less likely to encounter Charles sulking at some posting house when we change horses."

Darcy chuckled drily. "I would not enjoy such an encounter either. You are welcome to stay through tomorrow and beyond, if you like."

Caroline politely refused for both of them. "Louisa and I have much to contemplate, and a long journey is an ideal time for our reflections." After a pause, she asked, "Do you think Charles will take to heart anything we said yesterday?"

"Who knows? We have all embraced foolish notions, clinging to them as if they were part of our identity," he said.

Louisa said, "I shall pray that the contretemps with Miss Bennet pierced our brother's self-delusion."

≈≈≈

That afternoon, Darcy and Irene were playing chess in the library when Georgiana entered, waving a piece of paper. "Did you read poor Mr Bingley's note? It says you wrote to Miss Bennet's father asking for her hand in marriage."

"I threw his ridiculous note into the fireplace in my study," he said.

She responded to his implied censure, "My quill was broken, so I needed a new one. You should have a fire when you intend to burn something in your fireplace."

Irene sat back in her chair. *Why do I enjoy watching these two squabble when I find no comfort in arguing with* **my** *brothers?*

"Miss Bennet is a flirt who has collected the hearts of Bingley, Wickham, young Mr Selby, and lord knows who else! I believe she rejected poor Mr Bingley because his wealth does not match yours. She is a fortune hunter."

"She is not a fortune hunter. I proposed to her at Rosings, and she refused."

Irene looked at Georgiana. *Oh goodness, she is as surprised about that as I am.*

Georgiana declared, "You have given me a new reason to dislike her! What right does that encroaching mushroom have to reject a Darcy? And if you insist on pursuing her, it can only be for your vanity!"

"Miss Bennet had her reasons; I do not fault her for them. We have overcome our misunderstandings, and I look forward to making her my wife."

"How can you speak calmly about something that upsets me so?" She accused, "Your precious Miss Bennet hates me."

"You say that to justify **your** dislike of her. You have made your disapprobation a crusade that you demand the rest of us join. Why do you insist that I choose between Elizabeth and you?"

As Georgiana stared silently at her brother, her thoughts raged, *I don't **know** why I feel this way—I simply know that I cannot be happy unless ... unless **you** do what **I** want!* Her eyes were bright with tears. "I beg you, William, give up the Bennet creature."

In a cold voice, he said, "Do not disparage Elizabeth. I love her, and I shall marry her, whether or not you approve."

"I do not!" she turned away from his insistent gaze.

Smiling, Irene said, "Congratulations, Darcy!"

He was relieved to have at least some support. Gesturing at the chess board, he asked, "May we finish this match later? I need fresh air." Without waiting for her reply, he strode out of the library.

A moment later, Irene said, "He is gone."

Georgiana spun in a violent half-turn to face her. "You congratulated him."

"Do you not want him to be happy? You are jealous."

She sneered, "I have never heard you hope for the happiness of your brothers! *You* are jealous."

Momentarily taken aback, Irene said, "I am jealous that my parents value their sons over their daughter and that my foolish brothers have embraced their attitude. However, my sentiments are rooted in my family's treatment of me. You, Miss Georgiana Darcy, have *so* much, yet rather than appreciate your blessings, you endeavour to bend others to your will—for no better reason than a whim."

"My blessings? At least *you* have a mother and a father."

"In the eyes of the law, yes, I do. But my parents do not give me even a jot of the care that Darcy gives you."

"If you admire my brother so much, why did you allow the Bennet creature to steal him from you?"

"Steal him?" Irene chuckled. "He was never mine. I doubt you wanted him to marry me either."

"Well, since you insist on championing Elizabeth, you cannot be my friend. Do you prefer to return to Flint Rock Castle or the Harwich estate? As today is Monday, I trust you will have sufficient time to pack and farewell your friends at Oakland by Thursday."

"Dear Georgiana, I shall fill the tragic loss of your charming company by cultivating a friendship Miss Bennet. Also, it seems you are unaware that your brother. has told me I am welcome at Pemberley for as long as I wish to stay." Irene curtsied and left Georgiana to contemplate her frustration.

≈≈≈

Before heading their coach toward London on Tuesday morning, Louisa and Caroline called at Oaklands. They apologised to Elizabeth again for the rudeness that had tainted their conversations and asked her to convey their best wishes to Jane on her recent engagement. Caroline implored, "If you can suggest a better method for managing Charles, we are eager to hear it."

Louisa nodded. "We are all at our wit's end."

Elizabeth understood. The Bingley sisters could not warn a young lady in advance of their brother's infatuations, for who could predict when he would fixate upon a lady? Also, she had known ladies who would view the Bingley sisters' caution as a challenge to bring a rich young man up to scratch. "I am sorry, but I have no advice for you. Have you advice for me on how to win over Miss Darcy?"

Louisa said, "When we first met Georgiana—she was eight or nine then—she was a sweet child, but now ...." She trailed off, shaking her head.

Caroline said, "In London last December before the Darcys decamped to Flint Rock Castle, we encountered her and her brother twice in one week. At the first meeting, Miss Darcy complained that her gown made her look too young. When I said her gown was charming, she was offended. Having formed an opinion, she took any remark to the contrary as a personal affront."

Louisa recalled, "When next we met Georgiana, we both admired her bonnet. I would have been happy to wear it."

Caroline grimaced. "She claimed we were trying to curry her favour. *We* who have known her for years."

"Afterwards, we learnt that Miss Darcy called us fawning, insincere mushrooms. Yet, she vociferously championed a match between Charles and yourself," Louisa said.

Caroline added, "Not because she considered you two a good match—that was obvious. Rather, she was eager to separate you from her brother. Over supper at Pemberley on Sunday, while Charles took a tray in his room, we dined with Lady Irene and the Darcys. When Georgiana lamented Charles' treatment at your hands, we disagreed."

"We praised you! We told her our brother was a flirt and did not deserve a lady of your calibre," Louisa declared. "She was not happy to hear that."

"Her dislike of me is no secret," Elizabeth said glumly.

After the Bingley sisters departed, Elizabeth mused on how sincerely apologetic and pleasant their behaviour had been. As for their caution about Georgiana, she sighed. *It is quite embarrassing that my fiancé's sister is so public in her detestation of me. Nor does she give me so much as a hint as to how to repair our relationship.*

≈≈≈

While any excuse would do, Darcy had a perfect reason to call at Oaklands on the afternoon of the last day of June. He had received Mr Bennet's letter approving the engagement to Elizabeth and, to his delight, she had also received her parents' approval, so her effervescent mood matched his.

"A sensitive gentleman would confirm that the lady has not changed her mind." Darcy was joking, yet he felt a twinge of uncertainty.

"An overly sensitive lady might wonder if that remark is a sign that the gentleman has changed his mind." Elizabeth gave him an arch smile.

Gently clasping her free hand, he brought it to his lips and kissed it lightly. "I am convinced that my chance of happiness with you is far greater than with any other woman I know or have yet to meet."

Feeling secure in their affection for each other, they strolled automatically to the little wilderness as they discussed wedding dates and places. Darcy said he was happy to marry in Hertfordshire, that this was only fair as, afterwards, Elizabeth would reside primarily in Derbyshire. She agreed that she would prefer a Hertfordshire wedding and said she would ask her parents to arrange for the banns to be read in Meryton when a date for the wedding was fixed.

"Or I could purchase a special license," he suggested, hoping to become her husband sooner rather than later.

"Your relations will want to celebrate with you." Suddenly, she felt a twinge of uncertainty and thought, *Well, I **hope** they will celebrate our match.*

Darcy produced his pocket diary and pencil. "What are your thoughts about an engagement party at Pemberley on the eighteenth of July? Then we can travel together to Longbourn in the following week."

Hesitantly, Elizabeth asked, "Do you think Miss Darcy will have accepted me by then?"

"I love my sister, but her whims do not rule me—and I will not let her rule you either. Will you write to your mother this week about the reading of the banns?"

"Yes, allowing time for a letter to travel from Lambton to Longbourn—and allowing Mama at least two days to overcome her nervous flutterings at my news—I suggest we have our wedding in the last week in July."

"That seems very far away. I shall need kisses to sustain me," he said solemnly. She laughed as he pulled her behind the wide trunk of the Spanish chestnut, and they celebrated Mr Bennet's approval with delicious kisses before Darcy rode back to Pemberley.

≈≈≈

Fitzwilliam arrived at Pemberley shortly before supper. Over glasses of claret in Darcy's study, he said, "Anne has established an account for me in London, and she has already put fifteen thousand pounds in it. Thus, in addition to dealing with the paperwork—I trust that your men of business have kept you apprised—I have been acquainting myself with the servants at," he winced, "Daisy Meadows."

"You have not chosen a new name yet."

"Not yet," he touched his glass to Darcy's, "*I have an estate!* Now, what is your news?"

"Mr Bennet has given his permission for Elizabeth and me to marry."

"Congratulations!" He touched his glass to Darcy's again, and they drank. After a moment of contented silence, as both men savoured the feeling that All Was Right With The World, Fitzwilliam asked hesitantly, "How did Georgiana take your news?"

"I shall tell her at supper."

"And I will be with you." He left to settle into his room.

Now alone, Darcy refilled his wine glass and meditated on his history with Elizabeth. After meeting her in Hertfordshire, he had believed the Bennets would be poor role models for Georgiana. Months later at Rosings Park, he explained in his proposal that his affection for Elizabeth was stronger than his disdain for her family. (At that recollection, he winced.) However, in Derbyshire, he discovered her family encompassed more than a lazy father, a desperate mother, and silly younger sisters. As well, when circumstances forced him to recall his knowledge of Jane Bennet, he realised she was a pattern card of ladylike behaviour.

After being what he termed "properly humbled by a lady worthy of being pleased", Darcy had decided Elizabeth, with her kindness and experience as an elder sister, would be the perfect friend for Georgiana. *Why does my sister not see what I see in Elizabeth? Or is something in my behaviour the true reason for her unhappiness? Am I trying to fix a situation that Georgiana must resolve for herself?*

Darcy had no answer.

≈≈≈

Over a dessert of syllabub and shortbread, Darcy announced the news that Fitzwilliam knew, Irene suspected, and Georgiana feared. To the relief *and* disbelief of everyone, Georgiana calmly congratulated her brother.

No one believed her mood would remain so sanguine.

≈≈≈

The letter Darcy sent to Flint Rock Castle on the first of July began with the happy news of his engagement to Miss Elizabeth Bennet and the plan to celebrate with a ball on the eighteenth of July. He urged the Countess to bring her guests to Pemberley no later than the seventh so that the family could enjoy time together before the festivities.

≈≈≈

Knowing of Darcy's dislike of Upton Parnell, Georgiana had decided that since her brother persisted in spending time with a lady she despised, she would cultivate a friendship with a gentleman whom her brother despised. Thus, that afternoon, Georgiana drove herself and her maid drove to Lambton.

As Georgiana waited in the curricle, her maid entered the Parnell office. When she returned a few minutes later, Upton was following her. After Georgiana exchanged greetings with him, she told her maid, "There is a blue bonnet in the milliner's shop. Go there and inquire about the cost."

Puzzled, the maid said, "The milliner has several blue bonnets, Miss Darcy."

"Then have her make a list of the prices of *all* the blue bonnets. I shall wait here."

"Yes, madam." As the maid walked to the milliner's shop, she muttered, "Well, Miss High-and-Mighty couldn't just say, 'Leave me alone with this fellow', could she? And are these meetings with Mr Hands-On Parnell going to be a regular thing? That would put me in a difficult spot between Herself and Mr Darcy."

Upton's first thought was that Darcy did not know she was here. However, the solicitor was sufficiently curious to let Georgiana reveal her purpose in her own time. Within minutes, her chatter became flirtatious, and he responded in kind. Even before the put-upon maid returned with a note from the modiste, Georgiana and Upton had agreed to meet on the following day for a ride on the Parnell estate. Georgiana's desire to defy Darcy's authority matched Upton's desire to tweak his nose; neither knew whether their clandestine ride would be a one-time event or what might come of joining forces.

≈≈≈

Upton had never taken much interest in the familial estate. Although he was the heir, he still clung to the dream of living in London while his younger brother resided at Parnell Downs to guide a competent steward. Thus, when

Upton said he would close the office on Thursday to ride around the family estate, Baron Parnell was in alt, believing his eldest was finally taking an interest in his heritage.

Parnell Downs was one-quarter the size of Pemberley, and Georgiana met Upton at a well-known stile between the properties. After some bantering, they fell into a conversation that took an intriguing turn. In Upton, she found a sympathetic ear; he listened to her discontent without telling her that she was selfish or should be grateful for having such a kind brother. As he meditated on this younger-than-her-years lady, Upton realised that through her, he could wound Darcy without risk of reprisal.

When Georgiana bemoaned the insignificance of her brother's betrothed, Upton said, "You have more power than you realise, Miss Darcy. Miss Bennet will never be your equal, despite the consequence she receives through her association with your brother. I suggest you find a way to remind her of her inferiority."

She was intrigued. "How?"

"Oh, merely some gesture or action that shows your superiority. Think on it for a bit; you are a clever young lady." He smiled, "Shall I look for you at the market next Wednesday so you can tell me your progress?"

"Oh, perhaps, I shall be there," she replied flirtatiously.

On the ride back to Pemberley, Upton's words circled through Georgiana's thoughts. *A gesture or action that shows my superiority. I **am** a clever young lady and a superior horsewoman.* She also decided that she needed an ally—or, at the least, a dupe—whose presence would lend the appearance of innocence to her machinations. Thus, before supper, she sought out Irene.

As Irene listened to her cousin's apology for past incivilities, she kept her expression pleasant but non-committal. She did not trust Georgiana, but she was willing to act as if their friendship were restored.

≈≈≈

Georgiana invited Irene on a shopping excursion on the following day, and when the ladies chose new fans from the selection at the millinery, she paid for Irene's. Opening and closing various fans with a flick of her wrist, Georgiana said, "As Lambton is so near to Oaklands, I wish to call and invite Miss Bennet on a ride. William says she is not an equestrienne, but she has been practising. Poor dear! I doubt that even the best steed at Oaklands would equal the worst at Pemberley. I should like her to have the opportunity to ride a beautiful stepper."

"That's very kind of you." Irene thought, *The day is young,* **and** *Georgiana has purchased a new fan for me* **and** *suggested offering Elizabeth the use of one of Pemberley's fine horses. What next?*

"Help me select a fan for Miss Bennet. Uncle Kestevyn says that gifts always inspire people to reciprocate or, at least, to agree with you.

When the Pemberley ladies called at Oaklands a short while later, Elizabeth whispered, "Please join us, Mrs Susan. Miss Darcy unsettles me."

Georgiana had heard enough about the Selby household that she was not surprised when Mrs Harcourt remained in the parlour to pour out tea and make conversation. Presenting Elizabeth with a wooden fan painted dark green, Georgiana said, "Irene and I purchased new fans today, and because I had planned to call, it seemed only logical to bring you a fan as well."

"Yes, quite logical," Elizabeth murmured. "Thank you."

For an instant, Georgiana thought her hostess was mocking her, but a calming voice in her thoughts urged, *Follow your plan; do not be distracted by suppositions. You are her superior.* "Miss Bennet, will you come riding with Irene and me tomorrow? I am told you have been practising."

"I need more practice—years more."

"There is so much of Pemberley you have not seen, and some of the most interesting places are best reached on horseback. Do you not think so, Irene?"

At last—Georgiana has said something I agree with. "The estate is a treat for those who enjoy nature."

"Have a servant bring you to us. We will provide you with a suitable mount," Georgiana pressed.

"I am happy to accept your invitation, but I beg you to remember that I am a novice." Turning to Irene, she asked, "Is that your new fan? Join me at the window so we may admire them in the sunlight." After Irene followed her to the window, Elizabeth flicked open her fan and whispered, "Why is she being nice to me, Lady Irene?"

Irene opened her fan and said softly, "When she bought a fan for each of us, I pondered that very question. Georgiana has been angry with me lately, but yesterday she decided we should be friends again. Such a mercurial girl!"

≈≈≈

When Owain drove Elizabeth to Pemberley in the pony cart on Saturday afternoon, they were both quite impressed by the size of the stables. *Surely, there will be a calm, slow horse somewhere here,* she thought.

While Elizabeth **wished** to see Darcy, she **expected** to see Irene; however, Georgiana said the lady was resting with a headache. "Should we all ride together on another day?" Elizabeth wondered, *Do I sound hopeful?*

"Oh, Irene would not wish to suspend any pleasure of ours," Georgiana assured her.

Elizabeth waited with her hostess while grooms fetched their horses. "My mare is named Fortuna; William bought her for me last month. He is the best of brothers, eager to give me whatever he thinks will make me happy."

"You are a fortunate lady."

"And you shall ride Apollo."

"I look forward to the experience." She smiled as she lied, wondering, *What have I got myself into?*

≈≈≈

After an interminable ride, Elizabeth was relieved to see Georgiana calmly watching Fortuna drink from the pool beneath the trickling waterfall. The ride had been challenging, and she was grateful that her hostess was resting the mare. Elizabeth's own mount, a skittish sorrel stallion, had taxed her abilities and given her many frightening moments. She said breathlessly, "You overestimated my skills, Miss Darcy. I can barely manage this animal."

"Yet you presume to manage my brother—and through him, me, Miss Bennet."

"I have no intentions of managing anyone!"

Fortuna had finished drinking, so Georgiana urged her to a nearby oak. It was old and tall, and the birdsong from the branches was incongruous with the tension between the ladies. "Did Wickham tell you he intended to elope with me?"

"No." *She is afraid of what he told me.*

"I thought that if I eloped, my brother would realise what could befall me when he ignored me. But after Ramsgate, he saddled me with an albatross of a companion, Mrs Annesley, and then went haring off to Hertfordshire with Mr Bingley."

Is this the truth, or was Wickham's tale the real one? Elizabeth wondered. "What do you want, Miss Darcy?"

She gave an exasperated laugh. "I want you to give up William. I shall be miserable if he marries you."

I could ask why, but it does not matter. "Your brother makes his own decisions."

"You have bewitched him—although I cannot understand how! He will not give you up, so *you* must give him up. You will never be a Darcy. Do not expect to be noticed by my relations and our friends; you will be slighted and despised by everyone."

"Does Lady Irene truly have a headache, or did you bring me here to insult me, expecting me to slink away in shame?" She was not insulted; she was angry. "To tie your happiness to the behaviour of another is to invite disappointment. Thus, I am resolved to act in a manner that will constitute *my* happiness without reference to you or anyone else unconnected with me."

"But we would be connected by the name 'Darcy'."

"Do you not expect to marry, Miss Darcy?"

"Of course—and my husband will have a title."

"Do you envision a titled wife for your brother?"

"Yes—and out of love for her, he will use his connections to acquire a title for himself."

"Well, I am grateful you will allow him to make a love match," Elizabeth said sardonically.

"You do not understand people like us." She gave a dismissive sniff. "You are not of our sphere."

"You speak as if titled people occupy some exalted realm between humans and angels."

"You are determined to ruin my brother in the opinion of all his friends and make him the contempt of the world!"

"And you have a vivid imagination. *The world* has too much sense to scorn such an honourable man."

After a tense silence, Georgiana said, "I had hoped, madam, you would be more reasonable." Reaching into a pocket in her skirt, she took out an apple. Balancing it on her palm, she said, "This is for my horse, you see."

Suddenly, she threw it high into the tree. At once, the birdsong was superseded by frantic fluttering as the birds took flight in panic. Startled, Apollo bucked and reared.

Terrified of falling onto the rocky ground, Elizabeth struggled with all her strength to control the restive animal, instinctively gripping both pommels with her legs. When at last Apollo was calmer, Elizabeth unhooked her leg from the top pommel and slid out of the saddle, landing on unsteady legs. The horse quickly moved away, for her panicked handling of the reins had hurt his mouth.

Grateful to be on solid ground, Elizabeth sat on a flat rock at the pond's edge, trying to regain her composure. Only then did she notice Georgiana had ridden away. "I shall not miss her," she told Apollo. At the sound of her voice, the horse regarded her with an unfriendly gaze. Suddenly, a single, squawking bird burst from the leaves. While Elizabeth wondered why it had not flown off with the rest, Apollo reared again before racing away. She shook her head. "Truth to tell, Mr Horse, I will not miss you either."

During the ride, Elizabeth had noted landmark features, as was her habit; she had also brought her compass. Thus, although Georgiana was out of sight and Apollo soon would be, she knew she could find her way back to Pemberley. Balancing carefully on the rocky bank of the pond beneath the waterfall, she washed her hands and face and then took a long drink. After cooling the back of her neck with her wet handkerchief, she began the long walk to the manor.

Chapter 17

Within a quarter-hour of Apollo arriving at the stable without a rider, Fitzwilliam and a groom were racing to the waterfall. A second groom followed more slowly, for he drove a pony cart. The fact that Fortuna had not also returned with an empty saddle convinced Fitzwilliam that his cousin was less in need of rescue than Elizabeth. He told himself, *If I am lucky, I will find the ladies together.* He pushed aside any thoughts of what he might find if he were not lucky.

Some three miles from Pemberley, when he saw Elizbeth walking toward him, he thought, *Half-lucky—that's good enough.* Standing in his stirrups, he waved, and she waved back. Upon reaching her, Fitzwilliam dismounted with a cavalryman's skill and offered her a curved leather bag with a cork stopper. "Water mixed with wine in an authentic Spanish bota."

"Thank you, sir." She drank deeply.

"Are you unhurt, madam?"

"Apollo did not throw me, tho' he made a good effort."

"Have you injuries that need treatment?"

"No."

"Where is Georgiana?"

"I thought she would be at Pemberley by now. After she startled a flock of birds—on purpose to upset Apollo—she rode away." At his puzzled look, she added, "The oak near the waterfall was full of birds. When she threw an apple into the branches, birds seemed to explode from the tree."

Fitzwilliam took a moment to digest Elizabeth's account. *The lady has bottom! No hysterics, no rage.* "Well, I am sure she is uninjured wherever she is."

"I hope that is so, sir." After taking another drink from the bota, she considered Fitzwilliam's gelding. "Your horse is frighteningly tall."

"A cart is on its way. And if you are wondering about Darcy, he was still at a tenant farm when I left, but as soon as he hears of Apollo's desertion of you, he will come. Irene said she had expected to join the ride to the waterfall today but that Georgiana insisted on having a private conversation with you. Irene wanted you to know that she was unaware of Georgiana's scheme and hopes you are safe."

"Georgiana said Irene had a headache."

Seeing that Elizabeth seemed unsteady, he said, "I have a horse blanket here if you wish to sit, madam."

"Sit. Yes, I would." Without waiting for the blanket, she sank onto the grass. When he sat beside her, she asked, "Would you mind if I leaned against you, sir? I am tired."

Fitzwilliam put an arm around her shoulder and pulled her to him. "The cart should be here shortly, Miss Bennet."

≈≈≈

The groom who had driven the cart was now riding the tall gelding while Fitzwilliam piloted the vehicle. Elizabeth sat beside him, and they occasionally bumped against each other as they traversed the rocky ground; she found his nearness reassuring. Hesitantly, she said, "Miss Darcy says your family disdains me. Be honest with me, sir. Is that true?"

"Anne and I have praised you to my mother, and Lady Catherine has complimented you, although I do not recall her precise words. Irene likes you. We do **not** disdain you. You will bring a welcome liveliness to Pemberley."

"I will not be welcome there until Miss Darcy accepts me." A shuddering sob wracked Elizabeth. "Now that I am safe, I realise I could have been badly hurt."

Badly hurt or worse, he thought grimly. "I do not know how best to address this situation, but we will not allow any harm to come to you."

As if anyone could promise that, she despaired.

When the cart emerged from the trees atop the hill that sloped down to the manor, Elizabeth saw a horseman racing up to meet them. Fitzwilliam said, "There is Darcy, just as I predicted." Relief swept through her, but a sense of dread quickly followed when she thought of the difficult conversation she must have with him about his sister.

Upon reaching the cart, Darcy called, "Fitz, take my horse." He dismounted hastily and ran to Elizabeth's side of the cart. "What happened? Are you injured?"

"No injuries to see," she said, meeting his eyes. Her words brought him to a standstill.

Fitzwilliam said, "Take my place, Darcy."

It was the work of a minute for the former colonel to mount his cousin's horse and ride away with the two grooms, leaving Elizabeth with her fiancé. As Darcy claimed the reins, he said, "When we return to the manor—"

She interrupted, "Oaklands. I feel safer there. **Please**."

"Of course." *She does not trust me to keep her safe in my home. What if she is right?* With a gentleness he did not feel, he said, "Tell me everything."

While Elizabeth recounted her meeting with Georgiana and Irene on the previous day and her excursion with Georgiana today, Darcy drove at a leisurely pace. His ability to remain calm was severely taxed as he listened to her sometimes-tearful account of her difficult ride on Apollo. Several times, he had to remind himself, *She does not need me to go haring off in a fury now. She needs me to listen and assure her that she is safe.*

When she finished, she said sadly, "If you have to defend me constantly to your sister and your other relations, ours will not be a happy marriage."

The realisation that she was questioning whether they should marry shook Darcy to his core. "I beg you, my love, do not give up on us. Allow me time to discover why Georgiana is behaving this way."

"The Selbys will ask me about my ride with Georgiana, as will Rafe, who has been helping me become a horsewoman. I won't pretend I was not upset and very frightened."

Lambton is a small town, and gossip moves through it like a brisk wind. Georgiana is young and foolish. How can I protect her from .... Abruptly, Darcy pulled the cart to a stop. "At what age does one stop protecting someone from the consequences of their actions?"

After hesitating, Elizabeth asked, "Does that not depend on the circumstances?"

"How old is Lydia now? Sixteen? Might her current situation be different if, several years ago, she had been held accountable for her impulses?"

"I had hoped that was true, so I asked my father to curb her, but he did nothing until the reputation of our family was at risk. But your sister's motives are different from Lydia's, I think. Hers seem directed at you ... or us."

Oaklands was now in view, and they travelled in silence for the remainder of the drive. Leaving the cart in the stable yard, Darcy walked Elizabeth to the front door, his arm around her shoulders. "Tell the truth when you are asked about your ride. Georgiana does not merit your protection."

She nodded but said nothing.

"I will stay with you if that will comfort you."

Her eyes were bright with tears. "Thank you, but no. I am well enough." She tried to pull away from him.

Darcy kissed her forehead before releasing her. "Do not give up on us, Elizabeth." She nodded again, and tears slid down her cheeks as she hurried into the manor.

For a moment, he felt she was running away from him. Then he scolded himself, *It is selfish and stupid for me to see her actions as if I am at the centre of all her thoughts. She has had a terrifying afternoon. She needs time to collect herself—time to be angry and frightened—before she considers what I may be feeling.*

As Darcy drove back to Pemberley, Elizabeth's prediction circled through his mind: "If you have to defend me constantly to your sister and your other relations, ours will not be a happy marriage."

He mused, *Had Elizabeth accepted my proposal at Rosings last April, I would have expected her to separate herself from her family. Yet, so that I might preserve my relationships with my sister and other kin, she offers me my freedom. My vanity asks why she is willing to give me up, but my voice of reason is grateful that she understands the difficulties I face. Bless you, my dearest, loveliest Elizabeth!*

≈≈≈

Fitzwilliam slouched on a wooden bench set against a building in Pemberley's stable yard. His outstretched legs were crossed at the ankles, his hat was beside him, and he held a tankard of ale. When a landaulet bearing the crest of the Earl of Kestevyn rolled to a stop, he watched with interest. After a groom lowered the coach steps and opened the door, Anne de Bourgh emerged, followed by her maid. She called, "Have you behaved so abominably, Fitz, that you have been exiled from the house?"

"**Someone** has behaved abominably, but not I." Setting aside the tankard, he crossed to her and noisily kissed the back of her gloved hand. "I thought the Flint Rock contingent was not arriving until next week."

"True. However, from the moment Lordling Henry learnt of Darcy's invitation, he began pestering the Countess with a demand to drive the castle's landaulet to Pemberley. He was so relentless that I told your mother I would handle the matter. Thus, the landaulet and I are here."

"I am happy for your company."

"When the others arrive, I shall send the landaulet back to the castle, thus, depriving the Lordling **twice**. Irene will be pleased."

"Thwarted at every turn? Henry deserves that."

"The Kestevyn heir is no longer speaking to the Harwich heir. In fact, Nigel has taken his wife and children to the seaside for the summer."

Anne's maid waited patiently beside the two small trunks and other assorted luggage her mistress had brought. Anne gave her an apologetic smile. "Hannah, would you please go and grovel to the housekeeper regarding my unexpected appearance? Of course, I will grovel to Mrs Reynolds, too, but first, I must hear from Fitz who is behaving abominably."

Anne was an undemanding mistress, and Hannah felt fortunate to work for the de Bourgh daughter rather than the de Bourgh mother. She bobbed a curtsy and followed the footmen who carried Anne's luggage into the manor.

As the cousins sat on the bench, Fitzwilliam explained, "I am waiting here to ambush Georgiana when she returns."

"Where is Darcy?"

"Driving Elizabeth to the estate where she is staying with her relations. The lady was Georgiana's victim."

"Oh, my! Our little cousin has become quite the brat," Anne said. After hearing Fitzwilliam's tale of the disastrous excursion, she said worriedly, "Georgiana is worse than a brat. Elizabeth could have been killed."

Within half an hour, Georgiana rode Fortuna into the stable yard. Fitzwilliam and Anne noted the moment that she saw them—and they saw her fear. He told Anne, "Carry my hat; it's got something in it." Then he crossed quickly to Fortuna and grabbed one of the cheek pieces of her halter. "No escape for you, my girl."

In a haughty voice, she asked, "Do you speak to the mare or me?"

"Shall I help you dismount? Anne and I wish to speak with you." She dropped the reins, and a groom took them. Then Fitzwilliam lifted her down from the horse.

≈≈≈

In the stable's tack room, Anne sat in the only chair and held Fitzwilliam's hat in her lap while Fitzwilliam leaned against the closed door and Georgiana perched on a low stool. "Do you even care that Miss Bennet could have broken her neck?" he asked.

"I saw her dismount—awkwardly, I must say. But she was uninjured. And you know her annoying self-sufficiency."

"Why did you spook her horse?" he asked.

"I did no such thing," she protested.

He took the apple from his hat and knelt by her stool. "Look what I found beneath the *oak* tree near the waterfall."

"You advised me always to have a carrot or an apple for a horse when I go riding," she reminded him.

Anne looked at Fitzwilliam, who said, "Yes, that is my habit." Returning to Georgiana, he demanded, "Do you deny flinging this into the branches, sending the birds into a panicked flight? And then Apollo behaved as he always does. It is a miracle Miss Bennet wasn't thrown."

She shrugged dismissively.

"Do you deny abandoning Miss Bennet some distance from the manor?" he pressed.

"The lady is famous for her love of walking." Under his glare, Georgiana said, "Miss Bennet provoked me!"

"How?" Anne asked.

"She was too stupid to understand why she must relinquish her hold on my besotted brother. I was angry. *She* made me angry."

"Angry people are not always wise," Anne said.

Georgiana ignored her. "I could accept their misalliance if they waited until after *I* married. Help me persuade them."

"Why should you marry first?" Fitzwilliam asked.

"Those who are titled and wealthy have freedoms the rest of us do not have. But no titled gentleman will consider a match with me if William marries that Bennet creature first. She has family members in trade!"

"Is that why you dislike her so?" Anne asked.

"As if Aunt Catherine would permit you to marry someone with connections to trade," she sneered.

"My mother has come to accept that she has no say in whether or whom I marry."

Fitzwilliam said, "I find it difficult to believe, Georgiana, that you have nurtured your pique toward Miss Bennet simply because she would not give you a book you did not want—a book already in Pemberley's library."

"Well, I did not know it was there," she huffed. "I confess that my temper is resentful. William is the same way. I suppose it is a Darcy family trait."

"What is our family trait?" No one had heard Darcy enter, but when he closed the door forcefully, no one could mistake his mood.

Georgiana regarded him defiantly. "I have heard you say that your good opinion, once lost, is lost forever."

Her words sparked a memory of his conversation with Elizabeth in Hertfordshire so many months ago. *Is that who I am? A man who cannot forgive? A man who does not realise when he is blinded by his pride and prejudices against the Bennet family and Wickham?*

"I have learnt it is a weakness not to revise one's opinion when one has misjudged a person or a situation."

"You are so moody and changeable of late, brother."

I am moody and changeable? He was astonished by her charge. "Why did you change *your* mind and tell Irene not to join you for the ride?"

"I wished to talk with Miss Bennet privately."

She is wholly unmoved by any feeling of remorse! Darcy regarded her through narrowed eyes. "Did you put Miss Bennet on Apollo with the intention of harming her?"

"Of course not! How was I to know she was such an unskilled rider?"

"You knew!"

Georgiana exclaimed, "Must I have a reason for my behaviour? Many a time, I have not known what I would do until I did it. Have you never acted on your feelings?"

"So, how you feel at any particular moment guides your actions?" Anne asked.

"I don't know! People do as they please!" she wailed.

Darcy shook his head. "You are not who I believed you to be, Georgiana."

"Who did you think I was?" she challenged.

"A bit shy. Melancholy. That Wickham's deception broke your heart. Except that is not true, is it? You did not intend to elope with Wickham."

"Did Elizabeth tell you that? I told her she was a fool if she believed anything Wickham said!"

"Wickham told me that."

Running her gaze over her relations, she accused, "You are all against me!"

"It appears to me that you are against all of us," Fitzwilliam said.

"And Miss Bennet," Anne said.

Georgiana glared at Darcy, "If you marry her, William, I will leave Pemberley! Choose her, and you will lose me."

He said quietly, "Anne, Fitz, I wish to speak with Georgiana alone." As Anne passed on her way to the door, she squeezed his arm; Fitzwilliam followed her and patted Darcy on the shoulder before exiting and closing the door.

"Where will you go?" he asked his sister.

His calmness infuriated her as she paced agitatedly. "I do not know. But what will society say if you abandon your only sister for that sorry hussy, that country mouse?"

After a silence in which Georgiana felt her composure stretched to the breaking point, Darcy said, "You are using our familial connection to create an obligation, and you use the threat of societal censure to daunt me."

She protested, "I am not—"

"As you said, your home will be with your husband when you marry. You know I am not afraid of solitude, so my wish to marry Elizabeth Bennet is not because my own company bores me. She is the future I dream of; I love her very much. I will not be bullied by you or anyone who attempts to use convention or tradition against me. And I have encouraged her to tell the Selbys about your dangerous behaviour."

"I never intended to dislike or ... harm ... Miss Bennet, but when I am in her company, something in her manner makes me feel like a naughty child."

"That mysterious 'something' is in *your* thoughts, not her manner."

"Oh, please send me to Flint Rock Castle! If I could speak about my feelings with Aunt Beatrice and Aunt Catherine, they would help me."

"Everyone at Flint Rock is coming here. I invited them to the engagement party, so you may confer with your aunts when they arrive on Tuesday next."

"Everyone? Henry and Nigel?"

"Nigel has given up on Henry." Darcy crossed to the door. "I will tell the stable master you are not to permitted to ride any horse or to drive any carriage until I say so."

"I shall not join you at supper. I feel a headache coming on." Head held high, Georgiana flounced out of the tack room. Very quickly, her demeanour shifted from combative to contemplative. *If Nigel is not here, there will be one less meddlesome relation to notice what Henry and I are doing.*

After she left, Darcy remained in the tack room for several minutes, calming his mind. When at last he stepped into the stable yard, he found Anne and Fitzwilliam sitting on the bench. "Did Georgiana go in the house?"

Fitzwilliam nodded. "She didn't even try to steal a horse and run away. Ooof!" Rubbing his ribs, he told Anne, "What a sharp elbow you have, my dear."

She ignored him. "How is Miss Bennet?"

"Understandably shaken. Bewildered by Georgiana's intense dislike of her. And ... and she is having second thoughts about marriage because she does not want to cause a rift between my sister and me." There was anguish in his expression when he said, "I could lose Elizabeth."

≈ ≈ ≈

At Oaklands, Elizabeth relaxed in a hot bath and tried to settle her thoughts. When Darcy was foremost in her mind, she was gratified to have inspired his love. When she considered the Selbys, she worried about what to tell them about her ride. But when she considered Georgiana, a shiver ran through her despite the steaming bath water. *How is such a girl to be worked on?*

Casting a retrospective glance over the whole of her acquaintance with the Darcys, Elizabeth felt overwhelmed. *I love William, but my life would be intolerable in a household where his sister threatens my safety. Surely, the servants would be more loyal to her than to me. I would never know a moment's peace! I rejoiced when I believed William's and my mutual affection would lead to marriage, but would it be wiser to postpone our marriage until Georgiana no longer lives at Pemberley? That could be years away. She is not yet seventeen ... and who would want to marry such a troubled child?*

Sighing, she murmured, "And I have already written to Mama about the reading of the banns. Oh, heavens, this situation is horrible in every way!"

≈ ≈ ≈

After Sunday services, Darcy went to Oaklands. On the previous evening, Elizabeth had told Mrs Harcourt, Abelard, and Squire about her harrowing ride, so when Darcy arrived, he and Elizabeth were left alone in the parlour with the door open. When he offered her Georgiana's written apology, she regarded the folded paper warily. "Have you read it?"

"I have. Her words are more stilted than sincere, but because she needed to choose them carefully—this is her fifth version—at least she had to reflect on her actions. Shall we walk to the little wilderness?"

Elizabeth did not meet his eyes. "I prefer the parlour.

Sitting beside her on the sofa, Darcy thought, *A place where we cannot steal kisses.* He feared she was sincerely reconsidering her decision to marry him, and his heart ached. Quietly, he said, "I see your worry."

"Your sister is your closest family."

Leaning toward her, he touched his forehead to hers. "I never imagined she would demand that I choose between her and the woman I want for my wife." Pulling back, he stroked her cheek gently. "You know you are very special to me, but I suspect you are not special to Georgiana. I daresay she would create a reason to reject any woman I choose. She wants to bring me to heel. ***You*** want me to be happy."

"Something must have influenced her preferences. Can you truthfully say that you do not share them, sir?"

That is a fair question, Darcy thought. "I can truthfully say that titles mean nothing to me, and my fortune is sufficient to keep us in comfort for several lifetimes. As for your connections, I am deeply grateful to you for reuniting me with old friends. I feel privileged to know Selby, Squire, and Mrs Gardiner and her husband, who, I suspect, has championed our match. Mrs Harcourt has also shown herself to be a kind-hearted, intelligent lady; I am pleased to be able to count her among my acquaintances."

Elizabeth smiled. "They are such good people."

He held out his palm to her, and she clasped it. "You wonder if I will blame you should Georgiana separate herself from me after we marry. I would never blame you. If my sister chooses to reject me, that is beyond my control. ***You*** are my future, and I am yours." With his free hand, he tucked an errant curl behind her ear. "Remember ***that*** should you feel some misguided impulse to throw me over. I love you."

"I love you, Fitzwilliam Darcy." After glancing at the open parlour door, she kissed his cheek.

Chapter 18

The knock upon Darcy's study door was so faint that he was not certain he had heard anything; thus, he returned to the calendar on his desk and the cup of coffee at his hand. A moment later, the door opened, and Georgiana stood at the threshold. "May I come in?"

"Yes, of course." As he gestured for her to sit in the chair before his desk, he glanced at the clock on his credenza, which he had wound scarcely an hour ago. The sculptural setting for this timepiece was a rectangular marble base, and on either side of the round clock was a cherub cast in biscuit porcelain. The white clock face had gold hands and gold Roman numerals to mark the time.

She followed his look. "If Mother's clock were not so large, it would be too feminine for this room."

Darcy said, "It is scarcely a foot wide and nine inches tall. Not so large." Then he realised they were starting their conversation with a disagreement. "I enjoy having the clock here because it was Mother's favourite. So then, what brings you here at this hour?"

In mock offence, Georgiana said, "This is not the first time I have dressed before nine o'clock." Smiling winsomely, she added, "I want to discuss how things are between you and me before our relations arrive from Flint Rock Castle."

And now she surprises me for the second time in two minutes, for she never wants to discuss how things are between us. "Yes, I think that is wise."

"No doubt Anne and Fitz will tell everyone about my ride with Miss Bennet. And I **was** wrong to lose my temper. But that was three days ago, and I have not done anything so foolish since then."

Well, nothing that I know of. Then Darcy scolded himself for the thought. "I am happy to hear it."

Georgiana's expression showed this was not the response she hoped for. "I do not wish to be excluded from activities when our aunts and Henry arrive, so I request—I humbly request—that my riding privileges be restored."

"Humbly?" he repeated.

"Will-YUM!"

There is no point in making her a pariah within the family. "Very well. Your riding privileges are restored, and you may go beyond the estate. You may not, however, go to Oaklands or seek out Miss Bennet. Do you agree?"

"I agree. Thank you." She curtsied to her brother and left his study. He sent a footman to the stables to tell the head groom of his decision.

Within an hour, Georgiana was racing across the fields of Pemberley. Upon returning, she saw Anne and Irene conversing as she passed the open door of the garden parlour. Although she did not consciously think, *Ah, an audience,* she entered for exactly that reason. "Ladies, it is such a pleasant day for a ride! How dreary to be indoors."

More out of politeness than real interest, Irene asked, "Did you ride Apollo or Fortuna?"

"Fortuna, of course." Georgiana told Anne, "William presented me with a new mare after I told him Apollo was too skittish. He enjoys making me happy. He is the best of brothers—well, nearly so."

"Nearly so? What is Darcy's flaw?" Anne asked.

"He refuses to give up the Bennet creature, of course. She isn't even beautiful!"

"Miss Bennet is lovely," Anne said, and Irene nodded.

Georgiana sniffed. "As I shall never agree, let us speak of something else." She looked expectantly at her cousins, awaiting their suggestions.

Anne asked, "Is Fortuna an improvement over Apollo?"

Georgiana shrugged. "Well, Fortuna isn't skittish. Still, I would have preferred to choose my own horse. And I would give it a proper English name!"

Anne asked, "But other than the tragedies of the mare's name and the fact that your brother chose her as a gift for you, what is your opinion of the horse?"

"In truth, I am somewhat disappointed."

Irene said, "If you do not want Fortuna, I would be happy to have her."

Georgiana smiled. "You are jealous of me."

Irene grumbled, "You may think that if it pleases you."

"Even if I wanted to give you Fortuna," and in her brief pause, Irene and Anne heard the unspoken, *Which I don't.* She continued, "I could not. William would not approve. I suspect the mare is a bribe to inspire me to be more welcoming to Miss Bennet. She—"

Anne said, "Let us speak of something else. Your incessant complaints are wearying."

Georgiana gave a huff of annoyance. "I must change out of these riding clothes. Will you two be here when I return?"

"No!" Irene and Anne said in unison and with such force that all the ladies were surprised. Georgiana huffed again and strode out of the parlour.

In a quiet voice, Anne told Irene, "I do not know what your plans are, but if you wish to join me in seeing the annoyingly named mare, I welcome your company."

"No plans, only an aspiration to where Georgiana is not."

≈≈≈

When the travel coach of the Earl of Kestevyn rolled to a stop in front of Pemberley's portico late in the afternoon, Darcy, Georgiana, and Fitzwilliam were waiting to greet them. Georgiana asked, "Why is Henry riding with the coachman? He was supposed to drive his landaulet."

A footman lowered the coach steps, and Darcy stepped forward to assist his aunts while Henry climbed down from the box, muttering, "Damned hot way to travel."

"I am certain the coachman would agree." Darcy handed out the Countess of Kestevyn and Lady Catherine.

Sauntering onto the drive, Fitzwilliam greeted Lady Catherine and his mother with a kiss on the cheek. Then he asked Henry, "Why did you not ride in the coach?"

Henry glared at his grandmother and his great-aunt. "They would not let me."

The Countess rolled her eyes. "Oh, do stop whinging. We did not put you out until our first change of horses. And we only did so because you were babbling nonsense."

Georgiana, who stood on the portico, crossed her arms and stared at Henry. "Where is your landaulet? You were supposed to bring it, sir."

"Unfortunately, I—" he began, but the Countess quickly turned to face her grandson.

"Say *nothing*, boy! I refuse to be subjected to your idiotic ramblings until I have refreshed myself."

Darcy asked, "Tea in the drawing room in an hour?"

Lady Catherine poked his shoulder with her folded fan. "Beatrice and I need brandy—and I suggest you have a dose of laudanum ready to silence that ridiculous lad."

≈≈≈

Later in the drawing room, Henry Northam (who would use the courtesy title of Viscount Bowmont until his father, the Earl of Harwich, cocked up his toes) slumped on a small velvet-covered sofa that he shared with Georgiana. The Countess and Lady Catherine occupied a settee while Darcy, Fitzwilliam, Anne, and Irene sat in various chairs, eager to hear about what had obviously been a fraught journey.

Holding a glass of Darcy's best brandy, Beatrice began. "The first we knew of Henry losing his landaulet was when Nigel returned to Flint Rock Castle in a hired coach. Alone."

Expecting sympathy, Henry exclaimed, "Uncle Nigel enjoyed a solitary ride in a private barouche, but *I* had to travel in a crowded, smelly mail coach. So I got back to Flint Rock a full day after he did!"

Irene enjoyed envisioning her brother's misery. "To be clear, did you ride inside the coach or on top of it?"

"Inside, which I doubt was any improvement over riding atop the vehicle."

Fitzwilliam asked, "Who paid for your ticket?"

"Uncle Nigel," Henry grumbled.

"Because ...." Darcy drew out the word.

Henry huffed. "Because I gambled away my landaulet." At Georgiana's groan, he added plaintively, "Uncle Nigel has kept me trotting too hard. I needed relaxation."

Surprised, Anne asked, "Gambled it away? When Nigel returned to Flint Rock, he said you had made a wreck of things, so I assumed you had crashed your carriage. But Nigel left the next day, so I could not quiz him."

The Countess said, "He collected his wife and children from their townhouse, and they went to Southend-on-Sea."

Henry told Georgiana. "I expected Grandmama to let me drive the Flint Rock landaulet." Glaring at Anne, he said, "But *you* took it."

The Countess interjected, "Anne did so at my request, Henry. You were harassing me mercilessly. As if I would entrust a Kestevyn coach to someone so irresponsible! You might have gambled it away at the first posting house where there was a game of cards."

Irene asked, "Henry, tell me about the wager."

Feeling in control of the discussion at last, Viscount Bowmont said, "After supper at the coaching inn, Uncle Nigel said he was done to a cow's thumb, and he toddled off to bed as old men do."

Lady Catherine groaned. " 'Done to a cow's thumb'—this is the nonsense Henry used to torture Beatrice and myself."

Henry scoffed at their ignorance. "Done to a cow's thumb. Knocked up."

"Tired," Fitzwilliam explained. To Darcy, he added, "Old men. Recall, if you will, that Nigel is not yet forty."

Henry continued. "I was drinking in the pub at the inn when some chaps invited me to join their card game."

Darcy nodded. "Ah, yes. Some chaps who recognized a green lad in his cups."

Henry said crossly, "I am answering my sister's question, sir. No need to be rude." After a pause, he admitted, "I might have been a trifle disguised."

Fitzwilliam said, "Or drunk as a wheelbarrow."

Lady Catherine said, "I understand 'ape-drunk', but 'drunk as a wheelbarrow' never made sense to me."

"Nor me," the Countess agreed.

Henry said, "I was bored after those endless hours discussing estate ... things."

The Countess, "Ah, yes, the reason your father wanted Nigel to educate you."

Henry shrugged. "I admit that before Uncle Nigel took me under his wing, I drew the bustle too freely."

Lady Catherine held up her hand, indicating to Henry to be silent. She looked at Fitzwilliam, but Irene spoke first. "Henry had been spending too much money."

"Well, I was fairly flush in the pocket that night at the inn as I had not gambled in awhile. But when I lost my landaulet, Uncle Nigel called me a flat."

When Darcy said, "A person who is easily tricked," Irene snorted.

Henry scowled. "Uncle is wrong. I fly to the time of day."

When neither Irene nor Darcy could explain, Fitzwilliam said, "Henry says he is wise to the ways of the world."

Frowning at his audience's amused chuckles, he said defensively, "I believe the game was a havey-cavey business."

"Suspicious," Irene nodded. "What else, brother?"

He rubbed his forehead as if trying to uncover a memory, "I dimly recall having some bachelor fare sitting on my lap."

Georgiana demanded, "Some *what*?"

Anne said, "A barque of frailty, a bit of muslin, a wanton, a lady bird."

Irene added, "Bird of paradise, a light skirt, a Cyprian, a peculiar, a trollop."

To the surprise of Darcy and Fitzwilliam, Anne continued. "A Paphian, a prime article."

The Countess said, "I thought a 'prime article' was a fine horse."

"No, Mother. You are thinking of a 'prime bit of blood'," Fitzwilliam said.

Irene asked, "Why do you suppose there are so many words for ladies who earn their living by prostituting themselves?"

Anne said, "I'll wager it was not women who crafted these ... well, they hardly rate as compliments, do they?"

Henry ignored them. "Before I knew it, I was in the suds. As for the fellow with his pockets full of my blunt, he was as queer as Dick's hat band!"

Darcy said, "Henry was in trouble, and an ill-looking man had won his money."

Henry agreed. " 'Pon rep. I nearly flashed my hash."

"Vomited," Irene said.

"When I realised I was rolled up—no gingerbread to my name—I thought if I wagered my landaulet and cattle, I could win it all back."

Lady Catherine asked, "Is 'gingerbread' the same as 'blunt'?" Darcy nodded.

The Countess said, "I always thought 'cattle' was an odd term for one's horses."

"By sunrise, my windmill had dwindled to a nutshell." Fiercely, he said, "But I was within an ames-ace of winning."

While Darcy and Fitzwilliam exchanged looks of disbelief at Henry's optimism, Irene translated, "You lost everything, although you were certain you were about to win."

"Yes, I made a mull of it; that's what young gentlemen do. But I didn't shoot the crow—not with Uncle Nigel sleeping upstairs."

Fitzwilliam said, "He did not leave quickly without paying his debts."

The Countess skewered Henry with her gaze. "You are shockingly loose in the haft, sir." To Lady Catherine, she said, "That is someone who has many vices but no consideration for propriety. I learnt it from Nigel."

Henry continued, "Anyway, I swallowed my spleen and left the table. But I knew I would be in the basket."

Irene said, "Henry controlled his anger, which, no doubt, is why the men who cheated him did not thrash him."

Anne said, "To 'be in the basket' is to be in trouble."

Lady Catherine said, "And why shouldn't Henry be in trouble with Nigel?"

Fitzwilliam said, "You, my cock-sure lad, were lured into a game with sharpers. You were gulled."

Henry sighed. "They were dirty dishes for sure, Uncle Randal. So until my father gives me my quarterly allowance, I am below hatches." He smiled at Fitzwilliam. "I don't suppose you would be willing to raise the wind for me—"

"Lend you money? No, sir. And I am doing you a favour."

"Oh, and by the bye, Henry," the Countess said, "while you were babbling your way through this nonsensical story, my landaulet departed for Flint Rock. I would not have you near my coaches or my cattle for love or money."

Georgiana gasped and strode out of the room in a fury.

"I did not mean to set up her bristles," Henry muttered

Irene stood and shook out her skirt. "Well, I know all I need to about why Father's heir is on foot these days. Excuse me while I memorialize this conversation in my diary."

"Irene! Reenie!" Henry called after her as she departed.

The Countess told Lady Catherine, "I shall have another brandy. Will you join me?"

Lady Catherine made no reply; she simply raised her empty glass. As a footman refilled the ladies' drinks, the aggrieved young viscount complained, "I did try to explain this to you on the journey here, Grandmama."

The Countess told Darcy and Fitzwilliam, "You understand, I am sure, why we made the boy ride with the driver."

Lady Catherine shook her head. "It was as if he could not speak the king's English."

Henry exclaimed, "Fiend seize it, Lady Catherine! It's unkind to give me snuff, especially when I am already in a hobble!" He waved at the footman. "I shall have a brandy."

As Darcy shook his head, no, at the footman, Fitzwilliam explained, "Snuff is a scold. Hobble is trouble."

Henry scowled at Darcy and then told the footman, "Then I shall lush some slop."

The footman said solemnly, "The Viscount desires tea."

"Yes," Henry nodded vigorously. After the footman left, he said, "If I may open my budget—"

Darcy said, "Yes, speak freely, although I cannot imagine what more you have to say."

"It is not as if I am a peep-of-day boy!"

Anne asked Fitzwilliam, "Mischievous?" He nodded.

"But I would be pitching the gammon if I said I didn't want to be a neck-or-nothing young blood of the Fancy."

Amused, Darcy explained, "Viscount Bowmont would be lying if he did not admit his desire to be embraced by the Ton as a fashionable young nobleman."

"Too right," Henry said. "And if that puts you in a pelter, Grandmama, I am sorry, but I must be true to who I am."

Before Fitzwilliam could translate, the Countess said, "Yes, I understand. If Henry's vapid ambition puts me in an emotional state, he does not care. It matters only that he shows his independence by behaving like every other young idiot of his class." She told Henry, "If you think I shall make a fuss—" Then she paused and looked at her son.

He obligingly said, "Raise a breeze."

"But that is different from 'raise the wind'?" she asked.

"Yes, to 'raise the wind' is to raise money for something, and to 'raise a breeze' is to create a disturbance."

Beatrice told Henry, "If you think I am going to raise a breeze, lad, you are in error. Make all the mistakes you feel you need to, ideally *now* when you are of an age that people expect you to be stupid. Your actions are of no consequence to me. However, if you think Nigel or I will rescue you from your scrapes, you are even stupider than Nigel says. And you will not find an ally in your grandfather."

Darcy said, "I believe I also speak for Lady Catherine, Anne, and Fitz when I say that we will not rescue you either."

Henry leapt to his feet. "This is how you treat family?"

At that moment, the footman returned with a small tray bearing Henry's tea. "Your slop, my lord."

He hesitated and then sat. "Milk and lots of sugar."

Darcy took the tray and set it on the table beside Henry's chair. "If you can wipe your own arse, you can fix your tea." Henry grumbled that he did not see the similarity between the tasks, but he prepared his tea to his liking.

≈≈≈

When Anne entered the music room, Georgiana was practising the pianoforte. "I am busy," she said dismissively.

"No, you aren't." Anne pulled a chair next to the pianoforte and sat. "Darcy delivered your apology to Miss Bennet. I heard you had to write several versions until you produced one he thought was adequate."

"I know; I was there."

"You had to reflect on your actions. What did you learn?"

"Miss Bennet is a terrible horsewoman."

"Be sensible for a moment. What made you go to war against her?"

Sighing deeply, she dropped her chin to her chest. "I *have* been fighting a war, haven't I?"

"Yes, and like most wars, yours is a foolish waste."

Closing her eyes, Georgiana recalled the first time she saw Elizabeth. "I did not like how she stared at my brother. Then, at the bookshop, it was a game to see if I could coax her into giving me something *she* wanted. She was so inconsequential I thought no one would care how I treated her. But William gave her consequence, so I wanted to humble her. But it was *my* war; she never did anything against me."

Anne asked gently, "Georgiana, what is it you want?"

"Miss Bennet asked me that, too. Oh, Anne, how can I know until I have it—whatever *it* is—and discover whether I like it? What I want is to *know* what I want!"

"Why blame Miss Bennet for your unhappiness?"

"I suppose I was in competition, wanting William to care more about me than he cared about her. It seems stupid now, but I don't know how to stop."

"First, you cease behaving so uncivilly. Then when you are able, you apologise to Miss Bennet in person."

"I scarcely understand my impulses and moods."

"I doubt she will ask for an explanation, but if she does, tell her the truth. That you were jealous."

"I wasn't jealous."

"Yes, you were." Anne left when her cousin turned away and played random arpeggios. Then Georgiana began playing Beethoven's Piano Sonata 14, which flowed effortlessly from her touch.

Anne is right. I must stop my pointless war against Elizabeth Bennet. William will never give up the lady, and I do want him to be happy. After I elope, her presence will distract him. And if I apologise, she might become my ally. I will need allies when Henry and I face the Earl of Harwich. As for our transportation, well, I shall need Upton Parnell's help and a plan to convince him.

≈≈≈

When Georgiana and Henry went riding the next day, she led him to Lambton, where the Wednesday market occupied the village green. Seeing Upton walking disinterestedly among the stalls, she told Henry, "I have a plan for obtaining a coach so we can elope."

"Aren't we going to use one of Pemberley's coaches?"

"No, we need a landaulet, and ours is too old for a long journey. William says he plans to buy a new one, but as we have other carriages, he is in no hurry. So, I need you to go to the Mute Ploughboy over there and wait for me. The ale is quite good, I am told."

Eager for ale, Henry looked to where she pointed; then, he recalled his situation. "I don't have a feather to fly with."

With a moue of annoyance, Georgiana gave him half a crown. "There. Go." When she looked again for Upton, she saw him standing near, watching her. She urged Fortuna to him. "Mr Parnell, how pleasant to see you."

He nodded in the direction of the pub. "A new friend?"

"A second cousin. My two aunts are visiting, and they brought him along."

So then, not a rival, he thought. "Have you made progress in convincing Darcy not to marry the Bennet chit?"

Pouting, Georgiana admitted she had not. "I despise the thought of sharing Pemberley with her."

*Let's see how suggestible **this** chit is,* Upton thought. "Why not leave the difficult work to your brother's bride, whoever she may be? Did I never tell you of the four years I spent in London? They were the happiest years of my life. Do you not enjoy the pleasures of town?"

"I have not spent much time there yet."

"Oh, Miss Darcy, London is the most exciting city in the kingdom!" Gazing into her eyes, he spun an appealing fantasy of how much she would enjoy living in an elegant townhouse in a neighbourhood of peers. "Imagine it, my dear, you will be surrounded by dukes, marquesses, earls, viscounts and, yes, even humble barons like my father. There is no better residence than a townhouse. And I have heard Darcy House is quite fine."

"William doesn't like it. I daresay he will buy something to please Elizabeth after they marry."

Upton gave her a sly smile. "Then ask your brother to give you Darcy House."

Although she had intended this conversation to be a flirtatious interlude to imply her interest, Upton's suggestion intrigued her. *If Henry and I have our own residence after we elope, we will not have to go begging to our relations for a home.* "Perhaps I shall, Mr Parnell."

Georgiana urged Fortuna to walk to the Mute Plough-boy, and as she passed the apothecary's shop, she glanced through the window and saw Elizabeth.

When Elizabeth stepped out onto the paving stones, she saw Georgiana seated on her mare, waiting for her. Immediately, she was wary.

"Please allow me to apologise, Miss Bennet. I realise that you are not the reason for my discontent. I am sorry for my treatment of you when we went riding."

Elizabeth stared at her, wondering, *Ah, yes, when I could have been killed. Should I thank her?*

Georgiana continued, "My aunts say I am of an age when my sensibilities are erratic. They say this is natural, so it is unjust for me to blame you for my moods."

Elizabeth wondered, *Do I thank her **now**?*

Georgiana frowned. "Have you nothing to say?

"In truth, Miss Darcy, I do not know **what** to say. I appreciate your apology, but I am still confused about your dislike of me."

She replied airily, "Well, we will never be friends, but I shall not interfere with your plans to marry my brother and have a family. I confess that seems very dull to me."

Hearing her dreamt-of future disdained, Elizabeth said, "I also hope to travel and learn more of the world, whether I experience it first-hand or through Pemberley's library."

She sniffed. "Books are no substitute for experience."

"Sometimes books are the safest substitutes."

Georgiana shook her head. "Only experience can show me whether or not I like something."

"My ambitions may be more quotidian—" Seeing her annoyance, Elizabeth chose a simpler word. "More ordinary than yours, but I understand the desire for new experiences."

"Do you expect William to give you those experiences?"

Am I blushing? I hope I am not blushing! She cannot be thinking of the intimacies between a wife and her husband. "Your brother has the education, intelligence, and resources to introduce me to a larger world. But that is not why I love him. My affection comes from my admiration for his character. He is a good man."

Georgiana studied Elizabeth. "You love William."

"Very much."

"Good day, Miss Bennet. I sincerely wish you happy."

Elizabeth bobbed a curtsy, and Georgiana rode away.

≈≈≈

That night, Georgiana was relieved to find Darcy reading alone in the library, for she did not want Anne or Fitzwilliam to intrude in their conversation. He closed his book when she sat in the bergère that faced his. "I have reconciled myself to the fact that you and Miss Bennet will marry. I have apologised to her, and I will try to like her for *your* sake. But I will be uncomfortable living here with the two of you."

He studied her for a long moment. "I assume you have a proposal. What is it?"

"You do not like Darcy House in London, but I do. Even before you met Miss Bennet, you spoke about wanting to purchase a different place."

He nodded. "Elizabeth and I will choose it together."

"Then give me Darcy House. Please."

"You cannot think I would allow you to live there without a chaperone!"

"I have not spoken to Anne about this, but if we lived at Darcy House together—two female cousins and perhaps a companion sharing the townhouse would be respectable."

"Anne plans to travel to Denmark."

"What if Irene and a respectable companion—or two, one for each of us—shared the townhouse? Sophie could also live there. Plenty of room for all."

"And what happens when Sophie and Irene marry?"

"Who is to say that I will not marry first?"

Darcy shook his head. "Nothing you have described seems like a suitable solution."

"Will you give me the townhouse when I marry? You gave an estate to Fitz."

After some consideration, he said, "I will give you Darcy House when you are married. As to where you live after Elizabeth and I marry, that is a conversation to have with our relations. Perhaps they have an acceptable suggestion."

Chapter 19

At the assembly on the second Friday of July, the townspeople found themselves in company with more peers and honourables than at any time in living memory. In addition to the local baron, Lord Parnell, were the Countess of Kestevyn, Lady Catherine de Bourgh, Lady Irene Northam, Viscount Bowmont, the Honourable Anne de Bourgh, and the Honourable Randal Fitzwilliam. As the Pemberley party entered the ballroom, Georgiana grumbled, "We are their pitiful **commoner** relations!"

Darcy ignored his sister, something he was doing with increasing frequency when she lamented her Tragic Life. He was far more interested in finding Elizabeth in the crowd of attendees. As he, Anne, and Fitzwilliam seated the Countess and Lady Catherine at a table with a good view of the dancers, her ladyship said, "I expect you to invite me to dance, nephews; of course, I shall decline."

"I, too, expect your invitations, but I do not promise to decline them," the Countess said.

Fitzwilliam asked Anne, "What about you?"

"I shall dance with my cousins only if I do not receive better offers."

Within a quarter-hour, the Oaklands party (untitled but well-liked) arrived. Although Squire had not attended an assembly since the passing of his wife, he wanted to show his neighbours that he was as hale and capable as ever. *Or perhaps, as hale and capable as any man of my years who had suffered a terrible accident and now walks with a cane,* he thought, cynically amused.

Abelard walked beside Squire as they slowly ascended the staircase. Nervously trailing the father and son were Toby, Polly, Mrs Harcourt, and Elizabeth.

Elizabeth danced the first set with Darcy and the second set with Henry. When she complimented his skills, the viscount said, "I never much cared for dancing until last summer when I stayed at the estate of a friend from university. The fellow had three sisters, and they all loved to dance. Couldn't say 'no' to the ladies; I was their guest. They taught me what a pleasant activity dancing can be with the right partner. Besides, there wasn't much else to do in Ramsgate," he added with a shrug.

"Did you encounter Miss Darcy there?"

At once, his expression turned wary. After a silence, he shook his head. "Was she in Ramsgate? Didn't know of it."

Elizabeth mused, *Is Henry so inept at lying because a young man of his station so rarely has to explain himself?*

On the balcony, dimly illuminated by the spill of light from the ballroom, Georgiana and Upton had a quiet conversation. They stood in the centre of the balcony, believing that their distance from the French doors at either end protected them from view. Aware that they could be interrupted at any moment, Georgiana said, "I thank you for suggesting that I ask William for Darcy House. He has agreed to give it to me when I marry."

"I am happy I was of service, Miss Darcy."

After a hesitation, she said, "There is another service you could do for me if you were so inclined." Then, to Upton's surprise, she spoke of her urgent wish to marry before her brother did. She concluded, "While you and I have been acquainted for years, Mr Parnell, it is only in recent weeks that I could claim to know you. Yet, I feel there is such an affinity between us. Might you ... could you ever imagine yourself eloping with me?"

No doubt her desire to spite her brother exceeds her desire for me. Making a match with this prideful chit has no appeal, but I am curious to see how far she will go with this nonsense. "Would you think me presumptuous, my dear, if I confessed that I had already imagined such a future?"

When Georgiana giggled behind her fan, Upton brought his face down to hers. Excitedly, she thought, *He is going to kiss my cheek. He adores me! What a lark!*

"Miss Darcy? Who are you with?" Elizabeth's sharp tone abruptly ended the romantic moment. Upton faced the street below and moved a few steps away; however, those few steps put him nearer to Darcy, who was standing in the balcony's other doorway. Upton worriedly realised he had no escape from Fisticuffs Darcy.

"Elizabeth, please escort my sister into the ballroom," he said tersely.

Reluctantly, Georgiana followed her. Glancing over her shoulder, she saw her brother castigating Upton. *If William frightens off Upton, where will I find a coach?*

That prospect sent a surge of fury through her. Once inside the ballroom, she shoved Elizabeth with both palms, causing her to stumble into some empty chairs lining the wall. When Elizabeth spun around to face her, Georgiana demanded, "How dare you spy upon me?"

In an icy whisper, she replied, "I will not speak of your reckless behaviour, but I did nothing wrong."

"If your wanton nature had not compelled you to tryst with my brother in a dark place, my innocent conversation with a gentleman I have known for years would have gone unremarked. *You* put my reputation at risk, madam!" She snapped open her fan and stormed away, ultimately settling at a table near that of the Countess and Lady Catherine.

Elizabeth felt her face flush with anger, so she turned toward the wall. A few moments later, there was a gentle touch on her shoulder. Anne asked, "Are you well, Miss Bennet? We saw my brat of a cousin push you."

Now Elizabeth's face was flushed with embarrassment. "We, Miss de Bourgh?"

"My mother and Aunt Beatrice were also witnesses. Please know that you have allies among Darcy's relations."

Elizabeth turned to her. "You are very kind, madam."

Anne offered her arm. "While the musicians enjoy a respite, shall we take a turn around the room? My mother insists that ladies always appear to advantage when they stroll slowly, fan themselves languidly, and wear inscrutable smiles." Laughing, Elizabeth linked her arm with Anne's, and they began to walk.

Georgiana sat alone, fanning herself with a jerky motion. Seeing Irene being escorted by her partner from the last dance, Georgiana smiled at her. Irene returned the smile and then whispered to her escort. He nodded and led her to the table where Lady Catherine and the Countess sat. Georgiana's smile tightened, and she glanced around to see if Irene's snub had been noticed. She did not dance for the rest of the evening, coolly refusing the only man who asked her.

Not until after the Pemberley party left the assembly did Elizabeth remember she had not told Darcy of Henry's presence in Ramsgate last August.

≈≈≈

At Oaklands on Saturday morning, Elizabeth waited until Mrs Harcourt, Cassandra, and Squire left the breakfast room. Then, with only Polly present, she asked Abelard, "May I beg a favour, sir? Will you please dance with Mrs Susan at my party?"

Abelard stared. "I do not believe I can do that."

"I was told that you **never** say you cannot do something," she pressed.

"I have danced—well, I tried to dance. It was a disaster!"

"I believe you can manage a slow waltz, Abel. Polly will be your practice partner while I play the pianoforte."

"I do not want to shame Mrs Susan," Abelard said.

"We will make this as comfortable for you as possible. And if you cannot waltz, that will end the matter."

Abelard glanced at Polly, who nodded enthusiastically.

Elizabeth allowed him some moments for reflection. Then she urged softly, "Will you try, Cousin? For I have heard that Mrs Susan would dearly love to dance with you."

Contradictory thoughts tumbled through his mind. *I **do** want to dance with Susan, but people will pity her and* *laugh at me. I have survived being laughed at—and pitied, but if I can spare her that .... A slow waltz would be more scandalous than a waltz at normal tempo. Can I do this? Elizabeth and Polly would not put me in a situation where I would fail. If I reject their kind offer, I will disappoint them. If I do not risk failure, I will disappoint myself.*

After a long silence, he said, "Tomorrow, I will let you show me that your plan **could** work. But do not speak of this to Mrs Susan. If I become a dancer, I want to surprise her."

"Tomorrow," Elizabeth and Polly said in unison.

"Now I shall try to attend to my usual business, worrying all the while that I have committed myself to an activity that may be a disaster," he muttered. "Good day, ladies."

After he exited the parlour, Elizabeth asked Polly, "Have you asked Toby about being Mrs Susan's practice partner?"

"I have. He agrees. Did you tell Mrs Susan your plan?"

"I will tell her today."

Grinning, Polly announced, "I have a song."

"By all means, sing, madam!"

To the tune of "Yankee Doodle," she sang, "Mrs Susan has beau but thinks that we don't know it; Mr Abel cares for her, and we hope soon he'll show it."

"Yes, we do." Elizabeth laughed. "Well, **that** is resolved, for I cannot imagine Mrs Susan refusing to waltz. Next on my list is calling at Pemberley, which I plan to do on Monday. My purpose is to charm Mr Darcy's aunts."

Polly was impressed. "The Countess of Kestevyn and Lady Catherine de Bourgh? You are braver than I, madam."

"When Mr Darcy and I marry, the ladies will be my family, too." Elizabeth thought, *And if I cannot win over his sister, I must make an effort with his other relations.*

≈≈≈

While Darcy was in his study, having broken his fast earlier, the breakfast room at Pemberley was filled with his relations. The table seated twelve; however, the six of them were sitting at one end, with the Countess at the head of the table. At her right were Lady Catherine, Fitzwilliam, and Irene; at her left were Henry and Anne.

The Countess said, "The assembly was pleasant. No, it was **better** than that. The musicians were more skilled than expected, and the atmosphere was very cheerful."

"There is no shortage of pretty ladies in Lambton," Fitzwilliam said before gesturing to the footman. "Are there more scones?" The footman left to inquire.

To avoid being mocked or hit with a fan, Henry tried to avoid using cant in front of his grandmother and great-aunt. Thus, everyone understood him when he frowned at his plate and muttered, "I should have asked the footman about more ham. A man needs lots of meat in his first meal of the day."

Anne looked up from her dish of fruit, cheese, a single egg, and brown bread. She asked, "What is the longest time you have gone without eating meat? How many days?"

"Days!" he gasped. "If a fellow goes more than twenty-four hours without ham or lamb or beef or bacon, his muscles start to weaken! That is a medical fact."

Irene, whose breakfast choices mirrored Anne's, said, "Last night, you seemed to enjoy your dance with Miss Elizabeth, Henry. Is it because she let you blather about yourself as if you were an interesting person?"

"She is a good dancer—you could learn from her." Henry made a face, and she returned the grimace.

Georgiana entered, and as she took the empty chair beside Anne, she thought sullenly, *If Anne traded places with Henry, I could sit beside him.*

"Good morning. I saw you speaking with Miss Bennet last night," Anne said cheerily. *If you think your bad behaviour went unnoticed, little Miss Darcy, think again.*

When Georgiana looked at Anne, she saw the scold in her eyes. Feeling defiant, she replied, "Miss Bennet was quite rude when I interrupted her intimate tête à tête with William. I was shocked by her scandalous behaviour."

Fitzwilliam scoffed. "You are imagining things, my girl. Darcy and I spoke about **your** behaviour last night." His look warned her, *I know more than you think.*

At that moment, the footman returned with fresh scones. When he offered the plate, Fitzwilliam and Lady Catherine each took one. As her ladyship buttered the pastry, the Countess said, "You do know scones are made with rather a lot of butter."

Spreading marmalade over the butter, Lady Catherine said dismissively, "You are not my mother, madam."

She chuckled. "Oh, thank heaven."

When Georgiana asked Lady Catherine what she thought of Miss Bennet, she replied, "While I would prefer she had more suitable connections, I am not opposed to the match."

Surely a countess will know this is a misalliance, Georgiana thought. "Aunt Beatrice—"

"I have decided it is not my place to decide whom my relations should marry," she interrupted.

Fitzwilliam asked innocently, "Would you put that in writing for me, Mother?"

"Why? Do you hope to introduce an opera dancer to us?"

Lady Catherine choked on her tea. "Do not say that even in jest, madam! Ah—you rolled your eyes at me—such a vulgar gesture," she scolded.

"I am a countess. The only ladies at whom I should not roll my eyes are duchesses and marchionesses," the Countess said matter-of-factly.

"Such impudence!" However, when Irene and Anne laughed into their napkins and Fitzwilliam chuckled, the corners of Lady Catherine's mouth twitched into a smile. "Point to you, Countess."

Anne said, "You must give Miss Bennet credit for not being an opera dancer. Like yourself, Georgiana, she is a gentleman's daughter—and I have never seen Darcy so happy as he is in her company."

How dare you say that! Georgiana wanted to shout. Instead, she asked with sugared malice, "In your chat with Mr Selby last night, did you discuss your health tragedies?"

Anne tsked. "Tragedies? You have a passion for drama! We spoke of our interests rather than commiserating over matters beyond our control."

Lady Catherine said, "I suppose you told him you are running off to Denmark."

"I did mention it, yes."

"Well, Lady Irene and I will be so pleasantly occupied in Kent, we shall not miss you," Lady Catherine said airily.

Anne laid a hand over her heart and sighed. "How you wound me, Mama!" And then both ladies laughed.

Georgiana exclaimed, "You are taking Irene to Rosings Park?" Although she planned to be married before Irene set foot in Kent, she was unhappy not to have been invited. "What does the Earl of Harwich think of this plan?"

Lady Catherine gave a dismissive shrug, "Daughters are never of much consequence to a father. And to that I say such disinterest is a father's loss."

Irene said, "Aunt Catherine will prepare me for my come-out." Accurately reading Georgiana's expression, she smiled. *You are jealous of me.*

Feeling a fresh wave of spite, Georgiana told Anne, "I marvel that you spoke with Mr Selby for the duration of a full set of dances. I have great difficulty understanding him."

Lady Catherine tsked. "Because you do not listen."

"You are mistaken, Aunt," Georgiana said coolly.

"I am **not** mistaken. Yesterday, I told you about the popularity of our little libraries in villages throughout Kent. And did you ask anything about our efforts? You did not. You wittered on your new summer gowns."

Just in time, Georgiana stopped herself from admitting she was uninterested in her aunt's project. "But I know nothing about libraries."

Anne teased, "It is not as if one can ask questions when one is ignorant about a topic."

Georgiana said defensively, "I spoke of fashion because it is a topic of general interest. I was ... providing a service."

Lady Catherine said, "Irene and I will see the new fashions for ourselves when we go to my modiste in London, who will create a wardrobe for Irene."

In a faint voice, Georgiana repeated, "A new wardrobe?"

"When Aunt Catherine and Anne saw my insipid gowns, they generously offered me a wardrobe a la mode. And dear Darcy has assured me I shall have everything I need that is appropriate to my station." Staring at Georgiana, she thought, *Now you are even more jealous of me.* Her ladylike smile became a wide grin.

≈≈≈

That afternoon in his office, Upton ruminated on the advantages of eloping with Georgiana. When the idea first occurred to him, he entertained it as a joke; he had hinted at their running away together merely to amuse himself. Thus, when she indicated that she was amenable to his suit, his first thought was "no". Where was the pleasure in being leg-shackled to such an immature, complaining creature?

Upton stared out the window to the view that reminded him he was in Lambton, a boring, bucolic backwater where the sheep and cattle outnumbered the people. At that thought, he groaned. "Oh, the **people** one must endure in this hamlet." Then, he inked a quill pen and drew a vertical line down the centre of a quarter-sheet of foolscap.

On the left side of the line, he wrote, "Immature and complaining". On the right side, he wrote, "Very rich".

To the left, he added that Darcy disliked him. Then, smiling, he drew a line through that and rewrote it on the right side of his list. He also wrote that he could live in London in gentlemanly style—well away from his father and Lambton; give up his law practice if he chose; and have the resources to travel. After some consideration, he jotted:

"Darcy can't snub me; Georgiana pretty enough; might get an heir from her."

Putting aside the quill, Upton set his elbows on his desk and rested his chin on his interlaced fingers. *Even if Darcy changes his mind about giving her the family townhouse, the chit has enough blunt to buy a residence in the right neighbourhood. I will also have achieved a match that defeated Wickham and Trevor.* (He ignored the fact that neither man had a serious interest in her.)

"Eloping with Georgiana Darcy—with or without her enthusiastic consent—would give me the life I deserve," he murmured. "I can manage the young lady."

≈ ≈ ≈

In Lambton's small church, Upton watched with amusement—and from a distance—as Darcy orchestrated the seating arrangements of the Countess of Kestevyn, Lady Irene Morton, Viscount Bowmont, Lady Catherine de Bourgh, the Honourable Miss Anne de Bourgh, and the Honourable Randal Fitzwilliam. *Our Mr Darcy would have made an excellent sheep-herding dog.*

Georgiana stood apart from her relations, and when she saw Upton, he smiled briefly. She watched as he opened his prayer book and adjusted a piece of paper within it so that one edge protruded slightly above the cover. Then he placed the prayer book on an empty pew and strolled away. When he glanced over his shoulder a few moments later, he saw Georgiana tucking his prayer book into her reticule.

Later in the privacy of her bedroom, Georgiana read Upton's note, which contained no names, no dates, and no tell-tale clues as to the author.

I had never allowed myself to consider the possibility of a match between us. Despite the title I will inherit, I always considered you above my touch. Yet in our conversations— never long enough to suit my heart—you showed me what a remarkable lady you are. Is it any wonder I have fallen in love with you?

Because I love you, I will do as you ask. I await your instructions ... and hope that someday, you will fall in love with me, too.

≈ ≈ ≈

Irene appreciated the long afternoons of July. With her face shaded by a wide-brimmed, woven-straw hat, she sat on the marble bench in Pemberley's rose garden, which was opposite the front of the manor. Hearing footsteps on the gravel drive between the garden and the portico, she glanced at the source; when she saw Georgiana, she returned her attention to her sketch.

Georgiana stood behind her. "Your skills are improving."

She is cheerful today; I wonder what she is up to. She only seeks me out when she wants an audience. Without looking up from her sketch, Irene said, "That is the first compliment you have ever given me."

"Oh, are you keeping track?"

"Until now, there was nothing to keep track of."

"May I share the bench with you?"

Sighing softly, Irene moved the woven-reed basket containing her drawing supplies to the paving stones at her feet. "Yes, sit. What is it you wish to tell me?"

Too pleased with her plan to be sensible, Georgiana said, "I think that eloping would be very romantic."

Irene asked, "More romantic than wearing a beautiful gown at a traditional church ceremony witnessed by family and friends? A ceremony in which the man and woman declare to love and honour and forsake all others? And afterwards, everyone sits down to a magnificent breakfast where all the bride's favourite dishes are served."

*She is **still** thinking about food.* Georgiana flicked an annoyed glance at her. "The Book of Common Prayer does not mention a breakfast dictated by the bride's preferences."

"So then, if you were of a mind to elope, Georgiana, who would be your groom?"

"I have not decided. Suppose … suppose I eloped with Upton Parnell. What a fine joke on William and that Bennet creature if I married before them."

Irene shrugged. "Your brother and Miss Bennet are deeply in love; they would console each over the loss of you."

"What do you mean the 'loss' of me?"

"Darcy will never accept Upton as family. He as good as forced Upton to leave the assembly. Did you not see?"

"No," Georgiana said quietly. *Oh, dear, if William keeps Upton away from me, how can I manage the elopement? Without his landau, Henry and I cannot run away together.*

Irene had more thoughts on the subject. "Marriage lasts until death parts the couple; Upton could live a long time. Do you truly wish to have conjugal relations with a fellow who, when he is not sneering, looks as if he is **about** to sneer?"

Rattled but unwilling to show it, Georgiana said, "Well, I will have made my point to William simply by eloping. Upton and I can have our marriage annulled immediately." For reasons she could not explain, she found herself defending an elopement she had no intention of doing.

"You are a rich prize. I doubt Upton would consent to forego conjugal intimacies **or** your fortune."

"Upton likes a joke. I would tell him beforehand that this is a prank I am playing on my brother—not a true marriage."

Irene made an exasperated noise. "It does not matter what **you** decide; once you are married, you have no control over your person or your life."

"But if Upton signed a letter agreeing to my terms that ours was not a true marriage—"

"In the eyes of the law, you are too young to make such an agreement. The very fact that you decided to do something so foolish will prove you do not have the capacity to create a contract. Annulments are not easily gotten, and if

Upton insists on exercising his conjugal rights—whether or not you wish it—you cannot stop him legally or physically; you are his property."

"Then a divorce—"

"You know it takes an act of Parliament—and several years—to get a divorce," Irene reminded. "And if you cannot get a divorce, you *will* be married to Upton Parnell. I do not know him well, but he seems to be the envious, arrogant sort of fellow. Your misery would be certain with such a husband. And if you *did* divorce, society would snub you for the scandal." Irene tsked. "For a lady of marriageable age, Georgiana, you are woefully ignorant about the laws that control—may I say *limit*—our fate.

"Surely, my brother or the Earl of Kestevyn could intervene on my behalf."

"What will this prank achieve? Would you risk *everything* just to be spiteful?"

Georgiana scowled. "I merely said that an elopement sounded romantic. You have taken all the fun out of an imaginary lark." She turned on her heel and stalked away.

Chapter 20

As Inglesby escorted Elizabeth up to the drawing room on Monday afternoon, they passed Georgiana, who was coming down the staircase. *Her expression has the smallest curvature of one's lips that can still be considered a smile,* Elizabeth thought. She responded with an impertinent grin.

"Miss Bennet, always a pleasure," she said coolly, stopping one step above her.

"Miss Darcy, my thoughts exactly." Taking the volume of Wordsworth's poetry from her reticule, she offered it. "My Aunt Gardiner gave this book to Cassandra Harcourt, who is happy to lend it to you."

"Thank you, no, but you were kind to bring it. Good day."

"Of course." *Well, I made an effort, and now I can return this copy to Cassie,* Elizabeth thought with relief. Aware that she was being dismissed, her grin broadened. "And good day to **you**, Miss Darcy. I have come to call on your aunts and your cousins."

Although Georgiana had no interest in spending so much as a hummingbird's heartbeat in the company of Elizabeth Bennet, she was immediately offended. "You are not here to call on me as well?"

"I do not wish to impose upon your time. As you are the hostess to many guests, I realise my visit may be inconvenient for you."

Elizabeth and the butler watched as several emotions flashed across Georgiana's face before she spoke. "Inglesby, please send a tea tray to the drawing room. Miss Bennet, allow me to escort you."

As they entered the drawing room, the Countess of Kestevyn, Lady Catherine, Lady Irene, and Anne de Bourgh were having a lively conversation. Elizabeth saw welcome in the smiles of Irene and Anne and reserved politeness in the acknowledgements from the Countess and Lady Catherine.

The tea tray arrived expeditiously, and Georgiana poured out. However, after drinking half a cup, she excused herself, saying she needed to attend to some matters for her guests. Although she was the designated hostess, she felt no qualms about shifting her responsibilities to her other relations.

After Georgiana's departure, Irene relaxed and spoke excitedly of going to Rosings Park for an extended stay. Elizabeth said, "I am certain you will enjoy it. The manor is very elegant, and I took many delightful walks on the grounds."

The Countess smiled mischievously. "You must come to Flint Rock Castle, madam. I long to hear you praise my home as being superior to that of my sister-in-law."

Lady Catherine tsked. "Henry would call that fustian nonsense, Beatrice."

"I am sorry you could not see more of Kent during your visit, Miss Bennet," Anne said. "I fear you were constrained by Mr Collins' lack of a carriage."

"In truth, Miss de Bourgh, my only regret is that I did not visit any of the libraries the Rosings Park ladies established throughout the county."

"Do you recall meeting my companion, Lady Phillipa at tea?" Lady Catherine asked. "It was her idea. Unlike the Darcys, who have been expanding their collection for years, the de Bourghs are less obsessed with books."

The Countess said, "The Kestevyns are not great readers, but Sophie and I enjoy a good novel—one in which the author does not moralize one into a stupor."

"I believe the villages in Derbyshire would benefit from more libraries. Of course, I don't expect Mr Darcy to relinquish Pemberley's collection, but he has the resources to encourage the pleasure of reading throughout the county."

"Have you mentioned this to Darcy?" Anne asked.

"Not yet. He has asked what I would like as an engagement gift, and I am excited about creating a library in the nearby village of Eyam."

Lady Catherine wagged her finger in a "no" gesture. "You must tell Darcy you want a necklace, brooch, or another piece of jewellery. Certainly, you should encourage him to fund libraries, Miss Bennet, but that must be separate from your engagement gift. Do you not agree, Beatrice?"

"I do, yes."

Elizabeth laughed lightly. "Well, on the matter of advice, Lady Catherine, I would like to hear your thoughts about establishing small libraries. For example, how do you choose where to put them? I have brought paper and pencil to record your suggestions."

Lady Catherine glanced at Anne in surprise before replying. "I do love to be useful, so I shall tell you about our experiences."

Elizabeth used Wordsworth's poetry book as her desk for the quarter-sheet of foolscap on which she made notes in pencil. When Lady Catherine finished speaking, Elizabeth began asking questions. On some matters, her ladyship had no answers; for others, she was intrigued, so she asked Anne to make notes.

Just then, Darcy entered, and Anne said, "Your timing is impeccable. I need to borrow your pencil and a page of your diary."

"Borrow? Then, after you write on the paper, you will return it to me?"

"I forgot how fiercely you hoard your pages," she teased.

Elizabeth said she had several small pieces of foolscap. "I shall make a list for myself and another for my impertinent questions." At her arch smile, Lady Catherine chuckled.

"What is the purpose of these lists?" Darcy asked.

"The de Bourgh ladies' successes in creating small libraries throughout Kent could be duplicated in Derbyshire. You asked what I would like for an engagement present." She smiled self-consciously. "I thought I would ask for enough books to establish a small library in Eyam."

"But we do not approve," Lady Catherine said.

"Eyam is no longer a plague village," Darcy assured her.

"That is not the issue," Lady Catherine de Bourgh said.

"Do you approve of libraries only in Kent?"

"We encourage you to fund libraries, Darcy," Anne said.

"But jewellery is a more appropriate engagement gift," the Countess said.

"You have given me much to consider," he said gravely.

Irene asked him, "Shall I pour out tea for you?"

"Yes, thank you." He glanced around. *Where is Georgiana?*

As if reading his mind, Anne said, "She drank one cup and excused herself." Darcy frowned, *Worse and worse—her rudeness cannot be explained away.*

Eager to keep the mood light, Elizabeth asked Lady Catherine, "How did you decide which books should be in the libraries?"

"I selected books neither Anne nor I wished to read."

"Does anyone record which books are popular and which are not?" Elizabeth asked.

Lady Catherine said, "No, and I suppose charity isn't truly charitable if no one wants what you give them."

"No doubt some of the less popular books are of value. Is there someone in London whom you could entrust with selling them and purchasing books that inspire people to read?" Elizabeth asked.

Darcy said, "Three booksellers in town notify me when they receive books of interest. I am happy to deal with them on your behalf, Aunt Catherine."

"May I help, as well?" Irene asked earnestly. "I can assist in identifying books no one wants to read, as more than a few such tomes have been thrust upon me."

Teacup in hand, Darcy relaxed in a chair and listened to the discussion. *This party is carrying on pleasantly without my sister.* Abruptly, he realised that Lady Catherine was telling Elizabeth about the almost-betrothal between himself and Anne. "Darcy pursued her for years, but Anne decided that rusticating in Derbyshire would not suit her."

He stared wide-eyed at his aunt and then looked at Anne, who solemnly apologised for breaking his heart. Everyone present knew the almost-betrothal between the children of Lady Catherine and her late sister had never been more than casual speculation. Thus, they listened with amusement as Darcy said with equal seriousness, "I appreciate your acknowledgement of my pain, Anne, for I have waited many years for your apology."

After a brief silence, Irene also apologised for breaking Darcy's heart, saying, "I am sorry, Cousin, but we simply would not suit."

Before he could reply, Elizabeth said, "Mr Darcy, *I* promise I will never break your heart." Her tender smile and loving declaration in the presence of his closest relations sent a wave of affection through him.

A short while later, Elizabeth apologised for overstaying her visit, and as she farewelled each lady in turn, the Countess murmured, "I would enjoy playing whist with you but not against you. You are impressively strategic."

Darcy escorted his fiancée to the stable yard where the Oaklands pony cart awaited her. He was of a mind to say something endearing—perhaps even romantic—until she asked, "Did you know Henry was in Ramsgate last summer?"

"I did **not** know that."

"If Georgiana attempted to elope with a titled man, could Henry be that man?"

"He could, although Harwich is against such a match."

"If Georgiana wants Viscount Bowmont, do you think her influence over him is greater than the Earl's?"

Darcy groaned and rubbed a hand over his face.

≈≈≈

After Georgiana left the tea party, she sought out Henry. "I need you to deliver a message to Mr Upton Parnell, the solicitor in Lambton."

"Isn't that the fellow your brother doesn't like?"

"I have not yet explained the details of our elopement."

Henry shrugged. "I trust you. You are a clever girl."

Behind her smile, Georgiana thought, *And you are a lazy lad, but I am willing to overlook that.* She gave him a folded paper sealed with wax. "If Mr Parnell asks you anything about yourself, just tell him we are second cousins. If he asks you anything about me, say you are not certain. **Do not** have a conversation or join him for a drink at the pub. Simply deliver the note and return."

He looked at the letter she pushed into his hand. "You didn't use your personal seal."

"Henry, this is a secret. Secrets are more ... secretive when you don't reveal your identity. This note tells Mr Parnell to bring his landau to Pemberley on the night of the party. Then you and I shall borrow it for our elopement."

He looked doubtful. "This fellow who knows Darcy doesn't like him is going to lend us his carriage and cattle because you ask him to?"

"We should be ready to negotiate," she admitted.

≈≈≈

At supper, Darcy asked Henry how he had spent the day. The viscount shrugged. "I went riding. Visited Lambton. Might like to do a bit of fishing tomorrow. If I were as full of juice—um, as rich—as you, I would keep a pack of foxhounds and drink a bottle of wine a day."

The Countess gave him A Look. "Then you would drink a great deal more than you ought."

"How did you spend the day, Georgiana?" Darcy asked.

What does he suspect? She, too, shrugged. "Miss Elizabeth came for tea."

"Yes, I joined the ladies after you left."

"I had hostess matters to attend to but nothing to be concerned about."

After supper, Georgiana excused herself from joining the others for tea and coffee in the drawing room; thus, she was absent from the conversation but not missed. Darcy sipped his coffee and listened with pleasure as various family members recounted their approval of Elizabeth. His heart did whisper, *She did this for me. She did not want our union to cause a rift with my relations.*

≈≈≈

Later that night in the library, Darcy poured brandy for Fitzwilliam and himself. He sat in the armchair that was a twin of the one his cousin occupied. "Fitz, whom do you know with a title tha—"

"My mother, my father, my elder brother, my two elder sisters, my nephew, my—"

Through gritted teeth, Darcy said, "Whom do you know with a title *that* my sister might wish to marry?"

"Offhand, no free-ranging, eligible peers come to mind."

"I cannot understand why Georgiana is so determined to have a title."

"I daresay she thinks it will bring her power of a sort. She would also take precedence over her commoner brother."

"Trevor is one brother away from being a baronet. Upton is the heir to his father's barony. Henry is already a viscount and the heir to an earldom. You have spent more time with the Lordling than I have. Does he seem like the sort who always obeys his father?"

Fitzwilliam groaned. "He is the sort who has no interest in anything other than diversions and amusements. I cannot imagine any lady finding his indolence attractive."

"For the prestige of being a viscountess, some ladies would happily overlook his immaturity."

≈≈≈

For a change, Darcy's call at Oaklands lasted no more than the polite quarter-hour. In the parlour, he explained to Squire, Mrs Harcourt, and Abelard that he needed Elizabeth to arrive early at the party so that she could approve of last-minute changes; thus, he would send Lady Irene in a Pemberley carriage to collect her at seven on Saturday.

As Elizabeth walked Darcy to the stable, he asked, "Regarding that special dance you have planned, do you want the musicians to accompany you?"

"Perhaps. I will talk with them before the guests come."

"So many details, but I think we have everything organized." Darcy's expression did not reflect the confidence he professed.

"We do, sir."

After a silence, he asked wistfully, "Are you certain that you do not wish to elope?"

Elizabeth laughed. "You seem nervous, my love."

"I have an uneasy feeling. Am I being foolish?"

Smiling, she gave a small shrug. "I refuse to worry. Is there anything else?"

"No. *Yes!*"

She watched with amusement as he patted his various pockets. Then he exclaimed, "Ah, here. This." He produced a slim box covered in dark leather and offered it to her. "For you." On a bed of black velvet was a flower-shaped gold pendant set with small pearls and amethysts. Elizabeth gasped with delight and touched it with a light finger.

Darcy said, "I hope it pleases you."

Leaning close, she murmured, "This pleases me almost as much as you please me."

A sensation of heat flashed through him, and his groin tightened uncomfortably. For an instant, he closed his eyes to distract himself. Then, with a self-conscious chuckle, he said, "I look forward to moments when we can please each other in a more private setting."

≈≈≈

At Oaklands, a Pemberley footman handed Elizabeth into the coach where Irene awaited her. "I thank you for your company, Lady Irene."

"Are you nervous about the party?"

"More excited than anxious. You look particularly lovely this evening. Lemon yellow suits you."

Surprised, Irene said, "No one has ever said that to me. Um, thank you."

"What do people usually say?" Elizabeth was puzzled.

"Stand up straight. You should not have eaten a second dessert. Your hairstyle looks too old, too young, too ...." She made a vague gesture as she trailed off.

Elizabeth tsked. "Small minds have small thoughts. I hear so few opinions that are worth remembering."

"I agree." Irene laughed lightly. "So here is my opinion. Your pendant is very pretty with your lilac gown. Watered silk, is it not?"

"This was made from some cloth that my aunt and uncle Gardiner sent. You have an eye for quality, madam." She touched her pendant fondly. "As does Mr Darcy."

Darcy does. He chose Elizabeth Bennet, Irene thought.

At Pemberley, Darcy was pacing on the portico when the carriage arrived. He hurried down the steps to hand out the ladies. Then, with Elizabeth on one arm and Irene on the other, he escorted them to the ballroom.

Seeing Anne and Fitzwilliam conferring over the punch-bowl, Darcy said, "A Conclave of Cousins. Should Napoleon be worried?"

"We are wagering about who Georgiana will elope with."

"I am **shocked**!"

"As if you have never made a wager," Fitzwilliam scoffed.

"Not about my sister!"

"I have wagered on all of my siblings. Won a pony on Harwich marrying Martha, and I used those twenty-five pounds unwisely ... and quite enjoyably," he recalled.

Irene asked, "Was there some question about whether my parents would marry?"

"Indeed there was. Your mother was one of two ladies your father was considering," Fitzwilliam said. "Anyway, my money is on Upton Parnell. Georgiana knows how vexed you would be, Darcy, to call him 'brother'."

Irene said, "I would also bet on Upton. I cannot imagine Henry going against Father's wishes."

Anne shook her head. "My money is on Henry. He is young, lusty, and rather dim."

"I sincerely hope my sixteen-year-old sister is not so foolish as to elope with anyone."

Anne asked, "Has anyone ever told you that you have a charmingly optimistic innocence?"

"What matters," Elizabeth interjected, "is that we all remain vigilant this evening."

"Georgiana would never cause a scene at my engagement party," Darcy protested.

"Such innocence." Anne patted his cheek.

Eager to change the subject, he said, "At breakfast, Irene, it sounded as if Georgiana had moved beyond 'merely civil'; she seemed rather friendly."

Irene looked at him apologetically. "It did not seem like genuine friendliness to me. I think she is up to something. And as for using this party as a cover, remember that it is easier to hide in a crowd than in an open meadow."

Fitzwilliam exclaimed, "Open meadow! I nearly forgot to tell you I have chosen an estate name: *Andarby*. Anne's name goes first because this happy solution was her idea. Also, I prefer Andarby to Daranby or Beadaran."

Anne laughed. "As one would. So, 'dar' is for Darcy, and is 'b' for Beatrice?"

"Yes. After my mother visited the estate, she promised me five thousand pounds. She says I must improve the kitchen, my bedroom, and a parlour first."

"Ah, the musicians have arrived," Darcy said.

Elizabeth gently pulled away from him. "Please excuse me while I speak with them."

"What is that about?" Irene asked, watching her confer with several of the musicians.

"A secret she is keeping for Mr Selby and a promise she is keeping to Mrs Susan," Darcy said.

≈≈≈

The Selbys were among the first to arrive at the party; Abelard escorted Mrs Harcourt through the receiving line, and Squire followed. He was still accustoming himself to walking with a cane, but his sedate pace gave a measure of gravitas to a man who had always moved in a hurry.

Had Mrs Harcourt not known Abelard so well, she would not have seen his nervousness. She knew he was concerned about waltzing tonight, and as much as she wanted to alleviate his anxiousness, she was determined to surprise him with a scheme *she* had been refining for some time.

Following the supper set, Elizabeth took the place of the gentleman who played the pianoforte. The violinist gave her a knowing nod and joined in when she began to play a slow waltz. When no one stepped onto the dance floor, Darcy asked Irene, "Can you waltz at that tempo?"

"Watch me!" She took his arm, and he led her to the floor. Less than a minute later, Abelard and Mrs Harcourt joined them. He was a bit unsteady at first, but when he saw her confidence in him, he relaxed. As he guided her through a second turn, he began feeling confident in himself. Soon they were moving like long-time partners. Susan's heart did whisper, *He did this for me.*

Fitzwilliam did not realise Lady Catherine was beside him until she prodded him with her fan. "At long last, a waltz played at a sensible tempo. You may dance with me, Randal."

He grinned. "I am a fortunate man."

"You are an impudent scamp, but I forgive you."

To Fitzwilliam's surprise, a slow waltz was quite pleasant, and by the time the music ended, other couples had made the same discovery.

Abelard bowed to his partner. "I think we acquitted ourselves competently, Mrs Susan."

With a gentle laugh, she said, "How formal you sound! Did you enjoy the experience?"

Did I enjoy it? "I ... I did, once I overcame my nervousness." As he led her from the dance floor, he asked, "You practised with Elizabeth, didn't you?"

"To match your pace so that I did not embarrass you."

She feared embarrassing **me**? "Did you enjoy it?"

"What I liked most was that you held me in your arms." He stared at her, delighted by her candour. She continued, "We know what we feel for each other."

In her face, he saw the love and yearning that matched his own. "Will you come outside with me, Susan?"

They stepped onto a small balcony that was illuminated by the glow of a torch in a sconce near the doorway. Abelard leaned against the balustrade, his hands resting on the rail behind him. He gazed at her for a moment, wondering, *Am I supposed to be doing something?*

She said, "I intend to rectify an unfortunate situation. I wish to make an honest man of you. The scurrilous rumours about our reputations are becoming more widely discussed by all and sundry."

"But, Susan, I have not so much as kissed you!"

"I intend to rectify that as well." Before he realised her intention, she kissed him firmly. "Will you do me the honour of accepting my hand in marriage, Mr Selby?"

After a silence (which, by her estimation, lasted a hundred years), Abelard said, "I love you, but ...."

"You love me, **but**?" She rested her hands on his, standing even nearer to him than when they waltzed.

"But you are you certain—"

"There is no one else I want to be with. Only you."

Abelard's heart fairly shouted, *I was too timid to ask for what I loved most, and she did this for me.* He eased his hands out from under hers so he could pull her to his chest. "I have loved you for a long time, Susan. No buts. I humbly accept your proposal." After he kissed her brow, she raised her face to kiss his lips again. And again. He murmured, "I suppose our marriage will surprise no one."

"No one except you, Abel." At that, he grinned. She continued, "As a widow, I have some advice for you—for us."

"I am listening, Susan. I will always listen to you."

"Even when you marry the right person, there is no certainty of a happy ending. We will have problems we create unwittingly and difficulties we never imagined."

"Do you promise, my dear? For a boring, predictable life is not my idea of a happy ending."

Chapter 21

Elizabeth and Darcy waltzed with the skill of partners attuned to each other's movements. As Irene danced past them with a local gentleman, Elizabeth said, "I am pleased Irene's situation is settled. Will your sister miss her?"

"I have been trying to recall the last time Georgiana seemed content. We stayed at the Harwich estate last summer; good riding, a tolerable library, and a cellar full of excellent wines. My sister was fifteen then. She spent much time with the Harwich children. Well, Henry was one-and-twenty then, so I cannot call him a child."

Elizabeth said, "Then, in August, Henry and Georgiana were in Ramsgate. Why do you suppose that in December, the Earl of Harwich felt he needed to announce that he would not permit a union between his son and your sister? Did he observe a budding interest between them?" Suddenly anxious, she said, "Oh, goodness! Irene is waving as subtly as she can. She is there by the windows."

With sweeping steps, Darcy waltzed Elizabeth to where Irene fairly vibrated with worry. Even before they stopped in front of her, she said, "I saw a footman give Georgiana a note. Before I could explain to this nice gentleman why we had to interrupt our dance," she gave her partner an apologetic smile, "she had left the ballroom."

Deciding this was a family matter, Irene's partner said, "I hope we may dance again." He bowed and walked away.

"Which footman brought the note?" Darcy asked.

"I only know he was not one of Pemberley's, so he must have been hired for tonight."

"Irene, find Fitz. Elizabeth, please wait here for him." As Irene rushed away, Darcy found Inglesby at his elbow.

"Is there a problem, sir?"

Elizabeth asked the butler, "Would you have maids look in the retiring room and Miss Darcy's bedroom? She seems to have disappeared."

"At once, madam." He bowed and was gone.

"Yes, you are right. I may be worrying over nothing," Darcy said. When a firm hand grasped his shoulder, he made a half-turn and found himself facing Abelard, who stood arm in arm with Mrs Harcourt.

"My groom just sent word through your servants that Upton Parnell has arrived with a landau, a driver, and a bouquet of flowers."

"Is he at the stable?" Darcy asked.

"No, he is by the kitchen garden," Mrs Harcourt said.

Almost before she finished speaking, Darcy was striding to the French doors that opened to the rear of the house. Elizabeth asked the couple, "Please send Mr Fitzwilliam to the kitchen garden. And if you see Georgiana, keep her with you until we return." Then, with as much decorum as she could manage, she rushed after her fiancé.

≈≈≈

When Darcy saw his sister and two men arguing as they stood beside a landau on the dirt track bordering the kitchen garden, he slowed, uncertain of what he was witnessing. *Does Henry have my pistol? Is he rescuing Georgiana?*

Then Georgiana clarified the situation. "I promise you, Mr Parnell, we only need to **borrow** your coach. We will return it soon—within a week. Tell him, Henry."

"We will return it within a week," Henry said woodenly.

Even I don't believe that, Darcy thought.

"But you are supposed to elope with **me**, Miss Darcy," Upton complained.

"Is she?" Darcy asked loudly as he came near.

Startled, Henry jerked, and his finger slipped off the trigger. "Dammit, Darcy, you scared the wits out of me!"

"I want my pistol returned to me, Henry. So, Parnell, you mentioned running off with my sister."

"Miss Darcy wants a title. If she marries me, she will have one."

Georgiana said primly, "But only after your father dies, sir. When do you think that will be?" Then she smiled at Henry. "Viscount Bowmont and I are simply finishing what we planned last summer. He already has a title."

As if his identity were in doubt, Henry patted his chest. "*I* am a viscount."

"Why does a viscount need to steal another fellow's coach?" Upton sneered.

She sighed. "Because **someone** gambled his away."

"I think the fellow was cheating," Henry said sourly.

"Henry, **focus** your thoughts on our plan!" Georgiana barked. "No one is going to stop our elopement."

"Why are you so sure no one will stop you?" Darcy asked.

As if complaining about a mechanical defect, Henry huffed, "Your pistol only has one shot. Can't shoot **everyone**."

"Do you plan to shoot me?" Darcy asked as Elizabeth came to stand beside him.

"Henry, you are **not** going to shoot my brother," Georgiana said sternly.

Upton crossed his arms. "I accept that I shall leave here without Miss Darcy, but I will not leave without my landau."

"Henry, put the pistol on the ground and step away from it," Darcy commanded.

After a tense pause, the Viscount sighed deeply and did as he was told.

"A wise move, nephew." Fitzwilliam stepped from the shadows and took the pistol.

The tense moments of silent uncertainty ended when a breathless Irene stumbled to a stop beside Elizabeth. "What is going on here?"

"Georgiana and I are eloping," Henry said. "We love each other very much."

While Darcy and Elizabeth exchanged doubtful glances, Irene said exasperatedly, "Father will never accept that!"

"He despises scandal. He will accept the deed after it is done," Henry said confidently.

"Do you mean after you exchange vows at a smithy's shop in Scotland or after you consummate the sacred union your father has forbidden?" Fitzwilliam asked.

As Henry contemplated how best to answer, Elizabeth wanted to laugh at his shifting expressions. Georgiana insisted, "Viscount Bowmont, please *focus*!"

Darcy said, "Do not trouble yourself, Henry. Neither deed will be done. Parnell, get in your landau and go. I will be speaking to Baron Parnell about this very soon." Upton made no answer as he complied, but he was clearly worried.

Darcy continued, "Georgiana, you will retire to your room, and footmen will stand guard outside your door to ensure you do not leave. As for Henry, he will remain in the ballroom, and if he has to use the necessary, a servant will accompany him."

"There's no need to treat me like a child, Darcy. I give you my word of honour not to abscond with Georgiana."

"If you had honour—or common sense—you would not be in this idiotic situation." Fitzwilliam slung an arm around Henry's neck.

Watching her uncle lead her brother away, Irene said, "I am astonished that you want to marry Henry. He is such a nodcock, Georgiana."

"I am convinced that my chance of happiness with him is as fair as most people can boast on entering the marriage state." Seeing Darcy's stony expression, Georgiana said imperiously, "You may leave now, Irene." And she made a shooing gesture with both hands.

"I want to see what happens next," Irene said cheerily.

What happened next was that Georgiana complained about never being allowed to make her own choices. When her short rant ran its course, Darcy said calmly, "Here are your choices. Spend the rest of the evening in your room with one of your famous headaches. Otherwise, I will make a great joke to my guests about your ridiculous prank. I shall tell everyone you are so jealous of my fiancée that you contrived a pretend elopement to disrupt our celebration. **My** reputation can weather the scandal, but you will be forever known as the petulant princess of Pemberley."

"No one will believe you," she said falteringly.

"Everyone will believe me, but not because of **me**. Elizabeth is admired throughout the neighbourhood."

"I hate you both," Georgiana pouted. Noticing Irene's broad grin, she added, "I hate all three of you!"

"Perhaps you do, but I wonder if you hate yourself more," Darcy said. He escorted her to the house, bypassing the ballroom and taking the servant stairs to the family bedrooms.

As Elizabeth and Irene strolled back to the party, Irene said, "I have never been certain whether Henry is stupid or too lazy to consider the consequences of his actions. After tonight, I am inclined to think he is both. I shudder to know that the fortunes of our tenants and servants are inextricably linked to such a selfish fool."

≈≈≈

On the following day, it was nearly noon when the family meeting commenced behind the closed doors of the drawing room. By the time it ended, Georgiana was no longer speaking to Henry, as he had admitted that he was less interested in her than in having access to her fortune so he could support his pastimes of gambling and horse racing with his friends. Henry was less bothered by Georgiana's subsequent silence than by her earlier admission that she was more interested in sharing his title than his bed or his life.

After Fitzwilliam said he would take his nephew to the Harwich estate on the following day, the others filed out, leaving Darcy and Georgiana alone.

"**Where** are you sending me?" she asked unhappily.

"To Kyrewood Academy in Gloucester," Darcy said for the third time in fifteen minutes.

"I shall tell everyone that my cruel relations have cast me out—that I am, in essence, an orphan."

"If I could turn back the calendar, Georgiana, at what moment might I have said or done something differently that would have prevented this?"

"I do not know. You are supposed to be my wise elder brother."

"It seems I am your inattentive elder brother. If you and I had conversations about your feelings, I am embarrassed to say that I don't remember them."

Did we have such conversations, or was I waiting for William to notice, to ask me? This was too uncomfortable to contemplate, so she changed the topic. "I cannot imagine that Fortuna will be happy at Kyrewood Academy. She has formed a bond with the other horses in our stable."

Ah, yes, my sister's greatest worry is the happiness of her horse. Why can we not talk about this mad year when so many things I believed to be true were merely mirages? Darcy asked, "Do you wish to discuss Fortuna?"

No, but .... Georgiana winced but decided to brazen out the moment. "Yes."

How do I reach you? How can I know what you care about? Where do I start? he wondered. At last, he said, "No."

Georgiana was confused. "No, you do not want to talk about Fortuna?"

"I have heard you are disappointed in the mare, so I shall give her to Irene."

"Are you going to provide me with another horse?"

"No."

Glaring, she said, "So I have to make do with Apollo?"

"No. Fitz will take the stallion. As a cavalryman, he knows more about horses than anyone else in the family."

"Apollo is mine!"

"When I gave you Fortuna, you said I could do what I pleased with Apollo. It pleases me to give him to our cousin. I will continue to ensure that you have what you need, Georgiana, but you cannot reasonably expect me to understand you until you **talk** with me. I know Anne and Fitz have spoken to you about your behaviour, yet it seems that none of us have managed to reach you." After a short silence, he asked, "Do you want to talk with me now?"

Georgiana had many tumultuous thoughts, but she could not decide what to say. After a silence, she said, "No."

Darcy bowed and left her alone in the drawing room. Watching him leave, she thought unhappily, *I don't know what to do. I don't know what I want. Why don't I know?*

≈≈≈

When Elizabeth arrived in the Selby pony cart late in the afternoon, she found her fiancé sitting on the bench in the rose garden. At the sound of the cart's wheels, he looked up. Seeing her, he stood and touched one hand to his heart. A groom appeared to take custody of the cart after his master handed out the lady. As Elizabeth tucked her hand in the crook of his arm, Darcy said, "Had you not arrived within the hour, I was going to come to you at Oaklands." He kissed her cheek. "I am so relieved to see you, my love."

They began strolling along the paving stone paths winding through the rose beds. Elizabeth said, "You have spoken with Georgiana about last night, I presume."

"Nothing was resolved, but I think we understand each other a little better. Had you asked me at Rosings what Wickham's greatest crime was, I would have said that he broke Georgiana's heart. But that was a lie."

"Are there not moments when each of us sees or hears what we expect rather than what **is**?" She leaned against him for a moment.

Darcy gave her an arch smile. "For example, when I proposed to you at Rosings Park, certain that you would welcome my offer."

"Or, for example, when I learnt Lydia was so selfish that she would risk her reputation and that of our family to be the first to marry."

"I would suggest, wife-to-be, that we have only sons. But having been confronted lately with such sterling examples of venality and stupidity as Parnell and the Lordling—"

"And Knowles," she interjected.

"Ah, yes, the Poisoner Parson, the Criminal Curate. Perhaps we should follow Fitz's example and raise hounds."

Elizabeth laughed, but when he clasped her hands, she saw the seriousness in his expression. He said, "Regardless of how the Earth spins, you are my North Star. As for Georgiana, I shall send her to Kyrewood Academy. I do not know how to make her happy."

"You make *me* happy."

Upon hearing those words, Darcy had an epiphany. "Before we met, you already knew how to be happy. It was your happiness that drew me to you."

As they strolled in silence for several moments, he felt relieved, but Elizabeth felt a niggling worry. "What if Georgiana joins forces with Lydia?"

Darcy groaned loudly, and she laughed. "Even if they unite, their strength will never match ours. We are more formidable than any who are so foolish as to work against our well-being and joy." Framing his face with loving hands, she kissed him. And kissed him. And kissed him.

Epilogue

Happy for all their sororal feelings was the day in the last week of July when the two eldest Bennet sisters married in a joint ceremony. Elizabeth married Mr Fitzwilliam Darcy, and Jane married Mr Emery Warren, the kindly, sensible gentleman who had conveyed her and her relations to Hertfordshire in April.

Lydia Bennet and Georgiana Darcy were offered a brief leave from the Kyrewood Academy to attend the wedding, but only Lydia went. She and Georgiana did not—as had been feared—join forces. Georgiana tried to befriend her, believing that banishment from the Longbourn would make her an ally. However, Lydia had many fond memories of Elizabeth but no fond memories of Darcy; nor did she find Georgiana's arrogance endearing. Within a decade, a less-sullen Georgiana married a baron, and a less-impulsive Lydia married a friend of Aunt Morton's husband.

Elizabeth and Darcy returned to Derbyshire in time to attend the wedding of Susan Browning Harcourt and Abelard Joseph Selby. Squire stood up with his son, Elizabeth stood up with Susan, and Cassandra was the flower girl.

Squire did not adjust easily to the new housekeeper after Susan became his daughter-in-law. However, when she was carrying Abelard's first child, Squire saw how challenging her pregnancy was. Thus, he made friends with the housekeeper. In time, Susan and Abelard produced a daughter and twin sons, whom Squire loved as dearly as he did Cassandra.

The Gardiners discovered that resolving the difficulty with the Bristol warehouse ultimately resulted in an expansion of Gardiner Enterprises; thus, their youngest son was able to buy a small estate some thirty years hence.

After her presentation, Irene was declared a diamond of the first water. In her third season, she married a duke and enjoyed having precedence over her Earl and Countess of Harwich and Viscount Bowmont.

Anne de Bourgh remained in Denmark for three years with the friend she had made during her stay at the health spa in Epsom. When she returned to Rosing Park, she brought her Danish husband, the second son of a greve (the equivalent of an English earl).

Caroline Bingley married before Charles Bingley did, and she found satisfaction in her life with her husband and children, who had happy relationships with their Aunt and Uncle Hurst and cousins.

Baron Knowles sent his second son to be a parson in India, and Trevor died there of malaria before his fortieth birthday. Baron Parnell removed his first son from the line of succession, closed the Parnell legal practice in Lambton, and began preparing his second son to inherit. After Upton received a settlement from his father, he moved to London and had a better life than many felt he deserved. As for Righteous Jordan James, within a year of his confrontation with Elizabeth, Lambton's local madman accidentally poisoned himself with one of his concoctions.

About The Author

After a career of writing and editing business, marketing, and technical materials, I retired in Spain. Here, I wrote my first novel for the fun of it and to raise funds for animal rescue projects where I have volunteered.

Then I kept writing for the fun of it. My other books are:
- Elizabeth Bennet's Impertinent Letter
- Elizabeth Bennet and a Serious Proposal
- Five Weddings and Wickham
- Elizabeth Bennet, Heiress to Rosings Park

About Ergotism

Ergot poisoning still occurs, although most victims are livestock that have ingested contaminated feed. Compounds derived from ergot are still used in some medications for humans. In 1938, a Swiss chemist synthesized LSD in a research project to create medicine from ergot alkaloid. It is the dose that makes the poison.

According to some researchers, the ergot fungus may have been a factor in some historical events, including the Dancing Plague in Europe and the witch trials in Britain's colonies in North America. This is one of many stories about ergot poisoning in a French Village in 1951 that temporarily went mad. (www.mentalfloss.com/article/558020/pont-saint-esprit-france-1951-bread-poisoning-mass-hallucinations)